A Wicked Bargain for the Duke

"I can't wait," she replied, sounding breathless.

"Patience, Lavinia," he said in a sly tone as he leaned down to kiss her.

His mouth was so warm and his lips so firm. She felt as though she were melting into the bed as he pressed against her.

The fingers of his right hand were in her hair, tugging gently as his lips urged her to open for him.

She did, sliding her tongue into his mouth as she had earlier that day. Only now, with so much less clothing between them and so much more bed, it was infinitely more intoxicating. Her whole body throbbed with awareness of his, of the warm strength of him against her, his other hand resting at her waist.

Move up, she wanted to say, but she knew he'd remind her to have patience.

She did not want to be patient, damn it.

By Megan Frampton

The Hazards of Dukes
A WICKED BARGAIN FOR THE DUKE
TALL, DUKE, AND DANGEROUS
NEVER KISS A DUKE

The Duke's Daughters
THE EARL'S CHRISTMAS PEARL (novella)
NEVER A BRIDE
THE LADY IS DARING
LADY BE RECKLESS
LADY BE BAD

Dukes Behaving Badly
MY FAIR DUCHESS
WHY DO DUKES FALL IN LOVE?
ONE-EYED DUKES ARE WILD
NO GROOM AT THE INN (novella)
PUT UP YOUR DUKE
WHEN GOOD EARLS GO BAD (novella)
THE DUKE'S GUIDE TO CORRECT BEHAVIOR

MEGAN FRAMPTON

A WICKED BARGAIN FOR THE DUKE

A HAZARDS OF DUKES NOVEL

AVONBOOKS

An Imprint of HarperCollinsPublishers

Excerpt from *Gentleman Seeks Bride* copyright © 2021 by Megan Frampton.

A WICKED BARGAIN FOR THE DUKE. Copyright © 2021 by Megan Frampton. All rights reserved. Printed in the United States of America. No part of this book may be used or reproduced in any manner whatsoever without written permission except in the case of brief quotations embodied in critical articles and reviews. For information, address HarperCollins Publishers, 195 Broadway, New York, NY 10007.

First Avon Books mass market printing: May 2021

Print Edition ISBN: 978-0-06-302308-6
Digital Edition ISBN: 978-0-06-301098-7

Cover design by Patricia Barrow
Cover illustration by Victor Gadino
Cover photos © Nike Sh | Dreamstime.com; © Sean Pavone | Dreamstime
.com; © Valuavitaly | Dreamstime.com
Author photograph by Ben Zhuk

Avon, Avon & logo, and Avon Books & logo are registered trademarks of HarperCollins Publishers in the United States of America and other countries.

HarperCollins is a registered trademark of HarperCollins Publishers in the United States of America and other countries.

FIRST EDITION

21 22 23 24 25 BVGM 10 9 8 7 6 5 4 3 2 1

To Scott, who made sure I could make my deadlines even while dealing with surgeries, chemotherapy, and radiation (I'm good now!). I love you.

Little did I know, when I woke up that morning, that my life was about to change.

I'd thought life couldn't change more than it had; both my parents had died unexpectedly, and it seemed my father had made some very bad investments. I was hiding the truth, hoping some miracle in the form of an offer of marriage would occur to rescue me. I can admit I am quite pretty, and I was optimistic about my chances. While I was technically in mourning, I ensured every eligible bachelor in London had seen me walking in the park, holding a handkerchief while garbed becomingly in black. I had had many fulsome compliments, and even more appraising glances, but nothing tangible to save me.

I was on the verge of complete and utter ruin.

My Dark Husband by Percy Wittlesford

Chapter One

Ducal Duties
(to be accomplished within a year of assuming the title).
1. Learn the names of the upper staff.
    a. Learn the names of the lower staff within a year and a half.
2. Survey the properties and assess their efficiency.
3. Acquire a civilian wardrobe.
    a. No pastel colors.
4. Make connections in Society.
    a. Avoid any who seem to require a set strategy for dealing with them.
5. Secure the dukedom with the addition of a suitable wife and subsequent heir.

𝒯haddeus Dutton, Duke of Hasford, leaned back in his chair and folded his arms over his chest, glaring with dissatisfaction at the list he'd written.

Not that it was the list's fault; it was his entirely. The list was proper, in correct order, and comprehensive. *Disciplined.*

Like him.

Boring, his cousin Ana Maria had once said

in reaction to his respectable wardrobe—she would far prefer he wear fashionable pastels, for example—but he knew her opinion went beyond that at times. Particularly when he was managing her.

He felt his lips curl into a rueful smile and drew out another sheet of paper, plucking a pen from the surface of his built-entirely-for-efficiency desk. He'd ticked off all the proper items on the list; he had hopes that accomplishing #5 would invigorate both himself and his life. He put the pen to paper and began writing quickly.

A Suitable Woman Will:

1. Be unassuming in looks and manner.
    a. Be pleasant to look at.
2. Come from a respectable family. Her relatives must be as well-bred in blood and behavior as she.
3. Have a general knowledge of all topics but not be too obsessed by any one of them. Her first priority should always be her husband and, eventually, their children.
4. Be able to immediately handle her duties as his duchess.
    a. Running the household(s), appearing with him at Society events, and comporting herself with the utmost honor and respectability.

He took a deep breath before quickly scribbling the last item on the list.

5. Engage satisfactorily in sexual congress.

That was a daring line item, and one he cared deeply about, although of course there was no way to verify the candidate's ability until after marriage.

The only surprising thing about him lately, he thought exasperatedly, was his becoming a duke in the first place, when it was discovered that his cousin Sebastian's mother had secured the dukedom for her son through illegal means. His cousin, the former duke, was now plain Mr. de Silva, while Thaddeus had left his command in Her Majesty's Army to take up command in Her Majesty's Aristocracy.

Being a duke was not dissimilar to being a military officer.

There was the general ordering about of things and people; the awareness that you were the most important person in the area, unless you happened to be keeping company with royals or generals; and there was the knowledge that if you made a misstep, you could cause the loss of lives or livelihoods for thousands of people.

It was the last bit that made him snap awake at night, nearly as much as he had when navigating a tricky battle strategy.

But with a wife he would have a second-in-command, someone who would assist him with the general ordering about of things and people.

Who would be his equal in the bedroom, giving as much pleasure as she got.

He felt himself stiffen, though not just in *that* way, and hastily balled the paper in his fist, stuffing it into his top desk drawer, which he locked immediately. He was sitting in the library, which he used as his office. Although there were comfortable chairs and plush carpet in the room, Thaddeus only ever sat in one of the two straight-backed wooden chairs behind a solid wooden desk.

Like him.

"Melmsford!"

Why he raised his voice to yell when he knew his secretary was likely hovering just outside the door was beyond him.

"Your Grace?"

Melmsford was, if possible, even more efficient than Thaddeus. A tall, slender man with prematurely thinning hair, Melmsford's chief attribute was his encyclopedic knowledge of anything to do with the Hasford holdings. He'd been Sebastian's secretary, whom Thaddeus had inherited along with the rest of Sebastian's staff.

It had been Melmsford who had helped Thaddeus navigate the first few perilous months of his taking the title, and Melmsford who even now guided him through the more delicate minutiae of his new role.

If he and Melmsford ever spoke even once about anything not pertaining to business, he might even say he was a friend. But they had not, so he could not.

He should add *Converse with Melmsford about something besides business* to his list.

"Yes, come here." Thaddeus gestured toward the front of his desk. "Sit down."

Melmsford folded his long frame into the chair as he regarded Thaddeus with the proper mixture of deference and awareness.

"It is time to approach item number five," Thaddeus announced. Melmsford looked confused; of course, he hadn't seen Thaddeus's latest list. "A wife." Melmsford's eyes widened, but he didn't speak. "I wish to attend events where there is the greatest opportunity to meet suitable candidates."

"Of course, Your Grace." Melmsford rose to gather a sheaf of papers from the small desk he used. "I have several invitations in hand." He sorted through them, a frown creasing his brows together. "Might I suggest the Baron Raddleston's party? It is being thrown in honor of Mr. Percy Wittlesford, a novelist. He will be doing a reading, I believe."

"Novelist, hmm?" Thaddeus said with a snort. He gestured to the bookshelves behind him and on each of the walls in the library. Books that had yet to be touched by him. "There's no time for reading for pleasure, there's too much to be done."

"If I might, Your Grace," Melmsford interrupted gently, "Mr. Wittlesford's latest book is the current favorite of a certain group of young ladies, young ladies who would seem to fit your requirements." He cleared his throat. "I believe the books are of a certain type?"

Thaddeus frowned in confusion. "A certain— oh!" he exclaimed, realizing Melmsford's usual discretion was even more discreet. At least the reading would not be boring. Or disciplined, for that matter. "In that case, I will attend the Raddlestons' party."

"Excellent, Your Grace."

And if he was fortunate, he would meet a lady of excellent birth, a quiet demeanor, of a pleasing appearance, who was also sexually adventurous.

And while he was at it, he might try to find a black cat in a coal cellar, a needle in a haystack, and a duke who both did his job well and wasn't entirely dull.

"VINNIE, HOW CAN you possibly get away with it?" Jane's expression was horrified, her lovely eyes wide, her perfect mouth making a perfect O.

Lavinia nodded toward Percy, who sat in the corner of the drawing room, one lock of dark brown hair falling elegantly over his brow. He was the epitome of the tortured author—a pen in his hand, smudges of ink on his strong chin, papers scattered all over the table at which he sat.

It would be perfect if the papers he was working on was a novel of torrid prose and not the household's budget.

"He's the one who's going to have to get away with it." Lavinia shrugged. "I just write the books. I don't have to read them aloud."

Percy looked up, his remarkably handsome face marred by the frown creasing his brow. Although, Lavinia had to admit, that wasn't necessarily true, since Percy looked remarkably handsome no matter what. He got all of their father's looks, whereas Lavinia had inherited her mother's height (short), her figure (exceedingly curvaceous), and her ability to focus (her father had none, except when it came to his work).

"Are you trying to undermine my confidence, Jane?" Percy asked, getting to his feet.

The three siblings—or more correctly half siblings, since Percy was their father's child by his mistress—were in the drawing room before dinner, Lavinia choosing the passage of her work that Percy would read that evening, Percy reviewing the budget, and Jane observing, her expression anxious.

Jane's face fell at Percy's question, and Lavinia immediately rushed to her sister, sitting down beside her on the sofa and wrapping her arms around her. She glared at Percy, who rolled his eyes in reply.

"I'm sorry, dear." Jane was the most sensitive of the siblings, even including five-year-old Christina, who would sulk for hours if she were denied anything, even something she did not actually want. The last enormous sulk had been because she was denied a serving of oatmeal, which she didn't even like. She'd received toast sprinkled with cinnamon sugar—one of her favorites—but since her siblings were having oatmeal, she took umbrage.

Jane, Lavinia, and Christina were their family's legitimate offspring; Percy and Caroline were the illegitimate offspring, with Percy their father's mistake, and Caroline their late aunt's child, born out of wedlock to Adelia, their father's sister, and a minor European prince, Lavinia always forgot which one. Her father had taken both Percy and Caroline in when they were mere children.

The entire family, along with their parents and a few of their parents' older distant relatives, lived in an enormous mansion in Mayfair, any potential for being shunned by virtue of their family's various scandals offset by their father's incredible wealth, and connections—his financial acumen meant he was a financial adviser to Queen Victoria, who overlooked their family scandal. Their father frequently forgot his various children's names, but he could recall to a penny what the queen had spent on bric-a-brac in a particular month. And that was usually quite a large sum.

Their mother more than made up for her husband's lassitude with her ambition for her family's status.

"I wanted to be here to support you," Jane replied, her words muffled. She raised her head and looked at Lavinia, then over her head at Percy. "Both of you. And I wanted to be sure I wouldn't reveal the secret, and I thought I would be less likely to if I wasn't surprised this evening." She returned her gaze to Lavinia. "You're not going to choose anything too scandalous, are you?" she added in a hesitant tone.

Sometimes Lavinia wondered if Jane had been switched with another child at birth. Unlike her siblings, half siblings, and cousins, she was quiet, well-mannered, and very gentle. If it weren't for the strong resemblance to their parents, Lavinia would be concerned there was a reckless girl— her true sister—somewhere out there horrifying a staid family.

"Of course not," Lavinia assured her. The passage she'd chosen was the characters' first meeting in a rose garden, entirely exemplary behavior, although there were mentions of thorns and poking and blooming, mentions that certain listeners would comprehend entirely, while others—like Jane—would entirely miss.

Lavinia had borrowed a variant of her half brother's name to publish under because lady novelists did not sell as well as male novelists. Percy Waters had become Percy Wittlesford, and she had happily collected the royalty checks from her publisher.

But then her latest book, *Storming the Castle*, had taken the fancy of many Society ladies, and there was great interest, her publisher said, in the author. Lavinia and Percy had discussed how to proceed, and the two had settled it between them that Percy would pretend to be the author.

Once the interested ladies discovered Percy Wittlesford was actually Percy Waters, the handsome illegitimate son of one of London's sharpest minds—well, it wasn't long before Percy was being asked to give public readings.

Even though he would much rather be home working on numbers. He took after their father in that way, but his illegitimacy meant he could only work behind the scenes. That might change, now that Society believed him to be a successful author. Even the queen's propriety could bend if there was fame involved, which was why Lavinia had encouraged him to make public appearances and why he had agreed to do so. The only other person who knew that Lavinia had actually written all of Percy's four published works was Jane.

Baron Raddleston, at whose party Percy would be reading, was one of Society's most influential tastemakers. He and his wife prided themselves on launching the careers of a variety of artists, from Italian opera singers to Russian harpists to homegrown British authors such as Percy.

Lavinia would do anything for her siblings, even including oatmeal-sulking Christina. If her talent for writing meant that Percy could finally do what he truly wished to, she'd happily pretend forever, just making certain Percy was familiar with most of the plots of the books. It was a relief, honestly, not to have to write the books and be the public face of the author.

Plus there was Jane to be considered—all quiet Jane wished for was to marry the equally quiet Mr. Henry McTavish. He and his family were their neighbors, though the two families were complete opposites. The McTavishes, it had been explained many times, were entirely correct and would never allow their only son to marry any type of scandal, even though the "scandalous behavior" was from an earl's family, and adviser to the queen, no less. But there had been an incident many years past, and it didn't seem to matter to the McTavishes that the Capels were well-thought-of by many.

Recently, however, the McTavishes seemed to be weakening in their resolve against Henry and Jane since the two were so devoted to one another.

Which would be wonderful, except Jane and Lavinia's parents—or more specifically, their mother—had insisted Jane and her beauty be introduced to Society in hopes of landing a husband who was in the upper echelons of Society, not a mere neighbor's son who was respectable. Lavinia knew Jane would suffer anxiety at meeting that many people on her own, and she might end up accidentally engaged to the wrong person if Lavinia weren't there.

It was Jane and Lavinia's plan for Jane to be so quiet in Society that nobody would notice her. It wasn't working—Jane's dowry overcame her quietness—but thus far her only suitors were desperate men, and their mother would not accept a desperate man.

So, if the Season ended and Jane had not found a suitably important man to marry, their mother might be persuaded to change her mind and let Jane marry Henry, after all.

If Lavinia had made a list of all her tasks for the next few months—which she had not, since Christina had used all their paper on drawing pictures of apparently distressed goats—the list would read thusly:

Lavinia's List of Responsibilities

1. Keep Jane unmarried until Mama is persuaded to consider Mr. McTavish.
    a. Keep Jane unmarried until Mr. McTavish's parents are persuaded to consider Jane.
2. Try to keep the family out of any current scandalous behavior.
3. Secure Percy's reputation as an excellent novelist who is also sharp with numbers. Have him announce his retirement from writing to devote himself to his father's business.
4. Convince Papa to allow Percy to join the business.

5. Figure out which minor European prince is Caroline's father.

"Jane! Lavinia!"

Their mother stood at the doorway, glaring disapprovingly at them as she simultaneously gave Percy a warm smile.

It was a remarkable talent.

"Yes, Mother?" Lavinia replied.

"You should be dressing for the evening." Lady Scudamore glanced at the clock in the corner. "You only have three hours!" She advanced into the room as Lavinia resisted rolling her eyes too obviously.

"They don't need that much time to look lovely," Percy said, so obviously exerting his charm. Lavinia nearly snorted.

Percy was not, of course, Lady Scudamore's child, but she treated him better than she did her own children. Or at least better than she did her younger daughter. Lavinia thought it was due to Percy's appearance and that he was male.

It was entirely unfair.

"*You* don't need that much time, Percy dear, but I've heard the Duke of Hasford will be attending the Raddlestons' party this evening." Lady Scudamore pursed her lips as she regarded Jane, whose anxious expression had returned. "And there is only one reason he would be going out. He has been extraordinarily reclusive. He must be searching for a bride." She stepped forward to slide her finger down Jane's cheek. "And you are lovely enough to be a duchess."

Lavinia glanced between Jane and her mother, noting the panicked look in her sister's eyes as well as her mother's determined gaze.

Oh dear.

"What gown should I wear, Mother?" Lavinia asked.

Not that she wanted her mother's opinion, but she did want her mother to stop focusing so intently on Jane. Her sister was too delicate to handle the pressure, and there wouldn't be much that Percy could do in this particular situation— the reason their mother wanted her daughters to marry well was because elevating their status would ameliorate the scandal of having Percy and Caroline living with them in the first place. There was only so much a large amount of money and the queen's favor could do, after all.

"You should choose whatever you want," her mother replied, clearly dismissing the topic as unworthy of her attention. "Jane, you should wear the white satin and I will lend you my diamond earrings." She gave a happy sigh. "A duchess! It would be all I've ever dreamt of!"

Lavinia took Jane's hand, tugging her toward the door. Jane stumbled as though frozen in place.

"The white satin then," Lavinia echoed. "We'll just go start, shall we?"

"THE DUKE OF Hasford," the butler announced.

Thaddeus paused at the entrance to the ballroom, glancing around at all the people who were currently staring at him.

If there was one thing he hated most about being a duke, it was that everyone gawked whenever he appeared in public. That would likely ease if he appeared in public more often, but that would mean appearing in public more often, and he had little tolerance for frivolity.

A small voice in his head said perhaps he would be less rigid if he had more tolerance for frivolity, but he quashed that quickly. He couldn't manufacture a tolerance he didn't have.

Another impetus for getting married—he could settle at home with his wife, tending to his business affairs and working on begetting an heir.

Literally mixing business with pleasure.

He stepped into the room, schooling his features to look blandly polite as opposed to annoyed. He was here for a *purpose*, he reminded himself. He didn't want to scare off any potential duchesses with his stern face, which his soldiers had assured him was terrifying.

"Good evening, Your Grace." A woman fluttered up to him, the feathers in her hair nodding gently as she moved her head. "I am Baroness Raddleston, and this is my husband, the baron." A gentleman appeared at her shoulder, both of them wearing exceedingly pleased expressions. Likely because they landed a duke at their party, not because they were particularly delighted to see *him*.

Although to be fair this was the first time they had met, so why would it be otherwise?

Perhaps the baron would prove to be a marvelous friend, and the two of them would discover they had common interests such as—well, damn. He didn't have any interests. Or hadn't allowed himself to have any because there was too much work to do.

He made a mental note to add "develop interests" to his list. And "frivolity."

The Raddlestons' ballroom was elegantly decorated. Chandeliers hung from the ceiling every six feet or so, and the lit candles cast golden shadows throughout the room, lending it a certain mystery. The servants, garbed in unobtrusive attire and holding silver platters, wound their way through the guests, dispersing what appeared to be tiny bites of food and the occasional glass of champagne.

There was a string quartet playing quietly in the background, obviously just something to pass the time until the evening's main event—the reading of the lurid material.

"Mr. Wittlesford will be reading in about an hour," the baron said, as though privy to Thaddeus's inner thoughts. He hoped not, actually, since in addition to wondering when the reading would be, Thaddeus was also wondering how early he could leave and still be polite to his hosts.

"Meanwhile," the baron continued, "we have refreshments and beverages and plenty of other guests. I don't suppose you have met—"

"Baron!" a lady said loudly. She was about ten feet away, with a few people in between them, but her voice was piercing enough to make Thaddeus wince. Or more specifically, to make him wish he could wince, but he couldn't, because it would be rude to do so.

"Lady Scudamore," the baron replied, turning to the lady, who was pushing her way through the crowd, dragging two ladies behind her.

Lady Scudamore was a middle-aged woman

with a strong jaw and a commanding figure, even though she was short.

The ladies she had trailing after her, Thaddeus could now see, were younger, both likely in their twenties. The more beautiful of the two wore a bright gown of white satin, her golden hair glinting in the candlelight. The lady had a serene expression, her pale blue eyes looking not at Thaddeus but somewhere over his shoulder.

The other woman was short, with darker hair than the first, strands of it falling onto her face. Rather than staring fixedly in one spot, as the first woman was, her eyes were darting around the room as though she were cataloguing everyone within.

And then her gaze shifted to him, and he saw her look at him openly and brazenly, raking her eyes up and down his body until she settled on his face. There was something so active and engaged in how she looked it was appealing, even though the judgmental part of him thought she was forward.

He didn't intend to, but he couldn't help but notice how enticing her figure was; more lush than the other woman, who was slender and perfectly formed. This woman's bosom was impossible not to notice, the curved white mounds nearly spilling out of her pale blue gown.

He felt an immediate visceral response to her, something so nearly crude he was startled at his reaction. This lady wasn't someone one would make polite conversation with; she was someone a person would hunger after, making it impossible to speak at all.

This woman was someone he would have to steadfastly avoid.

He liked things and people he could place in their appropriate boxes: soldier, servant, wife. His friends mocked his adherence to efficiency and routine, but it was what made him good at being first a captain and then a duke. Someone who didn't fit, who made him question his own reactions, was too dangerous to his state of mind.

"Good evening, Baron. Baroness." The older woman spoke, taking hold of the first lady's arm and keeping her gaze fixed on Thaddeus.

"Lady Scudamore, a pleasure." The baron gestured toward Thaddeus. "Your Grace, may I present Lady Scudamore? And her daughters, Lady Jane and Lady Lavinia?"

All three ladies curtseyed, and when they rose, the first lady—Jane, it seemed—still had that serene expression, but Lady Lavinia's lips had curled into a mischievous smile, revealing a deep dimple in her cheek. Her presence felt like a tangible thing. Probably his immediate and visceral reaction was a blend of desire and envy—he wished he could be as vibrant as she seemed to be. To engage everyone around her with enthusiasm and electricity.

Another item to add to his list, perhaps?

"Good evening, ladies," Thaddeus said, bowing. "A pleasure to meet you."

The younger ladies murmured something indistinct in reply, but their voices were drowned out by their mother. "Are you here for the reading? It is our own Percy who is the author." She leaned forward as though imparting a secret. "Naughty boy, we had no idea he was writing such books."

Lady Lavinia made a quickly smothered noise as Lady Jane's cheeks turned bright red.

"Percy Wittlesford is the author of *Storming the Castle*," the baron said. "Have you read it?"

Thaddeus shook his head. "No, I don't get the opportunity to read for pleasure." *And if I did, I wouldn't read books like those.*

"His books are quite—" And the baron paused.

"Delightful," Lady Lavinia supplied, that impish look still on her face. Lady Jane's cheeks turned even more red, if possible. "Impossible to put down," Lady Lavinia added. "One might say the books are ahead of their time."

"I look forward to the reading," Thaddeus said, knowing how stiff and awkward he sounded. And yet unable to do anything to stop it.

"Your Grace, my Jane mentioned she was very interested in your former career in the military."

Lady Jane glanced quickly at her mother, then smoothed her expression again. It was obvious she had never expressed any such interest.

Thaddeus felt himself admiring her ability to keep her emotions in control. An attribute to be greatly desired in a powerful titled lady.

"Yes, Your Grace," Lady Jane said. "I wonder what it is like in battle. If you could describe it."

Thaddeus took a deep breath, preparing to summon the stock answer he gave when anybody outside of the army asked him when Lady Lavinia spoke.

"I imagine it is something very difficult to describe," she said, a sympathetic look in her eyes.

He gave a brief nod.

"Do try," Lady Scudamore urged.

"Mother." Lady Lavinia's tone was nearly reproving. Of course. Someone who was so obviously observant would have seen his discomfort. It was unsettling to have someone see him so clearly, and so soon after meeting him.

Someone who was so determined to keep someone else from discomfort that she was willing to speak back to her mother.

Definitely someone to avoid. As well as someone to envy.

Had he ever spoken to his parents like that? He knew full well he had not—his father had also been a military man, and carried that demeanor to his child. His mother had been just as rigid, showing her maternal love in ensuring he was properly fed and clothed. He could remember just one time when she had hugged him, or allowed him to hug her, and that was when his father had died.

"Battle is, as Lady Lavinia says, difficult to describe." He kept his focus on Lady Jane. Far easier to look at, not just because she was so classically beautiful, but also because she lacked her sister's direct gaze. She was easy to put in a box: beautiful, eligible young lady. Not nearly as disconcerting as her sister. "It is filled with chaos, and loud noises, and confusion."

"Rather like a Society party," Lady Lavinia remarked dryly.

Everyone but Thaddeus chuckled.

"But you are out of that now, thank goodness," Lady Scudamore said. "And now you can leave the protection of our country to others."

"Yes." Thaddeus spoke shortly, and he caught Lady Lavinia's quick glance at him. He wanted to squirm under her sharp notice, but of course he did not squirm. And even if he had ever squirmed before, he was absolutely certain that dukes did not squirm.

"If you will excuse me, I wish to get something to drink," Lady Lavinia said. "Jane, are you thirsty?"

"Indeed," Lady Jane said.

"Perhaps the duke is thirsty as well." Lady Scudamore spoke in an arch voice that made it clear what she wanted to happen.

"Mother," Lady Lavinia warned again.

"I would be happy to escort the ladies to the refreshment table," Thaddeus found himself saying. Lady Scudamore beamed at him.

He could not resist shooting a glance toward *her*, only to find her eyebrows raised in disbelief, her expression revealing that she was already disappointed in him.

And they had just met.

If you give her this, you will find yourself accommodating her forever, her look seemed to say.

Perhaps I am fine with that, he wanted to reply. *I am looking for a bride.* And why not Lady Jane? A lady of beauty and good manners who was clearly able to control her emotions.

You are entirely predictable, her look shot back. *And therefore entirely disappointing.*

It was raining that fateful morning, but it wasn't just rain—it was a torrent, a maelstrom, an outpouring of liquid from the sky as though someone was tipping a bucket.

I fretted as my maid got me dressed; how was I to possibly go out in such weather?

And yet I had to.

I had an appointment with the person who held my fate in his hands. Even though that terrible morning I had no idea he did. All I knew was that he had sent a note insisting we meet. The note said it pertained to my future, and that I would profoundly regret it if I did not go.

My Dark Husband by Percy Wittlesford

Chapter Two

Lavinia had certainly not expected the Duke of Hasford to look as he did when her mother first mentioned him.

If asked to suppose what he might look like, Lavinia might describe an average-sized gentleman with aristocratic features indicating his faultless bloodline as well as a supercilious attitude. Someone who was in command of his surroundings and was certain anybody else was not in command. Whose presence was overwhelming because of his status, not because of what he looked like.

But oh, how wrong she was.

His presence was overwhelming because of what he looked like, with his status very much of an afterthought.

The actual Duke of Hasford was tall and broad-shouldered, his physique obviously hewn from actual work rather than dilettantism. He wore evening attire, as was correct, but what was not correct was how seeing his thighs encased in his evening breeches made Lavinia feel.

They were strong, as were his features, his dark eyes holding a severe promise that made Lavinia shiver. It was the same feeling she got after writing a particularly passionate scene. She wanted to step forward and press her lips against his mouth, see if that spark she felt deep inside would flare to life with a kiss.

But of course she could do nothing of the kind. Not the least of which was that their mother had already decided she would marry Jane off to this man.

This man who was outsize in appearance, impact, and title.

He would eat Jane alive.

Although he himself did not seem to know he might affect a lady in his vicinity; his behavior and manner of speaking was absolutely correct, and she had discerned his discomfort when asked to speak about his past life.

But it was there, a nearly tangible passion vibrating through his entire presence. It was almost as though his suppressed emotions were about to pulse through his skin. It made her keenly aware of him, of every movement he made.

If he were anything but a duke, she would entertain certain thoughts that thus far she had kept at bay.

The three of them walked through the crowd, the duke in the middle, his arms looped through hers and Jane's. Lavinia tightened her grip, noting without surprise how strongly muscled it seemed.

"Are you all right, Lady Lavinia?" the duke asked, likely as a result of her squeezing him. His words were as stiffly self-conscious as they had been earlier. Perhaps she was the only one upon whom he had this remarkable effect?

She'd have to ask Jane.

Although perhaps she wouldn't. That might reveal a vulnerability she wasn't certain she wished to, despite Jane being her closest friend as well as her sister.

"I am fine, thank you, Your Grace." There. She had replied in the entirely correct way, and they were still walking, and she hadn't done anything like twist around so she stood in front of his impressive form and admire him fully.

"You do not attend many Society parties, do you?" Lavinia asked.

"No," he said, again in that terse tone he'd used before. But she noticed he'd stiffened, as though ill at ease. Was it possible he just wasn't comfortable in social situations?

In which case, he'd chosen the wrong profession. Although of course he hadn't exactly *chosen* to be a duke—more like the dukedom chose him.

"Why not?" Lavinia asked. "Unless it truly is too much like battle—all the skirmishing, and battle lines being drawn, and determined mothers bearing the weapons of their daughters' beauty." It wasn't the polite thing to say, she knew that, and yet she couldn't seem to help herself. She already sensed Jane's worry about what she had said.

Was she suddenly a conduit for everyone's feelings?

She hoped not, she definitely would not like to channel whatever her mother felt most days—frustration that her family didn't do as she wished all of the time, or regret that Percy wasn't actually her son and Lavinia was actually her daughter. Perhaps glee as she introduced Jane to men such as the duke here, men who could elevate their ramshackle family into something much more respectable. It was one thing to have vast wealth, and the queen's trust, but tamping down the family's disreputability with a duke would be a coup.

"I have been busy with business. Too busy to attend social gatherings."

He spoke in a stiffly uncomfortable tone. Lavinia wondered if it was because he knew he sounded like a righteous prig, or because he was aware it could be seen as a judgment on other people who weren't too busy to attend social gatherings or just because he didn't want to speak with her.

Well, that answered her earlier question. She was definitely not a feelings conduit or she would have known precisely what he meant.

"Busy with business?" she said in an amused tone.

She saw his jaw tighten as he hastily suppressed an eye roll.

It should not send a shiver up her spine that he was so easy to bait. And yet here she was, shivering spine and all.

They reached the refreshment table, thank goodness, before Lavinia could forget herself and ask him if he knew just how his appearance might make some women—namely her—feel.

"Lady Jane, what would you like to drink?"

Lavinia released his arm, trying not to pay attention to the slight feeling of regret at the loss of his touch.

Jane leaned forward to catch Lavinia's eye, pointing to the punch bowl on the table in front of her. "Vinnie, they have sparkling punch."

Lavinia looked where Jane was pointing. "So they do. Your Grace, my sister and I would both appreciate a glass of punch."

Jane gave her a relieved smile. Jane found it so difficult to speak to strangers that Lavinia—who had no such problem—usually spoke for her sister as well as herself.

Perhaps once Jane was safely married to Mr. McTavish that would change. Because the alternative—Lavinia having to tell Jane's husband how his wife felt—would be even more than someone as gregarious and outgoing as Lavinia could handle.

That likely would not be an issue, if only because Lavinia had observed that Jane and Mr. McTavish sat for an inordinate amount of time not speaking.

That situation would drive her completely mad, but then again, she was not planning on marrying Mr. McTavish. She was planning on *Jane* marrying him, which was why it was so crucial that the Compelling Duke not develop an interest in her sister.

"Thank you, Your Grace," she replied as he handed the glasses to her and Jane. He nodded, but kept his gaze on Jane.

"Thank you," Jane murmured, taking a sip from her glass.

Lavinia took a sip also. The punch was unexpectedly fizzy and perfectly cold, a delicious mélange of berry tastes, champagne, and sweetness.

She happened to glance over at the duke, who was also drinking. He swallowed, and Lavinia watched his throat work, then felt her eyes widen as he closed his eyes in apparent bliss, allowing himself to reveal just how pleasurable he found the beverage.

Oh my.

And then the moment ended as quickly as it had begun.

"Your brother's reading will be soon?" the duke asked, his tone betraying impatience, his expression returned to its previous implacability.

Had she dreamt his moment of pleasure? Did he even know himself he reacted like that to something so basic and intrinsic as drinking something delicious?

His moments of pleasure would not, apparently, extend to the reading. She didn't think he was so eager to hear the words. More likely it was that he was regretting having to waste time waiting for the reading that he didn't particularly want to hear.

Lavinia had heard him say he hadn't read her book, and she had discerned a faint hint of condescension in his reply. Of course that was true of most any male, and many females, who realized that some novels were merely entertaining, and therefore contemptible.

Misguided humans.

Dukes weren't so above everyone else that they couldn't enjoy a good book once in a while, she wished she could point out indignantly.

But this particular duke might be.

Or he was too busy stalking around exuding his presence, the presence that seemed to affect her in a particular way, to spend any time doing something as normal as reading.

For the first time ever, she wished her imagination wasn't quite so . . . imaginative.

Because she could see him as the dark hero in one of her books, a man with an inherent sense of command discovering just what he could do with a strong heroine. What she would willingly let him do.

It was fortunate she didn't have access to paper and pen here, or she would be off in the corner scribbling down the images that were flooding her brain.

"Vinnie?"

Jane's voice broke through her thoughts, and while she should be grateful she was brought back to the present, she nearly resented Jane for interrupting the quite vivid thoughts she was having and the book she was already plotting.

Not that he'd read the resulting product, she thought grumpily.

"Pardon? I'm sorry," she said to Jane. "I was thinking about something."

Jane's mouth curled into a wry smile. "I could see that, just like you do when you're—*oh!*" she said, putting her hand over her mouth.

"What was the question?" Lavinia asked quickly, hoping the duke wouldn't realize Jane had nearly spilled her secret.

"When the reading will begin. I wasn't certain. The duke asked."

Of course. Right before she had let her mind wander through a field of kisses, tall, dark heroes and willing heroines.

"I believe the baron said it would be in about an hour, and that was approximately fifteen minutes ago. So—forty-five minutes from now?"

The duke nodded as though pleased. She suspected it was not because he was looking forward to it but because she'd been almost militarily accurate as to the time.

She would imagine—because of course she couldn't stop herself—that his military accuracy would extend to every aspect of his life.

And now she was all shivery again, and it wasn't because she was cold.

THADDEUS SHIFTED AS he stood by the sisters, a prickly awareness crawling on his skin. It wasn't entirely unpleasant, but it was unusual. While he often regretted his change in circumstances—ludicrous though that sounded, he was a *duke*, for goodness' sake—he didn't ever feel as though he didn't belong.

Because he always belonged. Whether it was when he was an earl's heir, and then an earl, a commander on the battlefield, or a duke in his Mayfair mansion, he belonged.

But now it felt as though he wasn't quite sure what he was supposed to be doing or saying, and there was an extra element in the room that brought all of his prickly consciousness to one person—Lady Lavinia.

It was aggravating to his normally staid mien, because her sister Jane was definitely far more to his taste. She was elegantly beautiful, tastefully gowned and mannered, and clearly obedient. With the exception of the one item he would not know until after marriage, she was precisely whom he'd described in his list of requirements for a bride.

And yet.

There she was, standing beside her sister, looking like riotous exuberance in comparison to the thoughtfully staid Jane. Like a tiger lily poking its defiant orange petals amongst a field of quiet Easter lilies. She gazed around her avidly, as though soaking up the sun of everyone's personality.

Probably she thought he brought only rain, given their interactions thus far. If he were to go so far as to be interested in her, which he was not, he would likely find himself challenged and provoked, two things he did not want in a marriage.

But her sister Jane was indeed perfect for his needs. He hadn't expected to meet someone who would be suitable so soon, but like any good battle strategy, he had to be prepared to strike at any moment. It was clear, from her mother's obvious and nearly crass insinuations, that this Jane was searching for a husband herself.

It was almost too easy.

"Lady Jane," he began, "I have not been long in town, and the time I have been here has been filled up with my various business affairs." Could he sound any duller? "But perhaps you could recommend some places I must see now that my time is less compromised?"

Lady Jane's big blue eyes got even wider, and she glanced over at her sister. Was she so cowed by Lady Lavinia that she was scared to speak for herself?

He already felt protective of her, and they'd just met.

"Your Grace," the tiger lily replied, "Jane and I like to do many things. I am not certain, however, what types of entertainment you would enjoy. You mentioned earlier you do not read." She gestured toward where the musicians played. "Do you appreciate music?"

Thaddeus felt a surge of annoyance flood through him. No, he did not read for pleasure, but the way she phrased it made him feel as though he was lacking somehow.

Something that voice in his head had already pointed out to him. Her seeming to reference it made it even more galling.

"I do," he replied, trying not to make his tone sound as irritated as he felt.

He had never had such a visceral reaction to someone before. If this Lady Jane were to agree to become his bride, he would have to take pains to keep her sister far away from them. He did not want his peace disturbed, and he already knew she was—whether she intended to or not—disturbing his peace. And he wanted Lady Jane to be able to express her own opinions, not defer to her younger sister.

"And art?" she continued.

Thaddeus nodded. "Art, yes." Not that he had paid much attention to art in the past, but he supposed he liked it. He had fond thoughts for several of the paintings in his town house, pictures of land-scapes with clouds and trees and such.

"Jane and I like to visit the Royal Academy, al-though of course they don't exhibit any female artists," Lady Lavinia said. "And then there are a few music halls we go to, even though our mother would likely not approve." She leaned in to speak in a lower tone of voice. "But our brother Percy accompanies us. We are entirely protected."

"Ah."

What did one say to a young lady who had just admitted to scandalous behavior to a per-son they'd just met? And admitted to taking her clearly shy and completely proper sister there as well?

"A friend of mine," Lady Jane said, her cheeks turning a delightful shade of pink as she spoke, "often remarks that music is the voice of the soul."

Lady Lavinia turned to look at her sister in sur-prise. "My goodness, that is quite poetic."

So she *could* speak for herself, Thaddeus thought.

Lady Jane blushed even more. "It is." She gazed directly at Thaddeus. "I know it could be seen as inappropriate, but I love attending the halls. The people there come from everywhere, all united in their appreciation of music."

"Or their appreciation for the dancers," Lady Lavinia remarked dryly.

"I would like to hear the music, Lady Jane," the duke said, ignoring her sister's comment. "The soul's voice."

"I can draw up a list of the places we prefer," Lady Lavinia replied.

That was not what he wanted, and she knew it. Of course he had phrased it as he had because he wanted to hear the music with Lady Jane. It wasn't as though he was actually interested in entertainment, except as to how it might pertain to his eventual settling down.

Aggravating woman.

She raised her eyebrows in a silent defiant question, and he found himself meeting her gaze, having another one of those unspoken conversations with her.

You are not worthy of my sister, her expression seemed to say.

You don't know me. I am worth plenty.

That is not what I meant, and you know it.

Entirely aggravating. And clearly determined to thwart whatever nascent courtship he might wish to embark on. But why?

And why did he wish to know so badly?

I made myself presentable, ate a biscuit with butter, and ordered the carriage to take me to the address on the mysterious note I'd received.

Why did I go, not knowing either the name nor the why of the invitation?

Because I was desperate. All I owned was a wardrobe suitable for a young lady of fortune, my mother's pearls, and a doll from my childhood.

Everything else was either not ours to begin with or about to be sold to settle my father's debts.

My Dark Husband by Percy Wittlesford

Chapter Three

Lavinia smiled as she surveyed the group assembled for Percy's reading. There were several sighing ladies, a few gentlemen who appeared to be taking inspiration from Percy's disheveled locks and generally artistic appearance for their own wardrobe, and of course outliers such as the Duke of Hasford, who stood between her and Jane, his stance as though he were standing at military attention rather than in a Society ballroom.

The three of them were at the back of the room, Lavinia having navigated them to the spot so she could observe the crowd's reaction to her work, while Jane was always just as happy to be at the edges of something rather than in the middle of it.

Percy stood at the front of the room on a dais, Lady Scudamore seated directly in front of him flanked by other ladies of similar age and admiration. The crowd grew quiet as Percy began to read.

"They stood in the garden at dusk, the setting sun casting long shadows over the flowers.

"Bathsheba turned to face him, this man who was going to implement her ruin. The earl was a formidable presence, a veritable thorn amongst the roses. He lifted his chin at her regard, placing his hands on his hips as he returned her stare.

"Bathsheba mirrored his movement, straightening her spine as she raised her chin.

"'You cannot intimidate me,' she said, speaking in a firm tone.

"He stepped forward and she resisted the urge to step back. He would not know how he affected her. How she wondered if his arms would be like banded steel around her body, if he would prick her as easily as a rose would if she let it.

"His face was bathed in a Peter Natural light."

Percy's eyebrows drew together in a confused frown. "Peter Natural?" he repeated. "Who's he?"

"Not Peter Natural," Lavinia muttered under her breath. "Preternatural."

Percy's face cleared as he peered back down at the pages in his hand. "'His face was bathed in a preternatural light,'" he began, shooting a quick glance toward Lavinia, who wrinkled her nose back at him, "'and Bathsheba wondered if there was a spark of kindness in him that she could cultivate as the gardener tended the roses.'"

She really had overdone the gardening aspect, hadn't she?

But it seemed the listeners didn't mind; Lavinia could see how many of them were literally on the edge of their seats, leaning forward to catch every word—mispronounced or not—dropping from Percy's lips.

Or perhaps they were looking at Percy himself, who was rather striking.

If *Storming the Castle* continued its sales trend, Lavinia would have enough money to pay for a place of her own. Not that she didn't love her family, even her mother, but sometimes she wished to be alone, free from having to worry about everyone in her orbit. And her parents might give her enough money to support her desires, but she'd still feel obligated to them, and there was the concern that they might withdraw their support at any time, especially if Lavinia helped Jane thwart their mother's plans for her.

Once Jane was safely married to Mr. McTavish, Lavinia could finally relax.

She might still set up her own household, however, regardless of how shocking it might appear—it wouldn't be the most shocking thing her family had ever done, after all. And she would have plenty of time to herself.

Though she suspected she would then worry more about Percy, Caroline, and the other members of her family to compensate for not worrying about Jane.

She tilted back where she stood, peering behind the duke's back to catch a glimpse of Jane.

Her sister bore her customary serene expression, but Lavinia could discern the lines of tension in Jane's body—the extra rigidity of her spine, how her hands were clasped behind her back, her fingers twisting.

Lavinia felt her mouth tighten in dismay, and wished she could whisk Jane away from all of this, gather up Mr. McTavish, and march them both to a vicar.

She could and would not rest until Jane was finally wed to the gentleman she wanted. Not the duke their mother wanted, or anybody who might draw Jane out of her shell, even though that was what Lavinia might want for Jane. But Mr. McTavish, all quiet lankiness of him. Lavinia would be bored within twenty minutes of marriage to the gentleman, but what was good for Jane was not necessarily what Lavinia wished for.

And that brought up the difficult question of what Lavinia *did* wish for—her only hopes thus far had been for her various and assorted family members, not for herself.

But if she were wishing for something, she might hope for someone as immediately intriguing as the Duke of Hasford, albeit without the boring parts. He would be beyond her ability to resist.

So it was likely for the best that he did seem to be dull. And he did still represent a threat to Jane's happiness, so she was going to have to figure out how to navigate that, so it was also good that she wouldn't be blinded by his splendid presence. Merely reduced to a bit of a shivery spine and the occasional forthright image in her mind.

She caught the duke looking at her, and she shifted back to her previous position, snapping her eyes back to the front where Percy was finishing reading the passage.

> "'I will prick you with my love,' Bathsheba exclaimed, wielding the rose in front of the count's face.
> "'Poke away, my love,' he replied, leaning forward. 'I will bear the stings if it means you will be mine.'"

Lavinia winced as the words emerged from Percy's mouth. It was always difficult to hear one's words read aloud, but even more so if one's words were being read by one's stupidly attractive half brother to a group of sighing females and a few sighing males.

The duke snorted as Percy concluded, and Lavinia felt the hot burn of embarrassment coupled with anger at his derision.

He joined with everyone else in applause, however, and Lavinia tried to remind herself that he had no idea she was the author, although he did know she was related to the purported author.

But perhaps dukes were above such things as common courtesy? Or perhaps that was only men, or at least this particular gentleman.

"Did you enjoy the reading, Your Grace?" Jane asked in her soft voice.

The duke turned toward her, and Lavinia found herself holding her breath waiting for his reply.

Not that his opinion mattered to her, not at all. First of all, he had already admitted he did not read. Second, he was someone whom she had just met. Not anyone whose good esteem she valued. Third—well. Damn.

Third was that somehow, despite how clearly

annoying he found her, and how much she did not want to care, she did.

She wanted him to approve of her, even if it was just of her writing, which he did not know was her.

She was as convoluted and confused as one of her own heroines.

"Just call me Bathsheba," she murmured to herself.

"The reading was quite enjoyable," the duke replied.

Lavinia couldn't resist rolling her eyes. Jane had asked if he had enjoyed the reading, and he had said the reading was quite enjoyable.

If the real world had a constant editor, the duke would have been corrected for his overuse of the same words. The Duke of Busy with Business, after all.

Percy, meanwhile, had emerged from his cluster of fans and had made his way to the back of the room to where they stood.

"That was wonderful!" Jane exclaimed.

At least Lavinia had Jane's praise. And she'd used another word than *enjoy*.

Percy made an elegant bow, then ruined the effect nearly immediately by stepping forward to enclose Jane in an exuberant hug. He grinned at Lavinia over Jane's shoulder, and she smiled in reply—how could she not? He was her brother, he had just lent his handsome countenance to her work, and she adored him.

"Your Grace," Jane said, emerging from Percy's hug still pristinely and elegantly beautiful, "may I introduce my brother, Mr. Percy Waters?"

Percy and the duke shook hands, both of them making the appropriately male noises of greeting.

"Vinnie, it went well," Percy said, turning to Lavinia. His eyes were bright with excitement, and he looked even more roguishly handsome. If he ever wanted to give up his dreams of mathematics, he could likely make a good living on the stage. Judging by how the audience members were sneaking glances at him, he could likely make a great living.

But he wanted to join their father in his work, hiding his own beauty in ledgers and columns and other items that made Lavinia's head ache just thinking about them.

It was odd, she thought, that a person's appearance had so little to do with what was inside their minds—for example, the duke's appearance and general impact might indicate he was one sort of person, and yet he found no time for entertainment and seemed to have a rigid attitude on all the topics that had come up thus far in their short acquaintance.

And Jane, who had the looks and manners to be the sparkling center of attention at any gathering, wanted to hide in the corner dreaming of her equally quiet suitor.

While Lavinia—well, she didn't know how she appeared to others, except that it seemed she was never quite as good as either of her two admittedly spectacular siblings.

That was why it was so lovely to lose herself in her writing—when she put pen to paper, she could be the ravishingly lovely Bathsheba, or the equally stunning Count, or any number of characters who were noticed for the appropriate things.

"Thank you for your graciousness at appearing this evening." The baroness's expression was smugly satisfied, and Lavinia exchanged a secret smile with Percy.

Their subterfuge was a success, and undoubtedly Lavinia would sell more books the more Percy went out in public as her. Or, rather, as the author of her books.

"We have a few copies of *Storming the Castle*, and several of my guests have asked if you would be kind enough to sign it for them," the baroness continued, confirming Lavinia's thought.

Percy nodded, then followed the baroness to the side of the room where a small cluster of attendees stood.

"Lady Jane," the duke began, "would you do me the honor of allowing me to take you out for a drive tomorrow?"

Oh dear.

"Jane would be delighted to," their mother said, seeming to appear out of nowhere.

Lavinia compressed her mouth so she wouldn't interrupt and tell their mother—and the duke—that Jane had said no such thing.

"Thank you, Your Grace," Jane said, lowering her eyes. But not before Lavinia glimpsed the trepidation in her sister's eyes.

Damn it. If the duke decided Jane would suit him, how could Lavinia possibly thwart both his and their mother's desires?

There was only so much one person's imagination could do.

THADDEUS WAS ABLE to extricate himself from the evening without much difficulty, though he was uncomfortable with the amount of attention he was getting.

He didn't mind attention, per se, but he preferred that he earn someone's notice rather than just be entitled to it because of his . . . title.

The evening had been successful in one aspect, at least—Lady Jane was precisely the type of lady he'd had in mind when compiling his list. She was beautiful, well-mannered, had a pleasant personality, and seemed as though she would be compliant to a husband.

She was also of good family, though not all her family members seemed to be as excellent as she.

Her half brother, who was illegitimate, was penning salacious tales he seemed more than proud of to read aloud. Her sister seemed determined to quash Lady Jane's desire to share an opinion, and also gained attention because of the almost vulgar ostentation of her voluptuous figure.

Her mother was somewhat crass also, though Thaddeus would have to admit she would make a formidable general, maneuvering her daughter into the most advantageous position.

Although he knew, if he were being honest with himself, that he was entirely envious of the family. It was clear how much they all loved one another, even if they behaved oddly in their proving of it.

He wanted to have that kind of family. Or, more precisely, he wanted to have a family, one that loved one another. And the way to begin that was to marry.

If he decided Lady Jane was suitable to be his duchess, he could extricate her from the not so good members of her family and rebuild a perfectly correct family. He could bend the rules on his list—after all, it was his own list. No one need ever know that a quietly respectable family was one of his prerequisites.

Which brought him to the element he could not know about. He would just have to presume she would be compliant there, as well, though it irritated him that when he brought those actions to mind, it was her luscious sister, and her exuberances, whose image appeared.

He would just have to restrain his baser urges and marry the right female.

The carriage slowed, and Thaddeus dismounted without waiting for any of the seemingly endless number of servants he now employed to assist him. He vaulted up the many stairs to the front door of his town house, a place that was far too large for just one person. But might feel more comfortable if there was another person by his side living in it.

Because he was damned lonely.

"Your Grace." Melmsford popped out from the library, his eyes bright with obvious curiosity.

"Melmsford!" Thaddeus was honestly pleased to see his secretary; the man was the closest he could come to having a friend nearby, now that his two closest friends—his cousin Sebastian and their friend Nash—had gone and gotten themselves married to women they were apparently besotted by.

"Fletchfield, whisky in the library, please," he

said to his butler. Fletchfield's was the first servant's name he had learned, and he employed it often.

"In here," Thaddeus said, marching past Melmsford and into the library, taking a straight path to his usual chair.

Only he was not working now, was he?

He paused before sitting down, then moved to one of the small sofas at the edge of the room. Likely a spot for someone to read one of the many tomes that were in the room. It was placed in front of an enormous window, though the drapes were closed now, and there was a candleholder on the table next to the sofa, also likely for someone to be able to continue reading once the daylight had ebbed.

He had never sat in any seat but his office chair.

Melmsford glanced around in confusion, then took a few tentative steps toward where Thaddeus was seated.

"There," Thaddeus commanded, pointing toward the chair opposite the sofa.

He nodded, positioning himself so he was at the edge of his seat, his hands on his knees, his back straight, all of his attention focused on Thaddeus's face.

This would not do.

"We are not working now," Thaddeus said, gesturing to Melmsford as he himself leaned back against the sofa.

Melmsford frowned in confusion, then his expression cleared, and he slid his way awkwardly back so he could lean also.

He still didn't look comfortable, but Thaddeus had to be satisfied with that small bit of progress. Perhaps eventually Melmsford could be a friend.

As much as a duke could be friends with a secretary.

It was so much easier on the battlefield; yes, he was in command, but everyone there was equal in the eyes of the enemy.

"Whisky, Your Grace." Fletchfield stepped into the library, halting as he realized Thaddeus was not in his usual spot. He pivoted to place a small tray on the table between where Thaddeus and Melmsford sat. He made as if to pour, but Thaddeus held his hand out to stop him. "We can take care of it. That will be all for the night. Thank you, Fletchfield."

The butler bowed, then exited, shutting the door softly behind him.

"I might have met a suitable lady this evening," Thaddeus said as he poured two glasses of whisky.

Melmsford started to slide forward on the seat in his excitement, then obviously remembered what Thaddeus had just said and jolted back in his chair.

"Might I inquire who it is?" he asked.

Thaddeus held the glass out. "Lady Jane Capel," Thaddeus said. "Her family is not all I could wish, but other than that she is ideal. I have asked to take her driving tomorrow."

Melmsford's eyebrows rose. "The Capels. I have read of them in the papers. The father, the earl, is the financial adviser to the queen."

"Oh, is he?" Thaddeus asked. That could explain why it seemed Society tolerated the unconventional family—if the queen, usually a stickler for propriety, found Lady Jane's father essential to the running of her government, the rest of Society would overlook any eccentricities.

"I can look into the family, if you wish," Melmsford said.

That felt . . . devious. Besides, it didn't seem as if there could be much worse than Mr. Percy Waters's illegitimacy.

"No, no, thank you." Thaddeus paused. "I will, however, ask you to tell me what things a young lady might wish to converse about."

Melmsford's shocked expression would have made Thaddeus laugh if he weren't entirely serious about asking. And if he ever laughed.

"Ah," Melmsford said after a moment, realizing Thaddeus was earnest in his question. "Well, I do have a younger sister—"

"You do?" Thaddeus said. He knew nothing about his secretary beyond his efficiency.

If he were to cultivate Melmsford's friendship, he'd have to know more about the man than that he was very good at his job. And mercifully quiet.

"You and your sister," he continued, "are you close?"

Thaddeus was an only child, and it wasn't until he'd met Sebastian and Nash that he'd come close to understanding the concept of family.

Melmsford nodded. "Yes, although I have to admit I don't always understand everything she talks about. But let me see," he said, tilting his head back in thought. "As far as I recall, the things she talks most about are fashion, who is marrying whom, her friends' likes and dislikes, and things she will be purchasing when she gets money next."

Thaddeus frowned. "Nothing else?" Not that he had a wide range of conversation, but he at least thought about politics, and proper land use, and the importance of the military.

And sex, though he didn't think Melmsford's sister—or anyone respectable, to be honest— would admit to even thinking about that topic.

"She also likes to talk about books, I think," Melmsford added. He shook his head. "Honestly, it can be difficult to follow her sometimes. She flits from topic to topic like a butterfly amongst the flowers."

"You are quite poetic, Melmsford," Thaddeus said in surprise.

His secretary blushed—*blushed!*—as he took a hasty sip from his glass.

"I do like poetry, Your Grace," he replied, sounding abashed.

Another thing he had discovered about Melmsford this evening. Not only did he have a sister—and presumably a life outside Thaddeus's office—but he liked poetry, something Thaddeus didn't realize people actually enjoyed.

"Did you read the book from the reading I attended this evening, then? Or has your sister read it?"

Melmsford glanced to the side as though embarrassed. "Uh, yes, we both have. Felicity lent me her copy when she was finished."

"So would that be a suitable topic for discussion with a lady?" Although that would mean he'd have to read the book, didn't it.

Courting a lady was more work than he had anticipated.

"Some of it, yes. Though that subject might wait until you know the lady better."

Thaddeus nearly chuckled. He didn't, but he did permit himself a small smile. "So I will stick to fashion and what things she wishes to buy. I will save the discussion of who is getting married and novels for later."

"Excellent, Your Grace."

"You HAVE TO come with me." Jane spoke softly, but the vehemence of her tone was clear.

It was the day after the reading, and the sisters were in the drawing room, polishing off a tray of scones and some tea. Though, to be fair, it was Lavinia who was doing most of the polishing. Jane was too distraught to do more than pick her scone up and put it down again. At least half a dozen times.

"He is taking you driving, Jane," Lavinia pointed out. "That means he will likely arrive in a vehicle meant to seat two people, and two people alone."

Jane picked up her scone, and Lavinia waited to see if this time her sister would actually take a bite out of it.

And put it down. So no.

"When have you ever let a fact like that stop you from doing something?" Jane asked.

She had a point. Lavinia prided herself on breaking whatever rules were set out, from the rule that one's illegitimate half brother could not be accepted everywhere his legitimate siblings were, to the rule that an author should only write about things he or she knew personally, to the rule that one should always obey one's parents.

The first rule would punish Percy for the accident of his birth, the second rule would mean Lavinia could never write about love or kissing, and the last rule could be followed if one's parents were at all sensible. Which they were not.

"But while you are thin, and could squeeze another person like you onto the seat, I am a bit more upholstered than you." Lavinia half rose from her seat to look at her bottom, which had not miraculously shrunk in the past few minutes. Not that she minded the size of her bottom, per se; just that if hers was more like Jane's there would be a better chance of all three of them fitting.

Jane twisted her lips together disgruntledly. "We can squish. I do not want to go driving with him alone, Vinnie. What if he proposes? You know how I am when someone asks something! I always just agree." Now she looked genuinely upset, and Lavinia's usual tug of wanting to solve problems grew to a yank.

She took a deep breath. "Mother is not going to be pleased about it, not at all. I cannot imagine she will allow it to happen, actually." Because their mother had spent the rest of the evening crowing about having secured the duke's attention, and then went on to plan the wedding and detail just how many children and what genders the duke and Jane would have.

"You'll figure out a way for us to leave without her noticing," Jane replied confidently.

"I suppose," Lavinia replied. "But Jane, I won't be around you forever. Especially once you are married to Mr. McTavish. You should practice saying no so you can do it when I am not there."

"You are probably right," Jane said with a sigh.

"No, I am not!" Lavinia said, jabbing an accusing finger toward her sister. "Do not just accept whatever it is someone is saying, that is the whole point!"

Jane drew her brows together in confusion. "But you just said—"

"And yes, it is true you should practice, but you should not just accept whatever someone says as valid. Do you see what I mean?"

"So I shouldn't practice?" Jane shook her head. "No, I do not understand at all. All I know is that you are coming with me when the duke arrives to take me out for a drive."

"Yes. And we can practice having you refuse things later on."

"No, we won't!" Jane replied in a triumphant tone of voice.

Lavinia burst out in laughter, which Jane joined.

"Excellent. Now we just need you to practice enough so that by the time the duke asks for your hand in marriage you can refuse."

Jane leaned over to wrap Lavinia in her arms. "You are the best sister. What would I do without you?"

"Be married to a duke who is immensely wealthy, owns several properties, and is remarkably striking to look at?" Lavinia replied in a dry tone of voice.

Jane rolled her eyes. "Who is also not the man whom I love. You'll see, Vinnie, when you fall in love that there is nothing you won't do to be with that person." Her eyes grew dreamy as she pulled away. "Henry is everything I've ever wanted. I think I could even say no to him, if I wanted to. Not that I ever want to. I am certain that Henry will always make the best decisions for us."

Lavinia felt an anxious qualm go through her at her sister's words. But Mr. McTavish was a quiet, almost meek, gentleman. He would never abuse Jane's trust. All she had to do was ensure that Jane got to marry her dream gentleman.

Which, right now, meant that she would be joining her sister on an outing to which she was not invited and would most definitely not be welcome.

Sibling love and loyalty was getting pushed to its limits today. Similar to how the carriage seat would be when all three of them sat upon it.

The coach was able to make its way through the rain, arriving at the destination within fifteen minutes. The neighborhood was not one I habitually went to, but that did not dissuade me. If anything, it encouraged me to keep the meeting.

I alighted from the coach and told the coachman to go home, despite his protestations. He had been with our family since before I was born, and he was old. I wouldn't risk his health in addition to relieving him of his livelihood.

"It's not safe, miss," he said, glancing toward the house. It was foreboding, its many windows shrouded with black curtains, ravens resting on the roof as though conjured by a witch.

"I will be fine," I assured him, even though I wasn't entirely certain of that myself.

My Dark Husband by Percy Wittlesford

Chapter Four

Thaddeus slowed the horses as he neared the Capel house. He'd specifically asked for the smallest carriage so he would be able to carry on a conversation with Lady Jane without having to shout.

Fashion, what she wanted to purchase, and books.

None of which interested him in the slightest. Was that what marriage was? Wandering about trying to find something in common?

And if that was true, why did so many people seem to want to do it?

There must be more to it, and more than just the nighttime companionship. He didn't think either of his two closest friends would have been so willing to marry if they had nothing in common with their wives beyond what they did in the bedroom.

And thinking about it all just reminded him that he needed to find more to be interested in now that his military career was over.

Perhaps he should rework his list to include getting a hobby.

The horses stopped, and he tossed the reins to a waiting footman, then began to dismount.

"Good afternoon, Your Grace."

He froze midair as he heard that lady's voice greeting him.

And turned to see Lady Lavinia and Lady Jane standing outside, both wearing impossibly frilly looking gowns and hats that had bits of fabric dangling off them, moving in the breeze. *Bonnets.* That's what they were. Bonnets. He was very proud he had been able to retrieve the name from some dark cavern of his mind.

He could ask Lady Jane about her bonnet, and if she had plans to purchase any more.

That would knock two of the topic items off right away. Excellent efficiency, even though it might mean they had nothing to talk about after the first five minutes.

He would have to figure something out.

"Good afternoon Lady Jane. Lady Lavinia." He finished getting out of the carriage, standing on the pavement in front of the ladies' house.

It was an enormous structure, nearly as big as his own, with large white columns flanking the stairs. It looked newer than his, which would make sense if Lord Scudamore had had it built.

"Good afternoon, Your Grace," Lady Jane said in a quiet tone. She glanced toward her sister, who stepped forward to speak.

"Your Grace, Jane and I thank you for the invitation to drive today." She accompanied her words with a wry smile, indicating she knew full well he hadn't intended for her to join them. But he couldn't very well refute her words; it would be impossibly rude to contradict a lady, even one who was lying to his face.

"The carriage," he said, gesturing toward it, "only seats two."

"We can squash together. We are related, after all," she replied in a cheery tone of voice.

There was going to be no way of getting out of this, was there?

Thaddeus bowed, then met her gaze, allowing some of his irritation to creep into his expression. "We will be quite cozy. As long as you two are certain?"

Both ladies nodded vigorously, and he took a deep breath, resisting the urge to swear. Had he thought the mother was good at maneuvering? Clearly one of her daughters had learned as well.

"Let me assist you," he said, holding his hand out to Lady Jane. She stepped up into the carriage, then moved all the way to the furthest side. "And you," he added, holding his hand out to Lady Lavinia, who looked as though she was delighted to have played a trick on him. She leaped up to sit beside her sister, and Thaddeus wanted to swear even more, because now Lady Lavinia and not Lady Jane would be seated beside him.

He growled under his breath, getting up into the carriage and standing on the runner as he assessed how much room there was.

Not much.

He would be thigh-to-thigh with Lady Lavinia, who would be pressed up against her sister.

There was nothing for it but to sit.

She let out a surprised noise when his body met the carriage seat, and he half rose again.

"It is fine. I thought for a moment you were going to sit on my lap," she said by way of explanation.

"I would crush you," he replied as he took the reins from the footman.

"Not at all. I am made of hardier stuff, Your Grace," she replied. "You could place your entire body on me and I would not break."

Did everything about this woman immediately make him think about carnal things? He was fairly certain he didn't like the flare of prurient interest her words engendered.

He was in pursuit of Lady Jane. It wouldn't do to be thinking those kinds of thoughts about her sister, the one who did not let her sister speak, who forced herself into situations she had not been invited to, and whose appearance seemed designed to turn him into a lustful beast, which he most definitely was not.

Despite what he'd added to his list.

"Where are you taking us, Your Grace?" she asked.

He leaned forward so he could see both of them as he replied. Lady Jane's expression was eager, as though she was enjoying the ride even though she was pressed against the side of the carriage.

"I thought we would go to Hyde Park. I understand the gardens are lovely."

Flowers. Melmsford hadn't mentioned them, but ladies had to enjoy flowers, and enjoy talking about them. Didn't they?

"They are," Lady Lavinia affirmed. "The scene that Percy read last night was inspired by the roses in Hyde Park. Or so Percy says," she added quickly.

"Lady Jane," Thaddeus said, wishing he didn't feel quite so awkward, "do you like flowers?"

"What's not to like?" Lady Lavinia said.

"I do," Lady Jane replied.

"And fashion? Do you like fashion?"

He wished he had not had the bright idea of finding a bride. Perhaps he could save himself, and everyone around him, by committing to becoming a hermit duke, living alone for the rest of his life.

If it would spare him from this conversation.

"We both like fashion," Lady Lavinia answered. Of course she did. "That is what ladies enjoy, is it not?" Now her tone had a sharper edge to it. "Flowers and fashion?"

"Vinnie." Lady Jane sounded as though she were chastising her sister. Perhaps Lady Lavinia spoke for the two of them because that was what Lady Jane wanted? He'd assumed it was because Lady Lavinia was trying to outshine her more beautiful sister, but perhaps he'd misread the situation entirely?

Because Lady Jane wouldn't have felt free to reprimand her sister if that same sister was perpetually suppressing her.

"What other *f* things do ladies like, I wonder?" Lady Lavinia continued. "We like fun, and frivolity—though those are somewhat similar— and fireplaces, and friends, and—"

"Vinnie." Now Lady Jane sounded firmer in her tone.

"Fine," Lady Lavinia said, then laughed. "Fine! Another *f* word."

They had come to the entrance of Hyde Park now, and Thaddeus shoved all his thoughts inside a box so he could concentrate on driving—he wasn't accustomed to driving a carriage. He was far more comfortable on horseback, and driving while there were people and small children walking about required his utmost attention.

The ladies seemed to understand that also, because except for a few whispers, they did not speak. Not even Lady Lavinia.

Thaddeus followed the road as it curved around the park, hoping that the gardens would be somewhere along the way. Feeling befuddled by everything, which was not at all like him.

Lavinia had had to suppress her laughter at seeing how discomfited the duke was when he'd realized she would be joining them. Well, suppress her laughter as well as her chagrin. Because there was something about him that tugged her toward him, and she wanted him to be just as interested in her as she was in him, and it piqued her that he wasn't.

So she exerted herself more, which seemed to result in his pulling back more.

Lavinia didn't always realize it, but she was accustomed to being the center of attention, even if the more beautiful Jane was in the room. She was just too naturally curious, and talkative, and interested in everything and everybody to fade into the background.

She couldn't seem to help it, which was good when one wanted to express oneself, but not as good if one's intention was to attract a potential husband. She was too bold, too assertive, too *much* for most gentlemen.

Which was why she was planning on living out her days alone, finding solace in her writing and her family.

"Over there," Lavinia said, pointing in the distance toward the gardens. The duke nodded, then turned the horses in that direction.

At least he could accept guidance from a woman. Perhaps there was more to him than it appeared at first.

His thigh was pressed against hers in the carriage, and she could feel its strength and warmth. What would it be like to actually touch his body? To feel all his weight on her, as just nearly happened when he sat down on the carriage seat.

More fodder for her books, but less helpful for dealing with him in real life.

"Oh, the lilies are out!" Jane exclaimed as they approached the garden.

The duke made some sort of surprised noise.

"Do you not like lilies, Your Grace?" Lavinia asked. Yes, it was forward, and yes, she had to know anyway.

"Some of them," he replied. "Easter lilies. Lilies in more subdued colors. Whites and pale yellows, for example. I find tiger lilies to be . . . ostentatious," and he glanced over at her as though he meant more than he'd just said. And why did his look make her want to bristle?

"The flowers that are the most vibrant likely attract the most bees," Lavinia said, wondering why it felt so important to defend bright flowers.

"The bees that are easily swayed by a flower's appearance are not particularly discerning, then."

"So you're saying that there are bees who appreciate a more subtle flower? That that results in better tasting honey?"

What even was this ridiculous conversation?

"I suppose I am," the duke replied.

"I like all the flowers," Jane said in her soft voice. Of course Jane was trying to smooth things over. That was what she always did.

"Thank you, Jane." Lavinia leaned forward to meet her sister's gaze. "I am relieved you are standing up for the poor tiger lily, who just wants to be flamboyant in peace."

"The poor tiger lily," the duke echoed in a dry tone.

They were to the gardens now, and the duke slowed the horses, dismounting from the carriage as soon as they were fully stopped.

He held his hand out to Lavinia, who took it after a moment of hesitation. She hoped the electric spark between them wouldn't manifest into something physical, like the kind of shock one might get when being struck by lightning.

His hand was strong and warm, no shock at all, she was relieved to discover. He let go of her as soon as she was safely on the ground, holding his hand up to Jane in the next instant.

Jane was more cautious in getting down from the carriage, and he kept her hand in his for at least a minute longer than he needed to.

And Lavinia tried not to be jealous of her sister over a hand.

For goodness' sake. She'd never been interested in any of the gentlemen who had noticed Jane, and there was a substantial number of them, given Jane's beauty and dowry.

What was it about this gentleman that made her so responsive to him? To his presence, his appearance, and his words?

"Shall we stroll in the gardens?" the duke asked, gesturing awkwardly toward the flowers.

Lavinia looked at Jane with her eyebrow raised. She didn't want to answer all the time for her sister, but Jane made it difficult not to, given how reticent she was.

"Yes, please," Jane said after a moment.

The three of them walked into the garden, its borders marked by a low fence about two feet high. In addition to the lilies, there were roses, daisies, and rows of shrubbery with shiny green leaves.

The sun was hiding behind a few clouds, but it was still temperate, and Lavinia was pleased their decision not to bring shawls was the correct one.

She knew how the seating would be, and she didn't want to add any unnecessary bulk.

"Which are your favorite?" the duke asked.

Lavinia bit her tongue before answering. She truly did want Jane to speak up for herself. It just usually took so long Lavinia grew impatient.

Plus Jane preferred to stay in the background.

"Vinnie?" Jane said, sounding anxious.

"I suppose my favorites are roses. I like their beauty, and I also like the fact that when you touch them, they are just as likely to sting you."

The duke let out a startled laugh.

"I suppose your favorite food is artichokes, then?" the duke remarked, sounding almost amused.

"Because of the thistles? Oh yes, definitely," Lavinia replied, smiling at his tone.

Jane was smiling also, glancing between the two of them as though relieved that they were not snapping at one another.

Jane was always so sensitive. *Too* sensitive, to be honest. That was why Lavinia wanted Jane to be able to marry and settle down, where there wouldn't be surprises, like unexpectedly interested and powerfully presenced dukes lying about.

"Do you like artichokes, Your Grace?" Lavinia asked. "Or fish? Those bones can catch in your throat. Mushrooms? Rhubarb?"

"Rhubarb?" the duke said, sounding puzzled.

"The leaves are poisonous." Lavinia turned to Jane. "Do you remember when Caroline snuck into the kitchens and took some of the leaves from the kitchen garbage?" She looked at the duke. "She was sick for a week. The doctor said she would have been dead if she had eaten more of it."

"Caroline is—?" the duke asked.

"Our cousin," Lavinia replied. "Her mother was our father's sister. Our aunt is gone now— not deceased, but traveling," she clarified. "She had Caroline after she had gone to some foreign place. Jane, do you recall which one it was? It was on my list to figure out, only I haven't had time."

Jane shook her head. "No, just that Caroline has very light hair, so I've always assumed it was somewhere north. Like Sweden or Denmark, only not either of those places."

Lavinia shrugged. "It doesn't matter, just that she very nearly died." She smiled anew as a thought struck her. "Jane, we should host a Dangerous Meals dinner. We could serve all those foods, plus cherries, apricots, and a copious amount of alcohol."

Jane's eyes widened. "That sounds rather dangerous."

Lavinia nodded. "Of course! It's a Dangerous Meal." She peered at the plants. "I wonder if there is any hemlock planted here. Or nightshade!"

"Are you planning on killing someone?" the duke asked.

She waved her hand in dismissal. "Of course not, silly." Wait. Had she just called a duke a silly? "It is just fun to think about, isn't it? How perilous life is, if we aren't careful? Which means we should go out of our way to take risks, since we don't know what will happen."

The duke stared at her as if frozen. For so long, in fact, that Lavinia felt self-conscious, which never happened to her.

Which made her exhilarated, anxious, curious, and trepidatious all at once.

Perhaps the most dangerous item in the garden, for her at least, was the duke.

After a long while, during which it felt as though she could not drop his gaze, his lips twisted into a knowing smile. "Take risks," he murmured, making Lavinia's heart race for no explainable reason.

A woman greeted me at the door without a word. She was older than me, perhaps as old as my mother, with grizzled hair and the bearing of a confident house-keeper. Like the house, she wore all black, which was disconcerting—all the servants I had ever encountered wore light colors. She beckoned me to a room on the right where I could see candlelight spilling out into the dark hallway.

"Whose house is this, pray?" I asked.

She shook her head, refusing to answer.

So I went into the room.

You might wonder at my foolhardiness. I thought I was brave, but I know now that going into that room was a terrible mistake. One that would haunt me for the remainder of my life.

My Dark Husband by Percy Wittlesford

Chapter Five

Thaddeus felt as though he had been assaulted by a tornado after the drive. Lady Jane was a steady, pleasant breeze, but her sister—he didn't think he had ever had so many ideas and images and bizarre thoughts tossed at him.

She was a force of nature. He had to revise his opinion of her after their outing, however; it wasn't that she was determined to speak for her sister, it was that her sister didn't always care to speak.

The clear love the sisters had for one another sent a stab of jealousy to his heart. His parents had never seemed to care demonstrably about one another, and certainly not for him. He knew they loved him, as you were supposed to love your offspring, but there was nothing more than what was required by custom and good manners.

But everything the two ladies said to and for one another—it could not have been said by anybody but them.

He surprised himself by chuckling over the Dangerous Meal idea as he was driving home after dropping them off. He'd ascertained that both would be at the Prescotts' ball the following evening, and he assumed he had received an invite, and if he hadn't, well, a duke was welcome anywhere he chose to go.

He arrived back at his town house looking forward to speaking with Melmsford, even though his attempts at discussing fashion had been thwarted—one might almost say frustrated—by Lady Lavinia's sharp annoyance at his conversational gambit.

"Melmsford," he called as he stepped inside past Fletchfield.

His secretary, as usual, popped out from the library. Did the man ever stop working?

Perhaps he ought to order him to do so.

"Fletchfield, whisky," he called as he strode inside. "And two glasses," he added.

He went to sit on the sofa, as he had the previous night, and Melmsford sat opposite him, immediately leaning back against the cushions in what Thaddeus supposed was a comfortable position. Or at least it was designed to look like a comfortable position.

"Well, Your Grace?" Melmsford asked. Thaddeus was grateful the man actually seemed interested. Although he paid him enough and could order him to be interested, if it were that important to him.

But he wanted genuine interest, not paid for interest.

Likely that was in short supply as a duke. Even the few unmarried females he'd met who'd shown interest in him—with the exception of the Capel sisters—had his title and wealth as their goal, so their interest would, eventually, be paid for if they were able to marry him.

But he knew that the Capels themselves were exceedingly wealthy, so whatever interest they might show was not because of his holdings. Perhaps his title?

It was still early; he'd just met Lady Jane. He didn't need to rush into things.

But he saw the camaraderie between the sisters and their brother, and he longed for that himself. Nearly yearned for it, if someone as stoic as he could yearn. And it didn't seem to matter that Percy was the earl's by-blow; the three of them were family, as much as if everyone was legitimate.

The sooner he got himself married, the sooner he wouldn't be lonely. The sooner Melmsford wouldn't have to bear all the brunt of his conversation.

Fletchfield entered the room and set the tray with whisky and the glasses upon the usual table, then nodded to Thaddeus and exited quietly. It was good when a servant knew just what one wanted—he hoped he would have that in a wife as well.

He was nearly decided on Lady Jane as his bride already. Making decisions was something he was quite comfortable with, and he didn't see the point of fussing around when he knew what conclusion he would reach eventually.

"The drive, did it go well?" Melmsford asked.

Thaddeus rose to pour whisky into two glasses, handing one to his secretary. "It did." He raised an eyebrow toward Melmsford. "Though her sister also joined us. Lady Lavinia."

Melmsford's eyes widened. "Ah!" he exclaimed.

Thaddeus chuckled, taking a sip from his glass. "Precisely."

"Lady Jane is quiet, and respectable, proper in appearance—"

"Quite lovely, in fact," Melmsford interrupted, his cheeks turning a bright red as he spoke. The result of his boldness in speaking or the whisky he'd just taken a sip of?

"Yes, she is lovely. I assume she is capable of running a household, and of course she would have Mrs."—he hunted for the name in his mind—"Mrs. Webb to assist her."

"So you're decided, then?" Melmsford said.

Thaddeus gave a quick nod before finishing his whisky. "I am. I will see Lady Jane at the Prescotts' ball tomorrow. I will ask her then."

And then he wouldn't have to go to any more Society parties where he would have to listen to novels being read or have to dance when he always felt too big and awkward, as though he might trod on his partner's foot at any moment.

He could stay at home in his town house, visit his various estates, and concentrate on learning the land and fathering an heir. Not in that order.

JANE FLUNG HERSELF on the bed when the sisters were finally able to get away from their Very Inquisitive Mother, who only had about seventy thousand questions about the drive, only one of which was about what Jane actually thought of the duke.

And even then she started asking another question as Jane was answering.

"Are you all right?" Lavinia asked, sitting beside her sister.

Jane turned her head to look at her sister, her arms flung to either side. "I am fine. I just need to not be around people for a bit."

Lavinia started to rise, but Jane put her hand on her leg. "Not you, silly."

The reminder of which made Lavinia start to giggle, while Jane stared at her in confusion.

"I called the duke—the enormous, full of presence, very serious duke—a silly. Didn't you hear me?"

Jane's expression grew startled, and she gasped as she clapped a hand over her mouth and began to laugh.

And then the two of them were howling with laughter, clutching their sides as they rolled around on the bed.

"A silly!" Jane exclaimed after they'd settled down.

Lavinia nodded, wiping the tears of laughter from the corners of her eyes. "At least I didn't call him a blunderbuss or a jobber knot."

Jane sat up abruptly, wrapping her arms around her knees. "Where do you get these words, Vinnie? A jobber knot?"

Lavinia sat up as well, a knowing look on her face. "When you are a successful author," she said in a mockingly haughty tone, "you have to speak many languages." She shrugged. "I happen to speak pub."

Jane's expression grew shocked. "Vinnie. You have not spent time in a pub. Tell me you haven't."

Lavinia gave her sister a sly look. "Fine, then I won't tell you." She leaned over to whisper in Jane's ear. "But I did."

"Oh!" Jane said, grabbing a pillow from the bed and launching it at Lavinia's head. "How could you do that and not take me? You went with Percy, didn't you?"

Lavinia nodded as she dodged the missile. "I didn't think you would want to go. Also I know your Mr. McTavish is a bit of a . . ." She paused as she searched for the word.

"A what?" Jane said in a suspicious tone.

"A stick in the mud?" Lavinia replied. Not for the first time, she wished she thought before she spoke. "I mean, he is so proper, and quiet, and doesn't seem to always enjoy our family gatherings. What with their being so noisy and all."

Jane folded her arms over her chest. "You mean he's like me."

"Yes! And that is why you are perfectly suited for one another," Lavinia said in relief.

"I suppose." Jane sighed. "Though that means we really have to deter the duke. There is no possibility Mother will allow me to say no, and I can't even trust that I wouldn't say yes if he got me alone and proposed." She closed her eyes and pitched back onto the bed. "I wish I was more like you, Vinnie. Able to speak my mind, no matter what."

"You mean like calling a duke a silly? Inserting myself into a carriage ride planned for two?"

Jane opened her eyes to look at Lavinia, a warm look in her eyes. "You are always there for me, no matter what." She patted Lavinia's arm. "I'll even forgive you called Mr. McTavish a stick in the mud."

"If the mud fits . . ." Lavinia replied in a mischievous tone.

Jane hoisted another pillow and flung it at Lavinia. This time, it didn't miss.

"WHATEVER YOU DO, Vinnie, do not let him be alone with me."

It was the following evening, and the two sisters were at the Prescotts' ball. Jane had feigned a headache to try to stay home, but their mother had merely glared at her and given her all the headache powders in the house. Along with her evening gloves.

"I should have brought a sword or something," Lavinia replied. "At the very least I could have challenged him to a duel."

Jane rolled her eyes. "You don't just challenge someone to a duel and then get to dueling. Besides," she continued, frowning in thought, "duels are illegal, and they used to be done with pistols, not swords."

"Details," Lavinia said in disdain. "My heroes always carry swords and are able to duel at any time, night or day," Lavinia said proudly.

Jane just rolled her eyes harder.

"You have no appreciation for artistic license," Lavinia sniffed.

The two had been announced fifteen minutes earlier, and had quickly found a quiet corner behind one of the enormous statues studding the room every ten feet or so.

The Prescotts were similar to the Capels, in that both families were exceedingly wealthy and neither had quite the correct amount of respectability. They also had a daughter to marry off, although their Phoebe was not nearly as opinionated as Lavinia, nor as beautiful as Jane.

The room, therefore, was opulent in its decorations and provisions, making it clear that whichever gentleman managed to snare Phoebe would be getting a sizable fortune as well.

"Perhaps the duke will see Phoebe Prescott and decide she is suitable to be his bride," Lavinia remarked. The two scanned the crowd to find Phoebe, who was in the middle of the room with a cluster of suitors around her.

They also found Phoebe's laugh, which was louder than most people's laughs, and employed more often.

"Though I imagine the duke is not interested in a wife with a sense of humor. At least not one who demonstrates it as often as Phoebe does."

"If only I laughed more," Jane said in a mournful tone.

Lavinia nudged her shoulder. "You should never change who you are, whether it is in pursuit of finding a husband or avoiding one."

Jane exhaled as she nodded. "You're right. It's just—what if he speaks to Father first, and Mother finds out?"

"Father is out of town on business for the next few days, remember? And the duke wouldn't speak to Mother, not without first talking to him." Lavinia looped her arm through Jane's. "I will be by your side all evening, except for when you are on the dance floor." She leaned in closer. "That would be a bit odd, even for me."

Jane laughed, as Lavinia had hoped she would. She could feel Jane's tension, however, and wished that her sister had been born a bit less beautiful, and their father been a bit less successful in business.

Then she would be able to marry whomever she wished, and Lavinia wouldn't have to squeeze herself into carriage seats meant for two.

"Oh dear," Jane said. "Mother is coming."

True enough, their mother was approaching, the feather plumes in her hair nodding vigorously as she strode forward.

"Oh dear," Lavinia echoed, seeing her mother's smug expression.

"There you are, Jane. And Lavinia," she added, as though it was an afterthought. "The duke's carriage is outside." She stepped forward and raised her hand to Jane's face, beginning to pinch her cheeks. Jane flinched, and Lavinia put her hand on their mother's arm.

"Jane looks lovely, Mother," she said in a low tone.

Her sister's cheeks were bright red, not from the pinching, but from the embarrassment.

"Of course she does," Lady Scudamore replied in a loud voice.

"The Duke of Hasford," the butler intoned.

Everyone in the room turned to stare at the doorway, where the duke stood.

Lavinia did as well, unable to suppress her gasp as she saw him. He was framed in the doorway as though he was stepping out from a painting, one where the triumphant king overcame his adversaries through brute strength. He wore evening clothes, which should make him look respectable, but the power and force of his body and personality overcame his polite dress, making him look like a wolf in sheep's clothing.

Why did he have to be the man who made her insides flutter like one of her heroines? The duke who her mother had determined was for Jane, and who Lavinia was equally determined would not marry her sister?

The duke descended into the ballroom, greeting the hosts with a polite nod, his intense gaze searching the crowd. Landing on Jane, and then allowing a small contented smile to pass across his face.

No, you will not, Lavinia vowed to herself.

And then he began walking toward them.

THADDEUS WAS GROWING more accustomed to the stares, even though he still had to resist the urge to wince at all the attention. Attention he received only because of his title. In training, and on the battlefield, Thaddeus had gotten his share of stares and attention, but it was because of his command, not because of his name.

He didn't know if he would ever not regret the circumstances that led to him standing in a ballroom instead of in battle formation.

But he had plans to improve his current life, and she stood just a few yards away, looking lovely and demure in a gown of pure white. Of course her mother and her sister stood beside her, but he focused his attention on her.

She would bring a quiet respite to his life, assist him in performing his ducal duties while also bringing him a measure of personal contentment.

He took a deep breath and strode toward Lady Jane, deliberately avoiding eye contact with anyone in his path who might wish to speak to him.

"Good evening, ladies," he said as he reached them.

All three curtseyed, although Lady Lavinia was the only one of the three who did not lower her gaze.

He felt . . . exposed when she regarded him. As though his basest thoughts and deepest desires were revealed to her.

He did not like the prickly feeling he had when in her presence.

"And how are you this evening, Duke? My daughter Jane is looking beautiful tonight, wouldn't you say?"

Thaddeus saw Lady Lavinia grimace, just for a moment. He felt a sense of chagrin at witnessing her mother's clear preference, and felt immediately defensive of her.

"Both of your daughters are looking beautiful," Thaddeus replied.

Because it was true. While Lady Jane was once again the decorous lily, her sister was vibrantly and starkly gorgeous in a sky blue gown that matched her eyes. The gown was simple, its sleek lines emphasizing the curves of her figure. Her dark hair was piled up on her head, revealing the elegant lines of her neck.

"Thank you, Your Grace," Lady Lavinia replied, the wry twist of her lips indicating she didn't quite believe him.

"Lady Jane, might I have a dance? And Lady

Lavinia?" Because he couldn't very well ask one sister to dance and not the other.

"Of course, Your Grace," Lady Scudamore answered. She took Lady Jane's dance card and presented it to him, while Lady Lavinia fumbled with getting hers off her wrist. Lady Scudamore also gave him a pencil, which he used to scribble his name on the card, then did the same to Lady Lavinia's.

"I will return to claim my dance," he said as he bowed.

The ladies curtseyed all over again, and he stepped away, the familiar feeling of suffocation overtaking him as he realized many of the guests had been watching the entire encounter.

The sooner he was settled, the sooner he could stop being an object on display.

At first, I couldn't see anything in the room. I paused at the threshold, waiting for my eyes to adjust to the gloom.

Gradually, I was able to pick out a few things: a fireplace with no fire lit, a large desk at one end, a row of shelves holding books that looked as forbidding as the furniture. I doubted there would be any enjoyable reading to be found in this place.

And then I saw him.

My Dark Husband by Percy Wittlesford

Chapter Six

ady Lavinia?"

The duke held his hand out for her, his eyes seemingly fixed on . . . something over her right shoulder. She hoped it was another female who had attracted his interest, but she doubted that; Jane had returned from their dance together even more convinced he was going to offer marriage.

Which made Lavinia more convinced that she would have to do something drastic to prevent that. Their mother was also convinced, and it would take a lot to derail the marriage train the duke and their mother had apparently boarded.

And wasn't that a terrible metaphor. And she called herself an author?

Clearly this situation had fuddled her mind. The sooner it, and him, were out of her life the better.

"Yes, Your Grace. Thank you." Lavinia slid her hand into his, then placed her other on his shoulder. He hesitated for a fraction of a second, just long enough for her to notice, then put his hand at her waist.

It was warm, and it tingled where his fingers were splayed.

If she reacted like that to just this, what would it be like if—? But no, she couldn't even think that. Even though of course she was imagining it at this very moment.

"Are you enjoying yourself this evening?" he asked, beginning to move her around the dance floor.

He sounded stiff.

"Do you truly want to know?" she replied. She wished she could pretend she spoke without thinking, but she wouldn't lie to herself.

He exhaled, glancing toward the ceiling as though exasperated. She did have that effect on most people, with the notable exceptions of Jane and Percy.

And even Jane got exasperated with her every so often.

She shrugged. "I don't understand why we must always be so polite toward one another," she continued. "Wouldn't it be refreshing if we could say what we were thinking instead of what we were supposed to say?"

He met her gaze, his eyes wide as though startled. Excellent! She'd managed to surprise him!

Why that should be a triumph she didn't know.

And then, to her relief, she saw his lips curl into a tiny smile. "That would be a remarkable disruption of Society, Lady Lavinia."

"Precisely!" she exclaimed.

He chuckled, and she felt her insides warm.

They danced without speaking for a few minutes, Lavinia enjoying the feeling of his hand at her waist, his firm shoulder under her fingers. The musicians gave no indication the music would be ending anytime soon, and for a moment, she wondered if her mother had bribed them to keep playing, mistakenly thinking the duke and Jane would be dancing.

"I wish I were at home," he said abruptly, startling her from her thoughts.

"I'm sorry?" she said, pausing the dance.

"So am I," he replied wryly. He gestured toward the edge of the dance floor, and she nodded, tacitly agreeing the dance was over for them, if not for the musicians.

They stood watching the other dancers—Jane was partnered with one of the gentlemen who'd been most aggressive in his pursuit of her, only nothing would happen because their mother knew full well he was a fortune hunter, and his family didn't have the respectability she craved.

"Ever since I became duke—unexpectedly, you know . . ." At which she nodded, because of course everyone knew how he had inherited.

The Unexpected Duke might make a good book title, for that matter. He was already a good model for a hero, given his general stern stoicism and commanding presence.

And now she was having those feelings again.

". . . I have thought how much of a performance we are all required to give," he continued, oblivious to her reaction to him. "I just want to do what I am obligated to in terms of my holdings and legacy." His lips compressed into a thin line. "But apparently I am obligated to appear at functions like this. And the other evening at the reading."

Small wonder he was so clearly determined to marry, and quickly. He wanted to be done with all of this, but he couldn't until his legacy was secured. Meaning a wife and an heir.

For a moment she felt a thread of sympathy go through her for his situation—she knew he hadn't been raised with any expectations of inheriting, and had committed to a military career before being required to take over as duke.

But then the thread faltered as she thought about how he had chosen Jane, and how much his force of personality might make Jane accidentally say yes when he proposed.

Which made the fault her sister's, but it didn't diminish the fact that it would be devastating for her.

She didn't reply at first, and he cast her a quizzical glance. One with a measure of uncertainty as well, which made her feel sympathetic all over again.

"Lady Lavinia?" he prompted.

"Yes, of course." She bit her lip before responding. "I understand your feelings." She raised an eyebrow. "It is difficult to be under scrutiny for things you were not responsible for." She sighed, thinking of her family. Not that she'd ever regret Percy or Caroline being born, but their presence in her family came close to tipping them over the edge into nonrespectability.

Which was why their mother was obsessed with harnessing the duke's faultless respectability to their own through marriage to Jane.

"Your brother did write those novels, did he not?" the duke asked, misunderstanding her point.

"Percy's books are not what I mean," she said, speaking with some vehemence. "I am proud of him." *And myself.* "It's that when he appears in public people are reminded of what his parentage is."

"Ah. Yes, I apologize," he said, surprising her. Though The Apologetic Duke was a much less compelling title. "I am familiar with that because of Sebastian. Mr. de Silva, the gentleman who was the duke until he was not."

"Of course," she replied in a rueful tone. "I'd forgotten that." She tilted her head to regard him. "And you are still friendly with him?"

He jerked upright as though offended. "Of course. I would not allow Sebastian's situation to negate years of family and friendship. It is not his fault, it is his mother's."

"You are a good friend," she replied.

"I merely do what is right," he shot back.

Of course he did. He was trying to do right with the dukedom, when others might have just let it flounder because they didn't want it. He wasn't continuing his military career because it would put the title in jeopardy. He was searching for a wife because it was the right thing to do in order to secure the dukedom.

He would always do the right thing, it seemed. *The Dutybound Duke.*

"Lady Lavinia," he said, bowing as he spoke, "I am delayed for a dance with our hosts' daughter, Miss Prescott. If you will excuse me." Another responsibility he took to heart.

She watched him thread his way commandingly through the crowd, his head and shoulders above most of the other guests. Wishing he and her mother were not such powerful forces, and that Jane was able to speak for what she wanted.

But they were, and Jane wasn't, and it was up to her. It would always be up to her.

And she would do whatever it took to protect her sister at all costs.

SPEAKING WITH LADY Lavinia, sharing his thoughts with her, left Thaddeus feeling oddly vulnerable. And even more determined to get himself settled so he wouldn't be in a position of vulnerability ever again.

He escorted Miss Prescott back to her mother, congratulating her on the evening's success, then went in search of Lady Jane. His bride-to-be, if all went well.

Because he knew what he wanted, and he should say what was on his mind, shouldn't he? That's what Lady Lavinia had said.

It was unsettling to agree with her, he had to admit.

He spotted Lady Jane's blond hair in the distance and strode purposefully toward her, feeling himself grow oddly anxious.

What if she said no? Or possibly worse, what if she said yes, and it turned out they did not suit?

But they would suit, of course. She fit all the requirements on his list, at least the most important ones. She would learn the rest from him and his staff.

"Your Grace!" Lady Scudamore exclaimed as he appeared.

"Mis Ja—" he began, only to be interrupted by Lady Lavinia.

"Yes, Your Grace, you mentioned you would like to view the Prescotts' impressive collection of paintings."

He narrowed his gaze at her.

"Jane would like to view them as well." Lady Scudamore glared at Lady Lavinia, and Thaddeus nearly—nearly—felt sorry for her.

"Oh, but Jane is promised to dance with Mr. Robens, isn't she?" Lady Lavinia looked at the dance card attached to Lady Jane's wrist. "Yes, she is," she said brightly. "But I am not promised to anyone at the moment, so this would be the perfect time to show you the paintings. They are just in the hallway over there." A moment of silence as Thaddeus tried to figure out what to say without being incredibly rude. "You did say you like art, didn't you?"

"I do love art," Lady Jane added. She gave Thaddeus a hesitant smile. "But Lavinia knows much more about it than I do."

"That's settled, then," Lady Lavinia replied, looping her arm through Thaddeus's. "We'll just go see them for a moment. If you will excuse us."

Thaddeus's feet moved without his willing them to—the unfortunate result of being habituated to taking orders, albeit not usually from a young lady in an evening gown at a ball—and they walked toward the edge of the room, her guiding him through a doorway into a long, narrow hallway. There were a few other party guests there, but they were farther down the hall, all engrossed in staring at the walls. At least they would lend some propriety to what appeared to be a strange sequence of events.

The sconces on the walls illuminated the pictures. Thaddeus noted there was indeed quite a lot of art, most of it looking as though a child had painted it. If this was what Lady Lavinia appreciated, then—

"You can't marry my sister," she said, taking all thoughts of art out of his mind entirely. She had let go of his arm and turned so she was facing him. The hallway was too narrow to allow for much distance, so they stood face-to-face. Or face to chest, since she was much shorter than he.

"Pardon?" He glanced toward the other people, but her voice was too low for them to hear. Thank God.

Her expression grew exasperated. "My sister," she repeated in a slower tone of voice. "You cannot marry her."

Thaddeus bit back the natural reaction—"And why not?"—because it wasn't any of her business, damn it, and he would not be drawn into an inappropriate conversation.

"I can escort you back if we are not here to view—"

She grabbed his arm, gripping it tightly as she leaned closer into him. "You would eat her alive. She is not made to be a duchess, especially if the duke is *you*." Her words stung Thaddeus, and he didn't hold himself back this time.

"And what is wrong with me?" he said, his voice low and furious. He'd only just met this woman, but she had managed to get under his skin in a way nobody ever had.

Including his friend Nash, whose first thought was to hit someone rather than to talk it out. Thankfully, Thaddeus was just as big as Nash, so hadn't suffered permanent damage.

"You're—" she began, letting go of his arm and flailing her hands in a wild gesture, "you!"

Thaddeus looked up as he exhaled. "That is certainly illuminating. I am me." He returned his gaze to her, noting how her eyes blazed with emotion, how her whole body seemed to radiate an intensity brighter than the candlelight in the hallway.

"And it's obvious you are interested in marriage, which is certainly fine for someone like you, but you can't marry Jane." She grabbed his arm again. "I am begging you, just leave off."

He yanked his arm away, only to entangle his fingers in her wide skirts, the button from his coat snagging the fabric, inadvertently tugging on both of them, making her stumble.

He saw it unfold as though it were a terrible dream, a veritable nightmare, as her body crashed into his, making him fall back into some sort of furniture behind him, stabbing his back with a sharp blow, at which he made a loud exclamation.

And she was still on him, now covering him like she was a blanket, her arms flung over his shoulders as she struggled to remove herself. And his hands were against her, trying to push her off, only he'd just realized one of his hands had landed on her breast.

"Lavinia!"

Goddamn it.

Thaddeus closed his eyes slowly as he heard her mother's voice and the sound of approaching feet. Several approaching feet. She was still pinned on him, parts of her pressing into parts of him, and he yanked his other hand away, which made a terrible ripping sound as fabric—likely her gown, because this wasn't hellish enough—tore.

"Damn it," he heard her murmur as she finally extricated herself from his body.

And he opened his eyes to see the whole awful sight, as though it was a painting, a nightmare landscape unfolding in front of his eyes.

Her gown, now shredded on one side. Her hair, completely disheveled and falling around her shoulders. Her eyes, still blazing, her mouth open in shock, her chest rapidly rising and falling as she panted for breath.

Her mother, standing at the entrance to the hallway, an expression of dismay on her face. People on the other side of him having scurried down the hall at the noise, some of them making small noises indicating their shock, others just standing there gawking.

All of them making him acutely, keenly aware of what he was going to have to do.

"No," she said, shaking her head slowly as she met his gaze. "No."

"We have to," he replied in a low tone. "We have to."

And then her sister joined the group, glancing from him to her, then back again, her mind seeming to come to the same conclusion.

"Vinnie," she said at last, sounding horrified, "what have you *done*?"

"I DIDN'T DO anything!" Lavinia said, for likely the thousandth time.

Not that it mattered. Nobody was listening to her anyway.

All of them—Jane, her mother, the duke, and her—were seated in the Capel sitting room, the same one she, Jane, and Percy had been in a few days ago. When she barely knew the duke existed, much less—

"We'll get married in three weeks."

He looked grim, and Lavinia felt a moment of sympathy for him. But then recalled that his grim expression was because he felt as though he had to get married to her.

"We don't have to do this." Lavinia addressed her words to him, who was already shaking his head before she finished.

"But the scandal!" her mother exclaimed.

Lavinia arched a brow as she regarded her mother. "Seriously? All the scandal this family has had, and you think me not marrying the duke would be anything other than our usual goings-on?"

Lavinia turned her gaze to Jane as she finished, and her breath caught.

Jane was looking at her with a pained expression. Clearly not because she wouldn't be marrying the duke—of course not—but because . . .

Damn it. If Lavinia brought additional scandal to the family name, Mr. McTavish's stickler parents would never allow him to marry Jane.

The truth of it washed over her like someone had dumped buckets of cold water on her head.

She would have to do this. She would have to marry him if she wanted her sister to find any happiness.

"Lavinia," Jane said as she rose. "Could I speak to you alone?"

Jane's face had returned to its usual calm mien, and Lavinia braced herself to resist whatever it was her sister was going to say—because of course Jane would tell Lavinia not to marry the duke even though both of them knew what it would mean for Jane.

Jane was too good for this world. Lavinia just hoped Mr. McTavish was good enough for her.

"We'll return in a moment," Lavinia replied, holding her hand up to stave off her mother's inevitable objection.

They slipped out into the hall, walking swiftly to the dining room, which would be unoccupied this late in the evening.

It was eerie, the open windows allowing the moonlight to stream in, casting long shadows on the enormous table, suitable for the entire family plus whichever guest happened to be in the house at that time.

"You don't have to do this." Jane's tone was sincere, and it made Lavinia's heart hurt. No, of course she didn't; she was stubborn enough to just refuse, and there would be nothing anybody could do to persuade her.

But if she didn't—

"You know I do, Jane." Lavinia took her sister's hands in hers and squeezed. "Look, I can admit I find the duke . . . attractive"—which was a mild way of describing the powerful reaction she had to him—"and I am certain he will be a fine husband."

She swallowed the lump in her throat. "One of us should get the future she deserves."

Jane's face crumpled, and she wrapped Lavinia

up in a tight hug. And then both of them were crying, and Lavinia knew she was doing the right thing.

Because there was only so much scandal her family would withstand. Because her mother would make her life hell if she refused, and would also no doubt figure out a way to have the duke marry Jane, after all. Because when she was married to the duke, she could ensure Percy get all the opportunities he wished for. Because Jane would be able to marry her Mr. McTavish sooner than expected.

Because a tiny part of her wanted to.

Eventually, they withdrew from the hug, both of them wiping their eyes with Jane's handkerchief.

"We should go back," Lavinia said at last.

Jane nodded. She still looked beautiful after crying, while Lavinia knew she probably looked a fright, with bright red cheeks and eyes and a drippy nose.

Perhaps the duke would see her and run away screaming. That would solve the problem at least.

She let out a wry chuckle as she and Jane left the dining room and returned to her mother and the duke.

Back to her future. Back to her fate.

To say my heart raced at the sight of him would be an understatement. It galloped, trying to flee out of my chest entirely.

Not because he was hideous to look at; the contrary, really. But because his entire appearance was crafted to look as menacing as possible.

And I was definitely menaced.

My Dark Husband by Percy Wittlesford

Chapter Seven

*T*haddeus watched her—*his future wife!*—leave the room, resisting the urge to break something. *Anything.* He never reacted this violently—that was his friend Nash's job—but it felt as though he could see his future, the tiny hopeful piece he'd wanted for himself, was being closed out, and he would never get the opportunity to have it.

Never was a long time.

Instead, he would spend the rest of his life with a woman who irritated him, made him physically aware of everything, and who was apparently just as averse to marrying him.

Not to mention she was very against his marrying her sister. So there were at least two women she did not want him to marry.

Perhaps he could round up more ladies and make it an even dozen.

Goddamn it.

"Lavinia should be back in a moment," Lady Scudamore said, sounding anxious.

Of course. She had a duke on the line, and she didn't want to lose her catch.

"She is quite . . . lively," she continued. "She might not have the looks of her sister, but she is a delightful person in her own right." She did not sound convinced, and once again he felt that fierce defensiveness on Lavinia's behalf—even though she had proven well capable of defending herself. "Lavinia has always enjoyed books, and sharing her thoughts, and her most enduring strength is her loyalty to her family. She would do anything for us," she said proudly, sounding more confident in her words.

Which meant, at least to Thaddeus's ears, that she always spoke her mind—which he knew already—and her first allegiance would be to her family. Never to him.

The complete opposite of the attributes he wished for in a bride.

And he suspected she did more than "enjoy books"; he rather thought she likely was obsessed in reading them, which also meant she would have interests outside of being a proper duchess.

He had not missed her quickly hidden look of disdain when he'd admitted he did not read.

He didn't mind that people liked to read; he just didn't think it was appropriate for it to be an all-consuming passion outside of living one's life in a suitable manner. And he had no reason to change his mind—Lady Lavinia reading many books likely contributed to her having outspoken opinions. Opinions he likely did not share, and would not wish to hear.

"I had hopes of you choosing Jane," Lady Scudamore continued. Apparently oblivious to the truth that he hadn't been able to choose, but the choice had been thrust upon him.

Literally.

"But I am just as happy you have settled on Lavinia."

"Yes." He spoke curtly, and the shortness of his tone was reflected in the shift to her dismayed expression.

Not any more dismayed than I am, he wished he could say.

Although of course he could not; no matter how he felt about it, this was the truth. He was going to marry her, and she him.

As long as she did eventually return. Perhaps she would decide that escaping London was the better choice. Perhaps she and her sister were already on the run.

Because being disgraced and estranged from your family and your entire world was preferable to being the wife of a fantastically wealthy and powerful duke?

Even she couldn't be that idiotic.

He exhaled in both relief and panic as he heard the door open, and the two ladies slipped inside.

He rose on instinct, glancing from one to the other.

Apparently there had been some crying, judging by the ladies' red eyes and damp cheeks. He wished he had been able to join them—he'd like to howl his frustration at the sequence of events.

Why did she have to draw him away to that hallway? Why did she have to stumble into him? He knew it wasn't her plan to marry him—he could tell that by how stunned she'd looked when her mother and the gawking crowd had arrived. But everything had happened, and now they were both stuck. With one another. With a future neither of them wanted.

No wonder he wanted to break something.

"I will make all the necessary arrangements," he said through gritted teeth.

"You don't—" she began, only to be cut off by her mother.

"Of course he does," Lady Scudamore said. "My daughter, a duchess! Not the one I'd anticipated," she continued, glancing at Lady Jane, "but nonetheless."

"Lady Lavinia," he began, "I am pleased you have done me the honor of agreeing to be my bride." He didn't look at her directly. He couldn't. He was too furious, too aware that at any moment he might shout his frustration.

"But I didn't—"

"Now that this is decided, there are some things I must take care of." Such as finding a reasonable way to release his anger, speak to her father and finalize the details of their marriage, get a license, and become resigned to a life where his best hope at happiness was not finding her as infuriating as he did currently.

He nodded. "I will send word when the details have been worked through."

Thaddeus didn't look at any of them when he left the room.

"WHAT THE HELL happened?"

Thaddeus's cousin Sebastian, the former Duke of Hasford, stood in the parlor of the small home he shared with his wife. Sebastian's dogs circled

Thaddeus's boots, making him glare down at them in suspicion.

He had left the Capel home with the full intention of returning to his town house to present the problem to Melmsford so they would work on solving it together.

But he'd felt nearly suffocated as he came close to his home, and instead turned in a different direction, knowing if there was any hope of not being miserable about the situation, Sebastian would provide it.

Thus far, Sebastian had not delivered.

Granted, it was past two o'clock in the morning, and Thaddeus had banged on the door until a rumpled Sebastian had appeared. Thaddeus supposed even charming gentlemen like Sebastian had times when they were less charming, which for Sebastian appeared to be two thirty-eight in the morning.

"Seriously, Thad," Sebastian said in a softer tone. He wrapped his dressing gown tighter around himself and ran his hand through his disheveled hair. "What happened?"

Thaddeus shook his head, the bile in his throat preventing him from speaking.

"Sit down."

Sebastian pushed him forcefully down onto the small sofa, then took the seat opposite, leaning forward to rest his hands on his knees.

"It's not what I planned, Seb." He spoke in a strained voice. "I had a list—"

"Of course you did," Sebastian interrupted, a thread of humor in his words. "You always do."

"And this woman, this Lady Lavinia, is nothing at all like my list." He shook his head again. "Her sister is ideal—beautiful, quiet, pleasantly mannered, modest in her behavior."

"So her sister is hideous, spits when she talks, and walks around drawing attention to herself?"

Thaddeus snorted in spite of himself. "Not that bad." He could admit, if just to himself, that he did find her attractive. That a part of him, the fiercely brutal part, couldn't wait to get her naked in his bed.

He had just expected that would be but one of the benefits of marriage, and now it was going to provide the only opportunity for joy.

Although joy was the wrong word. An assuagement of lust, perhaps.

Hardly the basis for a relationship. And what if she didn't feel the same way? What if the thought of sexual relations with him horrified her?

Goddamn it.

"I'm glad to hear she is not a troll," Sebastian replied. "I believe you when you say there is nothing to be done but marry her." He paused. "So how are you going to manage it? Because just as much as I know you have a list, I know you have a plan."

Thaddeus felt his eyes widen. "You're right. A plan. I need a plan."

Sebastian clapped his hands together and got up to walk toward a small table, yanking open its drawer and withdrawing a pen and paper.

He held it out to Thaddeus with a flourish. "You'll feel better if you have a plan," he said.

Thaddeus took it, laying the paper on his leg and placing the inkwell on the cushion beside him. His fingers held the pen above the paper as though preparing to strike.

Though he had no clue what his plan would be. But his previous plan—marry an unassuming lady who would be the ideal partner—had blown up spectacularly in his face, so like any battle maneuver, he would have to adjust.

"LAVINIA, YOU CAN'T do this."

Percy had repeated the same iteration of words nearly a hundred times in the past week. And each time, Lavinia had found herself smiling wanly and shaking her head in tacit acceptance.

She hadn't yet gotten to the point where she had reasonable words to accept the situation; goodness knew she had tried, but everything she'd managed to say had sounded desperate and sad, and she would not do the duke the dishonor—even amongst her own family—of admitting to those emotions.

Even though Jane knew, of course.

"I've said the same thing, but she won't listen," Jane said in her soft voice. "I told her the McTavishes would see reason eventually. Henry tells me they might want to invite me to their theater box in a few weeks."

Lavinia felt her mouth open in a sharp retort—what right did the McTavishes have to lord it over Jane, who was too good for their meek son—but Percy caught her eye and shook his head in warning.

"Even without the McTavishes' approval, or

lack thereof," Lavinia replied, "the duke's reputation is also at stake." That had been made clear when word of the engagement got out, and the scandal sheets immediately began to revive how the duke got his title in the first place, implying that the duke's own heritage was stained by duplicity.

Even though it was obvious to anyone who'd met him that the duke was a man of honor. That he had been determined to marry her, despite their clear differences, and despite his preference for Jane, was proof of that.

"I can't do anything that could damage his reputation," she continued. "It would be one thing if he were the one to figure out a way for this not to happen, some sort of graceful exit that wouldn't harm either of our reputations."

Percy snorted. "I don't think even you are good enough of a writer to dream up that kind of scenario."

"Thank you?" Lavinia replied wryly. "So it is inevitable. And I need to make the best of it. At least because we need to marry quickly we won't have to have the usual fuss of a long engagement or engagement parties or that sort of thing."

"What do you like about him?" Jane asked. Of course. Leave it to Jane to try to see the best in someone.

"What do I like about him?" Lavinia repeated. Perhaps it would not be entirely correct to mention his thighs. "Uh—he looks as though he is strong enough to hoist me over a fallen log, should one be in our path." She paused. "And he says he likes art."

"A fallen log," Percy echoed in a dubious tone. "You will be basing your marriage on the downfall of a tree."

Lavinia felt her face heat. "It is not as though I can stop this. I am going to have to make the best of it. If pressed, I will add that I admire his honor." Perhaps she should make a new list—*Things I Appreciate About My Soon-to-Be-Husband*. "Even though it is to my detriment in this occasion," she added in a rueful tone of voice.

"When have you ever made the best of things?" Percy asked, not unreasonably.

Lavinia glared at him. Even though he was right—she was far more likely to rail against the unjust circumstances than accommodate them.

But still. This time, she would have to settle. She would have to make the best of things.

At least she had his thighs to look forward to. *Added to the list*, she thought with a wry smile.

He didn't speak, not at first. Instead, he stood in the middle of the room, his boots planted on what I could see was a worn, dark carpet.

His arms were folded over his chest and he was looking at me as one might a bug. Or a creature who wasn't deserving of any of his notice.

Naturally, being who I was, and already determined to see this thing through, I took that as a challenge.

"I am Lady Rosalind Faringsworth," I declared, holding my chin up as I spoke. "I am here on your invitation, I presume."

"You do presume, madam," he replied. His voice was a low growl, sending a shiver up my spine. He had an accent I was unfamiliar with, one that made his words sound even more foreboding. "And that is why I sent my summons."

My Dark Husband by Percy Wittlesford

Chapter Eight

"If I were writing my wedding day," Lavinia muttered, "it would be the stormiest day London had ever seen. Lightning striking everywhere, rain pouring down in sheets, branches swaying dangerously in the wind." She peered outside, wrinkling her nose in distaste.

The day was perfect. Unusually perfect. The sun was shining, there were only a few fluffy clouds floating in the blue, blue sky, and it was neither too hot nor too cold.

"What did you say?" Jane asked, pausing from adjusting Lavinia's skirts. "Stop moving, I need to take care of this," she added, yanking Lavinia back from the window.

There hadn't been much time to shop for a suitable "getting married to a duke because one was accidentally compromised" gown, but Lady Scudamore had persevered, dragging a reluctant Lavinia and a helpful Jane to their modiste of choice, who'd managed to rework one of Lavinia's evening gowns into a wedding gown.

It was nearly as perfect as the day, Lavinia thought ruefully. It was cream colored, with a low lace-edged scoop neck showing a reasonable amount of bosom, a wide darker cream ribbon encircling her waist, with an enormous skirt flowing out over her hips. Both the sleeves and the skirt had flounces of tulle added to them, elevating the gown to look like something a fairy might wear. If a fairy were to marry a duke in a hasty wedding.

She was being overly dramatic; she knew that. But she also knew that this was her life, her future, and it was now irrevocably entwined with someone she knew very little about.

What did she know about him anyway?

1. He appeared to be very fit.
    a. She found him exceedingly attractive.
2. He did not read.
3. He was determined to do what he believed was the right thing, even if that right thing was damaging.
4. His thighs. (Not truly a thing to know about him, but worth noting nonetheless).*
5. He was a former military man who still carried that military rigidity.

    *This should probably go under #1, but his thighs truly deserve their own line.

That was not much to base a marriage on, although obviously many people had based their marriages on less.

"Lavinia?"

"Oh, what?" she replied. Jane stood in front of her, a frown on her face.

"You were muttering again." Jane placed her hands on Lavinia's shoulders. "It is not too late to refuse to do this, you know."

Lavinia snorted. "It is too late." She wrapped her arms around Jane's waist and hugged her. "And you will be happy." She withdrew from the hug and met Jane's gaze. "Besides, he will not be the worst husband ever." Those thighs, after all.

"Hardly a recommendation," Jane replied, her lips twisting into a rueful grimace.

"Help me with the veil," Lavinia said, gesturing to the long piece of white gauze on her bed. The veil was simple but elegant, hanging from a coronet with orange flowers attached to it. It went from Lavinia's head all the way down to her knees.

It would take a bit for him to raise it up for the kiss.

The kiss. Oh goodness. She was going to receive her first kiss. In a church, in front of everybody, with a man she knew approximately five things about.

And then there would be the wedding night, during which there would be much more than kissing.

Oh dear.

"Lavinia?" Jane said, sounding worried. Her expression must have reflected some of her apprehension. "What can I do?"

Lavinia shook her head. "Nothing." She forced a smile onto her lips.

Jane gave her a skeptical look.

Lavinia rolled her eyes in exasperation. "I promise, if I am completely miserable, I will do something about it."

Jane regarded her for a moment, then her eyes widened, and she went to get something from the top of Lavinia's wardrobe.

"Do you swear it on this?" She held out a copy of Lavinia's first book, *The Darkest Lord*.

Lavinia laughed as she placed her palm on the book. "I do solemnly swear on this most holy of books—even though it has several juvenile turns of phrase—that if I am completely miserable in my marriage I will do something about it."

Jane nodded as Lavinia spoke, then tossed the book onto Lavinia's bed and grabbed her sister in a warm embrace. "You just do so much for us, and I don't think it's right," she murmured into Lavinia's shoulder.

"If you're happy, that will be well worth it," Lavinia replied, trying not to let the words choke on her tears.

"Girls!"

They exchanged aggrieved glances as they heard their mother's bellow from the floor below.

"I gather it's time to go to the church," Lavinia said. She gathered up the bouquet of flowers the duke had sent that morning, casting a final glance at her room, which would be her room no longer.

Tonight she would have a new bedroom, one which the duke would presumably enter.

She shivered in both dread and anticipation.

"IT'S NOT TOO late."

Sebastian crossed his arms over his chest, staring at Thaddeus with an expression he likely thought was stern.

Thaddeus stared back at him until Sebastian exhaled in frustration, turning his gaze skyward.

"We could kidnap you," Nash offered.

Thaddeus turned his glare toward him.

The three were in his bedroom, Thaddeus having dismissed his valet as he prepared for his wedding day. He wore a blue frock coat, a white waistcoat, and trousers in a ridiculous light purple color that his valet Hodgkins had insisted was proper attire for a groom. *No pastel colors.* That was the least awful thing he'd contradicted on his list.

"It's not a horrible idea," Nash muttered in response to Thaddeus's expression.

But it was. It would go against everything Thaddeus knew about himself—that he honored his commitments, that he would do the right thing no matter what the personal cost, and that he would not run away from a difficult situation.

And he would ultimately achieve his goals even though the method was not what he had planned; he'd have a wife, and presumably he would have an heir in a year or so.

"I've never met your bride-to-be," Sebastian said. "What is she like?"

Thaddeus paused as he considered what to say about her. Replying that she was precisely the opposite of what he'd envisioned would be dishonorable and inappropriate to share, even if it was to his best friends.

"She is . . . lively," he began. Sebastian and Nash shot speaking glances at one another. "And an excellent conversationalist." He took a deep breath. "She is quite pretty"—which was true, although she was not beautiful like her sister—"and is deeply loyal." *To her family*, but he wouldn't add that.

"We know you'll make the best of the situation. You always do," Sebastian said. "But you do have options."

"Besides kidnapping," Nash added.

"Such as?" Thaddeus ran his palms over the soft trousers. If it weren't for the color, he might actually like them.

"You can lead separate lives. You've got plenty of estates, I know that. You can send her to one of them."

Thaddeus arched an eyebrow. "Banish my new bride to one of my estates because she is not who I would have chosen?" He shook his head. "That would be unnecessarily cruel." Not to mention that if they were separated, there would be no heir in a year or so.

"You should ask her if it would be cruel," Sebastian replied. "Maybe she would prefer it. What if she has just as little wish to be with you as you do with her?"

Thaddeus strongly suspected she *did* feel the same way as he, which would be excellent if a husband and wife were united in their opinion of what to do when they found themselves in the same room at the same time, but not so much when they were united in their mutual antipathy, if not to each other, then to their situation.

Agreement that they wished not to be married to one another was not a good basis for a marriage. To put it mildly.

Though perhaps if they admitted to their feelings they could find a way to solve their situation. If he thought of it as a military strategy, then he would come up with a plan.

"Your Grace?"

The voice, Fletchfield's voice, came from the other side of the closed bedroom door.

"Yes?"

"The carriage is ready, Your Grace."

The carriage to take them to the church. Where he'd confront his future, one that looked a lot different from what he had pictured.

LAVINIA SWALLOWED AS the duke helped her into the carriage.

She was married. To him.

The ceremony and the wedding breakfast had passed in a blur of congratulations and confusion—the former from people who thought weddings in general were happy things, the latter from people who were well aware that the duke and Lady Lavinia had just barely met, and that the lady's sister was a far more appropriate choice.

Lavinia wished she could tell those people she entirely agreed.

Yet here they were. Alone together for the first time since the hallway incident, the one that had resulted in this.

The only moment of the ceremony that stood out for her, in fact, was at the end, when the officiant had informed him that he could now kiss his bride.

Did he hesitate, or did it only feel like that?

Eventually he'd raised the veil, drawing it up far more easily than she had imagined, leaning forward to place his mouth on hers.

A moment of too brief contact, lips pressing against lips, and then he'd withdrawn, turning to face the applauding crowd before she'd even registered she'd had her first kiss.

A disappointing first kiss. She hoped they wouldn't all be that way.

"That was . . ." she began. Faltering when she realized she didn't have the words.

Ironic, given what she did.

"It was."

He spoke in a firm tone, one that strongly implied the subject was settled, and in fact, she should not attempt any more conversation.

Well, she'd be damned if she'd allow him to control her already.

"The gentlemen who stood up with you—your friends? Your relatives?" One of them was also a duke, she knew that, but she didn't know which one. She tended not to pay attention if it didn't directly affect her family.

He made a noise of disapproval before actually replying. "Both. My cousin Sebastian and our friend Nash. Sebastian was the duke before me, only—"

"Ah." She knew the story of how he came to be duke, of course.

"Ana Maria, Nash's wife, is my cousin and Sebastian's half sister."

"Your family sounds as though it might be as complicated as mine." Perhaps they had more in common than just their mutual desire not to be married.

"Your family appears to be more scandalous." God, but he sounded like a pompous ass. "Except for your sister. Lady Jane."

Lavinia gritted her teeth. "I know we have only been married for perhaps twenty minutes, but we are going to have to agree on some things before we proceed."

He uttered a derisive snort. "Or what? There is no turning back, Lady Lav—that is, Your Grace."

Your Grace. She was a duchess now.

"That might be true," she continued, refusing to let him—or her new title—intimidate her, "but it is my belief that it is far better to establish things at the outset rather than holding back. It is the way my family deals with everything."

"Whereas my family is the opposite."

She arched a brow as she regarded him. "And how was that for you?"

His expression was fierce. It was a good thing she was not easily cowed. "It was—" And then he paused, taking a deep breath.

"It was not good." He hesitated, and she held her breath, wondering what he would say next. Not daring to move a muscle in case he balked at sharing anything personal with her.

But he'd have to, wouldn't he, now that they were married?

Wasn't that what marriage was?

And if it wasn't, what was it?

"It was very difficult," he admitted at last.

SHARING HIS HURT felt like he'd just ripped open his chest and shown her his soul. A secret part of himself he'd never shared with anyone before.

And it was just a mild reply to her question. What would it be like if he were asked to reveal deeper emotions?

Thank God he wasn't planning on having any deeper emotions for her. He didn't know if he could tolerate the depths of feeling that would engender.

"All the more reason we should have everything out in the open," she said in a reasonable tone.

A tone that, nonetheless, irked him to his core.

"We'll be home soon," he said.

"That isn't a response," she pointed out, sounding faintly amused.

Well. At least she was able to find him and his behavior humorous.

Which did not irk him more. Not at all.

"We can discuss it at home," she continued brightly.

Home. His home was now her home. *Their* home.

The entire situation coiled around him like a serpent, making him feel as though he were gasping, making him feel as though he couldn't catch enough air. Like he was drowning.

Squeezed by a snake and submerged in water.

He had an excellent attitude toward his marriage, didn't he?

He'd have to reconcile himself to it soon or it would bottle up inside him and eventually explode.

But if he did, he knew, she would be able to tolerate it—not cower from him like he was a monster. Not hide from any kind of display of emotion the way his parents had. How *he* did.

He turned to see her regarding him steadily—as though she was cataloguing his attributes and shortcomings. *Did she make lists also?* He resisted the urge to ask her what she'd concluded—it was far too early in their acquaintance, and further, he thought he might know what she'd say.

And he didn't think he would want to hear it.

"Thank you," she said, startling him.

"For what?"

She snorted. "For seeing this through. It would have been devastating if we had not solved the problem in this way." She gestured vaguely in the air around them, indicating their marriage. "When I was trying to find a way out, I hadn't thought it all through. How not doing it would affect everyone else."

Her family, clearly.

"But you knew. You'd thought it all through, hadn't you? As though it was a military maneuver, and you were anticipating possible outcomes." She sounded as though she admired him.

Hard not to respond to that. Perhaps this wouldn't be completely terrible.

"Though that must make it hard to react in the moment," she added in a tone that indicated she thought that was a failing.

So much for not being completely terrible.

"Your Grace. Your Grace."

The butler stood at the doorway, bowing as he held the door open.

Lavinia held her breath as she entered, keenly aware of him right behind her. That body, those thighs, would be sharing a bed with her tonight.

Or not. She wasn't reading into things to recognize that he was just as averse to their marriage as she was. Perhaps he would ignore her entirely, including during the evening.

Though she also wasn't reading into things to recognize that there was an attraction between them that didn't just originate from her; she'd seen his eyes track her figure when he thought she wasn't looking, and she'd felt the sparks when they'd conversed.

"The duchess is tired. We'll take tea in the sitting room," he said, taking her arm and guiding her to one of the many doors that opened into the main hallway.

She opened her mouth to retort that she wasn't tired at all, but he tightened his grip on her and leaned over to speak quietly in her ear. "I know you're not, but I want to give the staff time to prepare. They weren't expecting us for another hour."

Her anger dissipated in a moment. He was being . . . thoughtful? Of his staff?

He reached the door and flung it open, gesturing for her to enter, then followed, closing it behind them.

The sitting room was surprisingly cozy, a stark contrast to the definitely not cozy husband who had followed her in. Two sofas were arranged on either side of plush carpeting, and she could even see a window seat where one might—if one were her—like to curl up on and read all day.

She turned to face him, planting her hands on her hips. "Are you certain you're a real duke?" she asked. She accompanied her words with a wry tone to her voice so that he would—hopefully—know she was kidding.

"Why would you ask that?" he said, his brow furrowed.

Noted: her new husband did not always recognize humor.

"Because you care about the well-being and comfort of your staff," she replied. "That kind of consideration isn't very ducal." She raised her eyebrows. "They might blackball you at the next meeting of dukes."

He snorted, striding past her to a small table at the edge of the room. He picked up a decanter and poured a dark liquid into a glass, then turned to her with a questioning look.

"Yes, please," she replied. Because if she couldn't drink liquor on her wedding day to the Impenetrable and Possibly Humorless Duke, when could she drink liquor?

"Here," he said, handing her the glass. He held his glass to his lips, waiting, until she took a sip, sputtering as the whisky burned her throat. "Would you care to sit down?"

She nodded, her eyes stinging from the alcohol.

He sat also, taking the seat beside her on the sofa. She was conscious of the warmth emanating from his body. If she moved over just six inches, her leg would be pressed against his.

He stretched his arm across the back of the sofa, then jerked it away as his fingers touched her hair.

"It's fine," she said. "We are married, after all."

He grimaced, and she couldn't help but utter a rueful laugh.

"Much as we might regret that," she added.

His brows lowered, and he narrowed his gaze at her. "We *are* married. That means you are due my respect. I apologize if I have said or done anything that might indicate otherwise."

He sounded sincere.

"Is this the first time you've apologized?" she asked in a soft voice.

"I will be drummed out of the dukes' cabal if this continues," he replied. Perhaps he did have a sense of humor, after all.

"And I think it wise for us both to be open and honest with one another."

He had returned to his usual serious tone.

She clasped her hands in her lap. "Go ahead."

"What?"

She lifted her chin. "Be honest."

She braced herself as he began to speak.

The storm that had begun that morning had not yet relented, and it took the very moment that he spoke to issue a loud clap of thunder. I forced myself not to jump, but stood there facing him, both of us silent, both of us surveying the other.

I suppose I should describe the man who turned out to hold my future in his hands.

It would be comparable to describing the god Hades—a man who seemed to hold darkness in his very soul.

My Dark Husband by Percy Wittlesford

Chapter Nine

$\mathcal{I}$ think we can both acknowledge that we are in this circumstance—"

"If a marriage can be called a circumstance," she interrupted.

"We are in this circumstance through circumstances not under our control." He exhaled, well aware that he sounded like an idiot. An idiot with a vocabulary of one word. *Circumstantial circumstances.*

"And if we are to have some modicum of happiness, we should establish some guidelines."

"Like drawing up a battle plan?" she asked in a dry tone.

He bristled. Because that is exactly what he had done. "Being prepared for anything—"

"Any kind of circumstance," she said, deepening her tone to mirror his.

"Is wise in any situation."

Lord, could he sound more like a pompous ass? He imagined if he were to ask her, she would answer definitely no. *No, you could not sound more like a pompous ass, because you sound like the most pompous ass in existence.*

He wished he had a portion of her apparent ability to laugh at . . . circumstances.

"And if we accept that premise," he continued, knowing they both thought he was a pompous ass, but unable to alter his words, "then we can proceed to navigate our life together."

"Navigate our life together?" she echoed. "What does that even mean?"

He cleared his throat. His plan had sounded much better in his head. "It means that since we find ourselves here, we should agree on some parameters."

"Like a contract," she replied. "I think we should write this down." She gave him a sly look. "I like to get everything down on paper," she said as she leaped from her seat. "Do you have any?"

"In the drawer of that table," he replied, pointing to it. "I write a fair amount of lists myself." That felt like a more intimate confession than it should have.

She plucked a few sheets from the drawer he'd indicated as well as a pencil, then returned to the sofa, glancing around with an apparent look of confusion as she sat down again.

"Oh!" she exclaimed with a look of mischief on her face. "I can write on you."

He stiffened. "Write on me?"

"Yes, just there." She took a sheet of the paper and laid it on top of his leg. "See? It's quite hard." And then her eyes widened more than he thought possible in a human, her cheeks turning bright red. "I meant—"

"How about I get a book from the library?" he

said, biting his lip to keep from laughing at her. "You can write on that."

Wait. He wanted to laugh? That was unexpected. He did not laugh.

At least, apparently, until now.

And, even more intriguing, was that his new wife was knowledgeable about some things. What that meant for their life in the bedroom remained to be seen, but at least she wouldn't be completely surprised tonight.

If the negotiations went well, at least. He would not force anything on her, even if he was within his rights to do so.

He had thought it all out. Their not wanting to get married to one another in the first place, his duties as a duke, hers as a wife.

He retrieved a book from the shelf, carrying it back to where she sat holding her paper and pencil. She had a bright look in her eye, as though she was gleeful in anticipation.

He'd have to file that away in information about his duchess: *Appears delighted to engage in marriage navigation. Enjoys making a list.* As he did.

Although he didn't yet know if it was the navigation itself or the anticipated result that she was most pleased by.

He placed the book between them on the sofa, and she picked it up, setting it in her lap. She put the tip of the pencil between her lips, her tongue darting out to lick its point.

He felt the impact of that gesture everywhere, but most particularly *there.* The place that hoped, most urgently, that they could come to some sort of marriage agreement.

Because he'd like to fulfill at least one of the items on his list, and this one would definitely be the most pleasurable.

"Well?"

She spoke in an impatient tone, which made him bristle. "Well what?" he shot back. "It is not as though I am dictating our negotiations. We are . . . negotiating."

One dark eyebrow arched. "Negotiating our circumstance?" Her tone was wry as she emphasized the last word, which irritated him even more.

"Yes."

And then she rolled her eyes. If only he could act on what he was feeling now, he'd haul her onto his lap, grasp her round bottom in the palm of his hand, and kiss her so thoroughly that she couldn't speak, and not just because he was monopolizing her mouth. Perhaps he'd caress that same bottom and then smack it with the flat of his hand after asking if she thought she should be punished.

Goddamn it. He wanted her so much it felt as though it was a tangible thing. And he hoped she would be just as feisty and irascible in bed as she was in conversation—he wanted an equal bed partner, not a woman who would just lie there and let him do as he wished.

He doubted she would ever do as he wished.

Unless it also suited her.

Perhaps he should add that item to his list: *Engage in mutually satisfactory goals involving pleasure.*

"Your Grace?" He was giving her an odd look, one that was both tantalizing and alarming.

Though in his case, those two adjectives were nearly the same. At least when it came to how she reacted to him.

She was intrigued by his proposing some sort of negotiation, by the notion that he was thoughtful enough to realize that while both of them might chafe against their marriage, she had much less power than he in the course of it.

But perhaps that would ultimately give her *more* power. It was clear he was considerate, even if she found his attitude and behavior irksome. He cared about his staff, and now it seemed he cared about her. Or at least about her comfort in their situation—their *circumstance*, as he might put it.

"You should call me something else," he muttered.

"Something besides Your Grace?" She shrugged. "But you are Your Grace. As I am now, it seems. Do you mean you would be confused by all the 'Your Graces' in the house? I am certain we will know which one of us we are referring to." She couldn't help but tease him. His words and actions were so pragmatic—did he have a playful bone in his body at all?

"And what if one of the Graces was actually named Grace?" she continued.

He did not look amused. At all. Maybe he didn't understand? "What I mean is, if a person's given name was Gr—"

"I know what you mean," he said, sounding annoyed.

"Oh." She shrugged again. It would be unfortunate if her new husband did not share—or perhaps even *have*—a sense of humor, but it wouldn't be the worst thing. The worst thing would be if he tamped her down any time she let her humor show, and she already knew he wouldn't do that. Yes, he had just effectively shut her down, but he hadn't been brutally dismissive or callously judgmental.

Unlike some of her family members, she thought.

"So how should I address you?" She waved the still blank sheet of paper in her hand. "Is that one of the items we'll be negotiating?"

His eyes widened, and she burst out laughing at his obvious shock.

And then—miracle of marriage miracles—his mouth curled into a faint smile. Very faint, and she wanted to laugh even harder because he now seemed even more startled. At smiling? At finding her humor amusing in the first place?

"I am willing to negotiate with the proviso that 'precious' is completely off the table."

Added to List of Lavinia's Responsibilities: Call him Precious at least once.

"Agreed," she said. She picked her pencil up and began to write. "Is there anything else that is not up for discussion?"

He clamped his lips together in their customary straight line, then lifted his chin as though he were about to issue a command.

"Love."

She sucked in a breath as she stared at him, the word jangling around her head like an out-of-control billiard ball. *Love, love, love.*

"Who said anything about love?" she asked, trying not to sound defensive.

"I did," he replied. His tone was mild, god-damn him. "I have been thinking that since neither of us wishes to be in this circumstance," he said in a wry tone, which only served to annoy her more, "we will agree that this marriage is to be a practical one."

"Practical?" she echoed. She likely did not wish to hear his explanation, but it would torment her until she understood just what he was proposing. Not that he had proposed in the first place, which was how they came to be in this circumstance.

He nodded. "I owe something to my title, the title that became mine through unfortunate—" And then he paused, looking uncomfortable.

"Circumstances?" she supplied. Trying not to smirk.

"Precisely." He looked entirely nonplussed. "Which means I need an heir." He gave her a meaningful look, which sent shivers through her body.

"Yes, of course," she replied, trying to sound nonchalant as they apparently embarked on a conversation about sexual relations. Perfectly normal thing for a newly married couple, after all.

"Can we agree on that? That you will provide me with an heir?"

"It is not as though I can determine the sex of the child," she shot back.

He frowned. "No, that is not what I meant. I mean, can we agree that once we have an heir and a spare that we will go our separate ways? You can be the duchess where and however you please, as long as you promise not to cause any scandal." He cleared his throat. "I know this—

our marriage—is not what you would have chosen for yourself. I am suggesting a solution."

She blinked in surprise. "You are suggesting we stay together only as long as it takes for us to produce two boys?" She shook her head. "That could take years."

Years of sexual relations with him. In case she wasn't clear about what that meant.

"Hopefully not years," he replied.

Well, that was direct. He did not want to spend years with her. Understood.

She arched an eyebrow. "You do know how long bearing a child takes."

Had she thought he looked nonplussed before? Now he was nonplusseder.

"Since this is a negotiation," she continued, "let us negotiate. You've made it clear you do not wish to live with me for longer than required." It stung, but then again, she could say the same thing about him. "Perhaps we can settle on going our separate ways when we have an heir. Just the one boy. That way," she said as she calculated, "we could theoretically be free of one another in a year."

Although . . . "But who would have the rearing of the child?" she asked. Dreading the answer, but needing to know all the terms of the agreement.

"I would, naturally."

Already her heart hurt at not being able to live with the child she had not yet borne. He wouldn't be so cruel as to deny her seeing him entirely—but he would be raising the boy, not her. "And if we have a girl?"

He bent his head as though doing her a favor. "Yours to raise."

Bile rose in her throat at the offer he was making—and not so much an offer as a command. Because really, what choice did she have? She had no power. He was a man, first of all, and he was a duke. One with the upper hand—the *only* hand—in this negotiation. He hadn't asked her what she wanted, of course.

She supposed she should be grateful he hadn't just informed her what he planned. That he gave her the semblance of control in their . . . circumstance.

She gave a brief nod. "I agree. We will be together for as long as it takes to bear a son." She held her hand out toward him, which he took after a moment of hesitation.

His hand was large, strong, and warm. He met her gaze as they shook, and she knew without a doubt that he would honor his part of the bargain—he'd allow her to live as she pleased after she had done her duty.

And heaven help them if it took longer than a year. Because she was already chafing at how helpless she felt. There were moments where it appeared that living with him could almost be tolerable, but she strongly suspected those would be moments, not the majority of her existence.

She would have to figure out some way to wrest some control. She had a boundless imagination; her books were proof of that. How hard could it be to determine some things for herself?

It would at least give her a purpose for the next year or so. Beyond having as many sexual relations as possible to ensure the bearing of a child.

She didn't know what to expect from either scenario. Which to most people would be a source of anxiety, but for her was quite different—a challenge. A challenge to be taken on and conquered.

He was tall, taller than anybody I'd ever seen. He wore all black, like his housekeeper, and it was clear he had not shaved in recent days. The lower half of his face was covered with a dark, bristly stubble, framing lips that were surprisingly full. His nose was strong and patrician, but it was his eyes that were the most compelling: they were black, with strong black brows slashing over them. His gaze was intense, and it felt as though his eyes—those dark pools of mystery—were luring me in as Hades must have lured Persephone to her doom.

My Dark Husband by Percy Wittlesford

Chapter Ten

"Well," Thaddeus said as he released his hand, "it is now enough time for us to meet the staff. They should be ready by now."

His wife—*his wife!*—nodded, getting to her feet as he finished speaking.

He shouldn't be irked by her negotiating less time for them to be together—after all, it was he who had suggested the bargain in the first place—but he *was* irked. If things had gone as he had hoped, as he had planned, he would be anticipating a marriage with a modest, beautiful lady who would be his accommodating partner for the rest of his life.

Instead, he was permanently wed to a fiercely striking and opinionated woman who appeared to be delighted to be rid of him.

After they'd fucked enough to bear a son.

"Your butler's name?" she said, oblivious to where his thoughts had gone.

"Uh—yes. Fletchfield." Relieved he could still recall his upper staff's names. He hadn't forgotten his list entirely.

"Fletchfield," she repeated with an adorable look on her face.

Wait. Adorable? Who had he become, to think something so unlike him? He didn't think anything or anyone was adorable.

Much less this woman who had literally been flung into his path, resulting in an unwanted marriage.

He shoved those thoughts aside as they walked out into the hallway, where the staff—his staff—was assembled.

"Your Grace. Your Grace," Fletchfield said, nodding to each of them in turn.

He couldn't help but glance at her, feeling the unaccustomed lift of his lips as he met her amused gaze, recalling what she'd said about their names.

"Thank you, Fletchfield," she replied, to his surprise.

And then, even more surprising, was that she stepped away from him toward the line of servants arranged in descending order of importance in the hall.

"You are the housekeeper, I presume?" She smiled as she spoke, and Thaddeus felt a pang of jealousy. She hadn't smiled with so much warmth toward him, had she? Her mouth had twisted in amusement, but she hadn't actually smiled. Even when they'd kissed in the church, her face had been solemn. It had only been when she was laughing at the redundancy of their titles that she had laughed. And that had not been inspired by him, but by her own humor.

"Yes, Your Grace," the housekeeper—goddamn it, what was her name—replied. "I am Mrs. Webb."

Mrs. Webb, of course.

His wife—whom he still didn't know how to address—continued down the line, taking a few moments with each one of the servants, addressing them in a quiet tone that was clearly used to put them at ease. At least as much at ease as a new duchess could put a staff.

He found himself reluctantly impressed with her thoughtfulness. Perhaps this marriage wouldn't be the disaster he'd anticipated.

Besides which, even if it was, it would be only for a year. Or however long it took to birth a son. And he had to admit he did find her desirable; while her lush curves and vibrant looks didn't seem quite duchess-like, she was striking. It would be a pleasure to find out firsthand what those curves felt like under his hand. What her skin tasted like.

He was already anticipating his wedding night. And not just for procreation purposes.

Hours later, Thaddeus was pacing in his bedroom. He'd allowed Hodgkins to remove his wedding attire and garb him in nightshirt and dressing gown, but had dismissed the man when he'd started hovering. As though Thaddeus wouldn't know what was expected of him.

He was to go to her room, engage in sexual relations with her, and then return to his own bedroom to sleep. The steps weren't even long enough to require a list.

To be repeated until he had an heir to the title he'd reluctantly inherited. With the wife he'd reluctantly gotten.

When would he be able to make his own choices?

A ridiculous thought, given how many choices he could make should he choose—he was a duke, after all.

But one who wouldn't neglect his responsibilities, his honor, and his duty.

In the meanwhile, he had pleasure to seek.

He allowed his mind to give in to the attraction he felt for his bride: her curves, her wit and humor, her sharp intellect. The way her skin gleamed under candlelight.

He didn't doubt but that she would be responsive under his touch. And he would be the one to show her the delights of the bedroom, to slide his fingers along her skin and find out what touches would make her sigh in pleasure.

The images flooded his brain, making his cock begin to stiffen as his fingers tingled to touch her. *Patience, Thaddeus*, he cautioned himself. He didn't want to disappoint her, especially not the first time.

Not his first time, though it had been a long time. But a first time for her.

He took a deep breath and flung his door open, stepping out into the hall and making his way to her.

HE KNOCKED ON her door, hesitating to open it until he heard her voice.

"Come in," she replied. He stepped inside, taking in the flickering candles, the enormous bed with the covers pulled down, and her. Sitting in an armchair by the fire, her hair down, her feet bare, wrapped up in a dressing gown that seemed made for a lady twice her height.

Her eyes were enormous in her pale face. After everything she'd faced, was this the thing that cowed her?

He'd have to reassure her it wouldn't be that bad. That *he* wouldn't be that bad.

"Lavinia," he said, coming to stand in front of the fire.

He saw her toes making gripping motions in the rug, as though they were digging in sand.

"I didn't know if I should be in bed already, or to wait here. But being in bed seemed so awkward, and I'd be lying down, and I didn't think I could sit still. I dismissed my lady's maid, a lovely young girl named Nancy. She is Mrs. Webb's niece, and has been working for the Raddlestons, the people at whose party we first met? Anyway, she knew I would need a lady's maid and she knew Nancy would be more comfortable with another family member in the house."

He wanted to chuckle at her chatter. Apparently when his bride was nervous, she talked. A lot. For the first time since meeting her, he felt as though he were comfortably in charge.

After all, he was the only one of the two who had actually done this before.

"Come," he said, holding his hand out to her.

She took it, and he guided her to stand, the dressing gown falling to puddle at her feet.

She laughed as she saw him glance down. "This was all so sudden, so I had to borrow my cousin Caroline's. She is a bit taller than I, as you can see."

Her words were accompanied by a cheerful grin, and he exhaled in relief at the sign of her returning to her usual self.

Although he didn't need a reminder that her usual self was already proven to irk him.

But she would be more comfortable, which would be more satisfactory for both of them.

"Let's get into bed, and you can remove that tent that is masquerading as a dressing gown," he replied, doing his best to give her a reassuring smile.

She nodded, walking ahead of him, the dressing gown pooling at her feet.

The bed was big enough for them and most of his upper servants, although he would hesitate to invite either Fletchfield or Mrs. Webb. It wouldn't fall within their job responsibilities, to be sure.

She glanced back at him before hopping up onto the bed, sitting against the headboard, her knees up, her arms wrapped around them.

He walked to the other side, sitting up as well, stretching his arm out so it lay on her shoulders.

She jerked in surprise, then chuckled. "I suppose I will have to grow accustomed to that."

He placed his fingers on her shoulder and began to stroke her skin.

Softer, even, than he'd imagined. He could feel her begin to relax under his touch.

"I know something about what is to happen," she said, her voice sounding a bit higher than usual. "I just want to—"

"We will go slowly," he promised, knowing the promise was as much to himself as to her. He didn't have much previous experience with all this. Just enough to know he liked it, and that the women he'd done it with liked him to take his time.

"Thank you," she replied in a soft voice, turning her face toward his.

It was a clear invitation for a kiss, and he complied, leaning over to press his mouth against hers. Soft there, too.

Instead of the perfunctory kiss they'd had at the church earlier that day, however, this kiss was longer. He lingered at her mouth, getting to know the feel of her before opening his mouth to taste her lips.

She made a noise of surprise, but then allowed his tongue to enter her mouth, placing her hands on his upper arms to steady herself.

And then she tentatively licked at his lips, and the intense wave of desire swept over him, making him turn her squarely toward him, his fingers going to the ties of her nightrail, undoing them quickly as he deepened the kiss.

She didn't seem frightened at all now, thank goodness.

He tugged at the fabric of her nightrail in an unspoken wish, and she complied, taking her hands off him to reach toward the bottom of her garment and draw it up over her head.

He did the same, quickly removing his nightshirt, tossing it over his head onto the floor as he kept his gaze on hers.

She bit her lip as she regarded him, and he held his breath, hoping his body met with her approval.

He knew he was larger than the average man

in height and width, but he also knew he was stronger, muscled through years of hard battle training and his own need to improve himself.

He swallowed as she made a low humming noise deep in her throat, one eyebrow raised over a warm look of satisfaction.

Thank God.

"You look every bit as I'd imagined," she said in a low, husky voice.

He resisted the urge to preen. "So you've imagined me then?" he asked.

She gestured toward him. "You have to know that. Our spark, our attraction, no matter what we think of the other. That's been present since we first met." She raised her chin as she spoke, as if defying him to contradict her.

"It has." He shifted closer to her, his erection hard and heavy on his leg. He saw how she glanced quickly toward it, then back to him, her eyes far wider than seconds before.

"Well," she said, taking a deep breath, "let's see about fulfilling the details of our agreement."

THADDEUS ROLLED OFF her, entirely satiated, and entirely certain that he'd done his very best to satisfy her as well. She'd responded satisfactorily, emitting small noises of pleasure as he thrust inside, only making one small sound at the initial entry.

"I will return to my room shortly," he said after a few moments.

She shifted onto her elbow to look at him. "You don't need to—that is, you can stay here if you want."

"I don't want to inconvenience you more than necessary," he replied. He'd never stayed the night with any bed partner, and even though she was his wife, it felt wrong to stay the night now, given what they'd agreed to.

"Thank you?" She sounded hesitant.

"I think it is best that we keep our interactions brief. Except for—" And he gestured between them, because how did you reference sexual intercourse, even if it was to your wife?

"Brief." Why did it seem as though a smile tugged at her mouth?

"Well, then." He got out of the bed, quickly donning his nightshirt and giving her an awkward bow. "Good night, Lavinia."

"Good night, um, Thaddeus," she said.

He gave her another nod, then turned to walk out the door, wishing he didn't feel so discomfited, despite having just had sexual release.

Marriage was going to be far different than he had ever anticipated.

LAVINIA WAITED UNTIL the door had closed behind him, then she flung herself back on the bed, stretching her arms out to the side. "Brief!" she exclaimed, chuckling as she spoke.

She had not thought her first time would be so . . . brief. So mildly disappointing.

When she'd thought about what might happen between a man and a woman on their wedding night, she'd imagined extremes—extreme embarrassment, extreme passion, extreme pain, extreme satisfaction.

This had been none of that.

It was . . . fine. Like a tea that was moderately hot and not suitably sugared was fine. It was still tea, but it wasn't anything worth remembering, or worth striving toward again.

This was what the poets waxed rhapsodic about? This general pushing into one's body for a few minutes, then a gush of liquid and then that was it?

Entirely disappointing.

When they'd kissed, she'd felt the curling spark of desire within, licked into flame by his tongue. But the rest of it didn't live up to that, and she felt as though she'd been cheated somehow. As though the poets and the sighing young ladies and the wistfully longing young men had lied to her.

She sighed, getting up to reach for her nightrail, which had fallen onto the carpet.

At least she had a pleasant room. The bed was huge, definitely large enough for her, him, and the company of their choice. She wasn't sharing the room with anybody, and she could run around naked in it if she chose.

That was an idea.

What else could she do?

She giggled as she pondered. If they were to be together only until she'd successfully borne a child, and their striving toward that goal was to be this forgettable, she would need to figure out other things to engage her attention.

She sat up as she drew her nightrail over her head, hopping off the bed, now too engrossed in her own imaginings to sleep.

Paper? Was there paper and a pen here?

At least she would be able to find enough time to write her books, since he wouldn't take as much time as she'd thought he might to fulfill their bargain.

There was a desk tucked into the corner, and she yanked open the top drawer, snatching a piece of paper out of it. No pen. Another drawer yielded a pen and ink, and she smiled in satisfaction, sitting down at the desk, gazing off into the distance in thought.

Things Lavinia Will Do to Pass the Time:
1. Write books.
2. Good works.
    a. What kinds of good works? Would her husband give her an allowance toward said good works?
3. Developing friendships with people who were not related to her.
    a. Should she throw a party for potential friends? How would she identify them? Would her husband give her an allowance toward said friend development?
4. Persuade her husband to give her a generous allowance so she was able to do whatever she wished.
5. Get a dog.
    a. Possibly a cat.
    b. Or both.

She sat back in her chair in satisfaction. She could, and would, have a full, busy, satisfactory life despite what it seemed her husband wanted.

Her husband. She was married to him, the Grim Behemoth, for the rest of her life.

And what she'd thought would be the saving grace of her marriage was something she would likely forget by tomorrow morning.

Oh well.

At least if she got a dog, he or she would probably sleep with her.

She shrugged, tucking the paper back into the top drawer and returning to her bed, her enormous bed, where she pulled the covers up to her chin and tried to settle herself to sleep.

I was distracted by his appearance. Too distracted, I have to admit. I wanted both to step toward him and place my palm on the stubble on his face and turn around and run out the door and out of the house, never looking back.

"You cannot leave," he pronounced, as though he knew my inner thoughts.

I stood up straighter. "I have no intention of doing so," I said. "Not until I know why you asked I visit you."

His expression changed then. If I had thought him forbidding before, now he was absolutely terrifying. His mouth thinned, and his nostrils flared, and his eyes narrowed.

But I was not terrified. I was intrigued, God help me.

My Dark Husband by Percy Wittlesford

Chapter Eleven

"Your Grace."

Hodgkins accompanied his words with a clearing of his throat, an indicator that it must be later than Thaddeus's customary waking time. His valet stood beside the bed, holding a tray of what Thaddeus knew was coffee and plenty of cream.

One of his few indulgences.

And he'd just added another, hadn't he?

He rose onto his elbow, glancing at the clock on his nightstand. Eight o'clock already!

He flung the covers aside, nearly knocking Hodgkins over as he leaped out of bed, running his hand through his hair in surprise.

"I must have overslept be—" he began, then stopped, aware he should not say the rest of his sentence. At least not to his valet.

I must have overslept because last night was my wedding night, and I greatly enjoyed it. As did my wife.

His wife.

"Has the duchess risen yet?" He sounded strained. He should not sound anything other than completely confident, especially when speaking to his staff.

He should add that to his goals list.

Hodgkins bowed as he placed the tray on the low table that was at the end of the bed. "I believe so, Your Grace. I believe she has gone out."

Thaddeus frowned. "Gone out?" Where could she have gone to? Was she already returning to see her family? Her sister?

Why hadn't he asked if she would have breakfast with him?

Because he'd assumed she would be here, that he wouldn't have to ask for the pleasure of her company.

Not that he found her company particularly pleasurable. She continued to irk him, even though they had satisfactorily come to an agreement and he'd brought both of them satisfaction the previous night.

Satisfactorily. Satisfaction.

Was that all he was to be? Satisfied?

It would do for her, certainly. And basic satisfaction was all he had hoped for when he had first devised his goals upon assuming the title.

But now that he had felt the stirrings of passion and yes, of irritation, he knew there could be more to his life.

"Your Grace?"

He shook his thoughts free to see Hodgkins holding his cup out, likely for some time, judging by his valet's expression of exaggerated patience.

"Yes, of course," Thaddeus said, taking the cup from his valet's hand. He waved toward the door. "That is all. I will dress myself."

Hodgkins's mouth pursed briefly—Thaddeus knew full well his valet did not trust him to put together an ensemble appropriate for his position—but didn't say a word, just bowed as he left the room.

Thaddeus sat down in one of the two chairs that flanked the table, breathing in the aroma of the coffee with, yes, satisfaction.

Goddamn it.

He'd thought he would spend the day, or the morning at least, with his blushing bride who would need time to grow accustomed to her new privilege and position.

But it seemed his new bride, whether or not she was blushing, had taken herself off to parts unknown, leaving him to fend for himself.

As you've done for your entire life, a voice inside his head reminded him.

But there was a part of him, he could admit, that longed to partner with someone, to share thoughts and ideas and the essentials of running an estate and holdings as vast as his own with another.

He'd hoped it would be Lady Jane. He had almost physically seen her in the position, but then her vibrantly exuberant sister had interfered, and now they were stuck together.

Not that it was her fault any more than it was his, but he could still resent the situation.

At least they had come to an agreement about the future. And thank goodness he hadn't developed an actual attachment to her sister—his interest in Lady Jane had been from a practical point of view, not yet what it might actually mean to his life.

And at least Lavinia understood what was

expected of her, and he knew what to expect from her.

Though that wasn't necessarily true, was it?

He hadn't expected that she would have gone out the morning after her wedding night. A tiny part of him had hoped that she would have been so spent, so boneless from passion, that she slept in until noon, and then emerged with a blissful look of, yes, satisfaction on her face.

He shook his head in rueful resignation. Feeling almost as though he had not done enough to make her want to stay in the house. Though her not being here was what he wanted, wasn't it? Eventually?

After she'd borne a child. A *son*. An heir to carry on the title he hadn't wanted, but wouldn't disrespect.

"Good morning." Lavinia kept her tone as normal as she could, but her entire family's heads still all swung toward her on their respective necks.

The family was at breakfast, the time one could most rely on to find all of them in one place. Her father sat at the head of the table, his gaze already drifting away from her likely because he'd had a thought about something. Her mother, at the opposite end, was staring at Lavinia with an expression of shock, while Percy's mouth was already curling into a delighted smile and Jane had donned her customary look of mild concern.

"What are you doing here?" her mother sputtered. "Don't you have things to learn? Like running a respectable household or being with your new husband?"

Lavinia raised a brow, advancing toward her usual seat between Caroline and Christina. Her youngest sister was the least startled by her arrival, likely because she was five years old and was intent on sneaking more sugar into her teacup.

Caroline shifted to give more space to Lavinia, who sat in her chair before replying to her mother's question. It was unusual, certainly, for a bride to appear at her family's home the day after her wedding. More than unusual, if she were honest.

But if other members of her family could brazen out their bizarre behavior, then she could, too. She'd just have to pretend it was perfectly normal.

"I am seeing my family," she said airily, snatching a piece of bread from the basket in front of her. "The duke and I are on comfortable terms, if that is what is concerning you." Terms that she would not reveal included going their separate ways once an heir was born.

"But don't you have duchessy things to do?" Percy asked. Lavinia would have taken his question seriously if he hadn't asked in such an arch tone and an expression of mock judgment.

"Are you all right?" Jane said in a low voice.

"I'm fine. Truly." Lavinia bit into the bread, placing the rest on her plate as she gestured for one of the servants to pour tea for her. She chewed determinedly in the ensuing silence.

Her family never shut up, but now they were quiet?

It appeared she'd figured out how to halt conversation entirely: just marry a duke one day, and return home for a visit the next.

"I am not certain of my duchessy duties," Lavinia said, sticking her tongue out at Percy, who laughed, "and I wanted to make certain the McTavishes understood what the change in our family's circumstances would mean." Because the biggest reason for agreeing to go through with this marriage—in addition to wanting to glimpse the duke's naked thighs—was because she wanted Jane, at least, to be happy in her marriage. "Did you speak to Mr. McTavish, Jane? And did he understand?"

Jane's shy smile and slight nod was all Lavinia needed.

"What's it like being a duchess?" Caroline asked.

Even amongst the blunt Capel family, Caroline was . . . blunt. She had a remarkable talent for asking the right question at the wrong time. Or vice versa.

Lavinia shrugged. "It's not much different." Almost underwhelming, she might say. But she did have her list, didn't she? She could concentrate on fulfilling those items rather than finding joy in her union with the Brief Duke.

She smothered a snort of laughter, which made Percy give her a piercing look. Drat, she'd have to explain herself.

"Well, I think it is the height of impropriety for you to be visiting here this morning," her mother said, lifting her chin in disapproval. "You should be at *home* with your *husband*."

"My *husband*," Lavinia replied, echoing her mother's emphasis, "is busy doing dukely things." She spoke as if she actually knew that to be true, but she had to assume so—it wasn't as though he was likely to be doing anything other than what he was supposed to do.

More's the pity.

"Jane will be taking a drive with Mr. McTavish's aunt and sisters in an hour." Her mother sniffed. "You can stay until then." Her gaze narrowed. "But don't you dare look anything but pleased in case they see you. I do not want Jane to have to explain your choice to come here."

Lavinia wished her mother was wrong, but it was odd she'd come, and she knew the McTavishes would inquire.

Lavinia shot Jane a wry glance, then rose from the table. "Since I have so little time, would you want to go to the gardens with me for a bit, Jane?"

Percy leaped from his seat. "I'll come, too."

Lavinia opened her mouth to object, but shut it again—it wouldn't matter anyway. Percy would join them no matter what she wished, and besides, it wasn't as though she would say anything to Jane she could not also say to Percy.

She appreciated, especially at times like these, having such wonderful siblings.

"I won't be joining you," Caroline said flatly. She had risen from the table also, and was tucking all the spare bread left in the basket into the skirt of her dress.

Odd, but definitely not as odd as some things Caroline had done. Sometimes Lavinia wondered if Caroline's father, the minor European prince, had some habits that he'd passed on to his daughter, because she didn't recall her aunt being so eccentric.

Or perhaps it was the natural result of living in such a chaotic household.

In which case she might find herself pocketing random breadstuffs into her clothing.

That would likely be a scandal of some sort—the baked good sort—so she would have to curtail her tendencies until after Jane was safely wedded to Mr. McTavish.

Perhaps she could write a character with a few eccentricities so she could get it out of her system, and hopefully not embarrass her husband or her sister's future in-laws.

Lavinia nearly cackled aloud in joy as the ideas began to swirl through her head, and she took another bite of the bread before spinning on her heel to leave the dining room and find her cloak.

She heard Jane and Percy following after, as they usually did.

It was reassuring to know that despite all the changes of the past few weeks some things remained the same.

Once out in the hallway, Lavinia grabbed her cloak from the hook where she'd put it—refusing the footman's offer of assistance—and drew it over her shoulders, sliding her arms through the armholes.

It was warm, which Lavinia welcomed, since she felt cold most of the time, even in the height of summer. She thought it might have something to do with the bare arms and necks that were required for a fashionable woman's dress, and of course her mother had never allowed her to add more fabric to a gown that displayed at least two of Lavinia's more . . . memorable assets.

Not that those assets had directly gotten her a husband, she wished she could point out to her mother. Yes, she had directly smashed them against his chest in the hallway, but it wasn't the assets themselves that were at fault—it was her clumsy footing.

If she had been able to wear sensible shoes, perhaps none of this would have happened.

But then Jane would have been the one last night to wait in that enormous bed for the equally intimidatingly large duke to come to her. And she didn't think Jane would have handled the situation with as much aplomb, murmuring the occasional word of encouragement as she thought about other things.

When the three of them were safely out of earshot of their mother—or Caroline, who might repeat back the most salacious elements of the conversation without realizing that was what she had done—Percy grabbed Lavinia by both shoulders and gave her a gentle shake. "How is it? How is *he*?"

She knew exactly what he was talking about, and she knew it wasn't about his ducal house, his ducal staff, or about his ducal attitude.

It was about his ducal self. Specifically, the self that had joined her in bed.

She planted her hands on her hips and gave him a cynical raise of her brow. "You wouldn't rather discuss how I am already learning how to be a properly respectful duchess? How the servants already cower as I approach?"

"Don't be an idiot. We know nobody would ever cower before you."

"He's right, you know," Jane added.

"Traitor!" Lavinia exclaimed as she laughed.

She pointed toward one of the benches lining the walkway. A bench, she knew from experience, that could hold all three of them, albeit rather snugly.

They sat, Lavinia tucking her skirts in underneath her legs to afford her siblings more room. Jane and Percy sat on either side of her, all of them gazing out at the gentle paths winding their way around the various plants their mother had deemed appropriate for the Capel garden.

"We're waiting," Percy said in an impatient voice.

"What do you want to know?"

"Everything," Jane said, sounding both excited and trepidatious.

Of course. Their mother couldn't be counted on to share anything at all about it. Percy, as far as Lavinia would know—and she would know; she knew everything about him—had never done it either.

It was up to her.

"Well," she began, clasping her hands in her lap and attempting to look sedate, "it was—well, honestly," she continued, speaking in a rush, "it wasn't much of anything. He got into bed, I took my nightrail off, there was some kissing, and then some pushing, and then it was all over. And he went back to his room."

Leaving her dissatisfied and somewhat grumpy. Either all the love stories she'd adored through the years were lying, or he—he was just bad at it. Or strictly mechanical, which might be even worse.

"Oh."

"Oh," Percy echoed, slumping back against the bench. "I was hoping you'd have new experience to add to your books."

Lavinia shook her head slowly. "Not unless I write about the short dull moments of marriage."

"Oh no. Does that mean—will Mr. McTavish?" Jane began.

Lavinia turned to her sister and took hold of her arm. "I have no reason to believe the duke is representative of the species in that behavior. I have every expectation that you and Mr. Mc-Tavish, loving one another as you do, will enjoy yourselves far more than I did."

She shrugged again, wishing she had more to share with her siblings. Or at least more good things to share.

"Though," she began, remembering her list of the night before, "this means I will definitely have time for my books, as well as doing some good works. Something to do with people needing help or something," she said, waving her hands in a vague gesture. "And now that I am not living with you, and now that Jane is likely to move out also, I think it would be good if I were to develop some friendships. Not that you two are not all I need," she added hastily, seeing their scowls, "but we have to be realistic that we won't be in one another's pocket all the time."

Jane's lip trembled.

"And a dog!" Lavinia nearly shouted, hoping to distract her sister. "I am going to get a dog."

"But what are you going to do about the duke? And all of—that?" Percy said, tilting his head meaningfully.

"What can I—oh!" Lavinia said, her eyes widening. "I suppose it wouldn't do any harm to see if there could be improvements. I mean, it is not as though I am likely to be lowered in his estimation—this marriage isn't a love match, after all." She couldn't even say it was a *like* match, since she didn't think either one of them thought that highly of the other.

Jane took Lavinia's hand in hers and squeezed it. "Vinnie, I cannot thank you enough for what you have done for me. I will never forget it. If you need—if you ever need a place to live, after Mr. McTavish and I are—"

"Hush about that," Lavinia interrupted. She didn't want to share the details of her agreement with the duke with her siblings. Not yet, at least—they would feel even worse for her than they already did.

"How would one go about bringing up the subject?" Percy's tone was humorous, but his question was sincere; she knew that. "I know!" he continued without waiting for her reply. "You can write it all out, as though it were in one of your books. That will make it easier, won't it?"

Lavinia considered the solution. "I suppose so," she said slowly. The idea rattled around in her head as she considered the permutations. "It would work," she said, speaking with more confidence.

And then she could use her words to get what she wanted.

Wasn't that what she'd always done? Why should the marriage bed be any different?

It wasn't as though he would refuse to do his

duty—the whole point was to do it until they had a male child. If he refused to listen to what she said or suggested, she'd just have what she had now.

"I should give him the benefit of the doubt, however," she added. "What if he was just nervous? It was our wedding night, after all. I will engage enough times to be certain that this is the norm before bringing up the topic. It is a sensitive one, I would imagine."

"I would imagine," Percy agreed.

"And what about you?" Lavinia asked. "Have any of Mr. Percy Wittlesford's fans caught your eye?"

Percy's expression shifted into an uncomfortably awkward one, and Lavinia held her breath.

"You don't have to talk about it," she added as Jane squeezed her hand even tighter.

Percy nodded slowly. "I don't want to, not now. I just—" He sounded so unlike his usual brash self, Lavinia wanted to wrap him in her embrace and never let go. She didn't succumb to the impulse however, since the gesture would mostly be for her and not for Percy.

"Just know we love you and support you," Lavinia replied in a firm tone.

"And meanwhile," Percy began, sounding more like himself, "you have a duke to seduce."

Lavinia laughed, as she was supposed to, and the three of them got up to return to the house— Jane to go on her drive with the McTavishes, Percy to figure out what he wanted and how to tell his siblings, and her to write a script for broaching the subject of sexual relations with her taciturn husband.

"Sit." He nodded toward the sofa tucked against the wall on the right-hand side of where I was standing. He went and sat behind his desk, not even waiting for me to take a seat before sitting himself.

I sat, folding my hands in my lap.

"Sir," I began. "You know who I am, and yet I do not have the same pleasure."

He smiled, but not in amusement—it was as though he was a hunter about to capture his prey. "I am the Count Dramorsky."

"And—?" I replied, lifting my chin. "I am not familiar with you or your name."

His smile was predatory now. I swallowed against my fear.

"You will be. Because it will soon be yours."

My Dark Husband by Percy Wittlesford

Chapter Twelve

Lavinia carefully laid herself out under her comforter, placing her hands on top beside her body. She had allowed Nancy to assist her into a nightrail, but had removed it as soon as she'd dismissed her maid; after all, she would be removing it soon enough anyway.

It felt surprisingly wonderful to sleep naked. Until now, she'd shared a room with Jane, so she hadn't even thought about not wearing a garment to sleep in.

She hadn't seen the duke—her husband—until dinner, and even then they had been distant. Literally, since they had been seated at either end of a vast table that could have accommodated all of her family plus all of his servants.

It was a large table.

They'd attempted conversation, but it was awkward to shout, especially since there were servants all about.

She'd retired as soon as it was polite, wanting to test if last evening was an indication of future behavior. Hoping it wasn't, that it had just been nerves, but a secret, sinking part of her suspecting it was.

She braced herself as she heard the knock on the door. "Come in," she called, wriggling under the covers.

He stepped inside wearing his dressing gown, as he had the night before, his strong legs bare to the floor.

"I hope I am not too early?" he said in his gruff voice.

"Not at all," she replied, willing her voice not to squeak.

He nodded, approaching the bed as he removed his dressing gown. He wasn't wearing a nightshirt this evening, and she wondered if he'd reached the same conclusion about it that she had.

One thing they had in common, perhaps? Not wanting to waste time donning garments that would be removed soon anyway.

She shivered in anticipation of his joining her in the bed. His penis was already erect, and she blinked at the size of it—it hadn't felt that large when it had been inside her, but it was impressive out in the open like that.

"Are you cold?" he asked, sliding into bed beside her and taking her into his arms.

"Usually." Her voice was muffled since she was pressed against his chest.

He curled his arms tighter around her, and she burrowed into him, twisting her leg so it was intertwined with his.

"Are you feeling all right?" he asked.

"All ri—?" she began, then realized what he was asking. "Yes, thank you. I am fine." She sounded far too sprightly for the moment.

She was supposed to be luring him into a passionate encounter, not sounding as though she was responding with joy to the offer of a second lemon scone or anything.

Though she did love lemon scones.

He shifted to put his hand at her waist, splaying his fingers across her skin. Just under her breast, which suddenly felt heavy and aching.

Oh, yes, she wanted to say. *Touch me there.*

"Can I—?" he began, his finger edging upward.

"Yes," she replied, this time managing to sound more passionate and less sprightly.

His fingers moved onto her breast, his palm holding the weight of her in his hand. She shivered in reaction, and he snatched his hand away, leaving her bereft.

"You're cold." He sprung out of bed and walked naked to a chest of drawers against the wall, leaning over to pull the bottom drawer open.

She levered herself up on her elbow to gaze unabashedly at his backside.

It was all sorts of impressive, from the muscles shifting in his back to his firmly rounded arse.

Her fingers ached to touch him.

He turned back around, and she dropped her gaze so he wouldn't see her staring. He tossed a blanket over her, tugging it so it lay somewhat straight, then jumped back into bed and pulled her against him again.

"I don't want you to be cold," he said in a far more formal voice than the situation required. Given that they were both naked in bed together.

"I wasn't—" she began, then sighed. What was the point? She could either argue with him about her body temperature, or she could discover if he was intent on her pleasure or just on fulfilling their bargain as quickly as possible.

He turned so he could wrap his arms around her again. She felt his hard erection against her thigh, and trembled again.

Goddamn it. She did not want him to encase her in wool rather than make love to her.

Thankfully, it seemed either he didn't notice or decided to ignore her latest shiver.

"Lavinia," he said, then pressed his mouth against hers. She could feel the scruff on his face gently abrading her skin. It was pleasant in an odd way; a reminder that they were not the same at all, him with his size, muscles, and hair, and her with her curves, soft skin, and diminutive stature.

But lying down together removed some of those differences.

He put his hand directly on her breast now, squeezing her warm flesh as she pressed into him.

This was more promising, at least.

And then he drew his hand away, sliding his fingers down her skin to the apex of her thighs, pushing her legs apart as he shifted to get on top of her.

He took a breath, then pushed his erection toward her entrance, hesitating for a moment as his gaze met hers.

He looked . . . worried. Not passionate or intent on indulging in pure pleasure or any of the things she wanted.

"It's fine. I don't hurt," she said, trying to sound reassuring without sounding pathetic.

He grunted in reply, then thrust into her, her legs spreading wide to accommodate him.

She wrapped her arms around him, even though she didn't think it was possible to have him any closer. What with a part of his body being inside of her and all.

Her fingers met at the small of his back, and she felt her breath hitch at the thought that she could touch what she had just been ogling.

He began to move as he placed her fingers on his arse, and she felt a sizzle of something electric as she felt the muscles in his arse flex.

Holy goodness, he felt amazing.

But it wasn't enough. That part of her ached for contact, but his body wasn't touching her there, and she didn't think it would be enough even if she were able to wiggle into position.

Had he never pleasured a woman properly before?

She'd only done it to herself, but even she knew where all the important parts were. She'd have to talk to him about it, but perhaps her first words shouldn't be, "Do you even know where my clitoris is?"

THADDEUS FELT HIS climax rising, the urgency and intensity of his thrusting increasing. She lay beneath him, her arms wrapped around him, her fingers splayed out on his arse as he pushed. He grunted, giving one final push as he came, collapsing on top of her in boneless satisfaction.

A few moments passed as he allowed himself to breathe naturally—so often, especially since he'd become duke, he hadn't let himself relax, not an inch. To relax in the military could mean death for his soldiers. To relax as a duke would be less damaging, but wasn't something he would tolerate. His responsibility, his duty, was now the dukedom, which was why he and she had entered into this bargain in the first place.

But now, for just a little while, he could release his vigilance and enjoy the postcoital bliss.

He felt her finger tapping his shoulder. "Would you mind—?" And she wriggled to indicate he should move off her.

"Of course," he said, feeling oddly rueful as he rolled onto his back. "I did not mean to—"

"Oh, you weren't," she interrupted, sounding far brighter and far less sensuously languid than he would have liked. "I am tired. It has been a long day."

He kept his gaze fixed on the ceiling, folding his hands on his chest. "You left the house early this morning."

Did he sound accusatory? Or worse, possessive?

He frowned as he considered it. She was his duchess, he deserved to know where she was in the time they weren't together.

"I did," she replied, sounding amused. "I went to see my family."

He frowned more. Her family? Wasn't he her family now? At least for the time being?

"Well," he said stiffly, "I do hope you will remain in the house tomorrow. I believe Mrs. Webb has certain household matters to discuss with you."

"Yes, I spoke with her when I returned." A pause. "We've already arranged to meet after breakfast. And I will be speaking with Fletchfield after lunch." Her tone made it sound as though she were humoring a petulant child.

Goddamn it. This was not how he'd thought their postsex conversation would go.

He'd thought he would have pleasured her sufficiently to dull her sharp edges, make her . . . softer. More malleable.

She's not her sister, a voice inside his head reminded him.

But also, *perhaps you didn't sufficiently pleasure her. Did it seem as though she climaxed?*

He'd never thought much about any of that before, except to acknowledge it was a physical necessity for him. Hence his adding it to his list.

And his previous partners had seemed relatively pleased. But had they been pleasured? He had to admit he didn't know.

But he hadn't considered her, except to think about what would bring him the most gratification—a lushly curved figure, an accommodating woman who wasn't nervous about sex.

Basically her, but less aggravating when not in bed.

"Are you going to stay long?" she asked.

He rose up on one arm to glare—no, to regard her calmly. "Do you want me to leave?"

She shrugged. He did not like that shrug. "I'm indifferent, but I am tired, so if you are going to leave, I'd suggest to do it soon so that you don't wake me when you do."

He felt his breathing increase and his eyes narrow. But this was what he wanted, wasn't it? A relationship that didn't exist outside of their sexual relations?

He gave a brief nod, then sat up, reaching for his discarded dressing gown and tossing it on.

"I will bid you good night, then," he said gruffly.

"Sleep well, Thaddeus," she replied cheerily.

He suppressed a growl, then turned and strode purposefully—not angrily—out the door.

Marriage was already not at all what he'd expected.

LAVINIA WAITED FOR the door to shut before emitting a huge sigh. Marriage—at least this marriage, she couldn't speak for any others—was not at all what she'd expected. It was substantially less, in fact.

She'd hoped that tonight would be different, that last night was due to nerves, or an overprotective consideration.

But after a few perfunctory kisses and caresses, he had pushed into her, setting his own pace without, apparently, considering what she might like.

Not that this situation wasn't precisely what most women dealt with each evening; she wasn't so idealistic about it all to think her experience was an anomaly.

But she'd had such hopes, what with the attraction between them, how he stalked around as though he were likely to fling a woman over his shoulder and carry her off to his cave to ravish her into pleasure.

She'd like it if he flung her over his shoulder and ravished her to pleasure.

But it seemed as though the most she could hope for was a flinging of dressing gowns and then a few pleasured grunts. From him.

She shook her head as she sat up, walking naked to her wardrobe to pull out Caroline's dressing gown, which she slid her arms through before going to sit at the desk. The fabric pooled at her feet, which reminded her she should go shopping.

Her clothing was fine for a young lady from an eccentric family, but not up to the standards she knew a duchess would be held to. She hadn't missed her maid Nancy's look of surprise when she'd gotten dressed for dinner earlier.

At least there would be pretty dresses to wear.

She glanced around the bedroom, noting the blazing fire in the enormous fireplace, the heavy velvet drapes at the windows, the sumptuously plush carpet on which her bare feet rested.

And the room was nice as well.

So there were a few things better about being a duchess. It was just unfortunate that the part she'd most anticipated was so lacking.

But she would speak to him about it. It might be awkward at first, and he'd likely be defensive, but once they worked it out, they would both be much happier.

And in the meantime she would purchase gowns, dive into managing her own household, and get a dog.

Oh God. She froze as the thought struck her— was this disappointment why so many ladies turned to reading books like hers?

In which case, she should make certain to keep writing. If not for the money—because she was a duchess now, she wouldn't need it—but to satisfy people who might remain otherwise unsatisfied.

Once again, doing her part to give voice to the voiceless.

She chuckled as she picked up her pen, placed her inkwell on the desk, and drew a piece of paper from the drawer.

She would write a new book, one that would do its best to fill the void left by hasty husbands. One inspired by hasty husbands, albeit not in the way they would perhaps appreciate.

I was too shocked to say anything to him. Married?

My silence didn't seem to bother him; he began to pace, walking from one end of the room to the other in long, quick strides. It would have taken me twice as long to cross the same distance.

And then he stopped suddenly, directly in front of me.

"You have something I want," he said in his harsh accent. "And if I am to get it, we must be married."

I was on my feet before I even knew it.

This was what I had hoped for over the past few weeks. But not like this. Never like this. "I will not stay here to listen to this nonsense."

He walked toward me and pushed me back down on the sofa.

I stared up at him, scared for the first time in this odd encounter.

My Dark Husband by Percy Wittlesford

Chapter Thirteen

Thaddeus was up especially early the next morning. Not necessarily to catch her if she planned to go out.

Even though a part of his brain told him that was precisely what he was doing.

They hadn't discussed, mostly because he hadn't even thought of it, that she would be making her home here now, and that leaving the morning after their wedding could be seen as meaning she was not happy with their marriage.

But he had made it clear that their marriage was only for the time being, so was it even appropriate to question her choices as he had done the night before? Goddamn it.

He sat at the enormous dining room table, at least three silent footmen standing at attention as he sipped his coffee.

He wasn't accustomed to being under such scrutiny.

It was so early the papers hadn't been delivered yet, or at least Fletchfield hadn't presented them as he normally did.

So he was sitting by himself at a table meant to seat twenty people as three grown men stood in the room with him not speaking.

This was possibly the most awkward situation he'd ever been in.

Though he had just accidentally compromised a lady by falling into her bosom at a ball, so he might have to say it was the second most awkward moment. And he didn't have to marry any of these men.

He snorted at his own ridiculous thoughts, shaking his head as he drained his coffee. He'd barely placed it back in the saucer when one of the standing men swooped forward to pick it up.

"More coffee, Your Grace?"

Thaddeus met the man's gaze. "Yes, thank you."

The man nodded in reply, walking swiftly out the door.

Two left.

The door burst open, and then she was inside, her presence seeming to fill the room although the room was large and she was not. She wore a simple gown, at least to Thad's eyes, with a higher neckline than he would have liked.

Given how much he appreciated her bosom. But it likely wouldn't be appropriate for her to wear a gown like that in the morning.

Though if she did, and they had no plans, perhaps they could excuse themselves after breakfast for more child-making attempts.

Damn, and now he was hard. And thinking about having sexual intercourse in the daytime. Did people even do that?

Her expression was startled as she caught his gaze. Damn, he hoped none of his thoughts were on his face. "I didn't realize you were here,

Thaddeus," she said, making her way to the opposite end of the table.

He frowned. And where else would he be? "Would you care to sit closer?" he asked. Hoping he made it seem like a request, not a command.

She froze in the middle of lowering herself to her chair, then sprang up with what seemed like a true smile on her face.

"That would be lovely. Thank you for thinking of it."

Why did it sound as though she were indulging him?

And when had he ever thought so much about anyone else's opinion of him? Or done so much thinking at all in general?

This would not do. He needed to remind himself of their bargain. That they would mean nothing to each other beyond producing a child.

But since she was here, as was he, and now she was seated to his left, he would do his utmost to be polite and respectful, which was the only right thing to do.

"May I get you some tea, Your Grace?" a footman asked.

She glanced up at him, a dazzling smile on her face. Nearly blinding in its pleasure.

"Yes, that would be lovely. Your name is—?"

The footman gave a brief nod. "Smith, Your Grace."

"Thank you, Smith. I would like tea with a large splash of milk and a larger dash of sugar." She looked at Thaddeus. "I try to resist sweet things, only they are just so delicious."

They are, he thought, images of the past two nights in his brain.

"What are your plans today?" he asked.

Her eyes sparkled mischievously. What had he said to cause such a reaction? "Besides meeting with the housekeeper and the butler?"

Oh, right. He'd made the mistake of seeming to be proprietary of her time while reminding her of her duties.

While in bed with her after sex.

He was truly an idiot.

And he deserved her unspoken reminder of that.

"Yes, besides that." He grimaced as she spoke.

She reached out to pat his arm. "It's fine, I promise." Was she supposed to be so amused by him?

"Other than that, I had thought I might go to the shops. I need a new dressing gown," she said with a grin, "and I would like to order some new gowns that will suit the wife of someone as important as you."

She was definitely amused by him.

And—he didn't resent it, for some reason?

She took a sip of tea, closing her eyes in obvious pleasure as she swallowed. He was transfixed by her expression, by how she licked her lips to wring every bit of sweetness from her drink.

He hoped he would not have this strong a reaction to her every time she drank tea—they were British, after all, and there was a lot of tea-drinking.

"Would you—" he began. "Would you like some company on your shopping trip?" He wasn't sure what made him ask, but the thought of spending the day with this easily amused woman—who had somehow become his wife—seemed appealing.

She looked surprised as she nodded. "If you are certain you won't be bored. It will be a help to have someone else along. I normally have my mother"—an exasperated look—"and Jane with me so there is less of a chance I'll end up in something that makes me look like a tea cozy."

A choke of laughter burst out of him, making him cough. "A tea cozy? You could never look like a tea cozy." More like a teapot, one of the fancy kinds the other officers used when trying to impress one another. All curves and sparkle, carrying the warmth of what was inside.

Not that he'd tell her she looked like a teapot, for God's sake.

She chuckled as well. "I always imagine I am going to look like an elegant lady with a grand sweep of skirt, but I am too short to manage it. I have always envied those tall statuesque people who can put on a gown and instantly look like a queen. Not *the* queen, you understand. She looks more like me. But a queen in general."

The now familiar burn of protectiveness rose in him at the unspoken dismissal of her appearance. She was beautiful in her own right, from her dark, wavy hair, to the dimple next to her luscious mouth, to her extravagantly lush bosom that he already fervently admired, to her curved hips.

And none of it was striking until you added in the force of her personality, the nearly palpable spark of her spirit lighting up every bit of her.

He had never met anyone so compelling before. Even though he needed to resist her, resist being entangled in her alluring web. He knew none of it would last, that even if by some miracle they got along, it would end. It was best to keep his emotional distance, to engage with her only in the pursuit of procreation. That's what she wanted.

Had she said she wanted that?

And yet—and yet he had asked if he could accompany her to go shopping for her wardrobe, for goodness' sake. He wanted to clap his hand to his head in dismay. What kind of idiot was he?

He did not want to answer that.

Instead, he rose to his feet. "I will leave you to your breakfast. What time did you wish to leave?"

She wrinkled her brow as she thought. "This afternoon, I think. After I finish my meeting. Say three o'clock?"

He bowed. "Excellent. I will take care of some business until lunchtime."

"Excellent," she echoed, that knowing smile tugging at her mouth. He wished he knew what was making her so damned amused, but he was also probably glad he did not.

LAVINIA SUPPRESSED A smirk as Thaddeus strode out of the room. He tried to be all stern, but then he'd do something like ask her to move closer down the dining room table, or offer to take her clothes shopping.

It was endearing, truly. And welcome—until two days ago, she'd lived in a home where one was likely to encounter someone else at any moment, likely to be pulled into conversations ranging from variations in pickle recipes to how to spell certain economists' names.

"Is there anything I can get you, Your Grace?" It was the other footman—Not Smith. "I heard you mention you enjoy sweet things, and Cook has made some currant scones."

She gave an enthusiastic nod. "Yes, please. And your name is—?"

He bowed. "Powell, Your Grace."

"Thank you."

He went to the sideboard, returning with a plate filled with not only the most tempting scone she'd ever seen, but two dishes holding clotted cream and strawberry jam.

She could grow accustomed to being a duchess.

Had the duke eaten anything? She'd seen an empty cup; she presumed he'd had something to drink, but did he ever indulge?

Oh yes. He did. The first night they'd met, he'd escorted her and Jane to the refreshments table. The punch had been fizzy, fruity, and delicious, but what had been most intoxicating was what his face looked like as he drank—he'd closed his eyes in pleasure, and she'd gotten a glimpse of what he might look like if he let himself relax.

The recollection of that expression should be enough to motivate her to get him to drop his guard. To relax, to indulge, to swirl in hedonistic pleasure.

And the side effect of that would be her own pleasure, which she dearly wanted to own.

She'd have to speak to him about it sooner rather than later, before their evening activities had become routine. How did one approach such a conversation? Should she prepare?

She should definitely prepare.

She finished the last of her scone, extravagantly creamed and jammed, and rose, intent on returning to her room to make a list of discussion points.

At this rate, she'd write a whole book's worth of lists.

Discussion Points on Evening Activities
1. There should be more kissing.
2. It should take more time than it currently does.
    a. Be patient.
    b. Be curious.
    c. Be adventurous.
3. ~~It should be more fun than it currently is.~~
    ~~a. For me.~~
3. We should discuss what is most enjoyable. A frank conversation will yield the best results.

"AND HERE WE are again, for another meal," Lavinia said. She'd taken the seat near to him again, not waiting for him to ask. She'd spent the morning—after making her list—meeting with Mrs. Webb, the housekeeper, who had shown her more rooms than she could recall, and spoken with approval of the duke's direction in regards to the household.

Though she had also mentioned the duke had very few visitors—only his cousin, the former duke, his cousin's sister, and his friend, the Duke of Malvern, who was married to the cousin's sister. And even they didn't come by that often lately, since everyone was recently married.

He was lonely, she decided. Even if he didn't know it himself. Else why would he want to go dress shopping with her? He didn't even seem to particularly like her.

And she was fairly certain he wasn't coming because he cared about gowns.

"Have you had a good morning?" she asked when her first comment produced only a nod and a "hmm."

He shrugged, making her notice his shoulders. They really were massive. It was remarkable that he was packed with so much muscle—which she had seen for herself—given how large he appeared.

He would look truly elegant in a gown. Not like a tea cozy at all.

"What are you laughing at?" he said, gesturing to the footman—Smith, she thought—to bring a tray of something delicious-smelling over.

I was thinking of you in a fabulous ballgown. How your arms would bulge out of the sleeves, and your long stride would make the fabric flow like a river behind you.

He gave a dismissive wave before she had a chance to try to think of something. "Never mind, it's none of my business." He helped himself to what was on the tray, then gestured to her. "Would you like some?"

She nodded, trying not to be stung that he didn't want to know what she was laughing at, which she didn't want to tell him anyway. The item on the tray turned out to be chicken in lemon and rosemary, and she took a bite as he spoke again.

"And you still have to meet with Fletchfield before we go out?"

"Mmph, yes," she said through a mouthful of chicken. "It should not be too long. And it reminds me. I wanted to ask if we could throw a party."

He looked completely startled. As though asking to throw a party was tantamount to asking if it would be all right for her to play badminton indoors while naked.

"A . . . party?" he said, sounding as though he'd never heard the word.

Perhaps he hadn't, at least not in context of himself.

"You have had the title for six months or so?" she said, continuing as he nodded assent, "and now you have a wife, and it would be a good thing for you to introduce yourself more properly to Society."

He scowled. "They've met me." And didn't like me, his tone indicated. Or he them; she couldn't distinguish.

"But they haven't truly met you, which is to say that they haven't come into your home and eaten all your delicious food and drunk all your most excellent wine."

He continued to scowl, but emitted a terse "Fine."

"Good," she said brightly, ignoring his expression entirely. "I'll make the arrangements with Fletchfield and work with Mrs. Webb and the cook on the menus." She fluttered her hand at him. "You just have to appear dressed in your finest ducal garb."

He growled, muttering something that sounded like "no pastels," then tossed his napkin on the table, which one of the footmen swiftly picked up. "I'll see you after your meeting with Fletchfield. I'll be in my study. He can tell you where it is."

"YOUR GRACE?" MELMSFORD sounded concerned, which likely meant that this wasn't the first time he'd addressed Thaddeus.

"What? Yes," Thaddeus replied, willing his brain to concentrate on the papers in front of him and not on when she would sail through the door.

It was just that—just that now that she'd moved in, and he'd spent more time talking to her, it felt as though a light had gone out any time she wasn't in the room.

Which was a ludicrous thing to think.

"We can finish up the accounting another time," Melmsford said, putting his hand on Thaddeus's desk as though to gather the papers.

"No, it's fine." Thaddeus placed his palm on the stack. "I'm just a bit distracted."

Melmsford sat back down slowly, his expression as concerned as his earlier tone. "Is there—is there anything you wish to discuss?"

It was a tentative offer of friendship, an unusual gesture given that they were employer and employee. But Thaddeus didn't have anyone to talk to—his two best friends, Sebastian and Nash, were off being blissfully happy with their respective wives—and Melmsford had already shown himself to have a kind heart.

"You're not married, are you?"

Melmsford shook his head hastily. "No, but I do hope to find someone someday." He tilted his head as though searching for the right words. "The duchess is a good person. At least that has been my impression."

Thaddeus nodded. "She is. I just—" *She wasn't who I would have chosen. Who I did choose. And now I have entered into this bargain with her, and I don't know how to treat her while we are together.* But he certainly couldn't share any of that with Melmsford.

"I should just get back to work," Thaddeus said abruptly.

Melmsford's expression remained concerned as they returned to the discussion of land, livestock, and tenants' rents.

And Thaddeus's thoughts remained confused. He wasn't supposed to like her; he *didn't* like her. That would make it all the easier when they finally, and irrevocably, went their separate ways. But then he went and did something as muddleheaded as to ask if he could accompany her on a shopping trip. To wonder where she went the day after their wedding. To wonder how she was finding dealing with the household staff—did she need help? Would she even ask him if she did?

He had not anticipated marriage would bring about so much thinking. If he had known that, he might not have been so determined to change his bachelorhood.

Although then he wouldn't have known what it was like to kiss her. To slide his fingers down her body, to feel her soft warmth surrounding him.

Damn it. He was supposed to be reminding himself of the reasons he would be glad when she bore a child, not reminding himself of the passion of the marital bed.

Of how she looked entirely naked, of how she looked at him with desire when *he* was entirely naked.

Goddamn it more. Now he was starting to get hard, and it was the daytime, and he was sitting with his secretary, who now seemed to be explaining Norfolk four-course rotation, whatever that was.

It was not the time to be thinking about any of those things. Those things were to be relegated to the evening, when everything else had been completed.

And yet—

"Hello!" she said, bursting into the room, making both him and Melmsford jump.

She strode toward them, a lively expression on her face. "Are you done? I can wait until you are done if you are not." She spoke so rapidly Thaddeus felt as though he were at half-speed.

He rose from his chair. "We are done." Melmsford had risen also, glancing between the two of them as if waiting for something to erupt. Him? He would not erupt. He did not erupt. "That will be all, Melmsford."

"Excellent, Your Grace." The secretary bowed to Lavinia, then walked quickly out of the room.

She immediately sat in Melmsford's vacant chair, leaning forward to draw the various papers on his desk toward her. "Is this what you were working on? Goodness, all those numbers! Percy would be in heaven." She chuckled, her tone warm.

Percy? He felt a flash of unexpected jealousy, which ebbed when he realized she was talking about her brother.

"Both Mrs. Webb and Fletchfield mentioned how impressed they were at you taking responsibility for your duties so swiftly," she continued. "Your predecessor—your cousin?" she said, pausing to wait for his nod of assent. "He had his heart in the right place, but it sounds as though he didn't have your discipline."

Thaddeus snorted. "Until he inherited, Sebastian was most interested in—" And then he froze, because he wasn't supposed to talk about those kinds of things with a lady.

Though this was his wife. A wife who was very plainspoken herself.

"In—?" she prompted.

"Ladies," he answered.

Her cheeks turned pink. Was it possible he had embarrassed the forthright Lavinia Capel? Now Lavinia Dutton, Duchess of Hasford?

"Speaking of that," she began, drawing a piece of paper from her pocket, "there is something I need to discuss with you."

A tinge of uncertainty came over him. Which never happened. "What about the shops?" He drew his watch out from his waistcoat pocket to consult it. "They will be closing soon, won't they?"

She gave a decided shake of her head. "This is more important than the shops," she said firmly.

She spread the paper out on the desk and met his gaze.

"It's about our marriage."

Now THAT SHE had his attention, she realized even more that this conversation was one that he would likely be loath to have.

What sort of person, let alone a man, let alone a military man, let alone a military man who was also a duke, would want to hear that he was . . . insufficient in that area?

Oh dear.

She could just keep quiet about it all, just tolerate it until she bore a child. Assent gracefully to whatever it was he thought was appropriate for their evening activities together.

But then she wouldn't be fully satisfied. And she had already agreed to his terrible bargain. She had no choice, so to submit to this as well would make her lose her spirit. Not all at once, but slowly. Leaking out one disappointing encounter at a time.

"Our marriage?" His tone was sharp.

She tapped the paper. "Yes. Specifically the part that deals with the actions required to procreate." Had she just uttered all of those words in one sentence? If she had written that sentence in a book, she would have crossed it all out to write "let's talk about sex."

He shifted in his seat, and then it struck her how odd it was—he was seated behind his desk, his work papers still spread in front of him, her sitting in front of his desk as though she were a supplicant.

"Let's move over there." She scooped up her paper and went to sit on the sofa that was positioned in front of the desk area. Much more comfortable.

He joined her without comment, thank goodness, his large frame taking up a disproportionate amount of the sofa. His lovely thigh right in her line of vision.

She was here for his thighs.

"Our actions to procreate—by which you mean . . . ?" he began.

"Precisely." She took a deep breath. "I was under the impression that the activity would be enjoyable for both of us."

His eyebrows rose in shock. "It's not?"

Poor ignorant man. "No, it's not," she said softly. She paused, then spoke again. "Since we have agreed to leave one another once you have an heir"—*and I'll have to leave my child, but don't think about that now, never think about that*—"and that is the focus of my life here, I would like to have more fun doing it."

The words seemed to echo around the room, although of course they couldn't, what with there being books and carpet and heavy furniture to absorb whatever noises were made here.

He took a deep breath, but didn't speak. Lavinia braced herself for his reaction.

"I see."

More silence.

"And your list here is to help?" He held his hand out for the paper, which she gave to him, biting her lower lip as he scanned the page.

"More kissing?"

"Mmm-hmm."

"And it should take more time in general?"

She exhaled. "Yes."

"Patience, curiosity, adventure?"

"Exactly so."

He leaned back against the sofa and regarded her, an appraising, but not unpleasant, look in his eye.

Very much like the look she'd caught in his gaze when he didn't think she could see him. When he seemed determined to court Jane, but couldn't stop staring at her.

"I am to show patience, exhibit curiosity, and have a sense of adventure." His tone had turned almost predatory, and a part of her—the part that shamelessly admired his thighs, his heavy muscles, and how his arse felt—thrilled at the sound.

"And you will too." It wasn't a question.

"Absolutely." She sounded breathless. A very good sign.

"And we will discover—together—what is pleasurable?"

Dear God, yes. "Mmm." She could barely speak; her whole body felt tight and aching. She wanted to squirm on the sofa, but she knew that wouldn't relieve the ache.

His lips slowly curled into what Lavinia could only call a sensuous smile. It made his whole handsome face look appealingly dangerous, and she held herself back from leaping onto him that very second.

"I agree to your new bargain." He gave her back the list, then held his hand out toward her. "Let's shake hands on it."

She stretched her hand out, and he clasped it immediately, his warm skin covering hers. He kept his gaze on her face, and she couldn't help but emit a short breath, one in response to the anticipation—the yearning, desperate anticipation—she'd likely have until this evening.

It would be unbearably delicious, to explore this man, to discover what made him groan, to allow him to discover what would do the same to her.

And she was entirely relieved that instead of being resentful of her demands, he'd listened and agreed. It augured well for when they had the "frank conversation" that was on her list.

How could she possibly wait until this evening?

"So," he said, still with that smirk on his face, "should we go dress shopping?"

He absolutely knew what he did to her, and what he was going to do to her. And she could not wait.

"You do not know it yet," he said, still standing in front of me, his hands planted on his hips, "but you have no other choice but to marry me. Your father promised you to me, and I am here to collect the debt."

"My father would never have done such a thing!" I exclaimed, even though I had the horrible feeling he would have. "This must be some mistake!" I tried to get up again, but like before, he pushed me back onto the sofa.

"It doesn't matter what you know," he said, sneering. "You will marry me by midnight tonight. If you don't," he said, letting his words linger in a clear threat, "I will do what I want with you regardless." He shrugged. "And if you do marry me, I will leave you alone. It is your choice."

And that is how I came to be the Countess Dramorsky.

My Dark Husband by Percy Wittlesford

Chapter Fourteen

Thaddeus wasn't sure whether he should applaud her for speaking up, be appalled he'd not noticed her disappointment, or haul her over his shoulder to her bedroom now.

The conversation—or more specifically, what lay underneath the conversation—made his imagination run wild. If there were no constraints, none of the usual sexual protocol that he presumed was supposed to exist between husband and wife—what could they do? What couldn't they do?

He couldn't wait until the evening. But he knew she was just as anxious for it, and a tiny part of him wanted to tease her into a state of heightened frustration. Until they finally were alone.

So he forced his expression back to neutral, placing his hands on his thighs as he spoke. "Well! Thank you for airing your concerns. That was most . . ."

Her eyes were intent on his face, her teeth worrying her lower lip in unconscious reveal.

"Informative," he said at last. "Should we go shopping?" He rose as he spoke, holding his hand out to her. She took it, standing herself, beginning to release his grip when he tightened his hold on her and drew her nearer.

"But since you did mention it, I believe there was to be more kissing?"

And without waiting for her reply, he grasped her waist and pulled her closer, placing his mouth on hers.

At first she seemed too startled to respond. But he could be patient—she'd told him to be, after all—and he waited as her body's tension eased, and she slid her hands up his arms to clasp around his neck.

And then it sounded as though she chuckled, deep in her throat, and he licked at the seam of her mouth, and she opened for him, pressing her body against his at the same time.

Patience.

He held her waist, his tongue darting into her mouth to explore. Soft, wet, and delicious. She tasted like the tea she'd had, of warmth, of passion. Her tongue met his, as eager as he was, their tongues clashing in a sensuous game. First he licked and sucked, and then she would respond in kind.

His entire focus was narrowed to where their lips joined, to the physical sensation of touch between them, to the sensual urgency claiming his body, making him want to touch her everywhere, to draw up the skirts of her gown to discover whether she was wet.

To tease her with his fingers there.

Patience.

But that wasn't what she'd asked for, what she wanted to happen. She wanted exploration and curiosity. To speak openly about what they enjoyed.

And of course more kissing.

So instead of rushing through to the inevitable conclusion, he lingered on her mouth, paying close attention to what it seemed she liked; him sucking her tongue into his mouth, his nibbling on her lip, his thrusting his tongue inside to explore.

After a while, he didn't have to remind himself to be patient. There was so much pleasure, so much passion, in the kiss it was enough. It was entirely satisfying, even though he knew at the same time it would leave him hard and aching.

She gave a tiny moan, and he tightened his grip at her waist, keenly aware of her luscious breasts just above his hands.

He wanted to knead them in his palms, roll her nipples between his fingers. He hadn't paid enough attention to them before, and he wanted to know if she was sensitive there. If he could bring her closer to climax by caressing her there.

But it wasn't the right time.

He broke the kiss, putting his mouth to the tender spot just below her ear. "We could do that forever," he said in a low tone. "But I know you want exploration." He splayed his fingers, moving them a tiny bit toward her breasts. She shivered in response. "I want to explore all of you." He licked her neck, then moved his lips so they were right at her ear. "You are right to demand patience and curiosity." His cock was hard and heavy, straining against his trousers. "I will demand the same from you." He reached toward his neck, withdrawing one of her hands and bringing it down toward his aching erection. Slowly, so she could stop him if she wanted. Patiently, he thought to himself wryly.

But she didn't stop him, and then he'd put her palm on his cock so she could feel what just their kiss had done to him. "Later tonight," he whispered into her ear, "I'll want to explore you. And I hope you'll want to explore me."

He drew back from their embrace, slowly, her hand still resting on his penis, her eyes heavy with a sensual gaze. Her mouth wet from their kiss.

She met his gaze and he nearly held his breath—had he shocked her? Would she be outraged by what he'd said, what she'd touched, how he'd spoken?

And then her mouth—that lush, curved mouth—curled up into a smile, her dimple adding additional punctuation to her emotion.

"I will, Precious," she said with a sly grin. "I look forward to it." And then, without breaking their gaze, she removed her hand from him as her smile turned more wicked. "Let's go shopping, and you can tell me what you want me to wear." She gave him a wink as she turned to walk out the door.

He froze, mesmerized by that smile, that wink, and how confidently she walked away, then followed, muttering, "Don't call me Precious."

A laugh was her only response.

LAVINIA FOUND IT difficult to concentrate on anything after that conversation. Even the joy of buying a wardrobe suitable for a duchess wasn't able to distract her from the thought of what might happen between them that night.

But at least now she had a dressing gown that fit. The dressmaker, who Lavinia's mother patronized, had fallen all over herself to ensure Lavinia—and the duke—were happy with her choices, although the duke hadn't paid much attention to the proceedings beyond mentioning he didn't want to see her in pastel colors.

Something they had in common.

They'd eaten dinner hurriedly and mostly in silence, their occasional pointed glances reminding the other of what would be happening later that evening.

Lavinia had felt her toes already curling inside her slippers as she ate her meal.

And then finally it was time to retire, and she was wearing her new dressing gown, standing in the middle of the bedroom as she waited impatiently for him to arrive.

That kiss . . . that kiss had already gone a long way toward persuading her that there was a chance that this aspect of their marriage, at least, would be better.

She appreciated that he hadn't rushed things. That he had taken her at her word—and her list—that he should have patience. So much patience, in fact, that she had found herself wanting more.

Which was the whole point, wasn't it?

If she didn't think it would seem condescending, she'd congratulate him on being so responsive to her needs.

The door swung open suddenly, startling her

from her thoughts. Making her jump as she jerked her head toward him.

Oh.

Like before, he wore a dressing gown. The same one. His feet were bare as he advanced toward her, his walk predatory without being menacing.

She felt like a delicious treat he was looking forward to savoring.

Or more accurately, she wanted to be the delicious treat he was looking forward to savoring. *Savor me*, a voice clamored in her head.

"You're smiling again," he said, his voice gruff.

"Do I smile too much?" she replied, raising an eyebrow.

He shook his head slowly, still walking toward her. Her new bedroom really was quite inordinately large.

"I like it when you smile." His words sent a shiver down her spine. "I want to make you smile." And then his lips curled into—not quite a smile, but a wolfish grin.

She rather suspected she'd awoken a beast of some sort.

And she knew, rather than suspected, that she liked it.

She tilted her head back to gaze into his eyes as he came so close to her she could smell the soap he must have used—some sort of piney scent that made her imagine him out in the forest chopping trees.

With a large ax.

Preferably shirtless.

"How are you going to make me smile, Precious?" she said in a soft, low voice.

His eyes narrowed, and he grasped her upper arms, then bent his head to press his lips against her neck. She arched her back and let out a small gasp. His mouth moved against her skin, and she felt her breathing quicken. Her hand had somehow found its way to his chest, burrowing underneath the lapels of the dressing gown to the warm skin underneath. Warm, strongly muscled, and covered with a scattering of hair.

"You want patience, curiosity, and adventure," he said, then immediately swooped her up into his arms, making her shriek in surprise. He took a moment to wink at her, then tossed her onto her big bed, following her immediately after.

She collapsed in laughter as the bed bounced with his weight. He took hold of her legs and straightened them, then crawled up her body, taking care not to crush her, but still kept her pinned.

"Ooh, so this is the adventurous part?" she teased, beaming up at him. "A bed? Your Grace, what a provocative decision!"

She saw his emotions shift from annoyance at her impudence to amusement at her high-spiritedness.

"I don't want to assuage your curiosity all at once," he said in a growl. "We will build up to moving beyond the bed."

Now she was really and truly intrigued. She'd been teasing, and she hadn't really thought of any places beyond the bed—on the carpet? Against a wall? In the garden?

Oh, this curiosity thing was going to be good. For both of them.

"I can't wait," she replied, sounding breathless.

"Patience, Lavinia," he said in a sly tone as he leaned down to kiss her.

His mouth was so warm and his lips so firm. She felt as though she were melting into the bed as he pressed against her.

The fingers of his right hand were in her hair, tugging gently as his lips urged her to open for him.

She did, sliding her tongue into his mouth as she had earlier that day. Only now, with so much less clothing between them and so much more bed, it was infinitely more intoxicating. Her whole body throbbed with awareness of his, of the warm strength of him against her, his other hand resting at her waist.

Move up, she wanted to say, but she knew he'd remind her to have patience.

She did not want to be patient, damn it. She wanted to—but then she forgot all about what she wanted to do when his left hand slid onto her belly. Stroking her skin as he continued to kiss her deeply, ravaging her mouth as she did the same to him.

"Is this curious enough for you, Madam List Maker?" he asked, raising his mouth from hers.

She met his eyes, saw the desire flickering in his hooded gaze. Knowing her desire was equally strong in her expression.

Though she hadn't gotten to touch him. Not in the way she wished to, at least.

"It is a good beginning," she replied, reaching her hand up to cup his neck. "I appreciate all the kissing." She licked her lips deliberately, a secret thrill running through her as she heard him draw in a breath at her action.

"But I want to explore. I've been very curious," she began, trailing her fingertips along his broad shoulders, sliding the fabric of his dressing gown down his arms, "about how you feel." Her fingers caressed his skin, ran down to squeeze his powerful biceps, moved sideways to his chest. Stretching her palm out over his pectoral muscles, feeling his heartbeat under her fingers.

His breathing was ragged, and she could feel his hardness pressed up against her thigh.

"How do I feel?" he asked, lowering his mouth to her skin—this time, pressing his lips to the area right below her collarbone.

She dug her fingers into his chest muscle, reveling in the hard strength she felt. "Incredible. How do you keep—you know, never mind, you can tell me later." She didn't want to distract either one of them by asking how he maintained his conditioning.

Although perhaps later he would allow her to watch.

"You feel incredible as well." He slid his mouth lower, his lips nibbling at her breast, sliding lower, until he covered her nipple with his mouth and sucked in.

"Oh God!" she exclaimed, flinging her head back onto the pillow.

She heard a soft chuckle against her breast. He licked her, swirling his tongue around her nipple, making every inch of skin there respond with alacrity.

Meanwhile, she kept her hand on his chest, exploring the planes of his body, brushing his nipple with the palm of her hand.

She felt liquid and languorous, but also urgent and frantic; both wanting to slow down and savor the moment and rush to the inevitable conclusion.

Though, as she knew, his inevitable conclusion felt different than hers did, at least in the two times they'd done it.

So she had to be patient as well.

He continued to touch her until she needed to have him inside, urging him to climax as she continued to relish the feel of his big body on hers.

"Was that better?" he muttered into the sheets.

"Very much so." She patted his back approvingly. "It appears you are as good at taking orders as you likely were at giving them."

He snorted in response, which made her smile. Perhaps they could tolerate one another well enough for the next year or so.

And then—and then she would carve out her own life, having fulfilled her end of the bargain.

Jane would hopefully be happily married by then, and she would have fulfilled that promise as well.

All these commitments, all this satisfaction—and yet a part of her still felt empty. *Enough time to think about that later*, she reminded herself as she began to drift to sleep.

The rest of your life, in fact.

"I should return to my room," he said abruptly.

"Oh," she murmured sleepily. "You don't have to, you know."

She heard rustling of the sheets, and then the distinct sound of him rolling out of bed, muttering something inarticulate as he did so.

The bed felt much emptier now.

But that was how it should be, wasn't it? They were together for one thing only: to produce a child. Anything more than that would be breaking their bargain.

She curled away from him, drawing the covers up to her chin. Waiting until she heard the door close, then exhaling, feeling the wash of some sort of painful emotion crash over her. An emotion she couldn't identify, but one that *hurt*.

He was true to his word.

After the ceremony—conducted by a muttering priest who was most interested in the money my new husband dangled in front of him—he rang a sonorous bell and the black-clad housekeeper came in, her disapproving expression revealing I would have no allies in this house. "See the lady to her chambers," the count said. "I'll be back in a week."

And without saying a word to me, without even looking at me, he left.

I took a long look around the room, wanting to scream in terror or run out to find someone who would help me.

But no one would listen. No one would help.

I was entirely and completely alone.

My Dark Husband by Percy Wittlesford

Chapter Fifteen

"Good morning, Melmsford." Thaddeus strode into his office feeling unaccountably jaunty.

"Good morning, Your Grace." Melmsford rose from his chair, a sheaf of papers already in his hand.

"Put those down," Thaddeus ordered. He didn't want to waste his high spirits with paperwork. "How about we do something else?"

"Something . . . else?" Melmsford echoed, sounding entirely confused.

"Yes, something that doesn't require us to sit inside on such a lovely day." Both men glanced toward the windows, which revealed a sky full of clouds.

"Well. Perhaps not a lovely day, exactly." But lovely for him. It appeared that for the duration he'd be with his wife he would indeed get to fulfill one of the items on his list. Even if she wasn't precisely the modest female he'd had in mind when he'd created it.

"What do you want to do?" Melmsford asked.

Thaddeus shrugged. What had he done with Sebastian and Nash when he'd spent time with them?

Mostly drink while trying to prevent Nash from getting into another fight. And envying Sebastian's easy way with ladies.

Neither of those seemed as though they would suit what he and Melmsford might do.

"I think I would like to go shopping," he announced.

"Shopping?" From Melmsford's tone, it sounded as though he'd suggested parading through London wearing only a fruit basket.

"Yes. I'd like—" What would he like to do? "I'd like to purchase something for my wife."

Something that would indicate his pleasure with her, assure he wasn't angry about her broaching the subject of their sexual congress together, and because he simply wanted to.

Why he wasn't certain.

"A piece of jewelry?" Melmsford suggested.

That had been what Thaddeus had presumed, but now that Melmsford said it, it didn't seem to suit. Lavinia might like a new piece of jewelry, but he'd like something more personal.

Though he didn't know her well enough to know what that thing would be.

And he wasn't supposed to want to know her well enough to know what that thing would be. Because that would be contrary to their bargain.

Goddamn it.

He shook his head, his good mood entirely dissipated. "Never mind, we should get to work." He stalked over to his chair, yanking it out and sitting down with a grunt.

"If you're certain, Your Grace."

Melmsford hesitated for a moment, then retook his chair, giving Thaddeus a few furtive glances.

He'd chosen this. He couldn't blame anyone but himself. He'd chosen to be isolated, to distance himself from his wife because he'd assumed she wouldn't want to know him either.

He didn't want to buy her jewelry. He didn't want to get to know her better to discover what might make her smile.

Beyond more kissing, that is.

That was the extent of their relationship. That would have to be enough.

So why did he feel so empty?

A few hours later, Thaddeus felt more himself. Less . . . aching. He and Melmsford had been systematically reviewing the ducal holdings, assessing each one to ensure it was bringing maximum gain to his overall wealth.

He intended to leave the dukedom in a better position than when he'd gotten it. Sebastian had begun the work, but had gotten disinherited soon thereafter, and Sebastian's father had neglected most everything while Sebastian's mother had spent all of her time, it seemed, tormenting Sebastian's half sister, Ana Maria, and maintaining her own prestige.

This work was familiar. Numbers and strategy made sense. He didn't have to worry about whether or not the investments liked him, or if he was doing enough for them. If they would be hurt if he let them go.

If he could just apply his thinking to his life, he would be far better off.

It was the only way to survive.

LAVINIA BENT OVER her work, a delighted smile on her face as she scribbled frantically. This was how she would endure the next year or so—pouring her emotions onto the page, writing the life for her heroines that would be denied to her in real life.

It would be enough.

And her publisher would certainly be happy.

She jumped when she heard a knock at the door, glancing at the clock that was perched on her desk. Startled to see it was close to lunchtime—had she really been writing all morning?

"Come in," she called.

One of the maids opened the door and stepped inside, staring down at the carpet as though too nervous to meet Lavinia's eyes.

"It's Gessings, isn't it?" she asked.

The maid nodded as she looked up. "Yes, Your Grace. Thank you, Your Grace."

Lavinia waited.

"Lady Jane Capel is here, Your Grace. Waiting in the sitting room."

"Oh!" Lavinia exclaimed, leaping up from her seat. "My sister!" She walked swiftly toward the door, past the maid and down the stairs. "Fletch-field," she called, seeing the butler at attention in the hallway, "which way is the sitting room?"

"Here, Your Grace," the butler replied, leading her to the room. He opened the door to reveal

Jane perched on a sofa, jumping up as she saw Lavinia.

It had been only a few days, but it was the longest period the sisters had ever been separated since Lavinia was born eleven months after Jane. It certainly felt like a much longer time.

"Thank you, Fletchfield," Lavinia said before rushing forward to envelop Jane in a hug. And then immediately felt something twining around her legs, making her stumble.

She looked down in surprise, her eyes widening as she spotted the shaggiest, tiniest dog she'd ever seen.

"Oh my goodness!" she exclaimed, turning her gaze back to Jane. "What is this?"

"A dog. You said you wanted a dog," Jane said, giving her an enormous smile.

The dog leaped up, putting its paws on Lavinia's knees. It was a tannish color, covered in wiry hair with a tail that seemed as though it were airborne, waving back and forth.

"What is its name? And is it a he or a she?"

Jane shrugged, her eyes alight with laughter. "I think it's a she, and I don't know her name. You'll have to name her."

They both looked down at the dog, who returned their regard with a few enthusiastic yips.

A wicked idea came into Lavinia's head. "Precious." She bent down to gather the dog in her arms. She wriggled and licked Lavinia's cheek. "I'm going to name her Precious."

"Precious is an excellent name," Jane replied. "And there's more."

Lavinia glanced up, immediately concerned.

Not because there was anything to be concerned about, but because it was in her nature to protect Jane in general. "What is it? Is something wrong?"

"Nothing's wrong," Jane replied, her eyes starting to glisten. "Henry has proposed."

"And you said yes?" Lavinia asked, releasing Precious to stand back up again.

Jane nodded. "Of course I did, you ninny," she said, rolling her eyes.

Lavinia exhaled, relieved that nothing was wrong. "I knew you did, I just wanted to be certain." She took Jane's arm and guided her to sit on the sofa.

"Tell me all about it." *Tell me what it is like to love a person and have them love you in return. Since I will never experience that firsthand.*

Precious ran to the corner of the room to investigate her new abode. Apparently the bottom of the bookshelf had some fascinating scents.

"Well, first he had to speak with his parents," Jane began. Lavinia suppressed a frown—she already knew Mr. McTavish was unduly determined to adhere to his parents' wishes. That was why she had agreed to marry the duke in the first place, after all.

Not every family is like yours, she reminded herself. *And Jane is not you. She is clearly pleased at the events.* Though she did wish he could have proposed first, knowing that his family was almost certain to say yes.

But this was real life, and not something she was writing. Because if she had been writing it— and perhaps she would, eventually—she would have had him declare himself in some passionate way and then announce what he'd done.

"And then his mother invited me for luncheon. Mother is still grousing about—" And then Jane stopped speaking, her eyes wide in shock.

"About me marrying the duke instead of you?" Because Jane's beautiful appearance and modest demeanor were far more suitable attributes for a duchess. Lavinia didn't even have to hear her mother say it to know she believed it. She'd made her feelings about her younger daughter abundantly clear as soon as both girls were out in Society.

It shouldn't hurt, not after hearing it for so long. But of course it did.

A mother should support her children—all of them. Her throat got thick when she realized that her child—at least her male child—would not have the benefit of her support more than the occasional visit.

"Mmm," Jane murmured. "But she finally agreed to let me go, though she made me take Caroline." Jane rolled her eyes in an uncharacteristic judgmental way. "That was entirely awkward. Caroline was—"

"Being Caroline?" Lavinia supplied. "Did she ask Mr. McTavish if today was the day he would propose?"

Jane shook her head. "Nearly. But I was able to distract her with some buttered peas, thank goodness."

"Thank goodness for buttered peas," Lavinia cheered. "So what happened?"

Jane took a deep breath. "After lunch, Mr. Mc-

Tavish invited me to stroll in the garden." A tiny frown appeared on her lovely face. "It was raining a bit, but Mr. McTavish assured me he never caught cold."

Had he checked with Jane that she would endure the rain?

Focus, Lavinia. This isn't your story.

"And then we went out and he showed me a statue his great-grandfather had commissioned while in Rome."

"A statue."

"The statue is of the great-grandfather, and Henry looks so much like him." Jane blushed. "He's told me I should call him Henry."

Yes, because you are engaged. Precious is completely off the table. She smiled at the memory before returning her focus to Jane.

"What did Henry say?" Lavinia asked, impatient for the details.

"He said that his great-grandfather, and his grandfather, and his father all married women who would be an asset to the McTavish name, and he hoped I would do the same." She gave a pleased smile while Lavinia tried to suppress her unkind thoughts about Mr. McTavish. Hoped Jane would do the same? No mention of love, or how honored he'd be if she agreed to marry him?

She was definitely going to write this up far better than how it had happened in real life. There would be many more compliments and much more—

"Did he kiss you?" Lavinia said abruptly.

Jane looked shocked. Well, that answered that question. Perhaps she should make a list of demands for Jane, postwedding.

"No, he—you see, his family was watching us from the window." Jane's cheeks were bright red. "And we haven't been alone since." She reached out to clutch Lavinia's hands. "I am doing the right thing, aren't I? I mean, I've admired Mr. Mc—Henry for so long, and now it's happening, and I want to make certain." She paused, taking a deep breath. "Because you sacrificed so much for me to have this option."

"You cannot imagine being with anyone else, can you?" Lavinia asked.

Jane gave her head a vigorous shake. "No." She sounded firm, and Lavinia felt a sense of relief. "He's who I dream of at night. He's kind, and handsome, and intelligent, and—" She stopped speaking, her expression now one of complete and absolute joy. "He is who I want, Vinnie. Entirely."

What would it be like to be in love so thoroughly? And to have someone love her back?

She bit her lip, suppressing a sigh. At least now she had a dog.

"I'VE GOT IT!"

His wife burst into his office, her outrageously bright gown eclipsed only by her excited expression. Something small and furry bounded alongside her.

Melmsford rose, bowing in silence as he left the room.

"What do you have?" Thaddeus asked as the dog—for that's what it was, a dog—ran up to sniff his legs. "I mean, I can see. Is this . . . yours?"

She advanced toward him, beaming. "Yes, it is. Jane brought her. Isn't she perfect?"

Thaddeus gave a dubious look toward the dog, who was looking back at him. It—she—was small and exuded a fearsome energy.

"Perfect," he echoed.

"But that's not what I came in to talk about. Come here, Precious," she said, snapping her fingers.

Thaddeus's eyebrows rose. Precious? She'd named it Precious. But she hadn't stopped talking so he didn't have time to dwell on the nuance of that. "Our party. We'll throw an engagement party for Jane. She's gotten engaged to Mr. McTavish, he's the reason—" And then she froze, her eyes widening.

"He's the reason . . ." he said, rising slowly to his feet. "He's the reason for what, Lavinia?"

He likely didn't want to hear what she was going to say, but he knew it would haunt him if he didn't.

She went to plop down in Melmsford's vacant chair. She was biting her lip, only not in sexual anticipation this time. Precious—why had she given the dog that name?—leaped up onto her lap, and she began to stroke the dog's fur, her gaze distant.

"He's the reason I married you." She flung her hands up in apparent disregard for his feelings. Or the dog's desire to be petted. "It was my inclination to accept the scandal, but Mr. McTavish and his dreadful family made it clear they would not allow any son of theirs to marry a scandal."

"Your sister has never been a scandal," Thaddeus replied, feeling suddenly defensive of his wife's sister, not to mention her entire coterie of bizarre relatives.

Who had he become?

Lavinia gave him a look that somehow managed to imply he was an idiot without actually saying the words.

"But I have been. And Percy, and the fact that we have other illegitimate relatives as part of our family."

"Oh."

He couldn't deny the veracity of what she was saying. But still—he'd known, of course, that she'd married him for reasons other than actual liking; their interactions prior to their wedding was obvious. But he hadn't anticipated he'd have heard the truth from her so soon in their marriage.

"It's good to have these things out in the open," he said after a long moment of silence.

She nodded. "Yes, it makes things so much clearer. Like our bargain."

"Right. Our bargain." The one that said they would separate after she bore an heir.

Suddenly he wasn't so eager for a male child as he had been a week ago. He still didn't particularly like her, but he had to admit the house was a lot more lively and certainly his evenings were more pleasurable.

Marriages, real where the husband and wife stayed together, were built on less.

But he still preferred to be alone. Didn't he?

Again, not a question he would want to answer. He'd barreled into the bargain, not worrying about whether or not she would care one way or the other. He couldn't then take it back as though he were deciding things based on how the wind was blowing.

Or how her mouth looked after he'd kissed her.

"So this party," he continued, drawing a fresh piece of paper from the pile on the side of his desk, "is to celebrate the engagement of your sister with Mr. McTavish."

"Precisely." She picked Precious up and put her down on the carpet. The dog immediately returned to her investigation of Thaddeus's leg. "I know you were not exactly thrilled when I suggested a party, but a party with a purpose—surely you can see the efficiency of that?" There was a glint in her eye that indicated she might be finding some amusement in all of this.

He had no idea what she might be amused by.

Nor would he ask.

"Yes." He tapped his pen against the paper. "The party will have the dual benefits of introducing you as my duchess, plus will celebrate your sister's upcoming marriage."

"As I said—efficient," she said with a wry smile.

"What is wrong with efficiency?" Damn it. He'd sworn not to ask, and yet here he was, not two minutes later, wanting to discover what was so damned amusing.

That was the problem with having someone around, someone as intriguing as she was.

She lifted her eyebrow, giving him a rueful look. "You admire efficiency, don't you? It's all part of your military training. Or perhaps it was there before, and that is why you were drawn to the military."

Why did it feel as though she were criticizing him?

"Is there something lacking in that?"

And why did he respond as though he were being criticized?

She shrugged, still with that knowing expression on her face. "There are times when it isn't necessary to be entirely efficient." She hesitated. "Times, in fact, when it is better to take one's time. So to speak."

He didn't think they were talking about a party anymore.

"I can slow down when necessary," he replied. If she was going to call him out—again—he would meet her bluff.

She arched an eyebrow. "Oh, you can." She shrugged again. He was beginning to hate her shrugs. She wasn't looking at him, but at the papers on his desk. As though it was their fault he was good at doing his job. "It's just that it feels as though you are marking the time until you can get back to being efficient."

And then she met his gaze, and he saw the challenge in her eyes.

"Marking time?" he growled, getting up from his chair. He saw her expression change from knowing to mischievous. As though she knew what she'd done, and she was delighted about it.

He stalked from his side of the desk to hers, moving slowly so she would have time to object if she wished.

She did not. Instead, her eyes widened and she licked her lips, staring intently at him as he advanced, getting up from her chair slowly, now biting her lip, a decidedly wicked gleam in her eye.

"It seems," he said, removing his pocket watch from his waistcoat and glancing at it briefly before meeting her gaze again, "that I have some time now to work on an ongoing project." He held his hand out to her. "Would you like to work on it with me, Lavinia?"

HE WAS GOING to kiss her, wasn't he?

And it wasn't that she didn't want it—she most definitely did—but it didn't feel right. If he kissed her here in his office, if they flirted with one another, and challenged one another, then where would it end? She knew for her it would be heartbreak.

Even though she had started all of it today with her talk about efficiency. Waving it in front of him as if it were a red cape and he were the bull.

She was already finding herself wanting to spend time with him when they were not engaged in sexual congress, wanting to get to know him as a person and not just a husband.

She'd always been curious about people, and this particular person was fascinatingly complicated: efficient, passionate, honorable, gruff, and surprisingly considerate.

But assuaging her curiosity would be to break their bargain.

"Stop," she said, ignoring his outstretched hand and putting her palm against his chest. "We can't—you told me that love was off the table. This," she said, gesturing toward them, "is the behavior of people in love. I know this is all my fault, I acknowledge that, but we just can't," she said, shaking her head. "I cannot speak for you, but I am not strong enough to withstand strong emotions, emotions such as love, or even liking." She swallowed as she met his gaze. "And I am finding it difficult not to like you."

He froze, his expression hardening. He snatched his hand back, putting both of them behind him.

Precious, completely oblivious to the emotions swirling in the room, had jumped onto the chair she'd been sitting on and was grooming her paws.

"I see," he said. His tone was cold. Had she hurt him? Likely only his pride—hurting his feelings would imply that he had feelings for her, and she knew, since he had told her himself, that he didn't. He saw her purely as a vessel for childbirth, whereas she was equally insistent he provide her some pleasure if she was to be used as such a vessel.

It was a bargain, with both sides receiving something from the other.

"I apologize if I—that I did appear to be leading you toward this," she said, feeling as though her heart was beating faster than usual. "It is my fault. I will endeavor to keep our future dealings impersonal. Except for—" And she paused, lifting her chin as she didn't say what they both knew to what she was referring.

He bowed. "Of course, madam. I will not overstep the boundaries."

My God, he sounded furious. How could he be so angry? This was what he had wanted, what he had demanded as the terms for their marriage.

She set her jaw and stepped toward him. "I am only behaving as you wish me to. As a proper wife would when her husband requires she behave a certain way." Now she was furious as well—one of the few things they had in common.

They stared at one another for a few moments, and then he nodded toward the door. "If you will excuse me, I find I have more work to complete. I will see you at dinner. Proceed with the plans for your sister's engagement party as you wish. I will leave everything up to you."

If his tone was any colder, there would be icicles hanging from his formidable nose.

Fine. It was her fault for bending their rules; she would accept the responsibility. And she would maintain her distance from him, except when they were in her bedroom at night.

To do otherwise would be to risk her heart.

"Come, Precious," she said, regretting her choice of dog name as they left the room.

For the next week, Lavinia pushed all her emotions regarding him to a separate box in her brain—a box she did not allow herself to open, not even after they'd spent time with one another in bed.

Because of course they were still doing *that*, and he was still learning what pleased her, and she was taking what pleasure she could from the experience. They hadn't quite achieved perfect personal pleasure for her, but they were making great strides. And he was persevering, which she appreciated.

Sometimes, when the box seemed to be opening just a fraction, she wondered if his enthusiasm for their nighttime activities was directly related to how much he didn't want her in his daytime life. The sooner she was with child the sooner he would be able to go his own way, allowing her to do the same.

But she knew that wasn't all there was to it; there were times when she'd look at him, his closed eyes, his intense, focused expression, and know that she was responsible for his few minutes of unrestrained passion.

It was intoxicating. Which made it all the more dangerous to appreciate. She wanted to bring him to that level of mindlessness, to help him lose himself in their pleasure.

So while she was planning the party that would announce Jane's engagement as well as present them as an official couple, she was also perusing the pages of certain books that were to be found in discreet bookstores. She justified her scandalous reading by knowing it was doing double duty in assisting with her writing—not that she would write those specific scenes, but just knowing those things were in the realm of possibility was helpful.

If she could tell him anything about anything, she would share it with him as an example of her own efficiency. But she knew he would be horrified to discover she was the author of the books he clearly loathed. It was bad enough that it was Percy, but if he discovered it to be his own, albeit temporary wife?

Oh dear.

She stifled a nervous giggle at the thought.

But she kept looking at her latest book, a collection of interludes that were as shocking as they were salacious.

She found fault with some of the various authors' choice of words, but she couldn't fault them on what they chose to describe—even now, when she was supposed to be making a guest list for the party, she couldn't help but peer over at the book that was on the right side of her desk.

"Your Grace?"

Lavinia snapped the book closed as she looked up to see Mrs. Webb, who stood at the doorway of the room Lavinia had claimed as hers.

It was on the ground floor, like his study, but it was smaller and much more cozy. She'd had Mrs. Webb change out the dark, velvet hangings for a much brighter fabric so she didn't feel as though she were sitting in a coffin. And she'd hunted down a desk in the attic that appeared perfect for her writing so she didn't always have to hide away in her bedroom to do it.

The bedroom, she'd decided, should be for one purpose, and it was not to get creative with words. Written on paper at least; she hadn't thought about their talking during the act. It was generally silent, with a few grunts and moans.

Perhaps she should look into that, as well. It could enliven the experience even more.

"Oh, yes. Mrs. Webb, I am sorry." *I was thinking about sharing some choice words and possibly some directions with my husband.*

"Your sister is here. She says you have an appointment?"

Lavinia leaped up, yanking her pornographic book from the desk and tucking it under her arm as she headed out to the hallway.

Jane was there, wearing an adorable walking outfit in a pale shade of lavender, a bonnet with a few silk flowers on her head. Her face practically glowed, and Lavinia felt a spark of envy—that glow was from being affianced to a gentleman who adored her, not someone who had to marry her because of an unfortunate stumble.

But she couldn't envy Jane, not really, because she was so happy for her.

This was why she had married the Incongruous Duke—duty by day, devilry at night.

"Good afternoon, Vinnie," Jane said, smiling. "Are you ready?"

"Yes, just let me go up and put this away." She did not want anybody to know what she was reading. Which was generally true, since most people judged ladies who read novels as being somehow lesser than ladies who read nothing.

It had never seemed fair to her, but then again, she didn't make the rules. Women never did.

She ran up to her bedroom, tucking the book into the bottom drawer of her desk. Nancy bustled in quickly after, beginning to apologize for not being in the room already.

Lavinia held her hand up. "For goodness' sake, I don't expect you to anticipate everything I might do." Because that would be unnerving, as well as be far more intrusive than Lavinia would ever want. "I am going out with my sister. Are you free to accompany us?"

Nancy looked startled to be asked, but gave a short nod.

"Excellent. I will need some sort of hat and a cloak—it appears to be a bit windy today. And you'll need something also."

Nancy was already on her way to the wardrobe, where she withdrew a bonnet with an extraordinary amount of plumes. It was dark purple, and it looked like something a modern-day queen would wear. Again, not the actual queen, since she was more known for her discreet mode of dress, but a queen in general.

Lavinia smiled as Nancy put it on her mistress's head, tucking her hair under the bonnet. "I don't think there is any worry someone won't know I am a duchess, not in this hat," she said.

Nancy returned the smile as she met Lavinia's eyes. "No, Your Grace." She stepped back to view her handiwork, then gave a satisfied nod. "I'll just go fetch our cloaks and be downstairs in a moment."

"Thank you." She called after Nancy. "Oh, and collect Precious. She'll be glad of a walk."

Lavinia twisted toward the full-length mirror in the corner of the room, frowning as the drawn drapes made it too dark to see. She yanked the drapes to one side, and the sun streamed in, lighting up everything in the room.

"There, that is better," she murmured. She wanted there to be light everywhere, nothing hidden from view.

Well. Except for the secret that she was actually the author Percy Wittlesford, that she read scandalous books in her own home, that she wasn't afraid to demand what she wanted from her husband, and that she would never wear pastels.

Though that last item might be obvious.

"Mr. McTavish and his family are so pleased you and the duke are giving an engagement party for us," Jane said.

The two sisters had decided to walk toward the shops, even though it was a fair distance, at least for ladies who did nothing but ride in carriages all day. But both Jane and Lavinia were accustomed to long tramps through the city, and Lavinia had been chafing at the lack of exercise in recent days.

Nancy trailed along behind with Precious, giving Lavinia a soft smile any time she turned around to look at her. Of course it made her feel awkward to have a servant following her—she hadn't bothered with that before, she and Jane were always together, and she didn't care about the scandal—but she didn't want to risk having anyone speak ill of the duke's duchess. She owed it to him, for the time being at least, to behave circumspectly.

"I am glad. The duke has left it all up to me, which I have to say is a bit daunting."

"Do you want assistance?" Jane asked, sounding worried.

"No," Lavinia replied. "I have Mrs. Webb, the duke's house—That is, my housekeeper. She is a remarkable person, quite organized."

"And the guest list?"

"I was working on that this morning"—*when I got sidetracked by a scandalous book about sexual relations between a man and a woman*—"but I would appreciate you reviewing the list."

"Could . . ." Jane began hesitantly. "Could the McTavishes review the list as well? They want to be certain that all the right people are invited."

Lavinia felt herself start to bristle at the implication, but then forced herself to settle down. The McTavishes were the epitome of propriety; of course they would be concerned their ramshackle neighbors would have inappropriate friends.

Lavinia actually found herself wishing she had *more* inappropriate friends—her best friends were her siblings, and Percy was only inappropriate because of his birth.

"Of course. Listen," she continued as the thought struck her, "how about we have everyone to dinner soon? Our family and the McTavishes? That way we can all get to know one another without having to worry that Caroline will appear in one of her re-creations."

In addition to out of context questions and the love of buttered peas, Caroline liked to make her own fashion out of things she found.

Her branch gown was the stuff of legends.

"And we also won't have either family jockeying to be the one to host. Lavinia, you are a genius!" Jane exclaimed, kissing Lavinia on the cheek.

The housekeeper—a Madame Kolstoff—arranged for my things, few though they were, to be sent from my house. I wrote a note letting the servants know what had happened, and Madame Kolstoff gave me more than enough money for their severance.

"The master left enough for you to live on, and quite well," she explained. I tried to get her to answer my questions—who was the count? How had my father known him?—but she refused to answer, refused to speak to me beyond telling me when it was time to eat.

I was quite lonely. But I also had plenty of time to think.

And make plans.

My Dark Husband by Percy Wittlesford

Chapter Sixteen

"Good evening."

Thaddeus rose as Lavinia entered, seeming to light up the room as usual. How did she do that? Was she somehow lit from within?

"Good evening," she replied.

Her dinner gown was cut nearly low enough for Thaddeus's taste, her creamy skin set off by the rich gold of the fabric. The fabric had various whirls and patterns set in it, so it shifted in the candlelight.

She sat, giving a quick smile to the footman who pushed in her chair.

Thaddeus sat also, still looking at her. He'd tried his best to pretend he didn't care about her when they weren't in bed together, but he had to admit he'd failed.

He managed to be in the dining room when she took her breakfast, and also knew when she went out or was meeting with one of the servants.

It was damned distracting, and he was looking forward to when she was out of his life.

Of course he was.

"Please," she said to Fletchfield, who'd approached with a tureen. They both watched as the butler ladled soup into her bowl.

She picked her spoon up as Fletchfield filled his bowl as well. "I've had an idea." Her eyes were sparkling, and he couldn't help but shoot a wary glance toward the servants. Her last idea had been to throw an engagement ball, but the idea before that—well, that one couldn't be spoken in front of anybody but the two of them.

She laughed as she caught his expression, then raised a pointed eyebrow as she took a sip of the soup. "I assure you, I don't have those kinds of ideas every day."

A pity, Thaddeus thought before he could censor himself.

"No, my idea is that we host a dinner party for my family and the McTavishes. They're the family Jane will be marrying into," she explained. She shrugged. "They are horribly proper," she said, sounding as though that was a bad thing, "but they are likely to be very impressed with you." She also made that sound like a bad thing.

But her opinion of him shouldn't matter, should it? They were nothing more than partners in the mutual goal of bearing a son. As well as the mutual goal of having fun while doing it.

"Jane and I thought that if the two families were here rather than at one or the other's houses there would be fewer opportunities for argument."

"Argument?" Thaddeus prompted.

Lavinia's response was a long-suffering sigh. "Yes, there is literally nothing upon which the two families agree. How long to trim the hedges, when to stop being loud in the evenings, what to pay the servants—that one caused many of their workers to come work for us." She twisted her mouth up in thought. "The only thing we seem to tentatively agree on is how wonderful Jane is." She met his gaze. "Which you agree on as well, I believe."

Ah. They had never directly addressed the conversation before the incident that had required their marriage. Was now to be the time then?

She bit her lip as she looked away. "But never mind that," she said hurriedly. "Is it all right with you if we have a dinner party? We can discuss the details of the engagement party with both families so hopefully there won't be too many hurt feelings to manage on the actual night."

He raised an eyebrow. "As long as it is not a Dangerous Meals dinner." At her blank look, he spoke again. "You recall when we went for a drive, you spoke about serving poisonous foods like rhubarb and something else."

She lit up as she spoke. "That would solve the problems between families, certainly." Then she gave him a wry look. "But there's no guarantee the right people would be affected."

"It seems very difficult to have a large family," Thaddeus remarked. He took a sip of wine. "When I was growing up, it was only me and my parents. That is probably why I became so close to Sebastian and Nash."

She turned her gaze back to him, a soft smile on her face. "They are your family then. Like Jane and Percy are mine."

He blinked at her words. He hadn't quite thought of it that way. "I suppose they are," he said slowly.

"Which is why you are so lonely now," she replied, making it sound as though it were a known fact and not a criticism.

"I'm not lonely," he said, lowering his voice.

She glanced over his head at Fletchfield. "The duke and I will serve ourselves, if you don't mind."

"Certainly, Your Grace," the butler replied.

Was it Thaddeus's imagination or was the man amused?

The door shut, leaving them alone.

She picked up a bowl of green beans and put some on his plate, then put some on hers.

"I didn't ask for these," Thaddeus said, knowing he sounded petulant and yet unable to stop himself. "I am not lonely!"

She paused before setting the bowl back down on the table. "You are. Why else would you want to come shopping with me, of all activities? Why else do you meet me in the morning at breakfast time? It is not as though you like me." She made a rueful noise. "You have made that very clear. From the first moment we met—'I don't get the opportunity to read for pleasure,'" she said, her voice dropping to imitate what he must have said.

"It is not as though that is an indictment of your person!"

She waved her hand. "It doesn't matter."

"But it does," he said, maintaining a measured tone. "It obviously matters to you, and so it matters to me."

She gave him a sharp glance. "What are you saying?"

He swallowed. "I'm not certain. I just—I just think we should try to get along."

"While we're together, you mean," she replied. She sounded prickly.

"Yes, but, what if—?" he began, not sure of what he wanted to say. Just that he wanted to feel something different from how he felt every day—wanting to spend time with her, but holding himself back from it. Wanting to know more about her, but not wanting to engage her unnecessarily.

"I suppose you're right," he said wearily. "I am lonely." He held his hand out to her. "Would you help me to be less so?"

She stared at him for a few fraught seconds, then placed her hand in his. "I will."

Somehow it felt like more of a binding oath than their marriage vows.

LAVINIA COULDN'T SAY precisely what she ate after that.

His words, his expression, played on repeat in her mind, even when they were discussing the details of the dinner party—in a week, with more servings of vegetables than usual because Lavinia's mother was trying to reduce.

The dessert was something creamy and delicious, and she blinked as she realized she'd devoured the whole thing without noticing.

"Do you want more?"

Thaddeus held a spoon aloft over her plate. The dessert, she saw now, was some sort of whipped confection with chocolate drizzled over it.

"Yes, please."

He gave her a few generous dollops, then scraped the remainder of what was in the dish onto his plate.

She arched a brow. "There's a lot there. Are you certain you can eat all of that?" She gave him a mock appraisal that encompassed his entire body. "Don't tell me that is how you came by all those muscles."

He slid a spoonful of the dessert into his mouth, keeping his eyes locked on hers as he did. Licking his lips clean as he swallowed.

Suddenly the room felt far too warm, even though moments ago it had been perfect.

She picked up her own spoon and dipped it into her bowl. Leaned in toward the bowl, lifting the spoon to her mouth.

Her lips curling up as she slowly opened them to allow the spoon entry.

Wrapping her mouth around the spoon as she sucked the cream off it into her mouth.

He hissed in a breath, and she suppressed a delighted giggle.

"Christ, woman," he said in a growl. "Fuck dessert, let's go to bed."

Then she did laugh, allowing him to yank her up out of the chair and upstairs, both of them walking quickly, sharing sly glances before separating into their respective bedrooms.

"Five minutes, Lavinia," he said, making it sound like a delicious threat.

"Five minutes, Precious," she replied.

"I NEED TO get out of this. Quickly," Lavinia said as she entered her room. Nancy sprung up from her chair, advancing toward her. Between the two of them, she was undressed in just a few minutes.

"I'll do the rest, thank you," Lavinia said. She wore her shirt and her stockings, and she'd pulled down her hair.

"Of course, Your Grace." Nancy bowed, then went to the door, making a surprised sound. "Your Grace! I didn't—excuse me," she said, rushing past him out the door.

He stalked inside, slamming the door behind him.

"It hasn't been five minutes," Lavinia said, nodding toward the clock.

He wore his dressing gown, just barely belted so she could see his wide chest above and his strongly muscled legs below.

He was definitely the dessert she was craving.

Perhaps tonight she would practice some of the activities she'd read about in her book.

"I couldn't wait." His eyes held a dark promise. "I was lonely," he said in a wry tone.

She held her hand out to him. "Come to bed, husband."

He took her hand, allowing her to pull him to the bed. Somehow his dressing gown was shed before he got in, and she took in the sight of his strong back muscles bunching as he moved. "Gladly." He took a deep breath as he rolled onto his back, folding his hands over his chest. His erection tented the sheet. "And I'll try to be as inefficient and take as much time as possible."

She felt a shiver trail over her, as though he had reached out and touched her skin.

"Excellent," she said, getting into bed with him.

My husband returned over a month later.

By that time, I had developed a routine for my life: in the morning, I took my breakfast in one of the few rooms whose windows allowed for light to enter. Then I would read, and in the afternoon I would stroll in the park opposite the house, always accompanied by my new maid, a young girl who spoke no English.

In the evening I would have my dinner in the vast dining room and retire to my room, where I would plot various ways I could escape.

But escape to where?

My Dark Husband by Percy Wittlesford

Chapter Seventeen

All Thaddeus wanted to do was spread her legs and push inside her, thrust rapidly until he reached his climax.

But that was the Thaddeus who didn't care about her pleasure. And he found now that he cared very much indeed—he wanted to make her climax, wanted her to shudder and call his name as she came.

Which meant he had to take his time.

Anything worth doing is worth doing well. A long-forgotten reminder from a past captain whose meticulous attention to detail made him an aggravating, if educational, leader.

And she was well worth doing.

Captain Hastings would be proud of him.

Thaddeus turned onto his side so he was facing her. The sheet was pulled up over her shoulders, and he put his fingers to it, resting them there as he met her gaze. The candles were lit on either side of the bed so he could see her face. She was smiling as if in delight, that intoxicating sparkling gleam in her eye letting him know she wanted this nearly as much as he did.

Nearly.

But if he took the time, if he did the job well, she would want it more.

Dear God, he wanted her to want it more.

"Can I—?" he asked, gesturing to the sheet.

She nodded, biting her lip. "Please."

He drew the fabric down slowly, his fingertips trailing on her soft skin. Her eyes fluttered shut for a moment, and then she swallowed.

He brought the sheet to her waist, revealing her upper body—those breasts that tormented him every evening in her low-cut gowns, her soft belly, the gentle curves of her neck.

He wanted to kiss every inch of her. Take his time as his mouth got to know the map of her skin.

"What are you thinking?" She spoke in a low, husky voice. He met her gaze, noting the stain of color on her cheeks, how her lip was swollen from where she'd been biting it.

"I'm thinking about how beautiful you are," he replied, his voice rough with honesty.

She gave a shy smile, and then put her hand on his shoulder, cupping it with her palm. "I could say the same about you."

He felt his eyebrows rise. "Me? Beautiful?" He shook his head. "I've been called many things, but beautiful is not one of them."

She chuckled as she brought her face closer to his. "Let me guess some of what you have been called." She put her mouth to his neck, sucking it gently. "Arrogant," she said, accompanying her words with a light kiss to the same spot, "determined," she continued, licking a bit higher, "stern," she said with a laugh as she pressed a kiss to his jaw just below his ear, "and extremely efficient." The last few words were punctuated by kisses moving along his jawline, until her lips were poised above his. "And of course breathtakingly handsome."

And then she lowered her mouth to his, claiming it with as much determination as he had earlier. Opening her lips and thrusting her tongue inside his mouth, her fingers tightening on his shoulder, running down his arm, then over onto his chest. Her fingers spread out to caress the planes of his upper body as she kissed him with all the passion he could hope for.

His fingers were on her breast, kneading it, rubbing the nipple under his palm, feeling it harden. He caressed the soft, round flesh, felt how she responded to his touch even as she continued to kiss him with abandon.

This was what he had hoped for. Or no, actually—this was beyond what he had hoped for, to find a woman who was giving, enthusiastic, and sensual. A woman who didn't seem ashamed of anything to do with what they did at night.

He was very lucky.

His hand gave her breast one last squeeze, then he moved his hand down lower, slowly, running his palm against the soft skin of her belly to just above her mound. His fingers tentatively stroking the soft curls there, circling the spot he wanted to touch.

"Please," she pleaded, breaking the kiss for a moment as she took hold of his hand and placed it right there, right where she wanted it, and right where he wanted to be.

He felt the tiny nubbin of flesh with his index finger and began to rub lightly, his middle finger sliding farther down to find her wetness.

And then he pressed his palm against her clitoris as he slid one finger, and then two, inside her.

So wet.

She moaned low in her throat, and he broke their kiss, pressing his face to her shoulder as he worked for her pleasure.

Her fingers continued to grip him, so hard he knew he might have bruises. He craved the bruises as tangible proof of her passion. Her head was thrown back as he felt her neck muscles strain with tension. And then she started to shake, and he didn't stop what he was doing, just kept up the pressure and the sliding in and out of her soft wetness, until he felt her inner muscles grip his fingers and she cried out as she climaxed, her hand keeping him in place for what seemed like forever, but couldn't have been more than a minute.

And then she was gasping as her head dropped forward and he slowed his movement, then stopped it, waiting for her to recover.

His cock was iron-hard, and he didn't think he had ever seen anything as beautiful as Lavinia when she came.

He wanted to make her come again and again, keep her in that constant state of bliss.

"So you do know where the clitoris is," she murmured, startling him so he snapped his head up.

Her expression was mischievous, and he

blinked at her, his brain processing what she had said. His wife had said all of those words.

He'd never imagined he'd be married to a lady who spoke so boldly, and he couldn't help but admit he liked it.

But none of this was in service of bearing a son. *Don't get too attached. She'll be leaving you.*

He couldn't help but emit a quickly smothered groan.

"WHAT IS IT?" Lavinia asked. His expression had changed, his jaw clenching, the lines around his nose revealing he was breathing hard, and not in a passionate way.

He shook his head. "Nothing."

She arched a brow, but didn't contradict him. Of course it was something; one moment he had been clearly reveling in her bliss, and the next he had shut down.

Her husband was closed away from his emotions, so closed he likely didn't know he had them. The first time she met him she'd been drawn to what she perceived as his sensual nature, but then had realized he didn't know he had one.

But, she thought as she smiled to herself in postorgasmic happiness, he clearly did.

So she'd have to show him how to release his feelings. And she was fairly certain she knew how.

She began to kiss his neck again, as she had before, sliding her tongue over his skin and biting gently. Sucking his skin into her mouth as she explored his neck, his collarbones, the length of his shoulders. She put her hand at his waist, spreading her fingers wide as she moved lower down, now flicking her tongue over his hard nipple as he shifted beside her.

She bit him there, too, and he groaned, his breathing getting deeper. Good. His chest was a work of art—broad with muscle and a light sprinkling of hair that trailed down into the thatch of curls surrounding his penis.

She kept her fingers flat against his belly, feeling the indents of his musculature there also. Places she didn't even realize had muscle.

And then she moved slowly down, as he had before, her hand coming to grip the top of his shaft.

"Lavinia," he said in a hoarse tone.

She tightened her grip. "Do you want me to stop?"

He shook his head vigorously. "Fuck, no."

She stifled a giggle at hearing her buttoned-up husband use language he would likely be appalled at using in other circumstances. She slid her hand down his penis, then up again, curling around the top, and then back down.

He thrust himself into her hand and she kept hold of him as she lowered her head, kissing his belly, then the junction of his torso and his leg, and then moved to where her hand held him.

His body was still, taut with something.

"Do you want me to take you in my mouth?" she asked, her tongue darting out to lick the top of him. She'd read the act described, multiple times, and it seemed as though it would have quite an effect on him.

"Yes," he groaned, and that was all she needed to hear.

She opened her mouth wide, as wide as she could, and drew him in, licking the top of his penis as though it was a delicious treat.

Which it was. He tasted salty and musky, and she was surrounded by his scent, his warmth, and how his body was tense, his gorgeous thigh muscles flexing as he shifted.

She put her hand on him, covering the place below her mouth and slid it down, following with her mouth, then up again.

"God, just like that," he said. His voice was ragged and pleading, and she felt triumphant she had brought him to this state.

She kept moving up and down his shaft, licking and sucking as she went, breathing in his musky scent, her hair falling forward onto his lower belly.

And then she felt his hands at her hair, pushing it back over her shoulder. "I need to see you," he said. "See you taking me in your mouth, God, Lavinia, it feels incredible."

She could say the same thing—feeling this power, to have him so close to mindlessness, him who was so controlled, so controlling, not in charge now.

It felt intoxicating.

She kept up the rhythm, following his unspoken cues for how fast, how hard, how long to go.

And then she felt him tense even more, and then he shifted, withdrawing suddenly from her mouth, moving her so she was facedown on the bed. His strong hand cradling her belly, pulling her up onto her knees as he got behind her.

He slid his hand lower to where she was wet, dipping his fingers in as he groaned. "Is this for me?" he asked, rubbing that spot where she ached.

"Yes," she said, pushing back so her arse was against those thighs. His penis was hard against her, and she wriggled, wanting all the contact he could give.

And then he took his hand away and she felt his penis nudging at her entrance, his hand on her hip holding her steady for him.

It felt amazingly savage, as though she was his for the taking. And she wanted to be taken, wanted to be filled up with that throbbing penis she'd just had in her mouth.

He pushed in slowly as she shifted back to take more of him inside. This position was different from the other they'd done, with her on her back and him on top of her. Where he was inside her hit her differently, made her want to take all of him, as much as she could, and more.

"Yes," she murmured as he began to thrust. His movements were slow at first, his breathing labored. She had brought him to this point. She had made him turn into this sexual beast, brought out what she'd seen the first time she'd met him.

It felt glorious.

And then his movements increased, and his thrusts became more intense, and she pushed back to meet him, feeling completely filled and delicious and nearly as mindless as he must have been.

His fingers came back to her clitoris and began to rub, and then she felt it start, her climax, and she moaned as he stroked and petted her, giving her just enough pressure there. Coming so soon again felt amazing, and she had a moment of smugness knowing he likely could not do the same thing.

"Don't stop," she said through gritted teeth.

"I wouldn't dare," he replied, lowering his head to bite her shoulder.

His other hand was still on her hip, gripping her tightly as he began to move faster. "Are you close, Lavinia?" he asked, murmuring his words into her back.

"Yes," she replied, biting her lip as his fingers increased the pressure on her. "Just like that," she said. "So close," she added, feeling the orgasm building until it was inevitable—that blissful moment just before when she knew she was going to come, when there was nothing that would stop it, and the pleasure flooded her senses, made her moan louder until she was gasping.

And then it felt as though she exploded, her orgasm blasting through her whole body.

He kept his fingers there but then began to move much faster, much stronger, until it felt as though he was pistoning into her. And that felt marvelous too, especially in the aftermath of her orgasm, since she knew he was on his way as well.

And then he pushed all the way inside her and froze there as he groaned, and she felt the warmth of his ejaculate in her body.

And then he curled his arm around her body and dropped to the bed, turning her so they were back against front on the bed. Both of them breathing hard, his penis still inside her, his strong forearm against her chest.

"That was amazing," he said at last.

"It was," she replied, putting her hand on top of his arm. "And now I am so sleepy," she said through a yawn.

"I'll go then," he said, moving as he spoke.

She felt the absence of his warmth right away, and felt a pang of something as he shifted off the bed, picking up his dressing gown.

She watched as he put it on. "You could sleep here," she said in a tentative tone of voice. "I wouldn't mind."

More than that, she would like it. But she didn't want to tell him that for fear he was thinking she was growing attached to him. That she wouldn't want to live up to her side of the bargain when it was time.

It was a good thing she wasn't growing fond of him at all, she thought ruefully. Fond of his small kindnesses, how he always strove to do the right thing, how he was awkward in social situations, how he was trying to listen to her even though his first impulse was just to tell her to do something.

Good thing.

"No, I don't wish to disturb you." He sounded stiff, not at all like the man who'd just been groaning in her bed.

She watched him walk toward the door, heard it close softly behind him as he left, and then curled up into a ball, suddenly very sad despite what had just happened between them.

Because of what had happened between them.

Damn it. She was starting to fall in love with him.

THADDEUS WAS JUST beginning to anticipate what was to happen between them when she addressed one of the footmen.

"Smith, could you fetch my and the duke's cloaks? We are going out. Oh, and ask Fletchfield to order the carriage."

Thaddeus stared at her in surprise. "Did I forget an engagement?"

Lavinia's expression was mischievous, and he felt something unfamiliar spark in his chest. A feeling that he wasn't completely in control of the situation, and also the feeling that he was . . . fine with that.

Not something he had ever felt before.

"When we first met, you mentioned wanting to hear music." She shrugged. "I knew you wouldn't allow yourself a night off from work, so I spoke with Melmsford and he assured me you would not be neglecting anything if you took one night for yourself."

"So we are going out?" he asked.

They were alone in the dining room, all the footmen having rushed out presumably to gather their things and request the coach.

"We are." She spoke as though there was no possibility of his denying her.

And, honestly, there wasn't.

"ISN'T THIS WONDERFUL?" she asked, holding on to his arm as they entered the venue.

They were in the lobby leading to what Thaddeus could see was a grand open room, wooden chairs such as might be around a person's kitchen table lining the walls. There was enough light to see the dance floor and that there were people gathered inside, but not much else.

"Wonderful," he repeated.

"Don't be such a grump," she said, squeezing his arm.

They walked through the door into the hall, and now Thaddeus could see the musicians clustered together at the far corner of the room. All of them appeared as though they'd spent the day working, then gathered their instruments and come here. They were disparate in clothing, age, and gender; all they had in common, it seemed, was that they could play something.

Though that remained to be seen.

The music struck up, and she turned to him, a wide smile on her face. "Would you care to dance, Your Grace?"

Before he could answer, she had swept him up and onto the floor, laughing at his presumably dismayed expression.

But only a minute into the music, something changed. He found himself looking into her blue eyes, feeling the way they moved together in sync, nearly as perfectly as those other times when they were physical.

The music was good as well; she hadn't misrepresented that either.

And it felt wonderful, for once, to just do something without it being in pursuit of a goal—even their sexual relations were in pursuit of an heir, no matter how pleasurable he found the process.

But this? This was just for its own sake. Something he could lose himself in.

"You're having fun, aren't you?" Her tone was confident, but not smug; it was as though she had been worried he would not have fun, and found joy in his reaction.

She was so kind, he thought. Even though they were not supposed to have anything more than a transactional relationship, she'd remembered what he'd said when they'd met, and she'd done something to respond to that—something that didn't require that he do any work. Just that he go along with it.

As she did often in bed, as well. Something he also appreciated.

They danced for over half an hour, Thaddeus growing increasingly warm until he finally had to pause.

"Can we get a beverage and rest a bit?" he asked.

She looked up at him. Her cheeks were flushed, and her eyes were as sparkling as he'd ever seen them. "Can't keep up, Your Grace?"

He hooked her arm through his and led her toward where he'd seen a woman selling something liquid. "You know I can, Lavinia," he said in a low voice.

He felt her shiver. And he knew she was not cold.

SHE'D WORRIED AT first that he'd be so non-plussed at being forced out of his usual routine, made to do something fun, for God's sake, that he wouldn't enjoy himself at all. Or worse yet, refuse to go entirely.

But she had spoken to his secretary, Melmsford, who'd encouraged her plans, saying he too thought the duke needed a bit of a respite from all his work. And then Melmsford had ensured that all the possibly pressing things the duke might claim needed his attention were taken care of prior to that evening.

The duke had seemed skeptical at first—the music hall certainly wasn't grand in appearance—and he had made it clear he did not waste time on frivolous things like books and art.

But then the music had begun, and she had bolstered her courage and dragged him out onto the dance floor. Where he had begun to loosen up, and she knew he was having fun and enjoying himself, even though he might not admit it.

He'd relaxed enough to exchange a few sexually-tinged remarks to her, remarks that made her feel as though they were in a real marriage with desire and companionship and, yes, love.

He purchased two cups of wine for them and they sat down on two of the wooden chairs at the edge of the room, as far away from the musicians as possible.

"It is lovely, isn't it?" she asked, taking a sip of the wine. And then grimacing.

"I don't think you mean the wine," he said, taking his own sip, then shaking his head. "Not up to my usual ducal standard," he said, making himself sound like the worst kind of snob.

"But better than we ever had out on the battlefield," he added in his own voice, taking another big drink.

"And the music is quite good, I think. Percy and I went to a few music halls before finding this one. This has the best music, even if it is the least well-appointed."

He glanced at her, his eyebrows raised. "A few music halls? With your brother?"

She rolled her eyes. "It's not as though this is the first time you've realized I've got a scandalously wicked streak, Precious."

He gave an unexpected laugh, and she felt an answering warmth low in her belly. One that was different from the desire she felt when they were in bed. This was much more dangerous because it was so insidious—there almost without her realizing it, but if it left, she would mourn its absence.

"My parents never took me out to anything like this," he continued, gesturing to the room. "Of course they wouldn't have, this isn't something for their Society, but I mean they never even took me to events where it would be entirely proper for me to go listen to music."

He'd mentioned his parents before, and she'd gotten the distinct impression they hadn't been very loving toward him. Was that what was causing his loneliness? His inability to find the words to connect to people other than his two best friends and his cousin?

"What did they do with you?"

He shrugged as he finished his wine, then took her glass. "Not much. I had a tutor until I was sent to school, and it was understood I was to go into the military because my father had, prior to his inheriting. Unusual for a family like ours"—because most only sons would have been trained up to be the heir and eventual title-holder, not risked at battle—"but that was the way of my father's branch of the family."

He exhaled, and to her it seemed as though he was releasing something he'd kept hold of forever. As though he was trusting her with something. "Until I met you, I didn't realize family could be something other than duty and responsibility and coldness."

"What about those duke friends of yours?"

"I feel responsible for them as well, even though there are other emotions at play, of course. But I wouldn't have begun to care for them without my first having assumed that their problems were mine, and I had to solve them."

"Like you solved your needing an heir," she said in a soft voice.

"And now I realize family can be more than that." He reached over and took her hand in his. "Thank you, Lavinia. This has changed me in ways I didn't expect."

Her breathing faltered, and she had to resist the urge to fling her arms around his neck and kiss him. Tell him all about how her family, her true family of Jane and Percy, supported her in her own personal passion, her writing. How their time together was inspiring her to do her best work. But he didn't want that—he didn't want any reminder that they might be more tied together than he allowed. He didn't want love. He might be unexpectedly grateful for what she had showed him, and what they did together, but he didn't want her.

So she stayed silent, watching the dancers on the dance floor, feeling as though it must be her imagination that the music had turned slightly mournful.

One refuge I discovered was the library. It was filled with a variety of tomes, ranging from what appeared to be ancient harvesting manuals to the kind of frivolous fiction my parents used to deplore me reading. Not all of the books were in English; there were books written in what I presumed was my husband's native language, plus books in French, Italian, Spanish, German, and Latin. I could read the French and Italian passably well, and it was on one particular afternoon I discovered something that could be to my advantage.

A book of poisons.

My Dark Husband by Percy Wittlesford

Chapter Eighteen

*H*e'd assumed being married meant your spouse would be underfoot at all times. He'd assumed he would grow tired of constantly seeing the same person's face, listening to their thoughts and opinions until those too became tired.

But no. Except for the one night at the music hall, and the evenings, when they came together after dinner—not literally, but usually consecutively, he saw Lavinia only briefly, when she stopped to slurp a hasty cup of tea or snatch a scone from a tray. Other than their nights together in bed, which were beyond what he could have hoped for.

She was, according to Fletchfield, busy planning the dinner party. The dinner party that was tonight.

He suppressed an oddly light feeling when he contemplated having her around more in the upcoming days.

"The black coat, Your Grace?" Hodgkins said, not waiting for Thaddeus to reply.

Of course not. His valet knew far better than he what he should be wearing. If it wasn't for sitting astride a horse as he issued commands to his troops, he didn't know.

"And the evening breeches."

Thaddeus felt his mouth start to open in protest—he hated those damned breeches; they were so snug it felt as though he might burst through the fabric—but kept himself quiet. If Hodgkins suggested the evening breeches, it was not a suggestion, it was mandatory.

Hodgkins was giving a few final pats to Thaddeus's neckcloth when they heard a knock on the door.

"Enter," Thaddeus called as Hodgkins stepped back to regard him, giving one small satisfied nod.

Lavinia flung the door open and stepped inside, her eyes immediately on his face.

"If you will excuse me, Hodgkins," she said in a pleasant voice, not shifting her gaze. Thaddeus felt that look like a physical caress—her eyes held an appreciative gleam that he knew well enough meant she liked what she saw.

She'd made her appreciation for his appearance abundantly clear, both in words and in gestures. He had never much thought about how he looked, but it seemed as though he had a pleasing appearance.

At least according to his wife, which was the most important person to hold that opinion.

"Of course, Your Grace, Your Grace," Hodgkins said, making her eyes light with laughter.

"Shouldn't you be supervising the dinner or something?" Thaddeus tried to keep the resentful tone from his voice. He should not be pining over his wife's absence.

And yet here he was.

She walked up to him, sliding her arms around

his neck and pressing her body against his. She held something in one of her hands that pressed against his neck.

From this angle, he could see straight down into her gown, those full, gorgeous breasts for his viewing only.

She looked up at him with one eyebrow raised, obviously noticing where his eyes had gone. "You are very naughty," she said in a wicked tone.

He put his hands at her waist. She wore what he supposed was an elegant evening gown—it was a dark blue, so dark it was nearly purple, and had ridiculously tiny sleeves just barely clinging to her arms. The upper part was molded to her body, while the lower part was an abundance of fabric spilling everywhere, seeming to snake around his legs to entwine him.

He liked being entwined.

"I am here because I have something for you."

He arched an eyebrow, giving her a knowing look.

"Not that," she replied. "Though it is tempting."

Since that night a week or so ago, she had learned even more amazing things to do with her mouth, and he appreciated all of them, even though he never allowed himself to climax there. He owed it to her to make a child as soon as possible, and so he invariably came inside her body.

Not that he hadn't thought about it.

She leaned up and kissed him, those breasts pressing enticingly against his chest. It wasn't a chaste kiss by any means, but it was a comfortable one, not one that was designed to lead to anything more, just one that was a mark of a comfortable sexual relationship.

A kiss that would be shared between a husband and wife.

"Is that what you have for me?" he said as she withdrew from the kiss.

"No." She removed her hand from his neck, and he could see what she was holding—a small black box with a red ribbon tied around it.

"This is for you," she said, handing him the box.

He took it from her, undoing the ribbon and letting it fall to the ground. He opened the box to reveal a diamond stickpin, its simple elegance a perfect match for his evening wear.

"I thought it would match your evening wear," she said, sounding a bit anxious. "I don't know that I've ever seen you wearing jewelry, but then I thought perhaps you never had because why would you, what with being in the military and all, and that now you are a duke it wouldn't occur to you. And I've seen many other men who are much less attractive than you wearing jewelry, and somehow it helps them, not that I am saying you need help—"

He bent down and pressed his mouth against hers. "I love it. Thank you," he murmured against her lips. His chattering wife who kept talking whenever she got nervous. It was truly adorable, and he lov—No. Not that. Never that.

"Thank you," he repeated, straightening back up. "Would you put it on? I'd rather have you do it than Hodgkins."

She smiled, taking the stickpin from the box. "I'd rather have me do it also." She accompanied her words with a sly smile and a raised eyebrow.

His cock reacted predictably, and he returned her smile with one of his own. "You know what you're doing to me, don't you?" He took the hand not holding the stickpin and placed it on the front of his trousers. "If we didn't have guests arriving in fifteen minutes, I'd pull up your skirts and find that sweet pussy of yours and lick it until you came screaming my name."

Her eyes had widened, and she was biting her lip and dear God had he just spoken all those words aloud? To his wife?

"I hadn't anticipated liking you speaking that way to me so much," she said in a husky voice. "But I do, and you'll have to promise to do it again when we have more than fifteen minutes."

She squeezed his cock through his trousers as she spoke, and then she took a deep breath as she used both hands to slide the stickpin into place on his lapel.

"There," she said, looking up to meet his eyes. "You look even more remarkably handsome. Thank you for doing this. I know my family is not to everyone's taste." She paused, a wry expression on her face. "And I know the McTavishes are not to mine."

"We can tolerate them together," he said, taking her arm. "Shall we go downstairs to greet our guests now that I am properly attired?"

She smiled up at him, and it felt as though she had lit a thousand lamps. "Yes, please."

This was far more than he had ever hoped for, and it was terrifying to him. Because she would leave eventually, and then he would be alone again, only now he would know what he was lacking.

Perhaps he could persuade her—but he'd promised, and he knew full well that even though she was definitely her own person, and capable of speaking her mind, she was still dependent on him for everything because of who he was. He didn't want her to feel in the least obligated to stay, even if she didn't realize she felt obligated.

Goddamn it. He wished he wasn't so thoughtful of others. But if he wasn't, he wouldn't have listened when she'd asked for more consideration in the bedroom, and he wouldn't be having the best sex in his life. He wouldn't be learning what it was to draw pleasure from and for another person, resulting in complete and utter satisfaction.

He wouldn't be falling in love with her.

"LAVINIA!"

She pasted a smile to her lips at hearing her mother's falsely warm tone. Her family had arrived before the McTavishes, and the servants were scurrying about taking cloaks and coats and other garments as they all stood in the foyer.

In addition to her parents and Jane, the Capels had brought Percy, Caroline and one of her mother's cantankerous aunts, which was a surprise since Lavinia didn't realize either one of them was even aware she was married. This one's name, she thought, began with a *P*.

Her mother wore an exceedingly lovely gown in gold, amber drops in her ears, and an amber necklace clasped around her neck. Jane wore one of her debutante white gowns, one with lace and frills designed to enhance her ethereal beauty.

Which it did, of course; Jane would look lovely in a potato sack, which Lavinia actually knew, having dressed Jane in one for one of the family's amateur theatrical performances.

Percy was immaculately garbed also, his romantically handsome face set off by the severity of his evening wear.

"Goodness, this house is lovely!" Lavinia's mother exclaimed. Perhaps her mother had determined she would be on her best behavior. "You haven't had a chance to decorate, have you?"

Or not.

Percy caught her eye and smirked, making her suppress a snort of laughter.

"The house is lovely, Vinnie," Jane said as she handed one of the maids her cloak. "But you are by far the loveliest thing here," she continued, stepping up to Lavinia and kissing her on the cheek.

"You are!" Percy said in a surprised tone. "Are you doing your hair differently? Or something? You have this . . . glow," he said, gesticulating toward her.

"Marriage to a duke must agree with you," her mother said in a slightly acerbic tone. "Maybe that is why—"

Thankfully her next words were interrupted by a knock at the door, and Lavinia turned in relief.

She wouldn't say she was ever *grateful* to see the McTavishes, but this time she was mildly pleased, if it meant her mother didn't get the chance to fully speak her mind.

"Come in," she said as Fletchfield opened the door.

The McTavishes and Henry stepped inside, Thaddeus immediately making his way toward Mrs. McTavish and removing her cloak himself. He handed it to Fletchfield before turning to Mr. McTavish. "Good evening, sir. Thank you for coming to dinner. We are honored to have you."

"It's our honor, I assure you," Mrs. McTavish replied. She looked enraptured as she gazed up at Thaddeus's face.

Lavinia knew how she felt, only she was more likely to have that expression when she was looking at his body. Particularly those thighs.

"It appears we are all here," Lavinia's mother declared.

Thaddeus nodded to her, but then looked at Lavinia. "My dear?"

She felt her heart melt a little at his subtle reminder that she was the lady of the house, not her mother.

The countess's expression froze, and her eyes lit with what Lavinia knew well to be outraged anger. But the truth was, she was in the wrong here; it was Lavinia's home, and her daughter now far outranked her.

"Your Grace," she said to Thaddeus, "could you escort my mother into the dining room? My father will take me in."

The rest of the party assembled themselves to follow, first the McTavishes, then Henry and Jane, then the elderly aunt—Priscilla? Petunia? Pamela?—brought in by Percy and Caroline, one on either side of her.

Mrs. Webb had outdone herself with the dining room—there were flowers on the tables at four-foot intervals, while candelabras were between, sending a glowing golden light into the entire room. All the footmen were in attendance, which meant every guest had his or her own particular servant, while Fletchfield stood behind Thaddeus's chair.

If she hadn't already gotten to know them, she would have found even the servants intimidating.

She gave a quick glance over to her mother, whose awed face indicated the majesty of the evening had had its desired effect—if her mother was cowed by how impressive everything was, it was less likely she would state some sort of opinion that would be sure to cause an argument.

If they were fortunate, perhaps her mother would be too dazzled throughout the evening to say much of anything.

"This could have been yours, Jane," the countess said in a wistful tone, looking across the table at Jane.

Lavinia swallowed the clump of anger that immediately rose in her chest. Was it too much to ask that her mother be happy for her happiness for once?

And she was happy—even though she knew what her future was to be, she was happy now. She was glad to be spending time with Thaddeus, who'd proven to be everything she'd imagined him to be, even if he didn't himself know all of it: kind, generous, trustworthy, honorable, and respectful. Plus able to take direction when needed, she thought, thinking of certain times she'd told him to go faster or harder or press in a different place.

"We are here to celebrate Lady Jane's engagement to a gentleman I believe she has long admired. Aren't we, my lady?" Thaddeus spoke in a warm, firm tone, giving Jane a comforting look that did not hold a bit of regret.

He shot a quick glance at Lavinia, his eyes narrowing as though he were commiserating with her about her mother.

You see why I am like this? she asked silently.

It is a miracle you are as confident as you are, his gaze seemed to reply.

"Lady Jane has been our neighbor for so many years, and yet it was only recently—only on the advent of Lady Lavinia's marriage to you, Your Grace—that we considered her as a possible match for our Henry."

Oh, wonderful. Now Mrs. McTavish was joining in on the denigration of one of the young guests to uplift the other. She and the countess had a lot in common, though their objects of admiration were entirely different. And were engaged to one another.

"And we would not have considered it either until Lavinia married the duke. Jane's beauty and elegance would seem to indicate she had a much brighter future until—" And then the countess gestured toward Thaddeus and Lavinia.

Until the best prize was won by the worst daughter.

"I think it is time for the soup course," Thaddeus said in a commanding voice.

Are they always like this? his eyes asked.

Always, Lavinia replied.

How did you stand it?

I didn't. I got married to you.

Thaddeus nearly snorted aloud as he saw her expression, and Lavinia couldn't help but giggle, shaking her head when her mother demanded to know what was humorous.

"It must be one of those couples things," the countess asserted. "I can tell whenever my husband is out of sorts or has forgotten to eat."

"Because that is most of the time," Lavinia murmured, catching Jane's and Percy's eyes. Both of them smiled back at her.

"Eating supplies energy, my dear," Lavinia's father said, surprising them. It was a family joke that the earl could go for days without paying attention to anything, and then would suddenly pop up with some prescient remark that entirely solved a situation.

It was unfortunate he hadn't yet been able to solve the situation of his overbearing wife.

"It would be most useful if a scientist were to invent nourishment that didn't require the sitting down to dinner," he continued. "If there was a way to ingest calories while moving, so that no time would be wasted."

"You've just described a food stall at a market, Father," Percy pointed out in an amused tone.

"So I have!" the earl replied in glee. "See, now if we could just stop wasting time with sitting and having several courses—"

"Then we would not be getting to know one another so thoroughly," Lavinia said smoothly, giving the McTavishes a warm smile.

Their returning looks were wary, as though uncertain what else the earl might propose.

It was something the Capels were all accustomed to. Sometimes Lavinia wasn't so surprised the McTavishes had taken their family in instant and perpetual dislike.

Jane took Lavinia's arm and leaned her head against her shoulder for a moment, as though silently thanking her for salvaging a potentially awkward situation. Likewise, Henry looked grateful, glancing between Jane and Lavinia with an anxious expression on his face. Percy regarded her as well, an approving look on his face as though well aware of what she'd done.

Jane's and Percy's presence was a good reminder that this marriage, that everything she had done since that evening was to help them, the two people she loved most in this world. If all went well, Jane would be happily married to her Henry, while Percy could give up pretending to be a scandalous author and go to work with their father, his bastardy balanced out by the addition of a duke in the family.

And the queen, while particular about family and propriety, wasn't going to turn down as excellent a worker as Percy if there was a reason not to.

THADDEUS EXHALED IN relief as Fletchfield served the first course, a mulligatawny soup that would require everyone's mouths to be otherwise occupied.

He felt as he used to when on patrol—keenly

alert for any danger, wary about seemingly innocuous things that appeared in his vision. Things like the countess, whose sharp tongue and strong opinions seemed designed to cause one of those arguments Lavinia had casually mentioned.

At the time, he'd been certain she was exaggerating, because how could relatively respectable people argue amongst themselves? He'd never seen it done.

But then the countess had made her first words an assault on his wife, and for a shameful moment he'd wanted to clap his hand over the lady's mouth and tell her to stop talking. That all she was doing was hurting her daughter. *Both* her daughters, since he knew how the sisters felt about one another.

The earl wasn't any help; when he had offered anything, it was as though he was carrying on an entirely different conversation, one whose topic sentence related to math and human existence and the relationship between the two. When he was not speaking, he was currently seeming to test out all of the wines in Thaddeus's cellar. While working them into some geometric theorem, one that perhaps would result in longer lives for everyone.

And on the other side, Lady Jane's future in-laws were pointedly ignoring the wine while gazing about with avid curiosity. Every so often Mrs. McTavish would regard Lady Jane and her mouth would purse just the tiniest amount.

Thaddeus had to restrain himself from asking what she could possibly see wrong with that lady, since not only would it be rude, but it would remind everyone there that he had initially chosen Lady Jane as his bride, and he didn't want to subject Lavinia to any more of those comments.

"The soup is excellent, Your Grace," Mr. McTavish commented, his gaze darting between Thaddeus and his wife. "Your cook must command a pretty penny."

The countess snorted, and Thaddeus felt a rising sense of panic at what she was about to say.

"When you pay servants what they are worth, you get excellent service." She gestured toward the various footmen standing behind the guests' chairs. "Do you suppose you could find men of this quality who would accept wages that I wouldn't pay to a scullery maid?"

"Mother," Lavinia said, her voice sounding strained, "perhaps we could discuss the decorations for the engagement party. The duke has generously offered to host it and leave all the details to us."

"Meaning your family?" Mrs. McTavish interrupted. "Which means we'll likely have dancing bears and inebriated guests." She gave a pointed look toward the earl, who didn't seem to notice the implied insult.

"Bringing bears into a household such as this one would require a substantial amount of preparation," he said in an earnest tone. "Bears are not generally thought of as being for all polite company."

"What with refusing to wear proper evening attire and eating all the lobster patties," Percy said dryly.

"Oh, no, my boy, it is a falsehood that bears

eat lobsters! Bears live near fresh water, whereas lobsters are primarily in the sea. Salt water," he added, as though not everyone was as aware of the differences between oceans and ponds. "Not that they might not try a lobster patty, but it would not be their first choice at a party."

Mrs. McTavish's eyes and mouth were wide in horror, and Thaddeus was no longer surprised Lavinia was dreading the evening so much. It would be a debacle before they reached the main course at this rate.

"We will consult with your family as well, Mrs. McTavish," Lavinia rushed to reassure her. "I only meant to say that we have been given carte blanche to do what we wish."

Mrs. McTavish's eyebrows rose and her eyes widened. "Carte blanche? As Lord Scudamore gave whatever woman is this one's mother?" She jerked a thumb toward Lavinia's brother Percy, who was doing his best to bury his head in the soup after the lobster patty comment. Smart man.

"Mrs. McTavish." Lavinia's voice shook with emotion. "I would ask that you keep the conversation to things we can agree on, such as that the engagement of Jane and your son is a wonderful thing, and that we hope that they will be very happy."

"They will be happy if they keep far away from your family," Mrs. McTavish sniffed, apparently undaunted by Lavinia's pleading for politeness. Apparently also undaunted by the reality that their families would be united in marriage soon.

"Enough." Thaddeus placed both hands on either side of his plate and rose. He gave each of the parents a pointed stare, except for the earl, who was finishing his soup as though he hadn't noticed there was a war brewing. "You are guests in our home. Our home," he repeated, "which means you are required to exhibit good manners to both me and my wife, the duchess."

He turned to look at Lavinia, whose face was paler than usual. He wished he could tell them all how much it must hurt to have her mother dismiss her so soundly, to listen to the two families bicker about propriety when he knew that Lavinia, Jane, and even Percy—despite the stigma of his birth—were the only kind people in her family.

She must be concerned about Jane's betrothed, Mr. McTavish who had done nothing to thwart his mother's clear ill will toward the Capels. In fact, his expression had barely changed during the course of the dinner, and he sat facing ahead, looking at his betrothed rather than doing anything to interfere.

What would he do if—which was to say *when*—his mother took out her anger at her neighbors on her new daughter-in-law?

"Mr. McTavish," Thaddeus said in an obvious "I am changing the subject" tone of voice, "what are your plans after you marry Lady Jane?"

The gentleman shifted in his seat as he glanced toward his mother. Not a good sign at all.

"Well," he began slowly, "there was the thought that Lady Jane and I would live in the country. I find it to be so much more peaceful than London."

"That is true," Thaddeus replied. And the couple would be far away from their respective parents, which could only help the prospects of their union.

"Although I do not wish to be too far from Lavinia," Lady Jane interjected.

Lavinia gave her sister a warm smile. Thaddeus was nearly overwhelmed by the clear love between the two—no wonder Lavinia had been willing to marry him if it meant her sister could have happiness.

Could she have happiness, too? Could he make her happy?

Though that wasn't their bargain. She would be far happier on her own, away from him. Perhaps living in the country near her sister.

"And we do not wish you to go, not just yet," Mr. McTavish said with a nervous glance toward his wife.

"No, of course not. Lady Jane will require training in her duties."

"Training?" the countess said. "What possible training will she require?"

"Ah, the fish course!" Lavinia exclaimed, gesturing hurriedly to Fletchfield. He nodded in understanding, and the footmen removed the soup bowls from the table and began to put down new dishes.

"Our cook makes the most delicious fried soles," she said as the door opened to admit servants carrying large trays. "With butter, and breadcrumbs, and of course sole."

"Sole would seem to be a crucial ingredient in fried soles," Percy said to Lavinia, a twinkle in his eye.

"And that is why he is the author in the family,"

the countess said in a proud voice. "Such a clever wit! So quick to make a jest!"

Thaddeus saw a pained look cross Lavinia's face. Of course. Another example of her mother praising someone who wasn't her. Not to mention Percy wasn't even her own son. His heart hurt for her at how clearly her mother favored anyone but her.

"Speaking of which," Percy added, "my publisher is hoping to have a new book out soon."

Lavinia stiffened, and he wondered what the issue there was. Was it possible she did not approve of her half brother's writing? No, that couldn't be it. He hadn't missed her look of pride the first time they'd met at the reading.

"You met with him?" Lavinia asked in a strained voice.

"Yes," Percy replied. "He sent word that the last printing of *Storming the Castle* was sold out, and that the public is demanding more. He said there was a sizable bonus if you—if I delivered the book within a month."

"Oh," Lavinia said softly.

"That is wonderful news, Percy dear," the countess said. "What will you do with all that money?"

Lavinia snorted. "It is not as though it is all that much money, Mother. Not compared to what you would think was a substantial amount. Maybe just enough to purchase one's own home and set up a modest household." She sounded wistful, which was odd, given that she was speaking about her brother's money.

"You're not leaving us, are you, Percy?" the

countess asked. "I could not bear it if you left, and neither could your father."

She, Lavinia, Percy, and Thaddeus all turned to look at the earl, who had fallen asleep against the back of the chair. He emitted a soft snore as they regarded him.

"Yes, Father seems desperate to keep Percy around," Lavinia said dryly. At least she wasn't currently looking pained or being belittled by her mother.

"So what about it? Do you think I can deliver a manuscript within a month?" Percy asked.

Lavinia picked up a forkful of the fried sole and brought it to her mouth. "I suppose you could, as long as you are still able to help me with Jane's engagement party."

"And Henry's," Mrs. McTavish said sharply.

"Absolutely," Percy replied, sounding as though he were making a vow. "I will do whatever I can to make the evening a success. The party is—"

"We should have it on the same night the book publishes!" the countess exclaimed. "Or at least when it is about to be published. That would be excellent advertising for you, Percy, to do a reading during the engagement party."

"I don't think—" Mrs. McTavish began, a sour expression on her face.

"It is an excellent idea," Thaddeus said, surprising himself. But if it would take the attention away from Lady Jane, who was looking more and more uncomfortable, and give the countess something other to do than criticize his wife, it should be done. Percy could handle the attention, whereas it was clear Lady Jane could not.

Could she have handled the attention of being a duchess? a voice asked softly in his head. *Could she have handled the attention he was currently paying to her sister in bed?*

The answer to both of those questions, he would have to say, was no. She was remarkably lovely, and would have undoubtedly been modestly obedient, but she was obviously shy, and he suspected her choice of the much more subdued Mr. McTavish was a better one than he would be. Much as he would appreciate her delicate beauty, he found he liked it when his partner pushed back against him. Wasn't hanging on his every movement, had her own opinions for how things should be done.

Life with Lady Jane, while it was what he had thought he wanted, would likely be much duller than life with her sister.

"If I put my mind to it, I should be able to have at least a rough draft to my publisher by that day," Percy said, giving another quick glance toward Lavinia, who nodded in response.

"How do you come up with the ideas for all your books, Mr. Waters?" Mrs. McTavish asked. That sour look was still on her face.

Percy shrugged. "Daily life, I suppose."

"I hope I never live the life you seem to have, sir," Mrs. McTavish said with a sniff.

Percy leaned toward her, an arch look on his face. "But you did read my books." He sat back in his chair, his hands sweeping out in a broad gesture. "All any author wants is a reaction to their work. Good or bad. Just not indifferent." He gave a mock bow at Mrs. McTavish. "And I presume you did not enjoy the book, but it did give you an opinion."

"Quite." Mrs. McTavish spoke in a sharp, prim tone, glancing away from Percy's delighted gaze.

"Is everyone finished with the fish?" Lavinia asked, pasting what Thaddeus could now recognize as a false smile on her face. Not the sweetly satisfied smile she wore when he'd just made her scream. Nor the one when she'd done something unexpectedly piquant in the bedroom, as though she were delighted it was so effective.

But the smile she wore when she was struggling to maintain her normal good humor. How often had she worn that smile when living with her parents? At least that was one thing that had improved for her, it seemed—she wasn't belittled at every turn. Although she also wasn't living with her closest companion. If anything, he was a sexual stranger.

They knew only the barest amounts about one another. As it should remain, if they were to keep themselves unencumbered by emotion in their dealings. But he had to admit, as she had already said, that he was lonely.

Could they be friends as well as lovers during their time together? Would she even be willing to entertain the idea?

But she had to be lonely, too—she slept every night in that bed by herself, she was up and off planning things like dinner parties and engagement parties and only very occasionally seeing her siblings.

What was the worst that could happen if he

asked? She could say no, and they would be where they are now.

"No."

His stomach tightened. It was her voice, only he hadn't asked her yet, had he?

"No, thank you, Fletchfield, please serve the duke some of the roast capon first."

Fletchfield nodded, and approached Thaddeus, who let out a deep breath. *Thank goodness for being wrong.* Something he'd never thought before. Mostly because he never was wrong. "Your Grace?"

The last thing he wanted to do was sit here and endure more of this agonizingly fraught dinner not certain if the countess or Mrs. McTavish was the worst of the two squabbling ladies. If it was possible for the earl to drink down his cellar as Percy commented on the proceedings with roguish humor.

If Lavinia kept having that strained look around her eyes and mouth, a look he thankfully hadn't seen since their marriage.

But if she could endure it, he could also. He was the one far more experienced at controlling his emotions—he'd dealt with enough ridiculous government bureaucracy in his previous line of work to make it nearly second nature—and she was his wife, for the moment, so she deserved all of his support.

"Mr. McTavish, I highly recommend the roast capon." He gestured to Fletchfield to bring it to the gentleman. "The birds are bred at my country estate—or one of my country estates, I should say—and are brought in weekly so they are far fresher than what you will normally find in London."

"Have you visited your country estates yet?" Lady Jane asked in an interested tone. "I have rarely been in the country, but I am looking forward to living there. When we live there," she corrected hastily as Mrs. McTavish muttered something unintelligible.

"Not yet. I plan on taking Lavinia there when—" *When she is pregnant with my child. When we will lead separate lives.* But he couldn't say that. "At some point when the most urgent matters here are taken care of."

The most urgent matter being, of course, her getting pregnant.

"The country sounds appealing. Percy, you have written books set in the country, have you not?" Lavinia asked. At his nod, she continued. "But I wonder if it would get dull after a time. There wouldn't be nearly the same amount of different types of people, and that is one of the things I love best about London. Knowing at any time you might run into someone whose life here is so wildly different."

"Because not everyone is a duchess," Percy remarked dryly.

She rolled her eyes at her brother, one of the first times it had seemed as though she was letting herself relax during this evening.

"No, of course not. But I mean more than that—I mean seeing things that point up the varying ways people live their lives. Getting up when the rooster crows as opposed to when the maid comes in to light the fires, or choosing your own bread at the market instead of having a servant present it to you."

"It is possible to see those things in the country," Percy pointed out.

"It is, but London is where people of all sorts are thrown together because of celebrations, or church, or just trying to get to their destinations. Do you know the bookstore I buy from has a small section of mechanical engineering manuals? The shop owner wouldn't carry those if he weren't able to sell them, which means that somewhere out there are would-be engineers looking for instructions."

"And what does it matter, knowing those people are out there?" the countess asked, sounding bored.

She nodded when Fletchfield presented a tray to her, and served herself what Thaddeus thought was likely Cook's renowned fricandeau of veal.

"It matters because they are people like we are," Lavinia said in a passionate tone. "Because their lives are as important as ours, and we should respect them."

"Where are you going with this line of conversation?" Percy asked. This time in a mild tone, as though knowing it was important to Lavinia, and not wishing to insult her.

She gave a hopeless shrug. A shrug that cut through Thaddeus like a cold wind. As though she had seen things that had left her more unhappy, not less so. How was her experience so different from his? Why hadn't he seen what she had seen?

He had lived in relatively egalitarian circumstances prior to becoming a duke—yes, the officers bought their way into the military, but the rest of the men were rewarded because of their talent, not what family they were born from or what money they had.

But he hadn't thought much beyond that.

"This is delicious!" the countess exclaimed, sounding surprised. "Your Grace, did you instruct your cook to make this?"

This, at least, Thaddeus could control. "No, it was your daughter, my wife, who handled all of the details. And she has done a marvelous job, has she not?" He kept his gaze sharp on Lavinia's mother, not letting her slide off the compliment hook he'd just baited her on.

"She has. Good work, Lavinia," she said in a stiff tone. "Though I daresay Jane will do just as well when she has her own household."

Thaddeus burned with the desire to leap up and tell the countess just what kind of a daughter she had raised, despite her worst efforts. But that would upset Lavinia more than it would defend her.

"Which won't be for some time," Mrs. Mc-Tavish interrupted in a smooth tone. "We'll want them to live with us for a time before deciding if they truly want to live in the country."

"Fletchfield, I think we might want to skip straight to the dessert course," Lavinia said in a firm tone. A tone that belied the heightened color on her cheeks.

"Yes, Your Grace."

Thaddeus caught the butler shooting a sharp look toward the countess, although that lady was too oblivious to notice, thank goodness.

The desserts ranged from a variety of puddings to blancmange and cheesecake, along with a wide assortment of cheeses for the guests who preferred something savory after dinner.

Thaddeus couldn't help but watch Lavinia eat her dessert—she'd chosen a pudding with some sort of pink cream spread all over it, and he felt his cock harden at watching her obvious enjoyment of the treat.

Pink tongue sliding out to lick a few bits of the pink cream from her mouth, her closing her eyes as she swallowed, making a tiny noise deep in her throat.

Similar to the noises she made when he'd eaten her up.

For a moment, he imagined bringing a whole pot of that pink cream into the bedroom, him armed only with a spoon and his imagination.

She caught his eye as he was picturing it, and her eyebrow rose in clear comment.

You're thinking about that with all this family here?

I can't think of anything else, not when you move your mouth that way.

She chuckled, then bit her lip as she kept her eyes on him, bringing a spoonful of the cream to her lips and opening just enough to slide it in. Closing that perfect, plush mouth around the spoon and letting her lips curl up in pleasure.

He might've had to endure the worst evening of his entire life—and that included the nights he'd been on patrol during active shelling—but at least he had the most delicious treat waiting for him at the end of it.

At first I didn't understand what I was reading—the book was in Italian—and so I thought, mistakenly, it was a cookbook. But the recipes it held were not for enjoyable meals around the dining table, but for the permanent removal of a person you despised. Rhubarb and nightshade salad? With a side of mushrooms?

I wondered: Did I loathe him enough to kill him? Was that the only way I could get my freedom?

My Dark Husband by Percy Wittlesford

Chapter Nineteen

Lavinia felt as though she'd been tossed under a carriage and tromped over, repeatedly, by clumsy horses.

Or by her mother and Mrs. McTavish. Same thing, only with more ribbons.

But the evening was finally over, and she was back in her bedroom, staring down at her evening gown with trembling fingers.

She'd known she would be in a state after the dinner, so she'd told Nancy not to wait up for her, that she would undress herself. But now she wondered if she'd made the right decision, since the thought of twisting around and undoing all those buttons was as daunting as trying to get her mother to be quiet or Mrs. McTavish to be polite to Jane.

Ugh.

She slumped down on the bed, heedless of creases, and placed her head in her hands. It had been horrible. She'd expected that, of course, but it had been even worse than she'd imagined—and she did have an active imagination, what with being a writer and all.

Her mother never missing a chance to demean her. Mrs. McTavish casting aspersion on everything, including Jane, who was as close to a perfect human as Lavinia had ever known.

How was Jane going to survive that?

Her father spewing his usual random thoughts unrelated to what was actually happening, letting her mother run roughshod over everybody as he pontificated on one of his many theories. While also ensuring his wineglass was never empty.

That ancient aunt, at least, had not caused any trouble. She had seemed delighted to be out of the house, and it certainly appeared as though she liked the veal as much as the countess had. Penelope! That was her name!

At least she'd solved one thing this evening.

She heard a knock at the door. If it was him, she might have to tell him to go away. She was most definitely not in the mood to cavort with him, even if he had stood up for her that evening. She was too tired. Too worn out from worrying about everyone else.

"Come in," she said at last.

The door opened, and he stepped inside. Barefoot, as usual, and wearing his dressing gown.

She put her hand out in a "stop" gesture. "I don't think I can."

He didn't stop, just kept walking toward her, his feet making no noise on the plush carpet.

"Can't what?"

She glared at him. At least she had energy for that. "You know what." She gestured behind her toward the bed. "That."

His expression was thoughtful. Almost as though he was concerned. She supposed that might occur if two people lived together and had enthusiastic sexual encounters—one of the two might grow concerned about the other if it seemed as though there was some upset.

"Tonight was difficult, hmm?" he said. His tone made it both a pronouncement and a question—as though he knew how bad it was, but wanted to know the extent of it.

"Yes." It was a relief to say it aloud, even though the truth of it was bouncing around her brain.

"I didn't realize," he continued, sitting down beside her on the bed, "how little regard she has for you."

There was no question about who he was talking about.

She shrugged. "It doesn't matter." Even though of course it did, and both of them knew that.

"And your father is no help. Is he always so absentminded?"

She chuckled. "Always." She thought that was why there were so many relatives living with them—he'd forgotten who was there already, and thought there was room, and that it was his obligation to solve all the familial living situation problems. "Except when it comes to business," she added. "Somehow, his investments always work out. Not that an earl is supposed to discuss money, but as you know, he's so good at making more of it. That might be the only thing he recalls, honestly."

And he had a good heart, even though it seemed as though he might've accidentally left it somewhere at times.

Thaddeus put his hand on her shoulder and drew her into his chest. Her cheek pressed against his skin, the hair on his chest tickling her nose. "I am so tired," she said in a soft voice. "I don't mind people, I generally like them, it's just—"

"Family," he supplied. "Here, let me help you." He shifted her forward so he could bring his hands to the back of her gown and began to unbutton her, each undone button making her feel closer to relaxation. To sleep.

"What about your family?" she asked. He finished up the buttons, then slid his palms onto her bare shoulders, sliding the fabric off her arms.

She got up and shook the gown down, stepping out of it and sitting back on the bed in her chemise.

"I should call for Nancy," she said, looking at the crumpled gown on the floor.

"Or I could do something about it," he said. He rose and picked up the gown, folding it carefully over his arm before draping it on the back of one of the chairs. It wasn't perfectly hung up, but it would mean it escaped most of the wrinkles it would get if it were in a heap on the floor.

"Thank you," she said. He returned to sit beside her and put his hand on her knee. It was comforting. Not at all as though he was next intending to slide those clever fingers up her thigh and touch her there.

Just as though he was offering comfort.

It was frightening, how much she wanted that comfort. Much as she was coming to appreciate sexual relations with him, she craved more. The more he'd vowed he wouldn't give. But this gesture assuaged that craving just a bit.

"My family—my parents—were very different from yours."

"You mean your mother didn't disparage your every action and your father didn't imbibe wine while getting into a theoretical argument with some dead Greek?" she said wryly.

He shook his head. "They didn't care enough to do either of those things, I don't think. They both wanted me to be the ideal son."

"They would have been delighted to see where you ended up, then," she remarked.

"They would have thought I still did too much—after all, I insist on going over all the accounts myself, I hold myself responsible for the stewardship of the land and the title."

"But that is the right thing to do," she replied in a righteous tone of voice. "You always do the right thing. That is who you are."

He didn't speak for a moment, and she wondered if she'd somehow said the wrong thing.

"Thank you," he said at last. His voice was low and earnest. "I don't know that I succeed in always doing the right thing, but I do know I try."

As he'd tried to marry Jane. As he'd then had to marry her.

"Do you regret it? Regret this?"

He paused again, and she found herself holding her breath. What would it do if he said yes? There was no way to change anything. All that would happen was that she would know.

"You know what, never mind, I don't—"

"No, I don't." The hand on her knee tightened.

"Your sister is lovely, and intelligent, and kind, but—" And then he stopped, and her mind—her active writer's mind—supplied what he might say:

"but I like my wives shorter and more talkative."

"but I've decided I want to be on my own after all, and you are easier to leave."

"but I find I like it when my partner demands satisfaction in bed, and I doubt your sister would be as determined as you."

"But now I can't imagine being married to anyone else."

Oh. That wasn't what she had expected at all.

"Do you regret it?"

Of course he'd ask her the same question; she should have anticipated that. He was nothing but equitable—always making certain she had as many, if not more, climaxes than he did. Listening to her opinions and deferring to her in decisions involving dinner and engagement parties.

If it weren't that he'd forbidden it, she'd think she was falling in love with him.

And of course she was falling in love with him, whether he'd forbidden it or not. He'd risen to her defense this evening, and she had no doubt but that he would support her no matter what she did.

It was on the tip of her tongue to tell him the truth about the author Percy Wittlesford when he spoke again.

"Never mind the question."

She had hesitated too long, and now he must believe she actually did regret it.

"No, I—I—"

He rose slowly, and she felt the loss of his touch immediately.

She got up also, her fatigue forgotten in her wanting to speak the truth. At least the truth as she understood it.

She stood in front of him, her chin lifted as she met his gaze. "I don't regret it at all," she said in a passionate tone. She needed to make him *see*. His parents might not have valued him, but she did. She wanted to tell him the truth, no matter if their time together was limited. Despite what was their certain future. "I am a duchess. You saved me from certain ruin. And, as you saw for yourself this evening, you've saved me from my mother. That is something."

"It is."

"And what is more, I find I like running the household." Her hands made a frustrated gesture. "And it's not just that, but it's everything. You trust me to make decisions. You have never been anything but absolutely honest with me. I don't think many men would do that."

His expression was thoughtful, as though he was absorbing her words. "I suppose."

She took a deep breath. "Would you—would you stay here with me tonight? Just to sleep?"

He looked startled. Of course it was an unexpected request, what with being the absolute opposite of what their bargain had said—the bearing of children and no commitments. No love.

Her heart was racing as she waited for his reply. If he said no, she would understand this was exactly what he had said it was.

If he said yes, perhaps there was a chance for something between them.

"I will, if you want it."

She allowed herself to exhale, and smiled, at which his lips curled into his version of a smile as well.

"Thank you."

She stepped past him to the bed, drawing her chemise over her head and tossing it to the floor before getting into bed naked.

She held the covers open for him, and he slipped out of his dressing gown as well, then climbed in, the bed dipping under his weight. She curled onto her side away from him, and he drew up behind her, wrapping his arm around her with his hand on her lower belly.

His breath was on her neck.

She patted his arm as she closed her eyes. "Good night, Precious," she murmured.

A snort was all she heard before she fell asleep.

SHE FELL ASLEEP quickly, nestled in the comfort of his arms, her lush backside pressed against his groin. Of course his cock reacted, but he tried to ignore it, reminding himself that wasn't what she had wanted tonight. And, even though his cock might object, it wasn't what he wanted either. There was something so intimate, even more intimate than the most intense sex, about talking in bed, speaking quietly about thoughts and feelings. Sharing hidden truths that could hurt if they were exposed to the world.

She was insightful enough to glean what he hadn't said about his parents: that while they weren't neglectful, per se, they were indifferent beyond what he owed to their family.

He would suggest her family was the opposite, that the family members she loved most owed loyalty only to one another, not to the family in general. Even if things had happened as he'd originally hoped, he couldn't imagine that Lavinia would have let Jane marry him, no matter what their mother had to say.

It would have been an ugly situation, far uglier than what had occurred, but at least nobody would be actively unhappy. He knew now that Jane would have been actively unhappy if she had married him—he was far too rigid and she was far too obedient. They would have assumed the other wanted things done a certain way, when that way was what neither one wanted; it was just the correct way.

And both of them would have been miserable but hiding it through a facade of polite questions and delicate negotiation.

Jane would certainly never have barged into his private study to demand more satisfaction in bed. Presented him with a list of demands in that area, for God's sake.

Nor would he have pushed himself past what he thought was proper sexual behavior to bring her the utmost pleasure.

Since the moment he'd seen her in that ballroom, a vibrant blossom in contrast to her lovely lily of a sister, she'd changed him. She'd challenged him, excited him, and made him see possibilities he never had before.

Could he bear to lose her when the time came?

But to try to tame someone like that, someone as willful and strong-minded as Lavinia would be to try to change her essence, the very thing he admired.

He needed to enjoy her while he could.

And perhaps try to learn from her so he could infuse his own life with some of the joyful exuberance that seemed to be part of her very personality.

Their bargain hadn't said they would never see one another again, had it? It had been implied, because at the time neither one of them had wanted to see the other, but there was no obligation that required them to be apart forever.

He could bring her to town for their son's birthday, or the opening of Parliament, or anytime it seemed as though it might be appropriate and she might be willing.

It wouldn't be the marriage he'd written on his list of so long ago, but it might end up being nearly as satisfying.

He would bring it up with her as soon as she wasn't distracted with the preparations for this grand party they were apparently going to have.

I mused on the problem constantly, for well over a week. Even my husband, who paid next to no attention to me, noticed something was off.

"What is going on?" he demanded one evening over dinner in his usual blunt way.

Startled, I dropped my spoon into my soup, sending drops of consommé flying into the air and onto my face and my gown.

I rose quickly without answering, rushing to change, shaking as I realized how far I had gone in contemplating it.

I couldn't do it, no matter how much I chafed against my restrictions. Nor how much I missed being a free woman who could do what she wanted when she wanted.

That woman had been lost as soon as my parents had died—the count had, in his bizarre way, actually rescued me. I could not murder him.

But I could do something else.

My Dark Husband by Percy Wittlesford

Chapter Twenty

Lavinia woke feeling different than usual. Perhaps that was because she was held in his arms, not tucked up against Precious's wiry fur?

It felt wonderful. She was warm, and she felt safe and protected and—if she allowed her imagination to drift into the impossible—nearly loved.

The bed was enormous, but so was he. She felt him shift and knew he was awake. His hand was splayed on her belly, and she put her hand on top of it.

"Good morning," she said.

"Good morning." His voice was morning-gruff. "Did you sleep well?"

"Mmph."

"Thank you for staying with me," she said in a soft voice. "I love my sister, and a few other members of my family, but—"

"At least you'll be able to see your sister more often."

"What?"

He rolled over onto his back, pulling her onto his chest. "If she is able to persuade her Henry to move to the country."

"Why would I be in the country?" she asked, her tone wary.

He moved her off him, sitting up in the bed. "That's where you'll be after our son is born." He spoke as though it was a certainty. "I was thinking about it, and I do hope I can persuade you to come up to London every so often."

Frustrated anger bubbled up so quickly she thought she might choke with it. "I beg your pardon?"

"Come to London? We're getting along tolerably well, I thought." Now he didn't sound nearly as confident.

"Not the London part," she said through gritted teeth. She flung the covers aside and snatched her dressing gown from the wardrobe, shoving her arms through the sleeves.

He still lay in her bed, looking up at her with a confused expression. "What are you talking about then?"

She advanced toward him as she tied the dressing gown tight around her waist. "I have no plans to go to the country," she said. "Where would you have gotten that idea?"

He frowned, then flung the covers off himself as well. Even the sight of his bare thighs wasn't enough to distract her from her question.

"Our bargain?" he said slowly, as though it was simply that she hadn't understood. "Once we have a son and we separate? You'll go to the country." He picked his own dressing gown up from the floor and donned it. "I assure you, there are plenty of places you can go that will be quite pleasant."

She gave her head a vehement shake. "I do not dispute that the country is quite pleasant," she said, mimicking his voice as she spoke the last two words, "but I was born in London, I have lived in London my entire life, my family is here, and I have no intention of leaving."

His mouth dropped open in such a dramatic expression of surprise she would have laughed if she were not so irate.

"But—but—" he sputtered.

"But what?" she snapped, folding her arms over her chest. "I have sacrificed many things for this marriage."

It looked as though he were about to speak, and she put her hand up in a stopping motion. "No, it is my turn to speak. I will not be leaving London. You can do whatever you want, I assume you will, but I will not scurry to the country to become a neglected wife."

"You wanted this!" he exploded.

She drew back, her gaze intent on his face. "I did not. You supposed that I would not want to stay with you, that I would want to leave my child and apparently go on some sort of bucolic adventure in the country where I have never been, mind you, and—what?"

She was so furious she could barely see. How had he misunderstood so thoroughly? It was as though he hadn't even listened to her when they'd first hammered out their ridiculous bargain, which she'd only agreed to because she'd assumed she didn't have a choice. Because he was a man, and a former military officer, and a current duke. Three things that demanded subservience.

"And do whatever it is people do in the country." He spoke in a placating tone, which only served to make her madder.

Goodness, but there was something gratifying about being so thoroughly angry. As though the rage had burned through every insecurity she'd ever had, every doubt that had plagued her.

"Whatever it is people do in the country?" She swallowed against the pain. "Do you even hear how arrogant you sound?"

"Of course I'm arrogant," he replied, now sounding nearly as mad as she was. He advanced toward her, his nostrils actually flaring. She'd never seen anyone in real life flare their nostrils, and yet here he was. "It is my job to tell people what to do all the time. It is my responsibility, because without it there is chaos."

Her eyebrows rose in disbelief. "Chaos?"

"If I don't do my duty by the title, there will be chaos. I was forced to become a duke. I had no desire to do all this," he said, sweeping his hand out to indicate the room, the house, the title.

She scoffed. "Poor you. First you had to leave the battlefield for a London town house, vast wealth, and people kowtowing to you everywhere. And then you had to marry a person you absolutely did not wish to, but was able to find a solution to that by dismissing her as soon as she had done her fecund duty and borne an heir. What terrible thing will you have to endure next? Oh, I know," she said, tapping her mouth in thought, "you might have to have the raising of our son while I am banished from his life."

Of course she had chafed against that part of

the bargain, but she'd tucked her future pain away, knowing there was nothing she could do about it.

"I like being married to you," he said in a growl. "I know your sister would not have suited me nearly as well."

"Because of what we do in bed." She drew herself up to her full height. "There is more to marriage than that, only you will not get to discover it. You do not want to discover it." The lost possibilities washed over her in a heartsick wave. That night at the music hall—if she had gotten him to go deeper, speak more about how he felt and what he hoped for. If she had spoken about her own wishes. But she hadn't. "I was hoping—you know what, never mind what I was hoping," she said, waving her hand in dismissal. "But I understand you want to keep the bargain as we struck it." She took a deep breath. "So we should do our best to see it to its inevitable conclusion."

She advanced toward him, loosening her dressing gown as she did, wrapping her hands around his neck and drawing his mouth down to hers.

At first he was tentative, as though she might withdraw at any moment. And then he deepened the kiss, thrust his tongue into her mouth with a reckless abandon as his hands went to her hips and gripped her hard against him.

His penis pressed against her belly, and she felt it stiffen as he continued to plunder her mouth. She returned his kiss with as much savagery as he had, so it felt as though they were in battle.

She drew her hand away from his neck, down his arm, onto his hip, and then finally gripped the shaft of his penis, wrapping the head of it in her palm. Sliding her hand down as he raised his mouth from hers, his breathing hoarse and ragged.

"Get on the bed. On your back," she murmured.

He flung his dressing gown off his body, going to lie down as she'd ordered. His penis was standing at full attention, and she kept her gaze on it as she approached the bed.

"What do you want, Lavinia?" he asked. His hands were fisted at his side. "I'll do whatever it is you desire."

His chest was rising and falling rapidly with his rough, quick breaths. His eyes were fixed on her face, and his expression was intensely focused. As though she was the only thing that mattered in the world.

It was intoxicating.

She straddled him on the bed, putting her hands on his chest to steady herself. He placed his hands at her hips again, holding her.

She rose onto her knees, grasping his penis and guiding it inside, lowering herself down until he was filling her, stretching her.

"Lavinia," he said, his grip tightening. His stomach muscles flexed, and she lifted herself up, then brought herself back down.

"I am going to ride you now," Lavinia said, putting her hands on her knees and rising again. "I want you to come, Thaddeus. I want to fuck you until you can't bear it anymore and your climax bursts out of you."

He groaned at her words, and she allowed a satisfied smile to curl her mouth up.

"I want to touch you," he said. "Please let me touch you." His tone was begging, and it made her feel so powerful, so in control, to have this large, beautiful man pleading to put his hands on her body.

"Where, Thaddeus?" She kept her rhythm up as she brought her hands to her breasts, cupping them. "Do you want to touch me here?" She took hold of her right nipple and squeezed gently. "Or here?"

He kept his attention focused on her hand.

"There," he said, nodding toward where they were joined. "I want to touch you there. I want to bring you to orgasm as you ride me."

"Oh," she gasped, sliding her hand down to his where it rested on her hip. "Do it," she ordered.

He immediately brought his clever fingers to her clitoris, his touch as rough and urgent as she needed it to be.

She kept riding him, up and down, faster and faster, his fingers rubbing her clit as his body bucked under hers, showing her what he needed.

And then she was coming, she was flying, the orgasm wrenched from her as his whole body stiffened and he groaned her name as he arched his back underneath her.

She felt the warm rush of his semen inside her, and she slowed her movements, both of them sweaty and panting as they rode the crest of their respective climaxes.

At last she stopped moving, falling forward

onto his chest, his penis still inside her, his hands now clutching her arse.

"My goodness," she murmured after a few moments.

"We should fight more often," he said in a husky voice.

She smiled against his chest, already mourning the loss of him, but knowing it was inevitable. They were too different, and he was too stubborn. As was she, to be honest.

Even though she knew she'd fallen in love with him.

Damn it.

THADDEUS WASN'T SURPRISED to see Melmsford at his desk already as he entered the library. It was later than he usually arrived at his desk, thanks to Lavinia and her wicked ways, and he'd spent longer than usual in his bath, allowing himself to relive what had just happened. Not the argument, of course, but what happened afterward.

He'd assumed he was a man of normal sexual appetites, hence his putting his requirements on his initial list, but he was coming to realize that he wanted her all the time: when he was tying his cravat, his mind would drift to wrapping the fabric around her legs, holding her open so he could lick her to climax. When he was seated at his desk, thinking about bending her over it and entering her from behind, her gripping the edge of the desk. When they were at dinner, and she was enjoying a delicious dessert, her tongue darting out to lick a bit from her mouth.

Was that normal, or was that just her?

And did it matter? He was going to lose her. It was inevitable, thanks to his stubborn idiocy on insisting on their bargain. Assuming that was what she wanted when he hadn't even asked her.

And now it was too late—his continued idiocy at assuming she would retreat to the country had made her furious, glorious in her anger. He'd been relieved when it seemed she'd had the same reaction he had to their argument—he'd been aroused by her furor, wanting to channel it into sex, but it wouldn't have been right for him to initiate it.

Thank God she had.

"Good morning, Your Grace," Melmsford said, half rising from his chair.

"Sit, sit," Thaddeus said, gesturing to him.

He went to sit behind his desk, frowning a bit as he saw all the papers stacked up on it.

"Am I behind?" he asked, waving toward the stacks. "I had thought we were on top of what had to be done."

Melmsford's expression was sorrowful. "Apparently there are some matters we were not aware of until recently. Some of the holding's investments have run into problems, and we'll need to sort them out."

Well, that sounded entirely dull.

He wished he could just sweep all of the papers onto the floor and find her, hauling her back to bed so they could enjoy the novelty of daytime sex.

But of course he could not. He'd said himself he had a duty to the title, and that duty did include getting her with child, but it wasn't his most important task.

"Which should we start with first?" he said wearily.

This was to be his life: dealing with urgent, and urgently dull, matters related to the dukedom. Eventually he would have a son, but most of the day-to-day tasks of that responsibility would be left to staff.

At least, that was how his parents had done it.

"Melmsford," he said as the thought struck him, "how were you raised?"

"I beg your pardon?" his secretary said, sounding startled.

"I mean were your parents involved with your upbringing, or did you have nursemaids and a tutor?"

"Oh," Melmsford replied. "My father worked, but my mother took care of myself and my sister. She was a vicar's daughter, and had received a good education for a lady, so she was able to see to my education until I went to school."

Thaddeus drew his eyebrows together as he thought. "And was that a good thing? Being with your mother so often?"

"Yes, absolutely." Melmsford sounded as definite in his opinion as Thaddeus had ever heard him. "I think it is crucial for children to have both their parents in their lives. My father was a good father, but he was a solicitor who took on a lot of work to keep us well fed and housed, so he wasn't at home that often."

"Ah. Thank you," Thaddeus replied.

"NANCY," LAVINIA SAID as the maid entered the room, "I was going to stay home today, but I believe I wish to go out."

She *needed* to go out. Her thoughts were a muddle, and the only way she could possibly figure out what she was thinking was to talk it through with Jane or Percy, preferably both.

Did she even know what she wanted anymore? And this morning—that was not at all like her, and yet she'd enjoyed it thoroughly.

She would miss that aspect of marriage. As well as all the other things that she presumed came with a real marriage: love, respect, reliability, trust, and common goals.

"Do you have a preference for what gown you wear, Your Grace?" Nancy asked, thankfully interrupting her mental list of things she would never have in her own marriage.

Lavinia shrugged. "I am fine with whatever you choose," she replied. It seemed silly to concern oneself with frivolous things like gowns and appearance when one's entire life was an enormous question mark.

What did she know for certain?

"Actually, Nancy, can you give me fifteen minutes? I need to take care of something."

"Of course, Your Grace," her maid replied, laying a gown on the bed. She walked out of the room, closing the door behind her as Lavinia went to her writing table.

Things I Know Will Happen:
1. The next book will be finished by the engagement party.
2. Jane will marry Mr. McTavish and live happily-ever-after.

She stared at the page, racking her brain for more certainties. Only there weren't any. Just two certainties, and only one of them was directly under her control. Not that it really was a certainty, but the story felt as though it were flowing out of her far more easily than past efforts. Perhaps because she was able to draw on her own experience now?

She smirked to herself as she thought about what he might say if he knew how much inspiration she was taking from him. Thankfully, he would never read that sort of book, and the references were vague enough so that nobody but the two of them would know it was drawn from real life.

But meanwhile, she had other writing to do. She took another sheet of paper and laid it on her desk.

Things That Might Possibly Happen
  1. Pregnancy
      a. If a girl, we'll have to try again.
      b. If it's a boy, that will signal the completion of our bargain.
  2. Cat adoption
      a. Because why should Precious be an only child?
  3. Another dog adoption
      a. If I'm going to be alone, I want to have company while doing it.

She laughed as she wrote the last item. At least she could still amuse herself. She folded the list and tucked it into her pocket, then rang the bell to summon Nancy.

"IT TRULY WAS terrible," Jane confirmed when they had finally been able to leave the Capels' house together.

First Lavinia had had to endure a continuation of her mother's comments, and then her father wanted to get her advice on what to name a new economic theory he'd been working on, heartily rejecting her suggestion of The Too Confusing for Most People Theory as being not descriptive enough.

The two ladies strolled in the garden since their mother wanted Jane to stay close by in case, it was strongly hinted, another eligible duke stumbled by and was smitten with Jane, demanding her hand in marriage immediately.

Percy was out meeting with the publisher, presumably to share the news that the next Percy Wittlesford book would make its reading debut at the Duke of Hasford's London town house during the event of the Season. Lavinia wished she could have been there to see her publisher's excitement, but she already had enough to do, what with finishing the book in the first place and planning the party.

"Mother was awful," Jane continued, shaking her head, "and I hesitate to say it, but Mrs. McTavish was nearly as bad. I didn't realize she was so . . . opinionated."

"You're going to have to get used to that since you're marrying into the family."

At least she hadn't had to deal with Thaddeus's irascible and annoying relatives—as far as she knew, the only relatives he had were his cousins, both of whom were charming and both of whom were busy being besotted with their new spouses.

"I'm not as strong as you, Vinnie," Jane said, clutching Lavinia's hand tighter. "Last night when I was watching Mother and Mrs. McTavish squabbling, all I wanted to do was hide."

And your betrothed wasn't doing anything to help.

"Did you speak to Henry about it?" Lavinia asked in a soft tone.

Jane nodded. "Yes. I mean yes, I tried, but he just said he didn't want to have to take a side."

"Both sides were awful. You and I can admit to that."

"Yes, and I wish Henry had done something to help. It took the duke to quiet them all down." Jane's tone was admiring.

And then he had commiserated with her, and held her all night, and then this morning—

"What is it? Your breathing just got very loud," Jane said in a concerned voice.

Lavinia gave her head a rueful shake. And then took a deep breath, one nearly as loud as the unexpected one. "There is something I haven't told you," she began.

"What you're saying is you and the duke made this ridiculous bargain—"

"The duke made it, not me," Lavinia interrupted. "I just agreed to it."

"Whatever," Jane said, waving her hand. "The point is, do you really wish to separate from him? It seems to me that the two of you get along quite well. It certainly looked that way last night. I can't imagine anyone willingly going up against our mother if they didn't have strong feelings about it."

Lavinia shrugged. "He doesn't like injustice. He saw someone who was being a bully, and he reacted. I don't think he cares more about me than he does his secretary." She paused. "Actually, given how much time the two of them spend together, perhaps he cares more about him."

"I saw the way he looks at you, Vinnie." Jane spoke in a firm tone. "When he didn't think you were looking at him. Like he was wishing he could say something but just couldn't."

Lavinia tried to laugh, but it ended up sounding more rueful than amused. "Are we certain you don't have any books to write too? Because it seems as though that is just wishful thinking. Something that would belong in a romantic story, not in real life."

"Real life can be a romantic story," Jane asserted. "Just look at me and Henry."

Lavinia quashed whatever misgivings she had about her sister's betrothed so as not to spoil Jane's rosy visions.

"You and Henry are a special situation. You have so much in common—you both like to lead quiet lives, are just as happy being with one another as at a party. I know you will support him in your work, and that the two of you will make calm, reasonable parents."

"I suppose. But you and the duke have many things in common as well—you both have strong moral codes, you are both direct in your opinions, you are generous to people who deserve it. Neither of you holds grudges, at least not for long—imagine if the duke had resented having to marry you after that incident, and taken it out on you? But he didn't. He offered you a respectable way out, one that would preserve both of your reputations."

Lavinia had never realized that while she was sitting quietly, Jane was also analyzing people's behavior and patterns. She should have made use of her long before this to write her books—then some of her readers wouldn't have called her characters' actions inconsistent.

"We're both not monsters," Lavinia agreed. "But is that the basis of a marriage?"

Jane folded her arms over her chest and looked nearly argumentative. "What is the basis of a marriage?"

Lavinia considered before replying—her usual flippant remarks weren't suited to the tone of the conversation. "Love would be what everyone says. But love can be damaging, and it also isn't entirely necessary. Mutual respect, admiration, thoughtfulness, and an interest in the other person." A lump formed in her throat. "We have most of that, only here we are. As soon as I have a son, we'll lead separate lives. Oh, and I didn't even tell you the worst part! He told me I would get to see you often because we'd both be living in the country."

Jane looked puzzled. "That is the worst part?"

Lavinia exhaled in frustration. "Not the seeing each other frequently but the living in the country part. He assumed that I would go hide away when our bargain is finished."

"I can't see you in the country," Jane agreed. "You'd end up arguing with everyone in your vicinity without new replenishments."

Lavinia paused. "Am I that bad?"

Jane patted her arm reassuringly. "No, but you are decided in your opinions. That is why you were able to save me from an impossible marriage—I mean, impossible for me," she corrected hastily.

"I know what you mean," Lavinia replied. "And you're right. If you were married to Thaddeus, you would be miserable."

"You're not miserable." It wasn't a question.

"I'm not." She felt her throat tighten. "Jane, I think I might be in very real danger of falling in love with him. Just when he has shown himself to be an impossible ass."

"Isn't that when we know we love someone? It's easy to love someone when everything is going well. It's the 'through thick and thin' part that causes problems."

Lavinia shook her head in wonder. "How did you get to be so insightful?"

Jane looked embarrassed. "Well, I had to do something when I was sitting in the corner being quiet. You know I don't like to talk much, but I do like to observe things."

Lavinia wrapped her arm around her sister's shoulders and drew her in for a hug. "I wish I had told you all this before. Perhaps you could have figured out a way out of this situation. Now I think it's too late."

Jane nudged Lavinia's hip with hers. "It's never too late. Once the engagement party is over, we'll find a way for you to keep your husband as your husband."

"And meanwhile—?" Lavinia said, giving Jane a wry look.

"Meanwhile you should enjoy all the pleasures that marriage has to offer," Jane said, her face turning red.

Lavinia did laugh then, giving her sister another hug as the warmth of possibility filled her senses.

But it couldn't be her who made the first move— she'd already as good as told him she'd agreed to his bargain under duress. She would not return to him to compromise on something she hadn't wanted at all in the first place. Because if she did that, she would always be in a disadvantaged position, and she was already disadvantaged, what with being a woman and his wife. And therefore his property.

Just the thought of it was enough to make her stomach tighten.

After the engagement party. She could forget about it all until then, couldn't she?

"And now we should discuss the party," Lavinia said, taking Jane's arm. "I want it to be what you want, not what Mother or Mrs. McTavish wants."

"I'm more optimistic about your chances than mine, honestly," Jane said in a wry tone.

If only Jane were able to stand up for herself, Lavinia wouldn't have been married to the duke at all.

So was she relieved her sister was the way she was or regretful?

She shouldn't answer that.

*I could make him fall in love with me.
I began the campaign that evening.*

My Dark Husband by Percy Wittlesford

Chapter Twenty-One

"What the hell happened to you?" Sebastian asked, his gaze assessing. "Is it the dukedom? I know you didn't want it, but you surely didn't have to give up sleeping and eating for it." He squinted at Thaddeus's face. "And shaving."

Thaddeus had done the bare minimum of work at home before dismissing Melmsford and heading to Sebastian's house, which he shared with his wife and his dogs.

It was much smaller than the ducal town house, and felt much more lived in. Perhaps because Sebastian and his wife Ivy were so clearly in love?

And when had he become so mawkish.

"You look like a bear," Sebastian added.

Thaddeus resisted the urge to growl at his cousin. First, because he was always in control, he did not growl. Second, because he knew Sebastian would just laugh even more at him. And how was it possible for him to look so terrible just hours after the argument with Lavinia? Or were his feelings about it all—whatever they were, he wasn't even certain—written so obviously on his face.

"Marriage," Nash pronounced. Thaddeus hadn't even seen him in the room, but he emerged from the corner of Sebastian's study, wearing all black and holding a snifter of brandy.

In other words, being Nash.

"Sit down," Sebastian commanded, gesturing to the sofa.

Thaddeus's immediate reaction was to refuse, because he was the one in charge, damn it.

But he needed his friends' help. So he sat.

There was a first time for everything, after all.

Sebastian sat beside him, while Nash leaned against the mantel. "Is Nash right? For once?" Sebastian said, darting a quick glance toward their glowering friend.

Nash snorted, but didn't threaten to punch anyone. His own marriage had clearly softened him.

Thaddeus shook his head slowly. "Yes? No? I don't know."

"You're in love." Nash spoke flatly, as though it were a fact.

"I'm no—Goddamn it."

Sebastian began to laugh, throwing his head back and closing his eyes as his whole body shook.

"It's not that amusing," Thaddeus said.

Sebastian wiped a tear from his eye, his shoulders still shaking. "It is, though. You thought you had this all sorted, and your life could run with military precision, even though you're not in the military anymore. Isn't that right?"

Thaddeus glared at him. Yes, Sebastian was right; no, he didn't want to admit it.

"Since you are too stubborn to say so, let us offer some advice," Sebastian said, gesturing to include himself and Nash, who nodded in agreement.

"It's not enough to throw yourself on her mercy."

"It's not?" Because when Thaddeus had imagined it, he had imagined some sort of throwing-self-on-mercy scenario. It seemed the easiest way to achieve his goal.

His goal of having her stay with him in a real marriage.

Goddamn it.

If only he hadn't been so determined to keep their lives separate. If only he hadn't assumed he would never care for another as he had grown to care for her.

The people he'd cared for were in this room, and he certainly didn't want to be married to either one of them. Never mind that Ana Maria, the other person he cared about, was already actually married to someone in this room.

His inability to imagine what was possible, the pragmatism that had served him so well in the past, had let him down profoundly now.

"Well, you will have to throw yourself on her mercy eventually," Nash said slowly. "But first you have to show her how you feel. Not just tell her."

"Because anyone can tell her," Sebastian added.

The thought of anybody else telling Lavinia they loved her wasn't the point, and yet Thaddeus felt his muscles twitch in his desire to punch that mythical loving person.

Perhaps he was more similar to Nash than he'd previously thought.

"How do I show her?" He hastened to add to his question. "Do not tell me things to do—"

He made a vague gesture, and both his friends laughed harder than he'd ever seen before.

"While I would pay good money to have Nash educate us on his bedroom tricks," Sebastian said dryly after the laughter had subsided, "showing is not about that. We're men, we can't help but have our minds go there first."

"That's extraordinarily observant of you," Thaddeus replied. "How did you come by this knowledge?" he asked, his tone suspicious.

Sebastian's eyebrows rose. "That you have to ask that means you and your wife have not resolved your situation."

"Of course not, you idiot, that is why I am here!" Thaddeus sputtered.

"Right. I'd forgotten." Sebastian bit his lip, presumably to keep from laughing again. "You are married to a strong woman, much as Nash and I are. What you need to do is allow her to be strong on her own, treat her as an equal, but also treat her as someone more special than you."

Thaddeus processed that advice. "How can I both treat her as an equal and treat her as more special?"

Nash folded his arms over his chest and nodded. "That's the trick. Once you figure it out, you should be sorted."

"Exactly," Sebastian confirmed.

Thaddeus felt as though he was going to explode from frustration. "You haven't told me anything useful." He rose and began to pace.

"You should speak with Ana Maria to get her perspective," Nash added. Unhelpfully, since Ana Maria wasn't here.

Damn it. Not only did he want to punch someone—preferably one of his two friends here—but now he was pacing.

Had he turned into Nash by accident?

"You'll sort it out," Sebastian said in a reassuring tone. "Just treat it like a military exercise, one where two superiors have given you conflicting orders."

Thaddeus paused in his pacing. That made sense. Sort of.

"Right. Well, thank you two for being of little help. I will see you at that damned engagement party, won't I?"

"When is it?" Sebastian replied.

Thaddeus gave Sebastian a damning look. "You're coming. It's in two weeks, give or take."

Sebastian clapped his hand on Thaddeus's shoulder. "We wouldn't miss it for the world, would we, Nash?"

Nash grunted in assent.

IT WAS UNUSUAL for Lavinia not to speak her mind. But she was determined not to, no matter that agreeing to a different sort of bargain occupied the waking thoughts that weren't concerned with party preparation, finishing her book in time, and fussing over how adorable Precious was.

Thank goodness there *was* so much going on, or she would have stormed into Thaddeus's office and gone to sit on his desk until he agreed to have an actual conversation with her about everything.

Because he was barely conversing with her at all. He was continuing to visit her bedroom in the evening, but they didn't speak much then, and he hadn't repeated the one time he'd slept the entire night in her bed.

Despite how she felt and what she wanted, she was growing resigned to leaving as soon as she had done her duty—which in itself made her feel like nothing more than a vessel.

It was odd, though; even though he was barely speaking to her, he was being thoughtful in other ways. One morning she discovered he'd asked the cook to make her favorite meal for that evening's dinner; another day he brought her tea in bed, prepared precisely as she liked it; and then he took pains to mention how much he liked what she was wearing, even if it was a gown she'd worn before.

It was sweet, of course, but also entirely befuddling.

Normally she would have demanded that he say why he was doing these things, but she'd sworn not to address him in any personal business until he did.

Was she being unnecessarily stubborn?

Likely so.

Was she also remaining true to herself?

Also likely so.

If he would ever compromise on their bargain, he was going to have to take her entirely uncompromised. An irony, given that a compromising situation was what had landed them in marriage in the first place.

She wore a rueful smile as she reviewed the guest list for the party—she had yet to send it to the McTavishes, despite Mrs. McTavish's frequent reminders, because she did not want that lady's comments on how many of Lavinia's family were invited, even the ones who usually were not asked to such events.

It was a byproduct of having so many odd relatives; none of the ones who didn't go out in Society cared at all that they didn't, but they would care if they were not there to see Jane's engagement officially announced.

Lavinia had also included the queen on the invite list, although she doubted that worthy lady would find time to attend. She was apparently too busy bearing children and running the country to spend much time socializing.

But Mrs. McTavish could hope. Which was why Lavinia had included her in the first place.

"Lavinia."

She started, not realizing Thaddeus was in the room. She was downstairs in her salon, Precious napping at her feet. She had papers strewn all over the desk, ranging from the guest list to the menu to the schedule of what had to happen when for everything to work out properly.

"Uh, hello," she said, brushing hair off her face. It tended to come out of her coiffure as she worked, primarily because she would run her hands through her hair when she was stuck on something.

She was stuck a lot.

He looked devastatingly handsome, and she took a moment to appreciate his beauty since she would be subject to it much less frequently as soon as there was a little Thaddeus running about.

He had been letting his beard come in more, and she was entranced by the dark stubble on his cheeks, liking how it felt on her face when he kissed her or her thighs when he kissed her *there*.

"I have a question for you."

She turned so she was facing him more fully. "Of course. Is it about the party? I can go over all the details with you if you wish, they are right here, it is eas—"

"No, not about the party," he interrupted, his lips curling into a hint of a smile. It was good someone could still find something to smile about. "Or it is, but not what you mean. What color is the gown you will be wearing?"

Lavinia blinked in surprise. "I haven't thought of that yet, honestly."

His brows drew together in a frown. Was that a problem? Should she have known precisely what she was going to wear? Had she now failed some sort of duchess test and he would want to boot her out of the house even more quickly?

You are being an idiot, a voice said inside her head.

"Ah," he replied, clamping his lips into a thin line. "If you do happen to decide within the next day or so, could you share that information with me? You can send it via Melmsford, if you like."

"Of course." This was all entirely baffling. "So what are you wearing?"

Now *he* looked baffled. As he well should— gentlemen wore black and white evening clothes to parties; they seldom had a choice of color. "I think you should consider something that would suit your coloring," she continued, allowing herself to have a moment of fun. Perhaps she would even smile herself. "Purple would look marvelous with your dark hair, or perhaps a verdant green."

His lips twitched. "Something pastel, perhaps?"

Her eyes widened. "Precisely!" And then she couldn't help but laugh, because the thought of him wearing something that was not absolutely correct for the occasion was beyond her imagination.

"I will consider it, my—" And then he paused, and all the humor of the moment was gone. Had he been about to say "my love," but stopped himself when he realized she was not, in fact, his love? Had he been about to say "my wife," knowing that that wouldn't be quite true soon enough? Or was there something else she was missing?

But it didn't matter, because he was already stepping away from her. "Good day, Lavinia," he said abruptly before opening the door and shutting it firmly behind him.

She glanced down at Precious, who'd been awoken from her nap. "I don't know at all either," she said. Precious blinked sleepily at her. "But I will deal with it after the party."

THADDEUS CURSED UNDER his breath as he closed the door to her salon. He was doing a terrible job trying to woo her—he couldn't seem to find the right words, the words that would make her understand why he had said what he had and why he had now changed his mind. And his friends had said he should show her how he felt because words, apparently, were easy.

Not in his case.

And his showing her how he felt couldn't be in bed, since their sexual relations had begun well before he had realized he had fallen in love with her.

Because he had. Now that Sebastian and Nash had said it, it was glaringly obvious, and he was even more of an idiot for not realizing it sooner.

He loved how she was enthusiastic where he was restricted, loved how she barreled into things where he was more withdrawn, loved how she was fierce in her protection of the people she loved. As he was, in that case.

And he'd totally bungled up asking her what color she would be wearing at the ball—her expression froze and then dropped, as though he were testing her on something and she knew she was going to fail.

He'd had the thought of purchasing some jewelry for her. Something that would be personal to her, that would demonstrate he cared for her and wanted her to stay.

Not that he had a clue what that piece of jewelry would be. But he did know who might be able to assist.

"It took you long enough," Ana Maria said as she looped her arm through Thaddeus's. He grunted in response to his cousin.

"And now you sound like Nash," she continued in a reproving voice. "We're all supposed to use our words, not make noises like disgruntled animals."

He heard himself emit a burst of shocked laughter because Nash was like a disgruntled animal at times.

He hadn't known Ana Maria all that well prior to his taking the title of the Duke of Hasford. But when Sebastian was discovered not to be the duke, and Thaddeus was, he and Ana Maria had lived together in the ducal town house, the same house that he and Lavinia currently occupied. During that time, he had done his best to protect her, to provide for her as he knew Sebastian would like, although he hadn't been able to stop her from falling in love with Nash.

Judging from their respective auras of happiness, it was a good thing he hadn't been able to stop it.

Ana Maria was a wonderfully kind and sympathetic person, but more importantly, she had strong opinions when it came to things like clothing and color. She had redecorated her room in Thaddeus's home in an array of vivid colors, and while it wasn't to Thaddeus's own taste, he did know she had a discerning eye.

"What are we doing today?" she asked. "Nash told me of your conversation. I was wondering why you hadn't invited us over before. Was it because you assumed your bride would be leaving soon anyway? And you didn't want me to form an attachment?" She paused, then gave her head a definitive shake. "You are an idiot."

Words that had been said to him more in the past few days than ever in his entire life, and oftentimes had been said by him to him.

"I am."

Now it was her turn to laugh in surprise.

"I want to buy something for Lavinia. Something that will demonstrate how I feel. Something that will be personal and suit who she is."

"That is a tall order," Ana Maria said. "But in all cases, I would suggest something expensive. I don't suppose she needs another town house?"

Thaddeus shook his head. "The point is for her to stay with me, not to move out."

"Ah, excellent point," she replied. "Does she like to garden? Perhaps an exotic plant?"

"I don't think she likes to garden." Thaddeus frowned in thought. "I believe she likes to write. Her fingers are always smudged with ink."

"What does she write? Letters?" Ana Maria waved her hand. "Never mind, it doesn't matter. I propose you buy her a fine pen set."

"That doesn't seem very romantic. I was thinking about a piece of jewelry."

"A piece of jewelry would also be nice," she conceded. "I know! How about a piece of jewelry that looks like a pen?"

Thaddeus tried to imagine what that would look like and none of his images looked good at all.

"I think a pen set and a piece of jewelry."

"And here I thought you couldn't compromise," Ana Maria replied, squeezing his arm.

"Thank you, I think?" he replied, at which she merely laughed.

"Good evening."

The count muttered something under his breath as I held the dish of buttered turnips toward him.

"Can I serve you some?" I asked, keeping my eyes on his face.

He met my gaze, and I felt my eyes widen. How had I never noticed how strikingly intense his eyes were? They were so brown they were nearly black, and it felt as though he could see into my soul.

My Dark Husband by Percy Wittlesford

Chapter Twenty-Two

$\mathcal{L}$avinia smoothed her gown with damp hands. It was the evening of Jane's engagement party, and thus far everything had gone nearly as planned, except for the unexpected absence of flowers, because her mother and Mrs. McTavish had been unable to agree on roses or peonies.

Mrs. Webb, the housekeeper, had sent a few of the maids to the shops for ribbon, and then had tasked everyone who wasn't already working to make bows, so now there were ribbons in every color and pattern decorating every pillar, on the walls, and tied to the backs of all the chairs.

It was exuberant, and gaudy, and Lavinia adored it.

Even more so because she knew both her mother and Mrs. McTavish would loathe it.

She turned at the knock on the door.

"Lavinia?"

It was him. Of course. Was he here to critique the color choice she'd made for her gown?

"Come in," she called, returning her gaze to the mirror.

Instead of purple, she'd chosen to wear stormy blue, the color of the sky when it was just about to rain. It was made in a stiff satin, cut so as to enhance her bosom, bare of ornamentation except for the darker-hued blue lace at the bottom.

She'd asked Nancy to dress her hair more intricately than usual, with the result being a profusion of curls spilling onto her shoulders. Nancy had pinned several diamond stars in her hair, and Lavinia wore a stack of bracelets over her matching blue gloves.

For the first time in her life, she felt and looked dramatically bold. It was a fitting ensemble for a woman who wanted to make a final statement before being banished from the world she'd always inhabited.

He strode in, and she gasped as she took in what he was wearing.

All pastel. From his light blue waistcoat to his cream-colored jacket to the lavender trousers he'd worn on their wedding day.

And while it would seem as though he would look ridiculous—and others might certainly judge him to be so—she thought he looked incredibly and undeniably handsome.

"I—I did as you requested." His tone was low. And was it her imagination or did it seem as though his words held more impact than normal?

"I see." She took a deep breath as he stepped toward her.

"And I know now is not the time to speak on things, since your sister's engagement party is imminent, but I hope we can speak together afterward." His expression tightened. "I have some things I wish to say."

It felt as though her heart was caught in her throat. Could it be that he was finally breaking his silence to share his thoughts and feelings? Could it possibly be that he was going to ask her to stay with him, the bargain they'd made be damned?

If she were writing this, she would ratchet up the tension by making it seem as though that was what he was going to say, and then have him say something else entirely.

Thank God he was writing this, not her.

"Your Grace!" Even through the door, Mrs. Webb's voice sounded panicked. Very far from her usual calm demeanor.

"Yes?" Lavinia called.

"The ladies are here, and they are fighting in the ballroom. Your mother and that other lady? Would you mind very much coming down? Now?"

Lavinia rolled her eyes. Of course they were fighting—they had never stopped, not even when their respective children had declared true love for one another.

Jane was going to have a very difficult time navigating those relationships. Perhaps Lavinia could work on creating a list of possible ways to respond to cause the least amount of harm.

"If you will excuse me?" she said, wishing she could hear what he had to say now. It wasn't the interruption she'd imagined in her writer's mind, but it had the same effect.

"Of course," he said, gesturing toward the door. "Please let me know if you need help. And good luck separating the combatants."

She chuckled as she walked out, heading straight for the chaos.

IF IT HAD been any other evening, he would have said what he had to say right away, not hint at it as though he was teasing her. But it would be thoughtless for him to upend her world prior to this event, which he knew she'd worked hard on, and was important to her.

He left her room, pausing in the hallway as he heard the sound of upraised voices. Should he go see what he could do? Or should he wait until she asked for him? He needed to show her he trusted her to make her own decisions, to do what would be best without his interference or the force of his title.

I'll be there if she needs me. He walked down the stairway toward his office, wincing as he caught a glimpse of his ridiculous outfit in the tall mirrors that lined the entryway. But he'd seen how she'd reacted to it, and the expression on her face was worth the wearing of any number of light-colored pantaloons.

"Your Grace," Melmsford said, sounding surprised. "I thought you would be in the ballroom. I believe the engagement party is this evening?"

Thaddeus nodded as he went to sit behind his desk. "Yes, but the party doesn't begin for a half hour or so, and it appears there is a fracas involving my wife's mother and the mother of the gentleman betrothed to my wife's sister."

"Ah," Melmsford replied, sounding as though he understood. "I heard Mr. Percy Wittlesford will be previewing his next release during the party? That is quite a coup."

"Say," Thaddeus said as the thought crossed his mind, "you mentioned you and your sister read Mr. Wittlesford. Would you like to bring her to hear the reading?"

He wouldn't have thought of it when he'd first been married. But seeing how Lavinia always treated the servants—as though they were people, not just soldiers in service to the house—made him want to extend that same thoughtfulness to the servants he dealt with. Particularly Melmsford, who'd proven to be a good sounding board on all sorts of issues.

"That wouldn't be proper, Your Grace."

Thaddeus chuckled. "Melmsford, tonight we will have the most disreputable family in London as our honored guests. I hardly think having an honorable working man and his sister in attendance will make a bit of difference. If you think your sister would enjoy it."

Melmsford's expression lit up. "Enjoy it! She would like it above all things."

Thaddeus made a shooing gesture. "Then get going, go retrieve her and I will see you later."

Melmsford rose and bowed a few times, then scurried out of the office, leaving Thaddeus to think about how he'd changed since meeting Lavinia.

He hoped he would continue changing, perhaps finally becoming someone who didn't even need a list in order to run his life.

With her by his side, her exuberance and passion and fearless curiosity were things he would try to emulate, not deplore.

If they could just make it through tonight.

By ELEVEN O'CLOCK, two hours into the party, Lavinia could say she was officially exhausted. In addition to solving the argument between the mothers, both of whom had chosen to wear yellow, with each demanding the other return home to change, she'd dealt with her father insisting she weigh in on an argument on economic theory he'd been having with Percy, as well as shepherding her various addled aunts around the ballroom to ensure the ones who were in lifelong battles with one another were not seated in close proximity.

"It's going well, Lavinia," Jane said, taking Lavinia's arm and squeezing it.

"Yes, I think so. All we have to do is have Percy read, and Father can announce the engagement officially, and then this evening will be complete. Have you and Mr. McTavish finalized a date yet?"

Jane's lovely face got clouded. "I have tried, but he pushes back on everything I suggest. Apparently his mother has superstitions about certain dates, and then she suggests other dates, and I say fine, and then it turns out those dates aren't fine, after all."

"Jane, I know you might not want to hear this—"

Jane met Lavinia's gaze, sorrowful resignation etched on her face.

"But I have to tell him it is her or me." She sounded determined.

Lavinia exhaled in relief. "Yes. You cannot allow her to rule your life and your marriage. He will have to make a choice."

Jane nodded. "I will speak to him after Percy reads. I hope it's not too scandalous. Did you choose what he'd read?"

Lavinia shook her head. "There was no time. I just told him to find something that was short and that would pique people's interests."

"Oh good, so it will be a surprise to you, too."

A faint sense of dread crept up Lavinia's spine. What if—? And what if—? But no, Percy would choose something that was appropriate for the venue. There was no possibility Thaddeus would discover her secret.

Even though now she had to acknowledge she had kept a secret from him.

"YOUR GRACE."

Thaddeus smiled at Melmsford as he and a young lady who shared Melmsford's coloring entered the room. "This is your sister, I assume?" He took her hand and bowed over it. "I am the Duke of Hasford, and your brother is an excellent employee. I am glad you were able to attend tonight."

The party, as far as Thaddeus could tell, was going well; Lavinia had apparently quashed whatever argument was brewing between the two mothers, the wine was flowing in copious amounts, and there were several servants darting between the guests offering a variety of hors d'oeuvres.

"Thank you for having us, Your Grace." Miss Melmsford was probably about seventeen years old, with wide eyes that kept getting wider the more she looked around the room.

"I understand you are a fan of my wife's brother's writing," Thaddeus said in what he hoped was a kind voice. He knew his presence could be intimidating, and he didn't want to make her anxious. At least, not more anxious than it appeared she was already.

"He writes the most romantic books!" she enthused, clasping her hands to her heart. "And the endings are always so unexpected; I am always so surprised when it turns out who the real villain is."

"Ah," Thaddeus said. Of course he was not able to comment on the quality of Percy's writing, not having read anything the man had written. He suppressed a wince as he recalled how condescending he'd sounded when he'd first met Lavinia and her sister—remarking that he did not read those kinds of books or whatever.

Another way in which he'd changed. If Percy's books were romantic, perhaps he could pick up a few hints about how to treat his wife.

If she would stay with him.

Later, he reminded himself. He'd talk to her about it later, after the party.

He glanced at the crowd, unconsciously looking for her. There she was. She stood next to her sister, a determined expression on her face as they conversed.

And then he saw Lady Jane nod and walk away, her mouth set in a serious line. Not the kind of joyous expression one would expect of a woman who was announcing her engagement, but then again, he couldn't imagine being joyous, either about marrying that weak lummox or having to endure his mother as her mother-in-law.

But then again, he wasn't Lady Jane.

As he watched, he saw Lavinia spot him and begin to move toward him, her gaze shifting to the Melmsfords, at which point a warm smile curled her lips.

Thaddeus suppressed the unexpected stab of jealousy that pierced him. How dare she smile at someone else like that? Because he knew damned well it was just her nature to smile.

"Good evening, Mr. Melmsford," she said, taking his secretary's hand. "And this must be your sister? Welcome, Miss Melmsford."

That lady turned a bright shade of pink.

"Thaddeus, how clever of you to invite the Melmsfords! Mr. Melmsford, I do recall you mentioning you were a fan of my brother's work. I am sorry I did not think it myself."

She gave him an approving glance, and he felt as satisfied as he did after one of their more adventurous bouts of lovemaking.

Was this what love was? Feeling warmth when the person you cared most about in the world acknowledged a kindness?

And yes. She was the person he cared most about in the world now. Sebastian, Nash, and Ana Maria were his family, but she was his heart.

Dear God, please let him say the right things to convince her to stay. He wished he could drag Percy off somewhere and ask him to write a script or something.

Instead, he'd have to rely on his own words.

"If you would excuse us, it is time to have Percy read." Lavinia took his arm, and he nodded toward the Melmsfords.

"Do you remember the last time we were together at one of your brother's readings?" he asked as they walked toward the front of the room.

She chuckled. "Yes. I was trying not to notice your thighs as you were perusing all the single females for a possible duchess."

And I ended up with the best one.

"Wait—my thighs?" he said.

"They made the first week or so of marriage tolerable," she replied in a saucy tone of voice.

Oh, how he wished they were alone right now.

"I was just thinking I should try to read one of your brother's books."

"They are excellent," she pronounced. "Full of adventure and some romance and truly wonderful writing. If I do say so myself."

"You should. He is your brother, after all."

"Yes, of course." It sounded as though she had forgotten something, and he was about to ask if there was a problem when they walked up to Percy.

"It's time," Lavinia said. "Thaddeus will introduce you. That way neither Mother nor Mrs. McTavish will be upset, since he is the only thing upon which they agree."

Percy held his hand out for Thaddeus to shake. "Excellent to see you again, Your Grace. Thank you for hosting this party."

"Anything for your sister," Thaddeus replied in a gruff voice.

He heard her emit a soft "oh," and that eased the worry in his heart by a tiny amount.

He gestured to the musicians, who stopped playing. The crowd turned toward him.

"Welcome to our home. The duchess and I are grateful you have come on this festive occasion. Before the evening's announcement, however, we have a treat. Mr. Percy Wittlesford will be reading from his next book, entitled—" He paused and glanced toward Percy.

"*My Dark Husband.*"

Thaddeus's eyebrows rose. "Ah. We will be honored to hear an excerpt from *My Dark Husband.*"

The crowd applauded, and Percy began to speak.

> "*I did not know what he thought of me. Just that I was an inconvenience, and that he would rather I was not living in his house. If I could just get him to trust me enough, I would be able to steal away in the middle of the night. But I had no friends, no family.*
>
> "*I was entirely alone.*"

Percy paused, and several ladies in the audience emitted sympathetic sighs.

> "*Over time, we came to an unspoken agreement—a bargain, if you will. We kept out of one another's sight during the day, while in the evening we would sit together at dinner and I would watch him as he ate. Wishing he wasn't so compelling, that I didn't feel as though I was a spider in his web.*
>
> "*That I didn't want to discover what it was that he actually cared about.*
>
> "*So I could use it against him.*"

Again, Percy paused, surveying the crowd. Thaddeus had to admire his ability to keep everyone's attention without it being required—he had done the same in the army, but it had been a life or death situation.

Perhaps he should read one of Percy's books, after all. They seemed harmlessly entertaining, and it could be a respite from reviewing the constant stream of accounts and legal missives that demanded his attention.

Lavinia stood beside him, paying rapt attention, and he held his hand out at his side, moving it over until his finger felt the fabric of her gown. And then he drew his hand up to clasp her hand, curling his fingers around hers.

She looked at him, eyes wide. Of course. He'd never done such a simple demonstratively affectionate gesture before; it wasn't in the bargain, after all.

"Over time, I gained his trust. I spoke to him of his life, of who he had been before, and learned he was accustomed to being alone. He reciprocated by showing me all the passion that had been lacking in my life before.

"I hate to admit it, but I was falling in love with him. And I knew he would forget entirely about me once I had served my purpose, but he wouldn't yet tell me what that purpose was."

Her fingers were warm, and it felt right to be standing here in his house, with all these people, holding her hand. Having her as his anchor keeping him human, and connected so he didn't forget what was most important to him. That his duty to which he was so committed was because he cared about the people behind the dukedom, the servants and the tenants and the merchants who purchased the products of his farms. That his duty was to Sebastian so he wouldn't feel guilty about his mother having tried to destroy the dukedom for her own personal gains. To Ana Maria, who deserved something for having been an unpaid servant for so many years.

Even to Nash so that he wouldn't have the excuse of not being the best possible duke he could be.

> ". . . He stood in front of me in all his lividly angry splendor, his handsome face set in harsh lines, his arms folded over his chest while I could see his thigh muscles bunching as though he were going to barrel straight toward me. And do what, I had no idea."

Thigh muscles?

> "'When I tell you to remove yourself to the country, you will do it.' His voice was deep and harsh and I trembled to hear it. 'And there you will stay until I decide if you can return.' He stepped forward, and I began to shake. 'There is no need to be afraid of me,' he said, reaching his hand out to touch my cheek, 'after all, you are precious to me.'"

Thaddeus froze, his mind processing all that he'd heard. He dropped her hand as he heard her gasp, and he looked at her, hoping he wouldn't see the truth in her face.

But there it was.

Percy continued to read, and she looked entirely guilty. He nodded to her, a grim expression on his face, as he stalked toward where he saw Fletchfield.

"Bring me a big glass of whisky," he ordered before glancing back at her.

Her back was rigid, and it appeared she was about to turn to look at him when her sister ran up, her face crumpled up as though she was about to cry.

Thaddeus nearly returned then, but stopped himself—they were merely partners in an agreement, not trusting spouses. Not if she hadn't been able to trust him with this, clearly a very important part of her life.

Why had he thought they might have something together? He'd spoken to her at the music hall of how he felt as a child, how his responsibilities weighed on him. It would have been the time for her to share something about herself, yet she had been quiet. Quieter than usual after that conversation, he recalled.

It wasn't that she was an author of books he would never read that was the problem; it was that it was an essential part of her, clearly, and yet she had kept it hidden away from him.

What else had she hidden? Could he trust her to speak the truth, all of the truth, again? Could he trust her with his heart?

Percy finished reading, and the room exploded in applause. Thaddeus saw how Percy's gaze went immediately to Lavinia, a satisfied smile on his face as though he was glad she was able to hear that the audience appreciated her work even if she couldn't be given credit for it.

Goddamn it.

She deserved credit for it, too. From him, as well as all the other people in the room. But she hadn't trusted him with the information, as though he was just another one of the many guests they'd invited to their home and whose names they likely wouldn't recall tomorrow morning.

He wanted to snarl, to stomp around and break things to relieve some of the furious anger inside. But that would be totally unlike him, as well as being totally unsuitable for his position.

So he would tamp it all down, remind himself that their bargain was still intact, and that this would all be over when he and she had done their duty.

Because he would always do his duty. That was all he was.

It was difficult to get him to talk to me, let alone trust me.
  But he did, eventually, as I made my plans to escape,
leaving him and his wicked ways behind.
  Even though a part of me never wanted to leave.

My Dark Husband by Percy Wittlesford

Chapter Twenty-Three

Lavinia knew the moment he'd figured it out. He'd dropped her hand as though he'd been burned, and then he'd looked at her with the coldest expression on his face—colder even than when they had first met, and it was apparent he disliked her.

That had been shallow dislike, not based on anything but a feeling. But the emotion she felt exuding from him was deep. Not dislike so much as hurt. As though she'd betrayed him.

Which she had.

How had she not seen that? That even if nobody else knew that it was her actually writing the books that if he found out he would be hurt?

"Vinnie."

Jane's urgent tone snapped her out of her reverie.

"What?" She looked at Jane's face, now streaked with tears. Everything else faded away. "What is it?" She took Jane's hands and led her into a corner of the room, glancing around in an unconscious need to make certain nobody saw Jane's pain.

Jane took a few deep breaths as Lavinia searched frantically around her person for a handkerchief. Unfortunately, her evening gown wasn't equipped with anything close to storage, what with it being made for a frivolous occasion, so the only thing she could do was strip off one of her gloves and hold it out to Jane, who took it to dab at her eyes. She began to speak in a soft tone as she kept her eyes lowered to the floor.

"Henry. I spoke to him and told him as well as I was able that it was difficult to navigate between his mother and ours and me, and that I wanted us to be united in what we decided for our wedding. For our future." Jane lifted her gaze, meeting Lavinia's eyes. "And he said that he knew best what was to be done, and that his mother only had his best intentions motivating him, and that if we were to be married—*if* we were to be married," she repeated, emphasizing the *if*, "that he would be the only decision-maker."

She sobbed, and wiped her nose with the glove.

"And?" Lavinia prompted when Jane had settled herself.

"And I said I no longer wished to marry him, and to consider our engagement off."

Lavinia felt a traitorous sense of relief at Jane's words. She'd been uneasy with some of the events following their engagement—hell, even the way he proposed had made her uneasy—but she didn't want her sister to be miserable and alone for the rest of her life.

The only reason she'd married Thaddeus in the first place was to ensure Jane wasn't miserable and alone for the rest of her life.

Damn it.

"And then Henry told his mother, and his mother marched up to ours and told her, and then she said it was just as well, and that she would find me a husband herself straightaway." Jane swallowed. "Vinnie, I think she will, and she'll browbeat me into it. I don't want to be married to anyone I don't love."

"You won't." Lavinia took a deep breath as she thought it through. "It just so happens that Thaddeus and I have agreed that it would be best if I go to the country for a bit, so you and I will go together. I won't be alone, and you won't have to marry anyone you don't want to. A perfect solution." Perfect if one didn't consider that that meant that Lavinia was going to be leaving her heart behind in London.

But he wouldn't want her now, now that he believed she'd betrayed him. Of course he still wished for a child, but he could compromise and come to the country later on, as soon as she knew she wasn't already pregnant.

It was the least he could do. And she would tell him so.

"Vinnie," Jane said, her voice catching, "would that really be a possibility? I just—I don't know what I did to deserve a sister like you." She flung her arms around Lavinia and squeezed her tight.

Lavinia looked over her shoulder, searching for Thaddeus in the crowd. She saw him at the other end of the room, and their eyes met for a moment before he deliberately turned away.

Perhaps this would be easier than she thought. Even though she already knew it would be the hardest thing she had ever done.

"WE HAVE TO TALK."

It was hours later, and all the guests had long since gone home. There had been no engagement announcement, much to Thaddeus's surprise, and Lavinia had only said she would explain later.

Well, later was now, and he'd been waiting impatiently in his room for her to come speak with him, but he hadn't been able to wait any longer. He'd flung his dressing gown over himself and stalked across the hallway to her room, tapping on the door and entering.

She sat on the bed, her hair undone from the intricate hairstyle she'd worn earlier. Her elegant gown off, her bare toes peeking out from under her nightrail. She looked exhausted, and Thaddeus felt a pang of sympathy for all she had done—all fruitless effort, given the lack of an engagement during the engagement party.

But then he recalled Percy's reading, and the sudden realization that she had chosen to hide something as important as her creative expression, and his anger boiled up again.

"I can see you are ready to talk. If not explode," she said, meeting his gaze directly. Her expression was defiant, eliciting a feeling of admiration from him—few people who knew they were going to face his disapproval were as strong. And he had never allowed himself to exhibit pure anger before, so even he didn't know what would happen.

That she was ready to face it, to face him, made him admire her more. Goddamn it. And he was going to lose her—or not, since it seemed he had never had her in the first place.

If he had, she would have trusted him.

"Come sit," she said, gesturing to the armchair where he normally draped his dressing gown before getting into bed with her.

He began to walk to do as she said, then realized there was no possibility he would be able to keep still. "I'll stand, thank you," he said.

Her expression tightened. She folded her arms over her chest and rose, standing a few feet away from him. So close, but she felt so distant. As though he'd never touched her, never held her, never told her his secrets.

"Jane has broken her engagement," she said flatly. "I cannot say I am not happy about it, but of course Jane is devastated."

And he knew—because she'd said as much—that the only reason she'd married him was to ensure her sister could be engaged to that milquetoast.

Was she regretting it now?

She had to be. Lavinia was nothing if not independent, and of course she wished to make her own decisions—staying in London when they separated, or not having to get married at all.

"Ah."

She shifted her gaze to the corner of the room. He felt the lack of closeness even more now. "I know it is not what we agreed to, but I am going to take Jane to the country. I am not certain for how long." She looked back at him. "I can inform you if I am pregnant. If I am not, you can visit me there."

It was an order suitable for a queen. As though she was the one in charge, making the demands.

He felt the resentment at being spoken to curl up inside him, rising like a serpent about to strike, and just barely stopped himself from barking back at her. Insisting she stay here, where she belonged.

Until he realized she didn't want to belong here. That no doubt she had felt the same resentment at being ordered to do things by him. But she hadn't done anything but adhere to what he required, not even when it no doubt chafed at her wish for freedom.

"Fine," he said in a short tone. "Where are you going? It would be preferable if you were to go to one of my holdings, but—"

"That is generous of you," she interrupted. Even in the flickering candlelight he could see the stain of red on her cheeks. "I apologize," she continued.

That startled him. "Apologize? For what?" *For leaving? For taking my heart with you? For not trusting me with who you are?*

"For portraying you in my book." She made a helpless gesture. "I don't believe anyone will know it was you, but I understand if you are upset about my using you as inspiration."

He couldn't stop himself from advancing toward her. She didn't flinch, she just raised herself up to her full height—still many inches below his own—and lifted her chin.

"You think I am upset that you used me as inspiration?" His voice was a low growl.

Her eyebrows drew together. "Why else would you be upset?"

"Because," he began, clasping his hands behind his back, "you didn't tell me you are Percy Wittlesford. Because you let me tell you things about myself that I had never even thought to share with anyone before, and yet you didn't tell me something that clearly your brother and your sister know. That you didn't trust me, Lavinia."

Her eyes were wide as she stared at him, her expression frozen. And then her face crumpled, and he felt it like a tangible hit to his belly, and all he wanted to do was step forward and wrap her in his arms, but she wouldn't want that. Not now, not ever.

"Oh." Her voice was faint. "I didn't—I never thought you would care."

"Not care?" he said in an incredulous tone. "When you are my wife, and we are partners in this marriage?"

"Hardly partners," she shot back. "Unless it is an unequal partnership."

"Tell me what I did to you that was unfair. Unequal."

She swallowed, breathing rapidly through her nose. "You said we would separate after I bear you a son. You were prepared to deny me any role in the raising of our child, though you conceded I could have the girl if I was so unfortunate as to bear one before I gave you an heir."

He winced at how harsh it sounded. And it was true—he had said that.

"I am sorry too, Lavinia." The anger receded as quickly as it had begun, and now all he felt was hopeless. Because he'd been hoping for more from her, but how could she trust him when he had all the power? She was correct; it was an unequal partnership. Unfortunately, it was also an indissoluble one. "I shouldn't have presented it so bluntly."

"If you had been more nuanced it would have been the same."

He dragged his hand over his face, wishing he were better with words. Wishing he had half her skill in speaking and apparently in writing, too. "That's not what I meant." He took a deep breath. "I will leave you to your sleep. I want to apologize again for hurting you. I never meant to."

"Nor did I. I am sorry, Thaddeus."

He nodded in acknowledgment as he turned to walk out the door.

"How are you feeling?"

It was approximately the four hundred and seventy-seventh time Jane had asked her, and Lavinia always had the same answer: "Fine."

They'd arrived at Thaddeus's country estate in a town called Medcross a week before. The town was lively, a mix of farmers, merchants, squires, and a few ex-Londoners who'd decamped to the country.

It hadn't taken the sisters long before meeting the residents; first the vicar and his wife had paid a call, and then a Squire Haskins, his wife, and three of his daughters, followed by another squire (this one with two young sons), the doctor who served the town, and a group of ladies who were the organizing committee for the church.

At first Lavinia had wanted to shield Jane from such an onslaught of visitors, but it seemed Jane thrived in company, at least in small company, and soon they were walking to town every day.

The duke's servants had made them welcome as well, having been told of their arrival from Thaddeus, who'd sent a note informing them. The house was large and spacious, as were the gardens. The furniture in the house was at least a few decades old, but it was comfortable and felt as though some past Duke of Hasford had made this house a home.

It would be a good place to rear a child, Lavinia thought with regret as she looked out her window one morning. She and Jane had now been here for eight days, and thus far, her only communication with Thaddeus had been short, to-the-point missives that indicated he was continuing to take care of things. As it seemed he always did.

Perhaps that was his creative expression, she mused, as Precious tried to get her attention by rubbing her nose on Lavinia's ankles. Or his driving impulse, since he'd married her solely to take care of her, and by extension her family's, reputation.

For even more times than Jane had asked how she was doing, Lavinia thought about how she could have handled everything differently—if she had known she was likely to fall in love with him, perhaps she would have trusted him more at the beginning of their marriage.

But he had said, as nearly one of his first stipulations, that there was to be no love.

She should have realized that while he could order things to happen that it didn't mean they had to. And he should have realized that, also—she knew, even though he hadn't said anything, that he had developed feelings for her, feelings that would have likely overcome any previous bargain they had.

"I'm in a muddle," she said to Precious as she scooped her up and sat down in one of the comfortable chairs in her bedroom.

The room was even more spacious than her London bedroom, decorated with a lively floral wallpaper in tones of pink and pale green, scattered throw rugs in similar colors on the floor, while an enormous fireplace was at one end of the room.

The bed was spacious, too. Lonely. She missed him in her bed, missed having him wrap his arms around her as they slept. Even though that had happened only one night.

And yes, she missed the sex. That had been the one good thing in their marriage, once she had shared her thoughts about it with him.

Late at night, after everyone else in the house was sleeping, she allowed herself to think about all of that: how she felt, how his touch made her melt, while the sight of his body did very interesting things to her insides. How her fingers slid along the planes of his chest, lower to find his erect and impressive cock.

How he'd paid attention to her pleasure, had seemed to find as much joy as she did in her orgasms. He absolutely did know where the clitoris was now, she thought ruefully.

Once she knew for certain she wasn't pregnant she would let him know. And he might choose to visit her for the express purpose of having sex with her. But it wouldn't be the same, not now that she knew she loved him. And had hurt him so badly.

Precious emitted a little yelp as she unconsciously squeezed the dog. "Sorry, sweetie," she said, kissing the top of her wiry little head.

There was a soft knock at the door, and she was already smiling as she turned to speak. "Come in." Because it was now Jane's habit to come to Lavinia's room each morning so the two could discuss what they would do that day—Jane had stopped crying every day, and she was looking more like her usual self. Their mother was sending letters, sometimes two or three in one day, but thus far Jane had declined to read them, saying that there was nothing there that would be useful for her. Lavinia resisted the urge to applaud Jane's newly found fortitude.

"Good morning," Jane said as she came into the room. She wore a simple light blue morning gown and held a bonnet with blue ribbons in her hand. Her hair was pulled back into a low bun, and her expression was warm, her face radiant.

"How are you this morning? You look well."

Jane tilted her head in thought. "I am. I've been reading your book, the newest one—"

Lavinia winced. *My Dark Husband* had been released the day after the engagement party, and was apparently doing well, according to the publisher, but every time she thought about it her heart hurt.

"—and I wonder if you were thinking about the duke when you wrote the count?" Jane nodded. "There are several similarities between the two of them. Though I don't know what happens at the end, don't tell me."

I don't know either. But Jane was speaking about the book, not Lavinia's life.

"You miss him," Jane continued, going to sit down on the small footstool next to Lavinia's bed.

Lavinia opened her mouth to contradict her sister, but of course she couldn't. Not just because it wasn't true, but also because she had never lied to Jane and she saw no need to start now.

"I do."

Jane flung her hands out. "So why not go to him?"

Lavinia shook her head. "It's not that simple."

"Did you tell him how you feel?"

Lavinia paused. Had she? No. Not in so many words. But he—

But he was a self-sufficient, emotion-quashing man who had spent his whole life trying not to be hurt by the people he loved.

Goddamn it.

"No."

Jane raised her eyebrows. "Well, you're an idiot."

Lavinia gave a rueful snort. "It's too late. It's—"

Jane held her hand up. "I'm sorry, is this Lady Lavinia Capel—sorry, *Dutton*—saying something is impossible? I don't believe I am hearing properly."

"He is angry because I didn't tell him the truth." *And I was angry because he didn't see the truth.*

Jane leaped up, slapping her hands together. "So go tell him the truth now! Tell him everything—that you love him, that you want to stay with him, that you find it charming when he stands at attention as though he is in a military parade."

It was impossible not to laugh, especially when Jane did an imitation of Thaddeus's stiff posture.

"He does do that frequently, doesn't he?" Lavinia knew her tone was soft, and knew Jane could hear it, and hear the warmth and emotion she felt toward him.

"Go on," Jane urged. "Go today, let him know that the wonderful, exuberant, intelligent, and literary Lady Lavinia has fallen in love with him, and he'd be an idiot not to want you back."

"So we're both idiots now?" Lavinia asked.

"Something you definitely have in common," Jane replied with a smirk.

His kisses made my knees shake. His passion was all-consuming, and I found myself lost in it, as though he was a drug and I was addicted.

But, I asked myself, was this who I wanted to be?

A woman at the mercy of my husband? A husband who devoted himself to me with such intense commitment it felt as though I was the only woman he had ever known.

It was intoxicating.

But just as the morning after a festive evening, my whole body and mind cringed recalling all of it. How close to lost I was. How I could never be truly free.

Was my freedom worth sacrificing this ultimate pleasure?

My Dark Husband by Percy Wittlesford

Chapter Twenty-Four

She'd been gone long enough so that her bedroom no longer held her scent. And he knew that because he'd taken to sleeping in that enormous bed, even though she wasn't in it.

He tried to immerse himself in his work, but he was unable to focus. He missed her too much. His throat tightened whenever anyone mentioned her, and he felt the familiar chill of loneliness—the chill she'd displaced with her presence—return to settle back into his body.

But if there was one thing Thaddeus was good at, excelled at, it was persevering in a lost cause. He'd done it on the battlefield and he could do it in his life.

Which was why he was returning to finish up some paperwork, despite his secretary telling him it could wait.

"Melmsford!"

Thaddeus raised his voice as he strode toward his office. The door was open, but he couldn't see anyone.

Until a slender blob dressed in somber tones of gray leaped up, a surprised expression on its face.

"Melmsford, there you are." Thaddeus squinted toward the man. "But what are you doing?"

His secretary brushed his trousers free of dust. "I dropped my pen, and it rolled under your desk. I presume you've told the staff not to clean in here?" He sneezed as he spoke, punctuating his question.

Thaddeus frowned. "I don't know. Perhaps Lav—perhaps the duchess reminded the staff not to disturb me while I was working—" Another quiet bit of courtesy she'd done just because she was a thoughtful person. "I don't want to embarrass Mrs. Webb. How about we take care of this ourselves?"

Melmsford looked surprised, but in a pleased way. As though Thaddeus had confirmed something he hadn't expected.

"We don't have a broom, though."

Thaddeus whipped off his jacket and flung it onto the couch, striding toward his desk. "We'll need to get creative, then," he said. He glanced around the office, his gaze finally settling on the table where the whisky and glasses were kept. He took the linen underneath the whisky—likely to catch any spills—and then snatched a piece of paper from his desk, a recent bill he and Melmsford had already dealt with. Then he got onto his hands and knees and stuck the linen underneath the desk, dragging it over the floor in an attempt to catch the dust.

"You don't need to join me," Thaddeus said as he noticed Melmsford putting his hands on his knees on his way down to the floor.

"Solidarity in the task, Your Grace," Melmsford replied, at which Thaddeus snorted in response.

At least he had Melmsford. And Sebastian and Nash. They wouldn't be enough to ease the ache in his heart her departure had caused, but they would keep him from being entirely lonely.

Except that Sebastian and Nash already had wives they loved, and they'd soon have families, and Melmsford had his own life, and Thaddeus couldn't force his secretary to be friends with him. To keep him from utter solitude.

The rest of his life unfolded with startling clarity: Thaddeus, alone for the rest of his life, doing his duty, since that was the only thing that was valued about him. A duke, but not a beloved duke. Not beloved by the woman he wanted to be beloved by.

Goddamn it.

"Your Grace," Melmsford began in a hesitant tone as Thaddeus felt his heart constrict, "might I ask if there is anything you might want advice about?"

"I know you're not married," Thaddeus replied.

"No," Melmsford said slowly, "but I do observe people. It is rather my hobby. Well, that and reading books."

"Books like *My Dark Husband*," Thaddeus said, trying to keep the bitterness from his voice. But Melmsford didn't know it was actually Lavinia writing the books. And none of that mattered anyway, did it? The only thing that mattered was that he loved her.

"Yes. And as I said, I know people, and I know

that the duchess—though she is proud and stubborn—has feelings for you."

Thaddeus turned to glare at his secretary who, to his credit, did not flinch. "Why would you say this?"

Melmsford's expression was as dry as his normally cheery-faced secretary could make it. "Because she has gone to the country and I saw her face when she left and you are even more military than usual. The two of you are both suffering."

Thaddeus reined in his urge to growl—*growl!*—in Melmsford's face. Instead he asked, "What would you say I do, then?"

Melmsford raised his eyebrows. "I am so pleased you asked. Because in Mr. Wittlesford's last book, *Storming the Castle*, something similar happened, and the resolution was very dramatic: the heroine had to run through rosebushes to rescue her lover, and then when she got to him, she was all scratched and her gown was torn, but she told him how she felt."

"So you're suggesting I run through rose-bushes?"

Melmsford took a deep breath and glanced to the ceiling as though hoping for patience. "No, Your Grace. The point is to tell her how you feel. The rosebushes are merely a dramatic fillip."

Tell her how I feel. He had been about to tell her how he felt, how he wanted her to stay with him forever. Until the night of the reading, when he'd realized she'd kept something so important from him.

"The thing that all of the books I read tell us

is that it is important to talk. You can clear up a misunderstanding, either big or little, with a simple conversation. You can share your thoughts and feelings with someone else, perhaps clarify an action or a previous event with your words."

Thaddeus absorbed Melmsford's words, feeling the impact of them through his whole body.

Melmsford was right.

Perhaps Lavinia and he were both wrong—but was that any reason to deny each other happiness? If he told her the truth, laid it all out for her, then he would know for certain how she felt.

And if she still said no?

Then he could live out the rest of his lonely life knowing he had done the right thing, even if it wasn't the result he wanted.

He rose, putting the now filthy square of linen on his desk. Melmsford followed him up, brushing off his hands.

"You should be writing one of those books, Melmsford." He clapped his secretary on the shoulder. "I am going to do as you and Mr. Wittlesford suggest. I am going to talk to the duchess."

He took a deep breath. "And I am going to do it right now."

IT WAS ALL well and good to decide to make a dramatic exit to go tell your spouse that you are, actually, madly in love with them.

But dramatic exits were for people who didn't have to arrange the care and feeding of a pet— Precious hadn't yet warmed up to Jane—or for people who didn't have a carriage just lying about handily in the carriage house. Lavinia had sent back the carriage that had brought them to Medcross, because the town was within walking distance, and she saw no point in depriving the footmen of London active work, since she didn't plan on going anywhere.

Besides, she didn't want to be the kind of person who just kept a carriage on the vague chance that it might be needed. So when it was actually needed, it wasn't there.

Therefore, her dramatic exit was actually two days after she'd decided she would storm back to London and lay her heart bare. When she wasn't trying to persuade Precious that Jane was trustworthy, she and Jane were discussing the best way to get to London. She could take the train—but the nearest station was over three miles away, and the only conveyance the estate had was a small trap for errands, and it had a broken wheel. She could walk to the train station, but she'd need to carry a case with her essentials. Plus she'd be walking on her own, because Jane couldn't very well walk her there and then have to walk back alone for a total of six miles.

The mail coach still made occasional stops, but the next available seat in it was in two weeks, and that was far too long to sit around thinking about how you were madly in love with someone who was so far away. Besides which, it'd be odd to tell him, "I realized I felt this way two weeks ago, but then I had to wait to get to town."

It was hardly romantic to wait for an open seat.

And she wanted to see him *now*. She didn't want to wait for the train, or the trap to be fixed, or the mail coach. She needed to tell him how she felt.

"That's it," she said at last on the third morning after she'd decided. She and Jane were sitting outside on the terrace overlooking the garden. It was warm out, but it wasn't sunny. The view was still lovely, however, with the late summer flowers waving softly in the breeze.

"What's it?" Jane asked. Precious stood by her feet, looking at her expectantly. The dog had finally come to realize that Jane gave as many treats as Lavinia did, and now followed her around as much as she did Lavinia.

That was one thing solved, at least.

"I'm going to London." She rose with determination from her chair, putting her mug of tea down on the small table between them.

"How?" Jane asked, sounding not the least bit alarmed, as she had adjusted to Lavinia's ways. The sisters had always been close, but they hadn't always understood one another. Now, through lengthy conversations and promising always to tell the truth, they did a bit more. Lavinia wished Jane's own concerns hadn't made her choice of Mr. McTavish nearly inevitable, and she was just grateful that her sister hadn't been stuck in a terrible decision when it was too late to change it.

"I'm going to the vicar," she said. "He has a carriage he uses to pay calls on his parishioners. I'll borrow it."

"And take it to London?" Now Jane did sound skeptical. Likely because Lavinia had never really driven a carriage. But how hard could it be?

"Mmm-hmm. I won't tell him where I'm going. I'll be back before he realizes I've taken it for longer than I said."

"You're going to lie to a vicar," Jane said in a wry tone.

Lavinia planted her hands on her hips. "Look, I don't believe it's wrong to lie when you're lying for the right thing. And getting to Thaddeus as soon as I can is the right thing."

Jane shrugged. "Fine, but make certain to take some money and a warm shawl."

"Yes, Mother," Lavinia teased.

Jane wrinkled her nose, likely at being compared to their mother, but got up to where they kept their money—only a few coins, since the estate paid all of the bills. That had been one of the missives Lavinia had received from Thaddeus, assuring her she would be taken care of.

"I'll go up for the shawl," Lavinia said.

"I VERY MUCH appreciate this, Mr. Davis," Lavinia said. "And Mrs. Davis, I hope this doesn't inconvenience you too much."

The vicar and his wife stood in their front yard, arm in arm, as Lavinia spun some sort of story about needing to sneak away to purchase a birthday gift for Jane.

It was almost too easy, and Lavinia had to remind herself she was not writing a book, so she didn't need to overexplain what was happening.

"It is no trouble at all, Your Grace," the vicar replied. "We are glad to do what we can."

"And I am certain the duke will want to offer a donation to the church when he hears of your kindness." At least she hoped he would, and not punish the vicar for providing the means for his wayward wife to return. And if not, she'd send them earnings from her books after the next royalty statement.

"That is not necessary," the vicar said, his cheeks flushing.

"But it would be helpful," the vicar's wife added, darting a quick admonishing glance toward her husband.

"I will be back before you know it," Lavinia replied. She watched as the vicar's handyman brought the carriage around. It was small, smaller even than the carriage in which she, Jane, and Thaddeus had ridden in so long ago. It was clearly made for short trips, and she hoped it was sturdy enough to withstand the time it would take to get her to London.

The horse pulling it looked solid enough, however.

"What is your horse's name?" Lavinia asked. Since they were going to be spending so much time together, it would be good if she knew its name.

"Martin," the vicar's wife said. "Named after my late father."

"Martin," Lavinia repeated. The handyman held the carriage steady as she walked toward it, her bag looped over one arm. She flung it onto the seat, then took the handyman's hand as he helped her up into the carriage.

Please let me look as though I've done this before, she pleaded silently.

The reins were dangling in front of her, and she picked them up, glancing over at the vicar and his wife. The handyman stepped away, and she took a deep breath.

"Let's go, Martin," she said, slapping the reins on the horse's back.

The horse began to move, thank God, and she breathed a sigh of relief.

"Thank you again," Lavinia called over her shoulder as they walked down the lane.

She hoped the hardest part would be driving the carriage. She strongly suspected that attempting to change the course of her life so she wasn't miserable and alone for the rest of it would be a bit more difficult.

My mind waged war with itself for the next few weeks. I was enthralled by him, but I was also appalled; he was demanding, forceful, and proud. But he was also compelling, forceful, and determined.

He devoted himself to me with such fervor I barely remembered who I was anymore.

I didn't know how much longer I could stand it. Any of it.

I needed to decide my future.

My Dark Husband by Percy Wittlesford

Chapter Twenty-Five

"Good luck, Your Grace."

Melmsford stood on the steps of the town house as Thaddeus mounted his horse. He'd decided the fastest way to get to her was on horseback—not only did he not want to chafe inside a carriage as it made its lumbering way into the country, but then he wouldn't have to wait for all the inevitable preparations to be made, regardless of how much he might insist he did not need a basket full of food or clothes for any possible occasion.

Instead, he'd tossed his linens into a small pack like the ones he had used in the army and ordered his horse to be brought around. The only person who knew where he was headed was Melmsford, who had promised not to panic if he didn't hear from Thaddeus for a few days.

"If any of my friends or family visit"—namely Sebastian, Nash, or Ana Maria—"just tell them I was called away unexpectedly. They'll likely figure out where I've gone."

Because all of them had gone and fallen in love, too. He just hoped his ending would be as happy as theirs.

"Yes, Your Grace."

Thaddeus nodded to Melmsford once more, then urged his horse into a trot, the fastest he could go while still on London streets. He would make up time once he was safely away from the city.

He wasn't allowing himself to think any more about what might happen if she said no, even after he told her how he felt. After he'd apologized for insisting on the bargain in the first place, assuming she wouldn't want to try to make the best of things. After he'd told her it didn't matter that she hadn't told him everything about herself, especially because at no time had she any reason to expect that they had a future together.

What he was allowing himself to think about was what to say, how to express himself when he had so little practice with it. The only thing he was good at was giving orders and maintaining discipline, and neither of those things would work in this situation. In fact, it was safe to say that those things would have the opposite effect.

"Lavinia, my dear," he began as Crusader maneuvered past a cart full of fish, "I wish to tell you how I feel. I deeply regret—no, that won't work, I don't want her to think I regret her."

Crusader whinnied.

"Lavinia, I—I have—I am," he said, shaking his head at just how tongue-tied he was, even when his horse was the only thing within earshot.

How could he possibly persuade her?

He could show her. But how? It wasn't as though he could sweep her into his arms and kiss her—

they'd done all that, and done all that quite well, so how could he kiss her in such a different way to convince her of his true feelings?

And it wasn't as though he could refuse to kiss her, thereby making his declaration of love clear. That would be ridiculous.

He'd left the gifts he'd bought for her at home—he didn't want to remind her even more that he held all the wealth and bounty in their relationship.

But he didn't own the one thing he desired more than anything, and that was her. And even if she said yes, he still wouldn't own her. Nor did he want to; he wanted her to be her own proud, spirited self, capable of handling whatever came her way but generous enough to accept help when it was proffered.

He'd just have to trust that he would find the right words when he saw her.

"WE ARE DOING quite well, Martin," Lavinia said in satisfaction. She'd been driving for about two hours, and nothing untoward had happened thus far. She'd asked a few people along the way if she was traveling in the right direction, and they'd said yes, though all of them had given her odd expressions when she'd said she was bound for London.

Natural enough, since she doubted whether young women usually took off for London in a vicar's carriage. Perhaps more should. Then every woman, not just the ones with access to vicar's carriages and pocket money could find their true happiness.

So she wasn't expecting it when the carriage suddenly lurched, sending her flying over its side and onto the road.

She landed with a thump, but thankfully on her backside, so she wasn't hurt as much as she might have been had she landed on a less plentiful area. "I will never wish you to be smaller again," she murmured as she got to her hands and knees. Martin had stopped, and thankfully it seemed only the carriage was damaged—the side closer to her had a bent wheel, and the carriage itself was sitting at an odd angle. Martin shifted in the harness, and Lavinia scrambled up to get him out of the buckles or whatever they were called before the carriage had time to collapse more, possibly bringing Martin down with it.

Thank goodness Martin was so good-natured, because it took Lavinia some time to undo him. She was conscious the whole time that the carriage might spill over, bringing them both down, and she tried to work quickly, but the buckles were old and the leather was stiff, and her fingers were unaccustomed to the work.

"Mother should have hired a coachman to teach me all this instead of the piano," she grumbled. "This, at least, is something that is practical, whereas my piano-playing is only good for scaring dogs and small children." She chuckled at herself as she undid the last buckle—finally—and took Martin's bridle to lead him safely away from the carnage.

"Well," she said, giving Martin a skeptical look, "it appears I will be making the rest of the journey on your back."

She looked down the dusty road. She had no idea where she was, nor how long it would take her to get anywhere. There were no houses in sight, and the sun was sliding down from high noon, which probably meant it was around three o'clock in the afternoon.

Maybe you should have asked someone how long it would take to get to London.

Because that would have been a sensible thought. But if she had, then someone would know where she was headed, and people would likely pour out of the woodwork to stop her or try to give her advice.

That was the difficulty with being the new shiny thing in a small village—everyone was suddenly an expert on what you should do and when. As it was, the vicar and his wife were probably telling everyone they spoke to that she had borrowed their carriage, so when she didn't return within a few hours it would be the only thing the town talked about.

But meanwhile, the town was two hours by carriage behind her, London was however many hours by horseback in front of her, and she had to get moving or she'd end up confessing her love to Martin, which wasn't the point at all.

How was she to get up on his back? She hadn't ridden very many horses in her lifetime—she far preferred her own two feet as a mode of transportation—and when she had, there had been a groom and a box to help her up.

She flung her arms over Martin's back and jumped up, only to fall back down to the ground and scrape her front on his harness.

He uttered a low whinny, and she could have sworn he gave her a disdainful look.

"I'm going to try again, Martin." She stepped back, trying to give herself a running start, only to end up in exactly the same place. Only now Martin was outright glaring at her.

She took his bridle and sighed. "Fine. We'll do it your way. I'll walk."

This wasn't the romantic gesture she had been imagining—she'd hoped that she could triumphantly sweep into London and dash up the front steps to the town house, burst into his study and confront him with both her apology and her love.

Walking bedraggledly into London with an equally tired and more annoyed horse was not what she wanted.

But since she wasn't the author of her own story, she had to follow the plot that was being given to her.

So she kept walking.

And then she heard a distant rumble and looked up at the sky. "Rain," she muttered. "Of course it's going to rain."

THADDEUS KEPT UP a steady pace as he left London, Crusader clearly relishing the chance to run. The pace and the sun combined to make him feel as though he were about to boil, so he managed to tear off his cravat and use it to wipe his head of sweat before tucking it into his pocket.

But he must have put his hat back at an odd angle, because it flew off as soon as his hands were back on the reins. He glanced back at it, lying dusty on the ground.

"Forget it," he said. "She won't care if I'm wearing a hat, and it's not worth the time to go back and get it. Besides which, it's likely too filthy to wear."

There was no one within earshot except Crusader, who didn't seem to have an opinion on Thaddeus's headgear.

If he were not so focused on his mission, he would have enjoyed the ride; it had been months since he had allowed himself the joy of going flat-out on his horse. Because it had been months since he had received the dukedom, and there had been too much to do to indulge himself.

But he was focused, although he was dreading reaching her as much as he wished he were there right now, and not hours from now. He still didn't know what he would say. He definitely didn't know what she would say. Likely she'd have more and better words than he did, and he hoped that her words would give him the answer he craved.

Yes.

Yes, please.

Please, yes.

Yes. Yes.

And variations on those two words.

Crusader was laboring by this point, and Thaddeus realized they had been on the road for at least an hour—the sun was now hidden behind some clouds, offering some relief, and they had passed a few farmers' carts and squires' carriages, but now they were on the road alone. Thaddeus slowed his horse, then stopped him, dismounting and gathering the reins to bring

Crusader over to a patch of grass. Crusader took the hint right away, and Thaddeus gazed out at the landscape, wondering if there was some water nearby. He should have prepared for the journey by bringing something to drink. When he'd been in the army, he would have had just as few belongings with him, but he would also have had the benefit of a cook, a batman, and any number of subordinates to bring him what he required.

He really was privileged, both before when he was in the military and now that he was a duke.

But out here, with just his horse and a dry throat, he was Thaddeus. Just as simple as that.

It wouldn't matter that he was a duke with all the status and wealth of his position if he didn't get her back. If he didn't see a future with her by his side.

And also, he admitted ruefully, if he didn't get himself and his horse something to drink.

"Come along," he said to Crusader, taking his reins and starting to walk down the road.

He'd let his horse rest a bit and hope he ran into someone else out here who might be able to give him directions to water if the person didn't have any on them.

And then he heard the rumble above and winced as he looked up at the sky. "Rain," he muttered.

Once again, it appeared Crusader was indifferent to the topic at hand.

"Of course it's going to bloody rain," he said, shaking his head. His hatless head. So he wouldn't even have the meager protection that would have offered.

Why had he thought it such a good idea to leave right away? Not take time to prepare? Mount this campaign as he had so many before, albeit this time with a different purpose.

But no. He had to dash off without thinking.

He had never done that before. *Love has changed you*. And that was a good thing—he didn't need a list, or a plan, or anything but his heart and his words.

In some way, that realization made him feel better. Even though he—and his horse—were still thirsty, and were about to get rained on.

He just needed to get to her. Wet, hatless, parched, and humble. He needed her.

THE RAIN STARTED slowly at first, but increased until it was a literal deluge. At least the rain wasn't cold; the day had been warm, so for a bit the water was a relief. Until it was not. Lavinia was drenched within minutes, and Martin's reins were already wet, while his hooves plodded on the now moist earth, shooting up mud onto her skirts.

And she had no idea how much further it was to London. There had been a tiny possibility she could get onto Martin's back before, but now that possibility was nil; there was no chance she could launch herself onto a wet, slippery horse while standing on sodden ground.

There was nothing for it but to laugh. If she had written this scene in a book, she would have wondered if she had gone too far—the tortured heroine struggling along in the rain, guiding a stolen horse on a path that might take hours.

"You would have had to have a different name, though," she told Martin. "Perhaps something like Love's Forlorn Hope, or something like that."

She peered through the rain at the road ahead. It was ridiculous to keep looking, hoping to see another human who might be able to help her. And yet she kept looking.

"I seem to be an optimist," she commented to Martin. "I never knew that about myself. I've learned so many things in the past few months." Things like how far she'd go to protect her family, that she wasn't afraid to ask for what she wanted, and that it was just as easy to hurt someone who was emotionally reserved as it was to hurt someone far more open.

That last part stung. She'd have to apologize for it, for not telling him. But she hadn't thought he'd be interested, and it had felt as though she wanted to keep something of herself back from him, for fear that she would lose her heart and he would own her.

"Well, that did happen, so I was right to be concerned," she remarked dryly.

She exhaled, glancing ahead in her fruitless optimism, hoping this time she'd see someone.

And then she did. Her eyes widened, and her pace quickened, and she ran through all the possible scenarios in her head: the person would demand money to help her, the person would immediately locate an umbrella and hold it over her head, the person would bring her back to their home and settle her in front of a fire with a large mug of tea.

The one scenario she hadn't thought of was that it would be he.

But it was.

"Thad—?" she began, halting in her tracks.

Martin nudged her arm, as though to urge her forward.

But she couldn't move.

He was there. In front of her. Several yards away, of course, but she could tell it was him. Nobody but him was that tall and had such an air of command, even walking in the rain guiding a horse.

She saw when he recognized her, and her heart leaped at seeing his expression change.

And then she *could* move, she could *run*, and she did, Martin trotting along beside her, her skirts hampering her movements until she reached down to pull them up over her knees so she could run faster.

"Lavinia!" he shouted, and then he was running too, and then they both stopped short, just a foot between them, and she stared at him, a tiny part of her wondering if this was a thunderstorm-induced dream.

"Hello," she said, as though they were meeting in a ballroom and not on a muddy rural road.

"Hello," he replied.

He was soaking wet also, the rain plastering his hair down on his head.

"You don't have a hat," she remarked.

"No. Lost it."

"Ah."

"You don't have a saddle," he said.

"Never had it," she replied. "The carriage broke, and so—" she said, gesturing toward Martin.

"Where were you going?"

He spoke softly, but Lavinia heard every word.

"To you. I was going to you."

He stepped forward then, wrapping his arms around her in a tight hold.

She buried her face in his coat, which smelled of wet wool and him.

"I was going to you, too," he said.

"What do you want?" he asked.

I shook my head. I didn't know how to answer, not without revealing my true feelings.

He cupped my chin and raised my face up. His eyes glittered with a dark emotion I didn't dare name.

"Tell me," he demanded.

So I did.

My Dark Husband by Percy Wittlesford

Chapter Twenty-Six

Thaddeus didn't want to release her. Not now, not ever. But they still had to talk.

He drew away slowly, his hand sliding on her damp arm.

She looked up at him as she bit her lip.

"I'm sorry."

"I'm sorry."

They spoke at the same time, and then both of them laughed.

"You first," she said, nodding to him.

He took a deep breath. The rain had eased, but it was still falling, and there was moisture on her face, the raindrops sliding down as though they were tears.

"I shouldn't have insisted on the bargain," he began. He glanced away, hoping the words would come somehow. "I shouldn't have kept you at a distance." He looked back at her, at her lovely, vibrant face, at the damp strands of hair sticking to her skin and shoulders. "I didn't want to fall in love. If you recall, I insisted that love was entirely out of the question."

"Oh, I recall," she said dryly.

"But I was wrong. So absolutely, terribly wrong." He gripped her upper arms. "Lavinia, I am an idiot."

The corners of her mouth tilted up in a slight smile.

"I wanted to ask you to stay, but then I heard the reading, and I knew you had kept that secret from me—"

Her smile faltered.

"But I think I understand why you did it." He took a deep breath. "Not that it matters, that I understand. You are your own person, you can and should make your own decisions."

He paused.

"I just want to be with you when you make them."

Her eyes widened.

"I love you, Lavinia. Come home with me?" It was a question, not a demand.

She closed her eyes for a moment, and he felt his chest tighten, as though his heart was expanding in emotion. He wouldn't believe she would say yes until he heard the word.

"I have something to say," she said, then opened her eyes to meet his.

He held his breath in anticipation.

WASN'T SHE SUPPOSED to be good at words or something? She was standing here in the midst of a rainstorm with only two horses in attendance, able to speak her mind, to tell him everything that she felt about him, about them, about everything.

And all that she could come up with to say was— "I—" And then she stopped.

What did she—?

"Yes?" He sounded pained. Of course, he didn't yet know how she felt.

"I am an idiot," she said, her lips twisting at repeating his earlier words. "Because I know what it is to hold yourself back from the people you care about. I love Jane, but she doesn't always understand me. Though that is changing," she admitted. But that wasn't the point now. "I thought we could have the bargain you suggested without either one of us getting hurt. Or attached, for that matter."

The rain had nearly stopped now. But she was still dripping wet, her clothes clinging to her damp skin. She would be feeling entirely miserable if she wasn't also so intent on telling him how she felt. If her whole body didn't feel as though it was on the verge of exploding from her emotions.

"But we can't." She shook her head to emphasize her point, and drops of water scattered through the air. "It is impossible for me to know you and not to love you. I even love the annoying things—like how you are so regimented and determined, and how you spelled out precisely what I could expect in our marriage." She smiled up at him. "Even though you turned out to be absolutely wrong."

He raised an eyebrow. "I have never been told I was thoroughly wrong before." His lips curled up at the corners. "And I have never been so grateful to be wrong before." He took her back into his arms, his mouth finding hers as his hands wound their way to her back, holding her in possession. Though now she wanted to be owned.

Their kiss wasn't a soft kiss of apology; it was a passionate, fiery kiss that conveyed just how close they came to utter unhappiness. Lavinia bit his lip, then swept her tongue into his mouth as his hands slid down to cup her arse, pulling her body up against his hardness.

His tongue clashed with hers, and she heard herself actually growl, at which he chuckled low in his throat. She had one hand at the back of his neck, pressing him close, and the other hand at the small of his back, her fingers splayed to feel the strength of him.

"We cannot fuck out here on the road," he murmured against her mouth. "So I have to ask again," he continued, lowering his mouth to press a kiss against the base of her throat, "will you come home with me?"

She tilted her head back as she arched her back, pressing her aching breasts into his hard chest. "Yes, please," she replied, gasping as he yanked her up harder against him, positioning her so she rode his thigh, giving her the contact she craved.

"Come for me, Lavinia," he said as she began to move against him. "Use me, I'm begging you."

The ragged edge of his voice nearly broke her, and she bit her lip as she shifted to rub herself against him.

His strong hand held her up so she had no fear of falling, and his other hand was at the juncture of her hip, his hand clamped down on her, then moving in to stroke her there.

"Oh God, Thaddeus," she said as the orgasm hit her, and she closed her eyes as the passion swept over her in waves, his grunt of satisfaction the very best type of punctuation.

"Let's go home," he said as her shuddering stopped. "I need to get you in a bed. And out of these wet clothes."

"Yes, please," she said again.

"I choose you," I said.

For the first time since I'd met and married him, I saw him smile.

And knew I was truly home.

My Dark Husband by Percy Wittlesford

Epilogue

"I am never leaving this bed," Lavinia declared.

Thaddeus chuckled softly in reply. His hand was splayed on her belly, his leg was flung over hers so that even if she did want to leave this bed—which she did not—she would not be able to.

They were in the London town house, in her bedroom, and it was already past ten o'clock in the morning.

"We have to get up sometime," he said, kissing her shoulder. The whole room smelled of sex, wonderful, passionate sex, and Lavinia had been naked and in this bed for nearly twelve hours. Thaddeus had been naked for nearly the same time, only Lavinia had wanted him to keep his boots on—and nothing else—for a while. Just for fun, but it did have a few added benefits, most notably when he bent her over the bed and took her from behind.

They'd finally managed to make it back to Thaddeus's country house, collecting a smug and not very surprised Jane and a very excited Precious and making their way back to London. After drying off, of course. And with Thaddeus tossing his title around in order to quickly hire a carriage. Not to mention his making a hefty donation to the church for recompense of the broken carriage.

Jane had decided not to return to their parents' house, and she and Percy had taken up lodgings a few streets away from where Thaddeus and Lavinia lived. Henry McTavish had not only not spoken to Jane since the night of their engagement party, but he had also managed to become betrothed to one of Mrs. McTavish's distant relation's daughter.

Lavinia was just happy she never had to speak to Mrs. McTavish again.

"Do you think anyone would know if I put Mrs. McTavish in a book?" she asked as Thaddeus's hand moved lower. "Ohh," she said as his palm cupped her sex. His finger found her clitoris and began to rub in precisely the right way as she closed her eyes and relished how her body felt.

Until—"Oh!" she said in a very different tone, leaping off the bed and running for the washbasin. She reached it just in time, her stomach ejecting whatever was left from her meal of the night before.

And then he was there, behind her, wrapping his solid arm around her body. "Are you all right?" he asked.

She raised her head as she counted the days, meeting his gaze in the mirror above the basin.

"I am," she replied. A tiny smile creased her lips. "I think we're going to be having Precious junior in about seven months." She'd waited to be certain before believing it herself, much less telling him.

He froze for a moment, then his eyes widened and his grip tightened, and he had turned her around in his arms and was kissing her.

"I love you," he said between kisses.

"I love you," she replied. "And your thighs."

He snorted in laughter as he held her as close as he possibly could.

Don't miss Megan Frampton's next
tempting Avon romance

GENTLEMAN SEEKS BRIDE

On sale November 2021

Wherever your favorite books are sold

Chapter One

Life was always easy for Thomas Sharpe.

He was witty, gracious, and unexpectedly charming. He didn't enter a room so much as owned it; women wanted to be seduced by him, and men wanted to be him. He was tall, handsome, and excelled at everything he did.

Life was easy.

Until it wasn't.

He could recall, to a second, the moment when things shifted. When his father entered the family dining room, his hat in his hands, his face ashen.

When his mother half rose from her chair, one hand to her throat.

It was a cold, dreary day, one where the idea of the sun was just that—an idea, not reality. A day when you looked outside and imagined all the ways the world could go wrong, secure in the comfort of your home and the knowledge that what you were imagining was just your imagination.

Unless it wasn't.

His father looked directly at his mother. "It's gone, Matilda. All of it. Gone."

His mother's eyes widened, and she slumped back down in her chair, her hand now clutching her heart. And then her expression changed from one of despair to one of desperate hope.

Thomas watched, a growing sickening feeling in his throat as his mother's gaze shifted to him. She had a fierce look in her eye, a look that demanded attention.

"It's up to you," she said. She nodded toward his younger sisters. "What will happen to them? To us?"

Thomas glanced at them, at Julia, who was just about to make her debut, and had been talking about nothing but for weeks. At fourteen-year-old Alice, who was excruciatingly shy because of a bad stammer, who would likely never want to be seen in public, but would need to be cared for the rest of her life.

At his parents, who were already old. Their children had come late in life, and this investment—the one they'd staked everything that wasn't already entailed on—was supposed to see them through to the ends of their lives. Provide a dowry for Julia, who wasn't blessed with Thomas's good looks. A poor, plain debutante from a respectable family had as much a chance at making a good marriage as Thomas had of going unnoticed at a social gathering.

It was up to him. It was all up to him.

He didn't need her to explain; after all, Alice had pointed out, ladies had done the same thing for their families for centuries: marry someone wealthy to enable the family to survive. They had even joked about it, back when it seemed an impossibility that they would come to this point.

And now the joke had become reality, and it was all up to him.

How could he refuse his mother's plea? There was no other choice, not one that would provide for his family. Even though it made a fierce anger burn in his chest. The inequity of it, having to sell himself in order to ensure his family survived.

He nodded as he took a deep breath. "I'll do it."

And so, with those three words, Thomas set off on an heiress hunt.

It was nearly two years after he'd accepted his future and Thomas was no closer to finding the woman of his dreams. Specifically, an unmarried woman with enough of a fortune to keep his family in relative comfort. His earlier dreams—dreams where someone would keep his attention long enough for him to develop a lasting affection for them—had fizzled at the same time as his family's money.

Julia had made her debut, and had thankfully married a baronet's third son, a man who had secured himself a vicarage. She seemed happy, and had one child with another on the way. She was taken care of.

But his parents and Alice were not. And things were only getting worse. Alice was sixteen now, and still painfully shy. His father now walked much more slowly, while his mother had never been able to shake last winter's cough.

Doctor visits. Upkeep for the estate, which provided land for the farmers who paid rent, the family's only source of income now that they had no investments. No money in savings. A few nice things for Alice, who never asked for anything, and who was clearly terrified at having to survive alone when their parents died.

It all cost money. Money that was just out of Thomas's grasp. Money that went to other, less comely gentlemen in as desperate straits.

Despite—or perhaps because of—his undeniable charm, he hadn't been able to get a lady to commit to him for life.

He was someone with whom they flirted, or sometimes more, but take him as a permanent partner?

No.

It seemed that they thought that he might be so irresistible as to be irresistible to *everyone*. That a vow of marriage wasn't enough to halt the perpetual interest he seemed to attract wherever he went.

It was wearisome, frankly, to be charming but not too much so; to be witty without being too clever; to be as well-garbed as any other gentleman without seeming to make it apparent he was far better-looking than any other gentleman.

Which was why he was on the hunt. Again.

The room was full to bursting with the best Society had to offer: ribald chaperones who insisted on cavorting, drinking, and gambling more than their demure charges; patriarchs who had been forced to attend by their insistent wives and then quickly escaped into a back room to smoke cigars and inhale port; the demure charges whose sole goal was to attract a gentleman they could tolerate for the rest of their lives, and vice versa; and the eagle-eyed mothers, who could sniff out, to a penny, just how much a prospective husband had. The night air was crisp and refreshing, but inside it was stiflingly warm, a testament to the party's success.

And Thomas was in the middle of it, navigating through the party's rough course, adjusting his behavior depending on whom he was talking to.

"Miss Porter," he said as mildly as he could. The lady stood alone at the edge of the dance floor, close to a cluster of chatting debutantes. She glanced wistfully toward them as they burst into laughter. One of Miss Porter's hands held a shaky glass of punch, while the other adjusted her hair behind her ear, felt her necklace, scratched her nose, or simply dangled in the air as though waiting for the next task its owner assigned.

Miss Porter reminded him of his sister Alice— clearly shy, obviously in a form of mild agony at being in such a large company.

Unlike Alice, however, Miss Porter was of age to make her debut in Society, and she had, it sounded like, several sisters who needed their eldest sister to hurry up and get married so they could also make their debuts.

This evening she wore the pristine white favored by most of the young ladies in attendance, a signal to the single gentlemen that they had not yet been matrimonially acquired. Rather like waving a red cape toward a bull.

Thomas had responded to her signaling with paying her particular attention at parties, but not so much that other ladies believed he was taken.

But Miss Porter either hadn't noticed or was ignoring Thomas's gentle hints, and he didn't want to overwhelm her with his attentions or force her into anything just because she was naturally timid.

Yes, he needed a wife, and Miss Porter's family definitely came with enough money, but if she wasn't in complete agreement with his suit, if it wasn't what she wanted, then he would not pursue her.

It shouldn't matter, the lady's happiness, not if it meant he could rescue his family, but Thomas wasn't able to *completely* lose his humanity in search of a bride. In that he differed from other gentlemen in his situation; he'd lost a few potential wives to more aggressive suitors, ones who didn't seem to care if the lady they'd chosen actually liked them. And had seen as those wives had been worn down by their husbands' indifference, or worse.

He would not be that kind of husband, even if his motivations for marriage were the same.

"Yes, Mr. Sharpe?" Miss Porter spoke at last.

"May I take that? I would not want your lovely gown to be ruined." He gestured toward the hand holding the punch, which wavered even more as he spoke.

She nodded, a shy smile crossing her face.

Another burst of laughter. Another longing look.

And not at him. Not what he was accustomed to, but it was almost refreshing not to be the focus of attention for once.

"Miss Porter, might I introduce you to Lady Emily?" Thomas nodded toward the clear ringleader of the group, a young lady who was already betrothed to a gentleman back home, but was in London so she "wouldn't miss out on anything."

Thomas had deduced that Lady Emily enjoyed being admired, meaning she had something in common with everybody else in the world, but she had a very specific limit to said admiration. Thomas usually counted his compliments on the fingers of his left hand; if he reached his thumb, it was likely one compliment too many.

"Oh, yes, please," Miss Porter said.

"A moment, Miss Porter." Thomas lowered his head so he could speak close to her ear. "If you want to tell Lady Emily she looks splendid, or any such words to that nature, please observe the rules."

"Rules?" she replied back in a puzzled tone.

"No more than four such thoughts. Otherwise, Lady Emily gets snappish. Rather like when you feed too many treats to a dog."

She smothered a giggle, turning bright eyes up to him. Thank goodness—she seemed much more relaxed, much less susceptible to being unfortunately judged by the group of ladies, some of whom he knew could be quite judgmental.

Thanks to his mission, he'd paid scrupulous attention to each of the possible candidates that might save his family.

Lady Emily was off his list, but she was a valuable asset. Miss Hemingsworth would settle for nothing less than a title, which he did not have. Ladies Thomasina and Theodora were nearly indistinguishable from one another, even though they were not related.

He'd confused one with the other too many times for either to believe he was serious in his admiration. Both were inordinately silly, so a part of him wondered if he had confused them deliberately, so as to avoid having to possibly marry one of them.

He held his arm out for Miss Porter, who took it with her hair-adjusting hand.

"Thank you, Mr. Sharpe," she said again.

"Of course." He patted the hand that rested on his sleeve.

"Ladies," Thomas began as they drew up to the group, "might I have the honor of introducing Miss Porter? Miss Porter is desirous of making the acquaintance of the most beautiful and charming ladies in London. Naturally I brought her to you." He accompanied his words with a bow, keeping his eyes on Lady Emily, knowing how she reacted would dictate what the rest of the ladies would do.

"Oh, Mr. Sharpe," Lady Emily replied with a knowing smirk, "you are too kind."

"I am not being kind, merely truthful," Thomas said smoothly.

"Miss Porter, do not believe a word this rascal says," Lady Emily said. "Come here, let me speak to you a moment. I do not believe we have met."

Miss Porter released her hold on Thomas's arm, but not before mouthing "thank you" to him as she turned toward her new friend.

"If you will excuse me," Thomas said, "I will leave you to discuss my various attributes."

Smiles all around, and then Thomas strode over to a more discreet corner than the one Miss

Porter had been hiding in, taking a deep breath as he allowed himself to relax.

It was exhausting. *He* was exhausted.

He turned to see Miss Porter with a delighted smile on her face. His task was arduous, but if he could help someone along the way, it was nearly worth it.

And he'd promised himself a night off the next day.

tlemen. She got a small sum from one when he kicked her out for cheating on him and nothing from the other one because he threatened to send around the photos his private investigator snapped of her. Her name was variously Sharon Downes and Sylvia Tralins. I got this from two newspapermen. Just thought you'd like to know. Should I keep digging?"

"Definitely. I just wonder if Mainwaring knew about any of this."

He laughed. "The way you described how hooked he is—you think it would've made any difference?"

EIGHTEEN

THE COMMUNE WAS busy. Four or five people worked the sprawling garden, two two-man units were fixing drainpipes and a front door and two women were washing a van vivid with peace symbols in various colors. Grace Slick was urging people to violence (from her safe posh digs on the West Coast of course) and a dog was yipping his disagreement. I wanted to shake his paw.

As I walked to the front porch of the nearest house a few people looked me over and apparently decided I wasn't worth even sneering at. A Negro kid named Jim Ryan came out the front door carrying a toolbox. He was tall and fleshy but not fat. A few of the more ardent racists in town had hassled him many times. One time he decided to hassle them back. It turned into another case where Cliffie wanted to charge him but the county attorney's office said no, he'd just been defending himself. The good people of the town, who far outnumber the bad, wrote many letters to the newspaper talking about the "riffraff" that had picked on Ryan and given Black River Falls a name it didn't deserve.

Ryan had been one of those rare perfect clients—bright, quiet, amenable to following my instructions. Today he wore his "Power to the People" T-shirt and jeans. He smiled when he saw me. "Lot of people around here don't seem to like you much."

"It's the same in town, Jim."

He set the toolbox down. "I used to build homes in the summers. I collected a lot of stuff. You lookin' for Sarah?" He was talking loud, over Grace Slick.

"Donovan."

His dark eyes changed expression. "He's been in his room since early last night. He doesn't want anybody to bother him. I knocked once last night and he called me a bunch of names. Pissed me off. He's a nasty son of a bitch, way he runs this place. I'll be moving on pretty soon. Can't hack it here any more with him around."

"Any idea why he's holed up?"

"You're askin' the wrong guy, Mr. McCain. I never could figure him out except he's a jerk. I admit we need a leader here just to keep things running right. But we don't need an egomaniac."

A woman came out wearing a craftsman's denim apron. She must have been in charge of the music because it died just as I heard a "See you in the barn, Jim." She glanced at me. Her lips flattened into displeasure. She hurried on.

"Another admirer."

"They think you didn't defend us very well from all the bad publicity. Not all of them think that, not me and the majority. But some of them. They're lookin' for somebody to blame because they think maybe they'll all have to move because of some of the people in town. I kept tryin' to tell them that there wasn't anything you could do. But you know how stoners are."

"I guess I don't."

He grinned. "Sometimes they make me ashamed I enjoy drugs as much as I do."

The interior of the house had been cleaned up and painted. The furnishings in the front room came from the Salvation Army or someplace similar. The old stuff has faces—the weary couch, the tortured chair, the wounded ottoman. It was no different upstairs where air mattresses and sleeping bags ran three or four to a room. The smells ran to pot and smoke and wine and sex. A kitten so small she would fit in the palm of my hand accompanied me as I tried to find Richard Donovan. The walls of the hallway were colorful and baleful with posters of Che, Bobby Rush, Nixon, Southern cops.

My search ended at the only room with a closed door. I tried the doorknob and found that it was also locked. I knocked: "Richard, it's McCain. Open up."

So our little game began. I'd knock and he'd stay silent. I had my usual rational reaction to impotence; I kept rattling the doorknob. It would magically open; I just knew it.

Finally, he said, "I don't feel like talking. Just go away."

"If I don't talk to you, I'll talk to Mike Potter."

"Is that supposed to be a threat?"

"I've got a witness who saw you arguing with Vanessa right before she was killed."

The silence again.

"You hear me?"

"Yeah, I heard you all right and I bet it was that bitch Glenna who told you, too."

"Doesn't matter who it was. Now open up."

After a long minute he was in the doorway, shirtless, barefoot and sullen. He was doing a James Dean, his hands shoved deep into his pockets. From what I could see his room was clean and orderly, almost military in the precise way he'd laid it out. "So we argued a little. That's all it was."

"What did you argue about?"

"That's none of your business."

"I'm told she shoved you and started to walk away but you grabbed her by the arm. And then followed her into the barn shouting her name."

"You know the kind of lawyers my old man has access to? He'd take some bitch like Glenna apart on the stand."

"You're not convincing me you didn't kill Vanessa."

He leaned against the doorframe as if he might fall down if he didn't have support. His eyes went through three quick and remarkable expressions—anger, hurt, fear. "I shouldn't ever have hooked up with Glenna. She's psycho and I mean completely. Jealous of any girl who even looked at me."

"That why you broke it off with her?"

"I can't believe she still hates me. That was almost six months ago."

He took a minute to jerk a pack of Marlboros from his back pocket. He knew how to stall. He set a world record finding a book of matches in the other back pocket then getting the smoke lighted. "I had a little thing with somebody."

"Vanessa."

His body tensed at the mention of her name. "She and Neil were having problems."

"So you stepped in."

"She wanted it." The absolute lord and master of the commune was whimpering now. "I saw her in town one night and we ended up going to a movie in Iowa City. A French flick. She was a pretty cool girl for a hole like Black River Falls. Then we just started seeing each other—you know, on the sly." His gaze fell away from me. He got real interested in how his cigarette was burning. "I didn't want Neil to find out. I didn't want him to think I was moving in on his chick."

I forced the laugh back down my throat. "Yeah, you wouldn't want him to think anything like that."

This time his eyes tried to put burning holes in my face. "We were friends."

"You're a noble son of a bitch, no doubt about it."

He moved back, started to slam the door but I was too quick. In a past life I must have sold encyclopedias. I had my foot planted in front of said door and it wasn't going anywhere. "What happened when he found out?"

"Who said he found out?"

"Don't waste my time. Of course he found out. It's hard to sneak around in this commune or in town for that matter. Somebody must have spotted you."

He touched the fingers that held his cigarette to his forehead as if somebody had just driven a railroad spike into it. "Glenna followed me one night. She saw us and told Neil. He—" I wasn't sure if the shrug was meant to impress me or himself. "He was crazy. He threatened to kill me. Then I didn't give a damn about him anymore. And neither did Van. She was afraid of him in fact."

"Leading up to the night she was killed."

"What?"

"You still haven't told me what you were arguing about with her."

"You know every goddamn thing. How about you telling me?"

"That she didn't want to see you anymore and that there wasn't any point in bothering her the way you had been."

I wasn't sure if it was an illusion or whether his face had paled.

"That seemed to be the pattern. Whenever the guy got too close to her she got scared and walked away. And that's what happened to you, too, wasn't it?"

The scowl didn't work because he looked tired now. "You think whatever you want. But you better have some proof. Like I said, McCain, my old man has some very prominent lawyers. They'd eat you alive."

"I wouldn't go anywhere if I was you."

The scowl hadn't worked but he had more success with the smirk. "Sure thing, little man."

I withdrew my foot. The door slammed shut. I wondered how long it would take him to call his old man. The prodigal son returns home. In bad need of a big-time mouthpiece.

WHITTIER POINT WAS in favor when it was used by the kids of a grade school a block away. Then the grade school was consolidated with a larger school and

Whittier Point was left to lie fallow. The city kept the grass mown on the area around the large pavilion but all the playground equipment was gone. Without supervision the city would be asking for a lawsuit; hell, even with supervision there'd been lawsuits. Hot weekends families still trekked up here but on workdays it was often empty except for school-age lovers lost in their own obsession with each other.

Until nearly four thirty my only companions were quicksilver birds lighting on the empty picnic tables and two stray dogs who kept their noses to the cement floor as if uranium might be found under it.

For the first time I considered Richard Donovan a real suspect. Neil Cameron had been his rival for Vanessa. He'd been seen arguing with her not long before her murder. And he'd gone rich boy on me when I'd asked him if he'd killed her. Telling somebody you're going to get world-class lawyers to save you doesn't inspire confidence in your innocence.

And naturally I wondered why Nicole wasn't here yet. Maybe she'd changed her mind. Maybe she'd decided that she'd angered her father enough already by talking to me.

I got up and started walking around the area outside the pavilion. The birds had that day's-end sound and a cordial, solemn weariness seemed to settle on the trees and grass and the small lake just over the west side of the hill. There were moments when I wanted to be a kid again, hurrying home to my collection of paperbacks and comic books, the only realm in which I was really myself. My dad would still be alive and my mom and he would be laughing about something adult just as I entered the kitchen and asked when supper would be ready. I could even put up with my bratty sister whom I loved despite all my protests to the contrary.

Then I saw her.

The winding paved road ended up in a steep grade if you wanted to veer off and reach the pavilion. But she rode her ten-speed with energy and skill. As she drew near she waved; the gesture was girly and sweet. But then the front tire swerved and she was quickly dumped on the grass.

I ran over to her. She'd been thrown facedown but she was quick to roll over on her back with her arms flung wide. She was gasping for breath. Her eyes fluttered as if she might faint. I knelt down next to her and felt her racing pulse. Her breath still came in bursts and a whimper played in her mouth.

"I guess I should've taken the car." That she'd managed the sentence with such clarity reassured me she was all right. Still, it was strange that a girl of her age, in apparent good health, would be worn out to the point where she'd lost control of her bicycle.

I helped her to her feet and looked for any cuts or scrapes. She fell against me for a moment. I slid my arm through hers and walked her into the pavilion and sat her down. "I'm throwing your bike in my trunk and giving you a ride home. No arguments."

"They'll see us together."

"I'll let you off a ways before your estate."

"God, this is so embarrassing."

"It's still ninety degrees. Could happen to anybody."

"Our house isn't even a mile away." She touched her face. Body heat had emphasized the acne on her cheeks. Her white blouse was soaked in spots.

"I've got a cold Pepsi in the car that I've had about half of. How does that sound?"

"That sounds great."

She drank it in sips, which was smart. The drink relaxed her or seemed to. She leaned back and took one of those deep breaths that usually mean you're feeling better—even philosophical—about some problem. "I guess it was kinda stupid on a hot day like this." Then: "My dad *really* doesn't like you."

"That I know. But why did he kick Tommy Delaney out?"

She wiped her brow with the back of her tiny, corded hand. "Poor Tommy. I always liked him but I don't think anybody else did. Except Marsha. She told me one day how bad at home it was for him. His folks always argued and sometimes it got violent. I guess his whole life was like that. She said that was why he liked being at our place so much. It was peaceful and it made him feel special, you know, with my dad being so wealthy and all. The funny thing is, it was my dad who started inviting him over. He'd show him off to his friends. He always gave a speech, too, about how Tommy was going to put the Hawkeyes in the Rose Bowl. But Eve hated him. She thought he was a moron. And that was the word she used. She worked on Dad until he started to dislike Tommy, too. I guess when Van was killed he decided it was a good time to get rid of Tommy."

"Tommy's not handling it too well."

She fanned herself with her tiny hand. "That's what I figured. He really isn't some big dumb jock. He's real sensitive, you know? I think he was in love with Van for a little while but he was smart. He gave up right away. I mean it was hopeless. Then he fell in love with Sarah. Van wouldn't even listen to him when he was telling her that Neil was sorry for being so mad all the time and how much he loved her. Tommy felt sorry for Neil, that's why he stepped in. But I told him up front it wouldn't work."

"Why not?" But my question came automatically. I was thinking about Tommy being in love with Sarah.

"She wanted to humiliate Dad every way she could. And that meant being with a lot of boys. But I doubt she slept with more than one or two of them. She told me she hated sex because it reminded her of Dad."

"And this was all because your dad married Eve?"

"Well—" She perched herself on the edge of the bench. She pursed her lips, looked away for long seconds then said: "There was something else, too. But now it doesn't matter. Van's dead."

"Did this thing that doesn't matter anymore affect you the same way it affected Van?"

She inhaled deeply through her nose. "I really don't want to talk about it, all right?"

"It might help me."

"My dad said it's all over. That you're only out to embarrass him."

"At one time your dad and I were close to being friends."

"That isn't the way he remembers it."

There was only one way in. "Does Eve go out much at night—alone?"

Getting to her feet was an effort. She wobbled on the first two steps. I caught her wrist gently and eased her back.

"Please let me go. I really don't want to talk about this."

"I just asked you if Eve went out alone at night sometimes."

"What do you want me to say? Yes, she did."

"How about your dad? Did he go out at night alone sometimes, too?"

"Of course he did. And still does. He's an important man. He has to." She broke suddenly, hands to face, quick dagger of a sob. "You know about their arrangement, don't you?"

"Was that why Van hated him so much?"

This time she had no trouble standing. Or walking. She walked down the wall and finally seated herself on the low ledge at the end of it. She didn't say anything for a time. She wasn't crying now. She didn't even look upset. When she looked at me all she said was, "I need a cigarette."

I did the movie star thing and lighted smokes for both of us. I carried them down and gave her hers. She had her nice legs stretched out in front of her now. She was considering them. She didn't seem to have much pride in herself. I hoped she at least realized that she had perfect coltish legs.

She smoked eagerly. "How did you find out?"

"Right now that doesn't matter. How did you and Van find out?"

A bright smile. "We followed her. Private investigators. We wanted to get something on her. We thought maybe Dad would divorce her if we could prove to him she was unfaithful. And that was pretty easy. She went out with Bobby Randall several times. And we assumed there were others, too. It's funny how it worked out, though."

I waited until she was ready to talk again.

"Before we got to tell him, Van and I got the flu pretty bad. We were in bed because we were so sick. I was asleep late one night when Van came into my room. She was so sick she could barely talk. She said she'd started down the stairs to get some orange juice and then she heard something she couldn't believe. I was so groggy I wasn't even sure what she was talking about. She said that this party Dad and Eve were having tonight—the men were drawing numbers to see which one of them would sleep with another man's wife. I couldn't understand it at first. But Van wasn't just beautiful, she kept up on things. She said this was what they called wife swapping and she said Dad was having a great time. They were going to pair off then get together that weekend at Dad's house up on the river. It's three stories and sort of like a hotel. Then Van started crying. I helped her into the bathroom so she could throw up. She was that sick—sick about what Dad was doing. She got into bed with me—I used to do that to her when we were little. She just kept crying and I held her and rocked her and sometimes I'd cry too."

She turned and flipped her cigarette onto the lawn. "That was a couple of years ago and that's when she started running around. She'd never been like that before."

"Did Van or you ever confront your father about it?"

"Oh, sure. We could tell he was embarrassed. He promised he wouldn't do it anymore. We both wanted to believe him. But then after about a month or so he started going out alone at night the way Eve kept doing. We followed him. He went to the same motel Eve did. The women were wives of his friends. Van used to scream at him and threaten to kill Eve. She always said that Eve shouldn't ever have been allowed to live in the same house our mom did. I agreed with her completely. Completely." Then: "Pretty shitty, huh?"

"Pretty shitty." I don't know why I was surprised that the Mainwarings had lied to me about the girls not knowing.

"He said we'd understand better when we were older. But neither of us believed that. That isn't any way to live. It's like he's in his second childhood or something." Then: "I guess I'll take you up on that ride back home."

"You want to head back now?"

"Yes, maybe I'd better. I'm really wasted for some reason."

I remembered how she'd been in my car the other day, not at her best, either. But there were a variety of physical responses to loss and trauma.

"You feel up to walking now?"

"I'm not a baby." Sharp, angry.

"I was just offering to help."

"I know, it's just—I'm sorry. I shouldn't have snapped at you like that. I hate being bitchy."

"I can't imagine you bitchy."

Her whooping laugh was directed at me. "You're one of those guys Van always told me about—the ones who idealize girls. You don't want to be around me when I get bitchy. I was even worse than Van and that was pretty bad."

"Thanks for the warning. Next time I'll come armed."

A soft summer giggle. "Well, I didn't say I was *that* bad."

With that she shoved off the edge of the wall. "Thanks for everything, Sam. I really appreciate it."

I put my hand on her shoulder. "Let's go get your bike."

NINETEEN

THREE HOURS LATER I sat in a chair on Wendy's patio watching the day slowly fade into dusk. Wendy had given me a kiss, a beer and a promise that even though dinner would be late it would be something I really liked. She would meanwhile go visit her mother for no longer than an hour. Whenever her mom felt that nobody was paying her sufficient attention she had panic attacks designed to get her noticed. Since Wendy's sister lived in Portland, Oregon, it fell to Wendy to be the noticer.

Dusk is always a melancholy time for me and I've never been sure why. Sometimes I feel the loneliness that has always been my curse, a loneliness that nobody can assuage. Tonight for company I had Wendy's hefty cat Victor. He sat in the chair next to mine and swatted at everything that tried to assault his bastion from the air. He had yet to down a single firefly but he certainly kept trying.

I wanted to give myself up to the Cubs game that was just getting started on the radio. Misery loves company and nothing is more miserable than listening to the Cubs blow another season. But this was pre-game yak and so I was left to the dying day.

It would be nice to send my mind on vacation so that I could just sit here and be one with my surroundings but I was restless. I kept thinking about the night of the murder. None of the lovers Van had thrown over would have had a difficult time getting into that barn—there was easy access through the thin line of forest in the back. Anybody who'd followed her to the commune would have been able to swing wide and enter the barn without being seen.

I also thought about the effect Eve had had upon the girls. Imagine if you'd grown up with a sweet, attentive, understanding mother who died and was replaced by a stunning but vapid swinger. And even worse, that your father became a swinger, too. Hey, one Frank Sinatra is enough for this planet, man. Had Eve taken her vengeance out on Van?

Victor started purring when the back door opened, which meant his mistress and patroness had come home. She carried her drink on a blue cloth coaster over to Victor's chair and nudged him aside so that she could sit down. He went unwillingly. As soon as she was seated he jumped on her lap.

"Feeling any better?"

"Not really. So much up in the air."

"I ran into Mike Potter at the supermarket. I bought us some red snapper we can put on the grill tonight."

"He tell you I'm crazy?"

"More or less. And he's worried that you could get in serious trouble with the state if you keep pushing this."

"I just want to make sure we get the truth."

"I said that to him. He said, 'If Sam wants to waste his time it's up to him.' But he smiled when he said it."

"That was nice of him."

"How about a back rub on the bed?"

"Are you trying to seduce me?"

"Maybe. Or maybe I'm just trying to distract you. You need to take a break."

We fit just about perfectly as lovers. And when we finished, Victor was squatting on the bureau and watching us in the darkness scented with her perfumes and sachets and creams. We'd had an audience.

"I never did get that back rub."

"Too late, buddy. I'm going to grill us some red snapper. And you're going to set the table."

"This is just like the National Guard I go to once a month. Too many orders."

"Don't say that. They're talking about drafting you guys. I saw it in the paper this morning. You must've seen it."

"I'll start setting the table."

"So you're not going to talk about it?"

"They've been predicting that for two years now. I'll set the table."

I went inside and started grabbing plates, glasses, silverware and napkins. I was careful to limit myself to the second-best of everything. The plates had tiny chips and the shine was off the silverware. I didn't blame her. Her only real asset was this house she owned. She basically lived on the income from the trust her husband had left for her. It had been the largesse of a decent but guilty man. Not his fault that he'd fallen in love with one of the girls his bully-boy father would never have approved of. He'd married Wendy because he was fond of her and because his family approved of her family. The trouble was Wendy had been in love with him and had come undone when he'd been killed in Nam.

And Nam was on my mind now, as well. Not only
because I opposed the savage meaningless war—Ike's
"military-industrialist complex" warning coming true
in spades—but also because our post commander at
the Guard had given us notice that we might be called
up. I'd lied to Wendy. Nam was in the offing. A number of Guard units had already been sent there. At the
rate our troops were being killed the great dark god
that was slaughtering the lives of soldiers and inno-
cents alike was ever hungrier. It wanted more flesh
and blood and many of the men in the Guard were at
the right age for making patriotic sacrifices the chick-
enshit politicians could prattle about when reelection
time came around again.

But talking about it with Wendy was difficult. Her
husband had died over there. And that's what worried
her, the cheap irony of losing her first husband and
then her husband-to-be in the same war. I didn't blame
her for the dread she faced in her nightmares but I also
couldn't do anything about it. Maybe we'd luck out.
Maybe we wouldn't be called up. But as General West-
moreland told more and more lies and more and more of
our troops died, I didn't know how we would be spared.

She came in and opened the refrigerator. She slapped
two pieces of red snapper on the counter and started
preparing them for cooking. She was fast and efficient
and fun to watch. She didn't say anything.

"You not speaking?"

"No, because if I do speak you know what I'll speak
about and then neither of us'll feel like eating. You
know how worried I've been about it. The story in the
paper just made it official."

"Maybe it won't happen."

"Just let me prepare this fish and not think about anything else."

A good meal and two glasses of wine later we both felt momentarily invincible and loving. We sat in chairs on the screened-in back porch and held hands like high schoolers. Victor appeared and sat on Wendy's lap. The only music was the night itself, the breeze and the faint passage of cars and the even more distant sounds of airplanes approaching Cedar Rapids for landing. I felt old and logy and I didn't mind it at all. I even considered the possibility—combine alcohol and fatigue and you can come up with the damnedest thoughts—that maybe, just maybe, things were exactly as they appeared. Neil Cameron killed Vanessa Mainwaring because he felt betrayed by her. And then he killed himself. Judge Whitney wouldn't be happy with this because Cliffie would have won one. And even one would be too much for Judge Whitney. The Sykes clan represented all things evil to her.

"How about helping me clean up and then we go to bed?"

"Fine. As long as you can help me drag myself up from this chair."

"You were supposed to help *me*, Sam." She laughed. "God, we sound like we're eighty years old."

"Speak for yourself. I don't feel a day over seventy-five."

"I love this so much. It's so comfortable with you."

"Is that another word for boring?"

"What an ego. You just want a compliment."

"I love you so much because you're so 'comfortable.'
Not exactly inspiring."

She giggled. "And because you're so exciting to be
with and such a stud in bed and because all my girlfriends are jealous that I've been able to keep a heart-
breaker like you interested in little ole me."

"Much better."

"*Now* will you help me clean up?"

I concentrated on the grill and she worked on the
dishes. When I came inside she was just loading the
dishwasher. "See, that didn't take long." She tossed me
a towel. "How about you dry and I wash? I've still got
these pots and pans to take care of."

The kinds of relationships I'd had with women in
the past had been all sex and tension. Lots of breakups
and makeups. There hadn't been time in all the grop-
ing and battling to get domestic in any way. Wendy
and I were already married in an informal sort of way.
But sometimes I got scared it would all end for some
terrible reason.

She jabbed me in the ribs. "You haven't seemed to
notice but there aren't any more pots or pans to dry.
You've been standing there with that last one for a couple of minutes now. You must be thinking of something
really fascinating."

"I'm just hoping this doesn't come to an end any
time soon."

"You keep asking me to marry you and you say
something like that?" She smiled and kissed me. "Look,
Sam, I worry about the same thing. And that's why I
just want to wait a little while. We're crazy about each

other. I want to spend my life with you. But I just want to be careful about it." She took pan and towel from me and set them on the counter. "Maybe we'd better discuss this in the bedroom."

By the time we finished making love, neither of us had enough energy left for discussing anything. She fell asleep against my outstretched arm. The aroma of her clean hair was innocently erotic.

THE CALL CAME at 3:26.

The phone was located on the nightstand on Wendy's side of the bed—as was only right; it was *her* bed—and before I was completely aware of what was going on, she had the phone to her ear and was talking. She'd told me once that all the while her husband was in Nam, where he eventually died on his second tour, she had nightmares about the phone ringing in the middle of the night and a cold military voice telling her that her husband was dead. She told me that she woke up several nights to find the phone in her hand, a dial tone loud in her ear. She'd incorporated the nightmare into reality.

"It's Mike," she said, lifting up the Princess-style phone and planting it on my stomach. I took the receiver and listened. I asked him to repeat what he'd said, so he went through it once more. He said he was at the crime scene and that if I wanted to join him it would be all right. He said that Cliffie wouldn't be there; he'd called the chief but the chief felt that Potter could handle it. I could sense Potter's smile when he quoted Cliffie: "I think you've learned a lot from me since you've been here and I've let you handle a number of other things already. You just keep me posted—the morning's soon enough." This was the first time I'd heard Potter draw down on Cliffie. But it was late and the scene he was at had to be a true bummer.

"What's going on?" Wendy whispered. Since I was still talking to Potter, I held up my hand to wave her off.

"I'm on my way, Mike."

Wendy had slipped into the bathroom. I heard her pee and then start brushing her teeth. If the National Dental Society or whatever it was called wanted to give a trophy (a big shining jewel carved into a tooth) to the person who brushed her teeth the most times a day, Wendy would be their choice. Seven, eight times a day and that doesn't count flossing.

I got a light switched on and dressed. I used one of her hairbrushes to batten down my own dark mess. I was lighting a cigarette when she came out wearing a ragged old robe she liked. She managed to look tousled, sweet and very sexy.

She came over and took my cigarette from me. She inhaled deeply; exhaled in a blast. She held up a finger. "One more." After she finally gave me my smoke back, she said, "Mike sounded shaky. What's going on?"

"Tommy Delaney," I said, "hanged himself earlier tonight."

TWENTY

Cue the rain.

Halfway to the Delaney residence a hot, dirty summer rain shower started pelting my car. I had the radio turned up to KOMA in Oklahoma, still my favorite station. In the middle of the night this way the signal was stronger than during the day. A bitter anti-war song seemed right for this moment. I kept lighting one cigarette from another. I resented all the snug people in their dark snug houses as I passed street after street.

All the natural questions came to me. What had Tommy Delaney wanted to tell me and then backed away from? Was this going to be another murder disguised as a suicide? Had he left a note explaining everything?

The Hills had never looked better, the darkness a mercy to the crumbling houses and sad metal monsters parked curbside, all cracked windshields and rusted parts and political bumper stickers for men who had only contempt for the owners. The closer I got to the Delaney place the more lights I saw in the small houses. The people inside would have heard the sirens and seen the blood splash of emergency lights pitched across the sky. Most would have stayed inside; after all it was raining now and who wanted to get wet. But the vampires among them would have shrugged on raincoats and trudged out. Pain, misery, death awaited them and this was a tasty brew that would give them a fix of the life force they sought.

The local press was already there. The cops had shunted them to a corner of the action. A beefy part-time deputy stood next to them to make sure they didn't stray. I parked next to the ambulance and walked over to where Mike Potter was giving orders to another part-time deputy. The crowd numbered somewhere around thirty, not a sell-out crowd but not bad for a rainy four a.m. show that wasn't in 3-D or Cinemascope.

The air smelled of wet earth, exhaust fumes from all the vehicles, and a cancer ward's worth of cigarette smoke, my own contribution included. Two squad cars sat together shining their headlights on the front of the garage. The door was down so all I could see was the blank white wood with rust snaking down from the roof. Above the door was the basketball hoop where I'd seen Tommy Delaney shooting baskets that day.

As I approached Potter I heard a scream from inside the house. The piercing agony of it stopped me as I think it stopped everybody who heard it. I'd been surveying the scene the way an investigator would. The scream forced me to survey it now as a simple human being. No doubt one or both of the parents had found their son hanging from a crossbeam in the garage. A mad-ness would set in. They would blame themselves, they would blame him and they would blame existence it-self, a ramble scramble of rage and grief and even more rage. I'd worked with enough social workers to know how suicides like this played out.

Potter said, "I'd stay away from his folks if I was you."

"They mentioned me?"

Rain pattered on his police cap. "According to her, her son was a nice, easygoing kid until you started pestering him about the Mainwaring girl."

"That's bullshit."

He had a flashlight the size of a kid's baseball bat in his hand. "C'mon, I'll take you into the garage."

On the way in, I said, "Did you hear me? What she said is bullshit. I came out here twice. Twice. That's hardly 'pestering' him or whatever she said. In fact I'm pretty sure he wanted to talk to me about something."

"Then why didn't he?" The cop guarding the side door stood aside as we approached.

"How do I know why he didn't."

"But you're sure he did? He sent you some kind of mind message?"

The sarcasm ended the minute we stepped inside. The hard-packed dirt floor, the rain and cool air streaming through the glassless window frame in back, the smells of gasoline, oil, dirt, now joined with vomit and feces. Somebody had run the only car outside so that the police could bring in all the necessary equipment to nail down every aspect of the suicide.

The way Tommy's mouth was twisted, it was almost as if he'd been smiling when death had taken him, a grotesque smile that seemed fitting for his end. He wasn't twitching, anyway, twitching the way he'd been with his folks screaming behind him in what was likely their ongoing marital war. I remembered the tic in his left eye and the forlorn, beaten tone of his voice. Their voices would have been with him as he'd looked for shelter and solace somewhere else. The Mainwaring home would have provided that.

All he wore was his jeans; no shirt, no shoes. Puke streamed down his chest and his right foot had been splashed with his runny feces.

"He left a note."

"Let's talk outside."

Potter raised his eyes, studied Tommy for a time then looked at me. "Yeah, outside."

The rain was backing off to a drizzle and the action was slowing down to the point that some of the ghouls, soaked, were wandering home. The hardiest of them would stay to see the corpse inserted into the ambulance.

I felt somebody watching me and when I looked to my left I saw Mrs. Delaney hiding behind a kitchen curtain. Even from here her hatred was clear.

"I got on a ladder and climbed up and looked at the ligature marks, Sam. No doubt about this one as far as I'm concerned. He definitely killed himself. The ME'll examine him and make absolutely sure it's suicide."

"I didn't have any doubt about this one."

"Why not?"

"For one thing, the little time I spent with him he struck me as a pretty sad kid."

"Hell, he was a football hero."

"Not when you heard his parents shrieking at each

other. I stood on the front lawn and heard them. Tommy was coming apart. It was like shell shock. And that came from years of listening to them trying to destroy each other. The other thing was he wanted to tell me something—at least that was the impression I had. But he could never quite do it."

"Any idea what it was?"

"No. But he knew a lot about the Mainwarings."

He lighted a cigarette now that the rain wouldn't soak it. The smoke smelled good in the chilling air. "That note he left, he apologized to his parents for taking his life and asked them to pray for him. And then he said that he never had any luck with women and that he just couldn't go on."

"And that's all?"

Before he could answer, the back door screeched open and barked shut. I saw her coming at me. Nuclear warhead. No confusion about who she wanted and what she planned to do.

Potter saw it, too, and stepped in front of me. "Mrs. Delaney, I asked you to please stay inside."

She pointed a witch finger at me and screamed: "He killed my Tommy! He wouldn't leave him alone! Tommy was scared of him! Tommy'd be alive if it wasn't for him!"

"Please, Mrs. Delaney—please go back inside. This isn't good for you or your husband."

But it was great for the living dead, the remainder of the group already pushing their way toward the garage. Drama was almost as good as blood.

She flung herself at Potter, trying to get her hands

on me. "He should be the one who's dead! He should be the one who's dead! He killed my Tommy!"

Paralysis. I couldn't move, speak. I was afraid of what I might have done to contribute to Tommy's suicide—maybe he felt pressure to tell me something but was afraid to and my contacting him scared him—just as I was afraid of her. All that anger, all that sorrow. I wanted to say something to comfort her but anything from me would sound blasphemous now.

"Just let me tell him to his face!" She dove at Potter but a stocky, balding man in a Hawkeye T-shirt came up from behind her and put big workingman hands carefully on her shoulders and began the inch-by-inch process of extracting her from Potter's body.

He just kept saying, "C'mon now, honey; c'mon now, honey," the way you might to a small child you were trying to soothe. Soft words, loving words. Hard to imagine this was the same man I'd heard battling this woman when I came here the first time to talk to Tommy. This time he was saying the right thing in the right way.

When he finally drew her to him, she folded herself into his arms and wept. He put one of those big hands on the back of her head and began stroking her gently. This made her weep even more.

This time the paralysis wasn't just mine. Potter stood in place, too, just watching her collapse into her husband's keeping. Not even the ghouls said anything, or moved. I thought of a documentary I'd seen about a tiger cub born dead and the mother trekking the corpse nearly a hundred miles across scorching dusty Africa. Not wanting to ever give it up. Mr. Delaney showed that kind of ferocious protectiveness as he slowly guided her back toward the house. He kept muttering his mantra. She clung to him with a desperation that made them indivisible.

Potter said, "Nothing with kids. And Tommy was a kid."

We'd had this conversation a number of times, how he could handle just about anything but death scenes involving kids or young people. He said he'd seen too many such scenes in Kansas City. He never elaborated on any of them.

Then he got brisk and officious. He wanted to wrap things up. The ME could get here and give his benediction and then everybody—except one unlucky uniform—could go home and catch what remained of sleep before the six-thirty alarm clock.

The remaining ghouls began to fade. A light went on in a back room. Shadows against a cotton blind. A piercing sob then silence. The light went out.

"I hope this is the end of it," Potter said. Irritation was clear in his eyes and voice. "No more murders or suicides. My wife keeps reminding me that we moved out here to take it easy. Now my migraines are back, I'm downing a bottle of Pepto a day and I'm constipated."

"Pepto constipates you."

"I know, but it's either that or having heartburn that damn near knocks me out."

I stared with great longing at my car. It would take me away from here. I would be back in bed with Wendy. In the morning the sunlight would be golden and pure and maybe we'd make love in it and then have breakfast on the back porch and Wendy would be sweet and fetching and for a time I wouldn't have to think about everything that had happened in the past few days or whether Wendy was going to marry me sometime soon. Or if my National Guard unit would be called up for the war that was a farce and a cruel joke on the American people.

"You be sure and keep me posted if you hear anything," Potter said.

"I will."

As I walked to my car I saw Mr. Delaney in one of the kitchen windows watching me. I almost waved. Instinct. But in this instance waving would be more than slightly inappropriate. I got one quick good look at his face. He seemed to hate me as much as his wife did. Maybe more but he couldn't express what he was feeling the way she did. He just stared.

In my car I snapped the radio on. Then right back off. Wrong to listen to the radio somehow. Instead I smoked and drove fast. Very fast. I didn't go back to Wendy's, I just drove. It was one of those robotic driftings I went through occasionally. Wasn't aware of where I was driving or what I was seeing. Just driving, the act itself lulling me into a state where nothing mattered but the present moment—my fortress against any kind of serious thought.

The first time I became aware of where my car was taking me was down on D Avenue where the Burger Heaven and the second-run theater used to be. There'd been a used paperback store there for awhile, too. And a tavern where they kept their pinball machines in front so teenagers could play them and not get carded or thrown out. It was all gone now. A supermarket and a new Western Auto took up most of the block. No comfort in those.

Wendy was asleep on the couch in her pajamas when I came in. The TV was on and snowy. Victor dozed on the armchair. I went into the kitchen and got myself a beer and sat down in the breakfast nook.

She came in soon enough. "I tried to wait up for you." Sliding into the booth across from me.

"You should've stayed in bed."

"You ever think I was worried about you?"

"If you're so worried about me why don't you just say you'll marry me?"

"Boy, you're in one hell of a mood."

"If you say so."

"All right, I'll marry you. You set the date."

"Are you serious?"

"Yes. I've been thinking about it. We love each other and even though I'm scared about it I don't want to ruin everything by putting it off. I just realized that if you ever walked out the door I would be miserable for the rest of my life."

"Well, probably not for the rest of your life."

"Goddammit, you're in a bad mood. I tell you I love you and that I want to marry you and you just keep on bitching about things."

"Well, I'm happy about it. Of course."

She was out of the booth before I could say anything more.

"Go to hell, Sam. I don't want you in my bed tonight. You take the couch."

Then she was gone. It hadn't done me any good to take Tommy's suicide out on her. I gave it twenty minutes and then went into the dark bedroom and told her how much I loved her. She laughed and said, "I was wondering when you'd show up. Now get into bed."

TWENTY-ONE

I WAS IN court the next morning. A divorce case. By the time of the trial I'd come to pretty much hate both of them. Selfish people who'd forgotten that they had two very lonely and frightened little girls to take care of. He'd told me, quite earnestly, that as soon as the papers were signed it was "Nookie City for this guy." There are men who could have pulled it off and made you smile along with it. He wasn't one of them. He was, I suppose, good-looking in a big-guy sort of way but he was as vain as a starlet, always combing his hair and watching his biceps pop in his short-sleeved shirts.

One time when he was in my office, I went to the john and came back to find him sucking in his gut and putting the moves on Jamie. She was wily enough to say, "My dad wears the same aftershave you do." A thirty-eight-year-old self-described stud ("Hey, chicks dig me and Elaine could never understand that, the bitch,") being compared to a God-only-knows-how-old Granddad-type? He got back to business, which meant running down his ex some more and winking at me every time he mentioned "chicks." Number one, I hate people who wink and number two, his winks looked like tics.

The judge, a man who had no time for Judge Whitney

or me, called me to the bench and leaned over and whispered: "Am I right in thinking that these two are among the biggest assholes who've ever appeared before me?"

I nodded. "Thank you."

He settled mutual custody on them and ordered both of them to take parenting classes. They sputtered and spluttered and called "outrage" in the middle of which the judge brought the hammer down, stood up and left.

"Parenting classes? Who does that asshole think he is?"

"Maybe you'll meet some chicks there." I grabbed my briefcase and got out of the courtroom fast so I wouldn't have to talk to him anymore.

The sun was so hot at ten thirty I had a science fiction image of people staggering down the sidewalk and falling into the street, their hands waving desperately in the air like drowning victims. I smoked a cigarette and took my time getting back to the office. I passed at least six people who told me how hot it was. I wouldn't have known that otherwise.

My office is located in the rear of a building that has been many things up front. The current tenant who took the front section and thus eighty-five percent of the entire place was an auto parts store.

I walked alongside of the building and when I turned I saw Jamie sitting on the steps leading to our office. She had tears in her eyes. She smoked a cigarette and sniffled. When she saw me she just sat there. No signal of recognition.

"What're you doing out here, Jamie?" I said.

"He told me to sit out here."

"Who's he?"

"Mr. Mainwaring."

"What the hell's going on?"

Her blue eyes shone with tears. "I just did what he told me, Mr. C. He scares me."

"So he's inside now?"

"Uh-huh."

I took her hand. "It'll be all right. Why don't you take an early lunch and do a little shopping?"

"Will you be all right?"

"Never better."

"I really don't like him, Mr. C."

"I don't either. But now he's my problem, not yours. Now go have some good food at the deli and put it on the office account."

"Are you sure that's all right?"

"Well, I've talked to the owner of this here law office and he said it was fine with him."

She was picking tears off her cheek with a little girl finger. And now she smiled. "I always tell people you're the funniest man I've ever known, Mr. C."

I didn't have to walk all the way into my office. He half dived out of it to grab me before I reached the threshold. He used his size to shove me hard against the hall closet. "Where is she? Where did you send my daughter?"

He'd become a grotesque. The blue eyes were crazed and the words were cries. Drool trickled from the left side of his mouth. He was slick with sweat and it wasn't from the heat. And then his hands reached for my throat. I tried to push off the closet door but he was too quick.

I could feel the fingers on the sides of my neck. I had just enough room to knee him in the groin.

He didn't fall down, he just went into a crouch. He turned away from me so I couldn't see his misery. Even in this situation he was a man of great pride.

I went into my office and sat down at my desk. I pretended to be fascinated by all the pink phone slips waiting for me. He was resourceful. In less than a minute he started groaning out insults. "I'm going to see that you're in prison for a long time, you little bastard." And: "If she dies, you'll be an accessory to murder."

That one got my attention and bothered me. "What the hell are you talking about?"

"At least own up to what you did, you slimy son of a bitch." The voice was stronger now and he was out of his crouch. As he came through the door he winced with every step. But his rage was as good as several shots of bourbon. "I don't know how you could ever be so god-damned irresponsible. I knew you were dirt, McCain, but she's a seventeen-year-old girl."

He sank into Jamie's chair. His ferocity was wearing him down. He stretched a hand to her desk as if for support. The next sound was a wail. "He'll kill her."

"Paul, damn it. Look at me. Tell me what you're talking about."

"You know damn well what I'm talking about. She's going to have an abortion because you told her to."

"Paul, that's crazy. I didn't even know she was pregnant."

"Oh, sure. I suppose you didn't see her yesterday afternoon, either."

"Yeah, I did see her. And what we talked about most of the time was how she and Van learned that you were doing the same thing Eve was and that you were in a wife-swapping group. And how much she and Van hated it."

"Don't put the goddamn blame on me. This is your fault. She's looking up some butcher who'll abort her. She doesn't know about sleazy things like that. That's your territory. You and your great friend Neil Cameron. He's the one who seduced her."

I had my elbow on the desk. Now I rested my head on my hand and took a deep breath. There are moments when the brain can't—or refuses to—comprehend and process all the information it is presented. Pregnant. Abortion. Neil Cameron. My voice sounded mournful. "What makes you think she's looking for an abortion?"

"She told Marsha she was having one and was driving over to see some guy. This was about twenty minutes ago."

"Oh, God."

"No shit, huh? Finally sinking in, McCain? Maybe having second thoughts about what you told her?"

I slammed my fist so hard against the desk top that I numbed my hand. "I didn't know she was pregnant and I sure as hell didn't tell her to get an abortion. Do you understand that?"

For the first time clarity came into his eyes. The lunacy waned. "Then who told her about this abortionist?"

"I have no idea. And even if I get around with low-lifes sometimes, I don't know anything about an abortionist in Black River Falls. There was one but he's doing time in Fort Dodge."

Wailing now. "Then where is she?"

"Shut up for a minute."

I grabbed the receiver and started dialing. Kenny answered on the third ring. At this time of day he'd be working on his portable typewriter slamming through "Cannibal Warriors of the Third Reich!" or something similar.

"Yeah?" He did not like being interrupted.

"I've got a big problem here, Kenny, and I'm really in a hurry. Is there anybody you know of who's peddling abortions these days? I know it's been quiet since Thompson got sent up to Fort Dodge for killing that girl."

"Supposedly there's some guy in Milburn. His name is Windom or something like that. I don't know that for a fact. But I heard it from one of the kids who always comes out here to get his copies of my stuff autographed."

Even Kenny was a star of sorts. "That's all you know?"

"Yeah, I'm sorry, that's the best I can do."

"Thanks, Kenny. That's a start anyway."

Mainwaring was on his feet. "What did he say?"

"Milburn. Some guy named Windom. But he says the only way he heard it is that some kid who wants his books autographed told him."

"People want that trash autographed?"

This coming from Mr. Open Marriage and Mr. Wife Swap. But now wasn't the time to respond.

We took his Jaguar. Milburn was fifteen miles away.

We both smoked. Any time we pulled up behind a car or truck Mainwaring leaned on the horn as if he thought they'd be so afraid that their vehicles would just take flight and clear a path for us.

"If he laid a hand on her, I'll kill him."

"First of all, we don't even know that he's the guy. So it would make sense to stay a little cool until we find out."

"You don't give a damn, she's not your daughter."

"No, but believe it or not, I like her and I don't want some butcher cutting her up."

All I got was a snarl.

Despite the heat, autumn could be seen in the hills, the tips of trees burning into golds and browns and reds and that scent of fall on a few vagrant breezes. For all the stupendous colossal magnificence of the Jag, the damn air conditioning wouldn't work so we had the windows down.

Milburn runs to maybe fifteen thousand and is known mainly for the Pioneer Days celebration it throws on Labor Day, complete with costumed people and a lot of artifacts from the middle of the last century. It gets a lot of state press and some big national advertisers sponsor a good share of the expenses.

As we entered the town limits I had the feeling that the place was a big old dog lying on its side in the boiling heat. The shopping district which ran four blocks showed a lot of empty parking spaces and only a few people on the sidewalks. A tractor was ahead of us at a stoplight so Mainwaring went into one of his rants about how hillbillies should be shot-stabbed-set on fire for getting in the way of the movers and shakers who by divine right were running this planet. Since (A) farmers aren't hillbillies and (B) I'm pretty sure that there had to be some hillbillies in my bloodline dating back to the early 1800s, I started thinking about shooting-stabbing-setting *him* on fire.

Finally I saw a Sinclair station and said, "Pull in."

He swept the beast onto the drive and I was out the door, him shouting, "What the hell are you doing?"

I like gas stations. The smells of oil and gas and the clang and clank of the guys working on cars in the garage. I like good old gas station conversations, standing around and saying nothing much with a Pepsi and some peanuts and a cigarette with some other guys who are also saying nothing much. This time all I wanted was a phone book which, in the case of Milburn, was about as thick as a comic book.

The middle-aged guy in the green uniform who came out of the garage wiping his hands on a rag looked like the man to ask. "Can you tell me how I'd find Sullivan Road?"

"Sure. Easy to get to from here. You go down two blocks to the Woman's Shop—big store right on the corner—and you turn right and go straight for—let's see—eight blocks. Maybe nine. Anyway, Sullivan Street is off that road there. You'll see a street sign."

"Thanks."

"We don't see many of those around here."

He meant the Jag. "Yeah, but the air conditioning doesn't work."

He had a great Midwestern grin. "You're kidding."

"'Fraid not. Well, thanks."

"You took long enough," Mainwaring said when I got in the car.

"Shut up and listen."

"I'm not used to people telling me to shut up."

"Tough shit. Now listen."

I gave him directions. They were easy to follow but we went through the honking again. I wanted to find Nicole, too, but without a siren on the Jag other vehicles just weren't going to shoot up on lawns to get out of our way.

Sullivan Road was where houses went to die. Most of the homes were built in the twenties from what I could see, two-story white clapboards adjacent to garages not much bigger than closets. Porches leaned and chimneys toppled and shutters hung crooked. On a few of them you could see porch swings that hung from only one chain. The cars were also old, blanched colors and monster rust eating its way across the length of the vehicles.

"This is just the kind of place I expected it'd be," Mainwaring said.

"We're looking for 1724."

"Some rathole."

"We're on the 1600s now."

"If he's touched her I'll kill him."

"You already said that. There's 1702."

"There's her car!"

The way he grabbed the door handle I thought he was going to leap out of the car before he even slowed down. There was a space across from Nicole's silver Mustang. Mainwaring pulled in. I had to grab his shirt as he tried to vault from the car. "We don't know what we're walking into here. So let me handle this, you understand?"

"Take your hand off me. This is my daughter you're talking about."

"Yeah, well if you're so concerned about your daughter, then we go in there cool and calm." He was so pissed I reasoned that the only way to get his attention was to shock him. "What if he's operating on her? He hears us breaking in and he slips and makes a mistake? You want to be responsible for that?"

His eyes closed tight. An anxious breath. "Oh, God, my poor little Nicole."

"I'll handle things. All right?"

"All right."

"Let's go."

The white picket fence around the scorched grass leaned inward, in some spots so low it was only a few inches from the ground. The gate was missing. The walk to the door was cracked into jagged points. A variety of animals had used the east side of the lawn for a toilet. Apparently the right side didn't have any toilet paper.

Mainwaring dragged himself now, as if afraid of what lay ahead. He must have been still thinking of the image of the abortionist's tool slipping when he heard our invasion. He muttered to himself but I wasn't sure what he was saying.

In the short distance between the car and the screenless screen door I was already soaked with sweat. We were going to hit ninety-four today according to the dubious wisdom of the weatherman.

There was a bell but I stuck my hand through the frame of the screen door and knocked. The neighborhood was quiet. The loudest sound was the power mower we'd passed about half a block away.

I knocked again. This time a male voice behind the door said something. Then the man who I assumed owned the voice did a foolish thing. He went to the east window and edged the dirty white curtains back and looked out. Straight into my face. I jabbed a finger at the door. The curtain dropped back.

Just to annoy him I knocked again. This time he opened the door, a short, heavyset man who had more hair on his body than a papa gorilla. A white T-shirt only emphasized the thick hirsute chest and arms.

"Help you with something?"

Mainwaring's strength was sufficient to hurl me off the low doorstep and grab on to the hairy man with enough force to drive him back inside so fast I didn't have time to quite understand what was happening. I piled through the doorway right behind him. By now Nicole, who was seated on a badly soiled light blue couch, was pounding on her father's back as he bent over to smash his fist again and again into the hairy man's face. The man was on his knees. His face was already bloody.

I pushed Nicole aside so I could slam my fist into the side of Mainwaring's head. But he had true madness on his side. He was gone into a realm where only murder would satisfy him. Prisons are filled with men like him, men who pay for a single explosive moment with long stretches behind bars.

The hairy man was crying and pleading. Mainwaring didn't stop hitting him until I kicked him so hard in the back of his left knee that he slowed and turned just enough for me to hit him almost square in the face. The hairy man was smart enough to slide away.

Nicole was back on the couch, sobbing now, sounding as crazed as her father, striking her fists against her thighs again and again.

I shoved Mainwaring toward her. "Take care of your daughter."

Dazed, he stumbled toward the couch and sat down next to her. He still didn't know what to do. He just sat there, still trapped in the vestiges of his rage. Then she surprised both of us by throwing herself into his arms and finally he was her father again and he held her and began crying along with her.

I followed a trail of blood dots on faded linoleum to a small bathroom where the hairy man was splashing water on his face and cursing with a good deal of eloquence.

"That son of a bitch is gonna be payin' me a lot of money by the time I get through with him."

"Are you Windom?"

He whipped around and glared at me. "No, I ain't Windom. Windom moved about four months ago when me'n the missus moved up from Anamosa. She's at work and this is my day off from the railroad." He put a hairy paw to his nose. "This look broke?"

I stepped closer. "Doesn't look like it but I'm not a doc."

He was still trembling. So was I for that matter.

"I'm gettin' me a lawyer."

"I don't blame you. I'll help you find one. I'm Sam McCain." I put my hand out and he shook after hesitating. Blood bubbled on the left side of his mouth. "You need to go to an emergency room and get checked out. What's your name, by the way?"

"Ryan. Nick Ryan."

He grabbed a towel. Wiping his face he winced. "Bastard is lucky I didn't have my glasses. I can't see much without 'em." Finished drying his face he said, "She ain't been here but maybe fifteen minutes and I didn't know what the hell she was talking about. She said she was in trouble and didn't I know what she meant. Then she started cryin'. If the wife was here she woulda known what to do but you know how it is when women cry—especially a young one like her—I just got her a bottle of pop and an ashtray. Young kid like that, I felt sorry for her. Then her old man busts in and tries to kill me. What's this Windom s'posed to have done, anyway? This is the second girl come here since we moved in."

"He supposedly performed abortions."

"I'll be damned. I don't go for that, you know. Catholic."

"You go to the ER and they can bill Paul Mainwaring."

"Who the hell is Paul Mainwaring?"

He squinted at me when I laughed. "A very important guy. Just ask him."

"Well, I hope he's rich because I'm gonna sue his ass off. We need to fix this place up, that's why we got a deal on it. Place we had in Anamosa was real nice but then the job shifted down here. I make a good living."

"I've got an uncle on the railroad. He makes a lot more than I do."

"Yeah? Whadda you do?"

"I'm a lawyer."

This time the laugh was on me. "You should work for the railroad like your uncle. Honest work."

"Believe me, I've thought about it. Now let's go back to the living room."

I led the way. Mainwaring was helping Nicole to her feet. I said, "You owe this man a sincere apology. And you're going to pick up his ER tab. And unless you can make some kind of settlement, he's going to sue your ass off."

"He's an abortionist."

"Now you've slandered him, too."

"I told you, Dad, Mr. Ryan's been very nice to me. He didn't know what I was talking about when I said I needed help."

Mainwaring's eyes roved from hers to mine. "This is true?"

"No, we're making it up because we're all scared you'll go crazy again. Now apologize to him and then give him a ride to the ER and then come to an agreement about how much money you're going to give him." I glanced at Ryan. "I'm his lawyer."

"That's a surprise."

"I'll drive myself home, Dad."

"Can I trust you?"

"How about you? Can I trust *you*?" This was one

of those questions carrying a load of history with it—
Eve, open marriage, wife swapping and alienating his
two girls.

"Just go straight home."

"You're forgetting something," I said to him. "I don't
have a car here. I'll have to ride with Nicole."

She took the keys from her purse, zipped the purse
shut and then looked at me. "Maybe you should drive,
Sam. I'm still shaking."

"Just hope that Mr. Ryan doesn't have any serious
injuries, Mainwaring."

"Oh, great, now I'm the villain."

"Yeah," I said, "as a matter of fact, you are." If I'd
been a sadist I would have used the moment to tell him
what I'd learned from the Wilhoyt investigators about
his wife. But as much as I disliked him, he had more
than his share of grief. I didn't want to add to it.

Nicole, in her peasant skirt and blouse, led me out
of the Ryan home. As we walked to her car she said,
"Maybe he's learned his lesson. Maybe he'll change."

I didn't want to give her odds on that but I said,
"Yeah, maybe."

I drove at about half the speed Mainwaring had a
bit earlier. For a time neither of us spoke. "Van and I
used to play a game. We used to sit in the back of the
car when Mom and Dad would take us someplace and
look out the back window at license plates. For weird
ones, you know. One time we saw one that read 'I'm
cute.' We laughed about that the whole way to Cedar
Rapids." Her voice was wistful but pained.

After a time she said, "He wants to send me to my

aunt's house till I have the baby. Then we'll adopt it out.
That's what he says now, though. I'm trying to imagine
having a baby and giving it away."

"You want to go to your aunt's house?"

"Yeah. Even Sarah said I should go away, I mean
before she told me about Windom. She said I should
go away to school for a year. Try to forget everything."

"She told you about Windom?"

She patted her face as she sometimes did. Maybe she
was hoping that her acne had magically disappeared.
I used to have moments like that—daydreams—about
being taller. "She's my best friend. When I told her
that Neil and I snuck around and saw each other for a
month—and then I told her I was pregnant—she said
I should see this Windom and get an abortion and go
away to school. And try to forget everything. I think
the whole thing made her mad. She said that Tommy
was going to beat Neil up for her but she stopped him
and said she'd take care of it." Then, "Poor Tommy. He
was kind of a little boy in a lot of ways. But he was so
sweet." Her eyes glistened. "And Van and Neil—it's
just all so screwed up."

"You don't hold anything against Neil?"

"I want to but I can't." Her gaze was distant now. "I
knew he was with me just to make Van jealous. I even
told Van about it. But she didn't care. She thought it was
funny. She didn't know I was p.g. though. But it was my
fault as much as his. I always saw all these really handsome guys around Van. I guess I just sorta wanted one
for myself. You know, with my face and all. He was a

lot of fun, too. Took me places and made me think about things I never had. He was brilliant. He really was."

"You need to see a doctor right away."

"I know. I've been afraid to go. I'll probably go to Iowa City where nobody knows me."

"Fine."

"You know, I have a little crush on you. Not a big one. But a nice little one."

"Well, that's funny because I have a little crush on you, too. Not a big one. But a nice little one." Her laugh made us both feel better.

I pulled up next to my car in the small lot behind my office building.

She reached out and took my hand. "I hope I see you again."

"Me, too. And for what it's worth, I think you're wrong about not meeting any more handsome guys. I have the power to see into the future and from what I can see there're a lot of them waiting to take you out."

"I sure hope you're right."

I slid out of the car and started toward my door. Behind me she said, "Thanks for everything, Sam."

By the time I reached the commune a hot rain stormed across the prairie with mean intent. Humans and animals alike rushed to shelter. Lightning walked the land on glowing spider legs and thunder shook the earth. I pulled as close to the houses as I could and then started my own rush to get out of the rain.

With everybody inside temporarily the voices were almost as loud as the music, this time the Beatles' best album, *Rubber Soul*. I had to use a fist on the door to get any attention. A white kid in something like dread-locks came to the door. I told him who I wanted to see and he gave me a thumbs-up. Maybe in a past life he'd been a WW1 ace.

I took one of the two broken-back metal chairs on the porch and had myself a smoke. The laughter from inside was clean and young and I felt envious of them. Crazy and pretentious as some of them were, at least they were questioning the conventional wisdom of growing up, entering the nine-to-five, and setting aside money for your funeral when you turn forty-five.

I watched the rain drill the flower power bus and the other wrecked-looking vehicles. A sweet dog face could be seen underneath the bus, all wide-eyed and floppy-eared.

Then she was there. "God, this rain doesn't even cool things off, does it?"

"I wonder how old Cartwright is doing up there wait-ing to hear from God."

She took the chair next to me. "Sometimes I feel sorry for him, Sam."

"I would if I didn't know he was such a con artist. Hair tonic and diet crap and all that."

In her denim work shirt and jeans she was tomboy comfortable and purposeful. That was my impression, anyway. Except for the eyes. She couldn't hide her anxi-ety. I guessed she knew why I was here.

"Mainwaring and I followed Nicole this morning. She was under the impression she was going to have an abortion."

The old confrontational Sarah scoffed at me. "You're

not exactly being subtle. As far as I'm concerned, I gave her good advice and I don't give a damn if you like it or not. I've seen too many girls her age ruin their lives by getting pregnant."

"So have I. But that's not what this is about."

She leaned away from me. "Oh? So what's 'this' about?"

"I think you know."

She was quick, starting for the door before I got out of my chair. I'd never get her out of the ruckus inside. But then she turned and came back. I had the feeling she was as surprised by her move as I was.

She sat down again. I started to speak but she held up a hand for me to stop.

"I can't get over Tommy killing himself."

"Why do you think he did it?"

"Because of me. Because he was in love with me."

"And you weren't in love with him?"

She dropped her head, was quiet. "I loved him enough not to marry him."

"I don't know what you mean."

She sat back and ground the chair around so she could face me. "He wanted to run away and get married. Not even finish high school. I told him he was crazy but Tommy—Tommy got obsessed easy. Plus he just wanted out of his house. He used to cry like a little kid when his parents had had one of their battles. I hated them for what they'd done to Tommy. But I still wouldn't ruin his life by marrying him right now. I told him he should take one of the scholarships—he had three or four colleges offering him full rides because he was such a good football player. If we got married his life would be ruined. I loved him too much for that."

"So Tommy killed himself because you wouldn't marry him?"

"I don't like your tone there. You trying to say I'm lying?"

"Not at all, Sarah. I believe you. But maybe there was another reason Tommy took his life. In addition to you not marrying him, I mean."

"Well, then I sure don't know what the hell you're talking about."

"I'm talking about him knowing that you killed Neil after you found out that he got Nicole pregnant. You knew Neil had killed Vanessa but you decided to keep his secret. But then when Nicole told you about her pregnancy—" I tried to take her hand. She slapped mine away. "Nicole told me how angry you were when she told you about sleeping with Neil. But I noticed you didn't speak up for Neil quite the same way even before you found out about Nicole. It wasn't anything obvious but your tone definitely changed. I knew then that you were sure that Neil had killed Vanessa. I can't read your mind but I think it was probably then you realized that your brother was out of control and that he was going to keep right on doing what he'd always done. I cut him a lot of slack for what he saw in Nam, Sarah, but I suspect if you're honest you'll tell me that he was always this way growing up, smashing things and smashing people. That's the way it was, wasn't it?"

"You don't have any right to talk like that. I thought you were my friend."

"I am your friend, Sarah. I care about you. I just think you'll feel better if you tell the truth. There's been too much lying already."

She raised her head and stared at the ceiling of the porch. A whimper became a small sob. "He was my brother. He'd had a hard life. I loved him."

"I know you loved him. But you saw that he needed to be stopped. And when you found out about Nicole— You decided you didn't have any choice. You killed him and tried to make it look like suicide."

She picked up my package of Luckies from the arm of my chair. I handed her my matches. When she got her cigarette burning she handed them back.

"You don't know any of this for sure."

"I do now. And you know it, too."

"He attacked me."

"I don't believe that but it'll make a good defense."

"I don't want you for my lawyer anymore."

"That's a good decision."

"I thought you were my friend," she said again.

"I am. That's why I'll get you the best criminal defense attorney I can."

"I don't have any money."

"It can be worked out." I had no idea how at the moment but there on that porch at that moment it was the right thing to say.

"I didn't plan on doing it."

"All right."

"Don't you believe me?"

"Yes. But you'll have to work this through carefully with your lawyer."

She exploded from her chair as if she'd been blasted out of it. She stalked to the east end of the porch and lowered herself onto the railing. She inhaled hungrily. The tip of the cigarette was an evil little red eye. "You don't know what it was like with Neil. All our lives. He was always in trouble. He was in a fight or he'd stolen something or he'd smashed up something. I used to feel sorry for him because I loved him so much. He always said that people wouldn't accept him for who he was and that's why he was always in trouble. He was just paying them back. For a long time I believed that. But when he got into so much trouble in the service—"

"You mean what you told me about Saigon?"

"No. When they got back stateside he started stealing stuff from the other soldiers. Watches and jewelry they'd bought for their girlfriends and wives. One of them caught him at it and Neil nearly killed him. They had him see a shrink. The shrink said that he should get a dishonorable discharge but no time in the brig. He came to my little apartment off campus. He was so angry about things he scared me.

"He'd always taken advantage of people before— I was able to see that then—and he got some kind of thrill out of stealing and fighting and conning people. But I thought that with everything he'd gone through— I thought maybe he'd want to straighten out for the first time in his life.

"And at first when he came to the commune he was really laid back. Really cool in a way he'd never been before. I'd see him out back of the barn planting along with some of the others and I'd get tears in my eyes.

I really believed that God had granted him another chance. Neil always laughed when I told him that I prayed a lot. But I didn't care. I kept right on praying for him. And everything was fine until he fell in love with Van. She was so beautiful I couldn't blame him. But by then Nicole and I were friends and she told me how Van used guys to hurt her father. She wanted to humiliate him by being a whore. I tried to tell him that but he just accused me of being jealous. I just couldn't deal with him anymore."

She was more silhouette than person perched there on the railing. I said, "But you knocked me out so he could escape."

"I was afraid for him. I was thinking maybe he really did kill Van. I didn't want him to go to prison."

"But then you couldn't take it anymore when he got Nicole pregnant."

She flipped her cigarette into the air, a blazing rocket ship against the moon-bright night. "Nicole is a kid. That's why I liked her right away. She's kind of innocent. We had lunch in the city park one day and she brought along a bunch of Archie comic books and talked about how Veronica reminded her of Van in a lot of ways. I laughed about that for a week. She was like this goofy little kid sister I never had. And when he got her pregnant—he couldn't at least have used a rubber?"

I stood up. "Don't tell me any more. We need to get you that lawyer first. I'll start calling as soon as I get home."

"You going to take me in yourself or have the cops come out here?"

"You got a preference?"

She came over and slid her arms around me. "I'm really scared." She seemed to fight her tears at first but then she was crying so hard her fear and sorrow came in great spasms.

We said very little on the drive back to town. There wasn't much point in talking I guess.

TWENTY-TWO

I'D GONE TO law school with David Brunner. He was now a prominent criminal defense attorney in Chicago. You can correctly assume he was a whole lot smarter than I'll ever be. I explained the case to him and told him that we could cover his fees. The largesse was coming from one Paul Mainwaring. As Marsha explained to me over the phone, Nicole was near a breakdown worrying about her friend Sarah. Mainwaring had saddled her and her sister with a sneering, duplicitous wife and an open marriage so he now saw that he needed to save his daughter. Marsha also told me that Paul and Eve had had two warring days of shouting at each other and that Eve had suddenly packed three suitcases and had taken a room at the Drake in Chicago.

Brunner was in the middle of a trial but promised he'd have one of his assistant attorneys on a train within two hours, which he did. John Silverman was in my office by late afternoon. I briefed him and then took him to the police station to meet Mike Potter and Cliffie. Potter and he got along in a reassuringly professional way. A way that was spoiled when Cliffie came in and began to pontificate about the case and warn John that "out-of-town lawyers" never did well in Black River Falls. He also reminded me several times that he said from the beginning Neil was the killer. Potter and Cliffie left us then to wait for somebody to escort us to a room where we could talk with Sarah. "I can't fucking believe that guy," Brunner said. Twice. A mild reaction compared to some when Cliffie was the subject.

The good Reverend Cartwright was presently housed on the fourth floor of the Protestant hospital where he was making a fraudulent saga of being struck by lightning. He had been pronounced fine by the emergency doc and fine by his own doc but the Rev insisted he was suffering from terrible but unspecified health problems that only hospital rest could cure. He bravely broadcast from his hospital bed where he announced a "Fund Drive for the True Friends of Jesus." He said that God had told him he would recover at the same rate that money poured into church coffers. He never runs out of gimmicks and damned if most of them don't work.

Four nights after taking Sarah to the police station, I got home late and weary. I'd been in court all afternoon and the central air there had worked only intermittently. Everybody in Court B was in a surly mood, me included. During lunch assistant prosecutor Hillary Fitzgerald stopped on the step where I was eating my burger from the courthouse menu and said, "I feel sorry for your client, McCain. I've never seen Judge Hammond this nasty. Your guy is facing a DUI and I think Hammond is going to give him the chair." She had a winsome smile.

When I was coming up to the house, I saw that something was wrong. I hadn't been able to contact Wendy by phone. Now the lights were out and the house had a deserted look. Where had she gone?

Her car was in the two-stall garage. Had a friend picked her up?

I hurried to the back door and walked inside. We never locked up until we went to bed.

Refrigerator thrum. Air conditioner whoosh. All those inexplicable sounds of a house talking to itself.

Downstairs empty. Upstairs—

I went straight to our bedroom and there with the bloody sunset filling the window like a wound she lay in a tight fetal position in the center of the bed. Her blue walking shorts and white blouse were badly wrinkled, something she would ordinarily not have allowed.

The bedroom décor was all hers, of course. And it was very feminine with a canopy bed, a doll collection, a dressing table, enough perfumes to enchant a sultan, and three stacks of fashion magazines from her high school years. I knew this because one night when she was depressed she sat in a chair in the living room with several very old issues, going through them with great interest. I asked her about them and she said, "That was the last time my life was simple. Back when I used to sit next to you in homeroom."

I knew she was aware of me because the sound of her breathing came sharper now. But she kept her eyes closed. When I saw the envelope on the hardwood floor I reached down to pick it up.

"Don't look at it." Her eyes were still closed; she hadn't moved.

But I did pick it up. I knew what it would be of course. Her mood told me that.

"We're going to Canada."

"No, we're not, Wendy."

Then she was not only sitting up she was hurling herself off the bed and standing in front of me.

"Well, you're sure as hell not going to Nam, I'll tell you that. I lost my husband over there; I'm not going to lose you the same way."

"I have to go, Wendy. It's my duty. Other guard units have gone."

"Don't give me any patriotic bullshit. I don't want to hear it." I took it as significant that she wasn't crying. Her fury wouldn't allow for any softer expressions of pain.

I reached out for her but she jerked away. "Don't touch me. I can't believe you're just going to go along with this."

"What the hell choice do I have, Wendy?"

"Go to Canada. Or say you're a pacifist. Or say you're queer. Some goddamned thing. You're a lawyer, Sam. Start thinking like one."

She was doing me a kind of favor. By having to deal with her I didn't have to deal with my own feelings— fear and anger just like hers—that would be mine when I was alone.

"And think of your mother, Sam. How's she going to take this? She needs you just the same as I do."

I knew better than to touch her. "Listen, honey. Why don't you fix us a couple of drinks while I wash up?

Then we can sit on the patio and talk this through a little more calmly."

"Don't give me your calmly bullshit, Sam. That's what you always say when you can't think of anything else." Then she waved me off. "This is making me so crazy. I'm like I was after my husband died." She looked crazy, too. Then, "I'll go make some drinks."

In the upstairs bathroom I washed up and as I did I studied my face in the mirror. I knew what she meant about those old magazines. My face had been very different back then. If I survived the war it would change even more and probably not to my liking.

I'd been taking my time in the bathroom until I heard her weeping downstairs. Great harsh gushes that must have burned her throat.

I hurried up then. I needed to be with her for both our sakes.

* * * * *

REQUEST YOUR FREE BOOKS!

2 FREE NOVELS
PLUS 2 FREE GIFTS!

WORLDWIDE LIBRARY®
Your Partner in Crime

FAMOUS FAMILIES

YES! Please send me the *Famous Families* collection featuring the Fortunes, the Bravos, the McCabes and the Cavanaughs. This collection will begin with 3 FREE BOOKS and 2 FREE GIFTS in my very first shipment—and more valuable free gifts will follow! My books will arrive in 8 monthly shipments until I have the entire 51-book *Famous Families* collection. I will receive 2-3 free books in each shipment and I will pay just $4.49 U.S./$5.39 CDN for each of the other 4 books in each shipment, plus $2.99 for shipping and handling.* If I decide to keep the entire collection, I'll only have paid for 32 books because 19 books are free. I understand that accepting the 3 free books and gifts places me under no obligation to buy anything. I can always return a shipment and cancel at any time. My free books and gifts are mine to keep no matter what I decide.

268 HCN 0387   468 HCN 0387

Name _____ (PLEASE PRINT) _____

Address _____ Apt. # _____

City _____ State/Prov. _____ Zip/Postal Code _____

Signature (if under 18, a parent or guardian must sign)

Mail to the **Reader Service:**

IN U.S.A.: P.O. Box 1867, Buffalo, NY 14240-1867
IN CANADA: P.O. Box 609, Fort Erie, Ontario L2A 5X3

FFBPA12

REQUEST YOUR FREE BOOKS!

2 FREE NOVELS
FROM THE SUSPENSE COLLECTION
PLUS 2 FREE GIFTS!

YES! Please send me 2 FREE novels from the Suspense Collection and my 2 FREE gifts (gifts are worth about $10). After receiving them, if I don't wish to receive any more books, I can return the shipping statement marked "cancel." If I don't cancel, I will receive 4 brand-new novels every month and be billed just $5.99 per book in the U.S. or $6.49 per book in Canada. That's a saving of at least 25% off the cover price. It's quite a bargain! Shipping and handling is just 50¢ per book in the U.S. and 75¢ per book in Canada.* I understand that accepting the 2 free books and gifts places me under no obligation to buy anything. I can always return a shipment and cancel at any time. Even if I never buy another book, the two free books and gifts are mine to keep forever.

191/391 MDN FEME

Name	(PLEASE PRINT)

Address	Apt. #

City	State/Prov.	Zip/Postal Code

Signature (if under 18, a parent or guardian must sign)

Mail to the **Reader Service:**
IN U.S.A.: P.O. Box 1867, Buffalo, NY 14240-1867
IN CANADA: P.O. Box 609, Fort Erie, Ontario L2A 5X3

Not valid for current subscribers to the Suspense Collection
or the Romance/Suspense Collection.

Want to try two free books from another line?
Call 1-800-873-8635 or visit www.ReaderService.com.

* Terms and prices subject to change without notice. Prices do not include applicable taxes. Sales tax applicable in N.Y. Canadian residents will be charged applicable taxes. Offer not valid in Quebec. This offer is limited to one order per household. All orders subject to credit approval. Credit or debit balances in a customer's account(s) may be offset by any other outstanding balance owed by or to the customer. Please allow 4 to 6 weeks for delivery. Offer available while quantities last.

Your Privacy—The Reader Service is committed to protecting your privacy. Our Privacy Policy is available online at www.ReaderService.com or upon request from the Reader Service.

We make a portion of our mailing list available to reputable third parties that offer products we believe may interest you. If you prefer that we not exchange your name with third parties, or if you wish to clarify or modify your communication preferences, please visit us at www.ReaderService.com/consumerschoice or write to us at Reader Service Preference Service, P.O. Box 9062, Buffalo, NY 14269. Include your complete name and address.

REQUEST YOUR FREE BOOKS!
2 FREE NOVELS PLUS 2 FREE GIFTS!

HARLEQUIN®

INTRIGUE®

BREATHTAKING ROMANTIC SUSPENSE

YES! Please send me 2 FREE Harlequin Intrigue® novels and my 2 FREE gifts (gifts are worth about $10). After receiving them, if I don't wish to receive any more books, I can return the shipping statement marked "cancel." If I don't cancel, I will receive 6 brand-new novels every month and be billed just $4.49 per book in the U.S. or $5.24 per book in Canada. That's a savings of at least 14% off the cover price! It's quite a bargain! Shipping and handling is just 50¢ per book in the U.S. and 75¢ per book in Canada.* I understand that accepting the 2 free books and gifts places me under no obligation to buy anything. I can always return a shipment and cancel at any time. Even if I never buy another book, the two free books and gifts are mine to keep forever.

182/382 HDN FV54

Name	(PLEASE PRINT)

Address	Apt. #

City	State/Prov.	Zip/Postal Code

Signature (if under 18, a parent or guardian must sign)

Mail to the **Reader Service:**
IN U.S.A.: P.O. Box 1867, Buffalo, NY 14240-1867
IN CANADA: P.O. Box 609, Fort Erie, Ontario L2A 5X3

**Are you a subscriber to Harlequin Intrigue books
and want to receive the larger-print edition?
Call 1-800-873-8635 or visit www.ReaderService.com.**

* Terms and prices subject to change without notice. Prices do not include applicable taxes. Sales tax applicable in N.Y. Canadian residents will be charged applicable taxes. Offer not valid in Quebec. This offer is limited to one order per household. Not valid for current subscribers to Harlequin Intrigue books. All orders subject to credit approval. Credit or debit balances in a customer's account(s) may be offset by any other outstanding balance owed by or to the customer. Please allow 4 to 6 weeks for delivery. Offer available while quantities last.

Your Privacy—The Reader Service is committed to protecting your privacy. Our Privacy Policy is available online at www.ReaderService.com or upon request from the Reader Service.

We make a portion of our mailing list available to reputable third parties that offer products we believe may interest you. If you prefer that we not exchange your name with third parties, or if you wish to clarify or modify your communication preferences, please visit us at www.ReaderService.com/consumerschoice or write to us at Reader Service Preference Service, P.O. Box 9062, Buffalo, NY 14269. Include your complete name and address.

HIDIR12